ON BLUEBERRY HILL

THE 19TH-CENTURY
BOYD VS. BENDER FEUD

ON BLUEBERRY HILL

THE 19TH-CENTURY
BOYD VS. BENDER FEUD

A NOVEL

GREGORY J. LALIRE

SUNSTONE
PRESS

SANTA FE

Sunstone books may be purchased for educational, business, or sales promotional use.
For information please write: Special Markets Department, Sunstone Press,
P.O. Box 2321, Santa Fe, New Mexico 87504-2321.
Printed on acid-free paper
∞
eBook: 978-1-61139-760-4

LIBRARY OF CONGRESS CATALOGING IN PUBLICATION DATA
(ON FILE)

WWW.SUNSTONEPRESS.COM
SUNSTONE PRESS / POST OFFICE BOX 2321 / SANTA FE, NM 87504-2321 /USA
(505) 988-4418

DEDICATION

For my family, immediate and extended, past and present, and, especially, the future. No matter what this world dishes out to us, one thing is clear—family matters.

... "He seems to be thrifty; and hasn't he need,
With the mouths of all those young Lorens to feed?
He has brought them all up on wild berries, they say,
Like birds. They store a great many away.
They eat them the year round, and those they don't eat
They sell in the store and buy shoes for their feet."

"Who cares what they say? It's a nice way to live,
Just taking what Nature is willing to give,
Not forcing her hand with harrow and plow."

"I wish you had seen his perpetual bow—
And the air of the youngsters! Not one of them turned,
And they looked so solemn-absurdly concerned."

"I wish I knew half what the flock of them know
Of where all the berries and other things grow..."

—From *Blueberries*, a poem by Robert Frost (1874–1963)

INTRODUCTION

First came the wild blueberries and then the Indians, or vice-versa. After the Lenni Lenape (the "true people") but certainly not the berries had disappeared, the first Boyds arrived in 1811. The Benders came next, in the 1840s. Trouble followed as the two families strived—or, in some instances, didn't strive—to coexist on a hill south of today's Wurtsboro Ridge State Forest and just east of Wurtsboro, New York. The village of Wurtsboro remains the economic heart of the town of Mamakating. That's in Sullivan County, where canal boats and railroad cars once flourished and where automobiles and trucks now rule. Although only a couple hours from New York City by motor vehicle, the county has always been blessed with gobs of land too rugged, too rocky, too wet, too dry, or too otherwise uninviting to interest ambitious farmers, builders of four-lane highways, or developers of modern civilization. Through the years, Blueberry Hill has been on the edge of progress—not the cutting edge, by any means...more so the back edge, the one butting up against what was once a wilderness and is now largely a nineteenth-century backdrop.

This is the story of the Boyds and the Benders and that Hill on which they were once as divided as yesterday and tomorrow. It is a story of conflict. In the beginning there was only pioneer Handy Boyd and his young bride and their first born. In time things became much livelier on both sides of the Hill, and two great houses were built, one of stone, the other of wood. The families did not see eye to eye on most issues, the primary one being how the land should be used or not used.

It was the nature of the Boyds to let nature take its course; one nearly mythical family member often quoted her favorite line from poet-profit Walt Whitman: "Nature and Man shall be disjoined and diffused no more." Handy, who worked in moderation, believed the land should be more admired and enjoyed than used. He memorized these words from Henry David Thoreau: "The order of things should be somewhat reversed; the seventh should be man's day of toil, wherein to earn his living by the sweat of his brow; and the other six his Sabbath of the affections and the soul—in which to range this widespread garden, and drink in the soft influences and sublime revelations of

Nature." The Benders, with few exceptions, wanted to use the land and create an economic empire. One of their entrepreneurs was fond of saying, "I have ways of making money that you know nothing of," long before that quote was attributed to John D. Rockefeller.

The Boyds were on the west side, the Benders on the east side, and for the most part the two families lived their lives in accordance with Rudyard Kipling's famous 1892 declaration: "Oh, East is East, and West is West, and never the twain shall meet." There was more than half a century of feuding. Blueberry Hill reached an uneasy balance that figured to be broken beyond repair if given enough time. Instead, something completely different happened. Credit the capability of love. This then is that story, too.

Amazingly today, as was the case at the end of the nineteenth century, Blue Rock House on one side and the Bend on the other are headed by impregnable, independent-minded women. They each raised a son and a daughter without getting married, and they consider themselves merry widows though they aren't particularly merry and neither is technically a widow.

The Boyd matriarch, Basha, is eighty-one but could pass for sixty-five, especially when she dresses down in her holey jeans and long-sleeve hoodies. She was named at birth for the Basha Kill when it was a stream (indeed *kill* is Dutch for stream) before Hurricane Diane arrived in 1955 to transform it. The Pine Kill, a tributary flowing down the ridge to the west of the Basha Kill, turned into a menacing maelstrom that August, bringing tree trunks, earth, and stone to where it met the Basha Kill at Westbrookville. A boulder dam formed there, and, as a result, the pancake-flat country to the north turned into a wetland.

She also shares her name with the squaw of an old chief who lived in the area before the white man came. The chief was a marvelous hunter, and his beloved Basha would dutifully carry back to their village whatever he killed. One day he killed a large deer; she tied its legs to a stick and put the stick on her shoulders. The path home led over a stream that was crossed on a log that stretched from bank to bank. The exhausted squaw stumbled and then tumbled off the log with the deer on top of her. She did not drown, but the stick drove into her neck, and she bled to death. That was how the stream got its name. So, the history went this way: Basha the squaw gave her name to Basha the stream, which gave its name to a Boyd baby girl who grew up to take many walks in the Basha Kill Wetlands, head the family company producing the most blueberries in New York state, and cap off a thirty-year teaching career by becoming an emeritus professor at the SUNY College of Environmental Science and Forestry. *Basha*, by the way, is actually a Dutch word meaning "stranger." But as Basha's great-great-great grandfather Handy Boyd used to point out to his family: "To be considered stranger than the rest of mankind, I take as the supreme compliment."

The Bender matriarch, Myrtle, is eighty-two, but only looks it from the bridge of her nose to the nape of her neck. Each year she *re-tires* instead of retiring. Her premature gray hair is a thing of the distant past, replaced by vibrant silver curls that seem to bounce with her every deep thought. Her eyes sparkle like man-made blue goldstone. Her body, as elegant as the string of freshwater pearls she wears while working, tends to stay as still and straight as a Shaker chair. She shares her name with an evergreen shrub. The name was once more popular than it is today, but nobody ever told her why she was called "Myrtle," rather than, say, "Rose" or "Violet." She does know that in the early 1960s, her older somewhat troubled brother Paul started calling her "Myrtle the Turtle" after the Dr. Seuss character "Yertle the Turtle." Paul had always liked books that were full of pictures and rhyme. In truth, though, it wasn't only because of that book. At the time, he was constantly telling people that his little sister had a big fat trap, like the mouth of the snapping turtle he saw hanging out in a wet section of the long-abandoned Delaware & Hudson Canal. Myrtle never remembers that part, even though she went on to become a practicing Freudian psychologist and is still seeing long-time patients. Myrtle now allows Paul, despite his artistic tendencies and advanced age, to run the accounting department of the Handy Spring Water Co., but she oversees him in cooperation with her co-director, Basha Boyd.

Blueberry Hill's west side today remains most lively during the blueberry picking season, and the east side now fully recognizes the so-called Blue Season. Bottling of spring water keeps a handful of Boyds and Benders—but mostly hired hands—reasonably busy year-round. On some winter days, though, you hear more ghostly echoes and creaks than live voices at Blue Rock House. And there are times at the Bend when you can only overhear the private conversations between Dr. Myrtle Bender and her long-time patients. Atop the Hill, there are only remnants of the great stone wall that once separated the Boyd side from the Bender side. Newcomers to Wurtsboro and the surrounding region would be hard-pressed to suspect that two families once feuded over a berry-rich uplifted land with majestic trees and the best spring water, both families now agree, in the world.

Adam Everly,
Independent Historian,
Port Jervis, New York

1

THE SHE-BEAR

Sullivan County pioneer Handy Boyd was more than half a century old and as bald as a musket ball in the summer of 1811 when he hewed his way with his prized long knife through the brush from the settlement of Mahackamack on the Delaware River to the wilds of the upper Mongaup River. There, a she-bear chased him away from her three cubs, and he lost his sense of direction. As he ran willy-nilly, the late July sun beat down so hard that it flattened his straw hat and pricked his skull. His sweat-drenched beige pullover shirt weighed heavy against his narrow chest and slight shoulders, and his hot wool trousers were making his legs itch. There was no wind to speak of, only the breeze created by his pursuer. He dared not stop. He could hear the black bear breaking branches behind him. The ground shook.

Panting like the shaggy mutt he had owned as a boy, he also heard his dearly departed mother cautioning him, "Handy-boy, don't run with sharp objects, you'll fall and cut yourself." He kept going, even pleading with his mother, "I can't stop, Mama; if I stop, I die." Dropping the knife, which had a foot-long blade and a twisted cherry wood grip, was out of the question. It was a Revolutionary War gift to him from his father, Benjamin Boyd, who had never actually used the knife or even fought. But that wasn't the point. The knife was what passed as a family heirloom. Handy squeezed the handle so hard his sweaty right palm ached. He doubted he could actually stick the blade into the bear, but he wasn't going to drop the knife even if the beast took off his right arm.

In truth, before running from the she-bear, he had not been constantly hewing through the brush. He had often stopped to pick and munch wild berries and, where the pickings were slim, he had used his knife to crack open shagbark hickory nuts and pry out the sweet kernels inside. Nobody had ever accused him of being a trailblazer. Others had already carved out passageways in the thick woodlands of Minisink country. Wherever possible he had followed paths made by deer, trails made by Indians (akin to the last of the Mohicans), and even a few wagon roads made by soldiers, surveyors, and half-crazed hermits. Handy was no hermit but he had undertaken this "Great Home-Hunting Expedition" (so named by his sweet fifteen-year-old bride) because he wanted to find a safe haven far from greedy, lecherous, warlike mankind where he could take Henrietta after the baby arrived. Safe haven? Well, he certainly hadn't found it yet. He slowed down to look back. The bear was still coming but was only loping as if it was in no hurry to finish him off. Handy picked up speed and was amazed that his thoughts churned faster than his legs. Handy's whole life didn't flash before his eyes, but his only previous brush with death did. In fact, it more than flashed. It stuck in his head like one of those boulders deposited by a glacier—an erratic.

It had happened during the Revolutionary War when Mohawk Chief Joseph Brant, the most notorious Redcoat-loving redskin to ever plant a moccasin on the New York frontier, was creating havoc. Called "Monster Brant" or "the Mohawk Terror" by his enemies, the tomahawk-wielding Iroquois leader was fighting for His Majesty the King and had gained a foothold between the Delaware and Hudson rivers. Handy, at nineteen, had been one of the local militiamen who tried to loosen that foothold. He wasn't a fighter by nature any more than his father was, but thirty-two years ago what choice did he have after Brant's warriors and Tory raiders swept through Mahackamack? Some 120 militiamen had traveled in two groups north by land, parallel to the Delaware River, intent on catching Brant and punishing him or at least recovering some of the horses and cattle he stole. Things didn't work out as planned, not by a long shot.

Not hearing any noise behind him and desperate to catch his breath, Handy slowed down. He waited. Nothing but his own heavy breathing. He didn't feel safe on the ground, though; he was in danger of collapsing from exhaustion. A climbing tree was nearby, some kind of oak, so he sheathed his knife and climbed, managing to get three branches up. He was able to make himself comfortable. In another life he could have been a grey squirrel or more likely one of those sloths that curl up in branches. After a while he closed his eyes. He stopped thinking of that bear. Chief Joseph Brant popped back into his head. He recalled the July 22, 1779, Battle of the Minisink, in which Brant's bunch killed fifty men, some chopped down where they stood, others shot while trying to swim the Delaware. Brant, who had gone to school in Connecticut and visited King George III in England, spared only the life of a Captain Wood, believing him to be a fellow Freemason. Sometime after the battle, the chief came across Handy in a cave preparing his last supper— stirring cracked corn into heated water and then adding five handfuls of fresh blueberries to form a simply delicious pudding called sautauthig (pronounced *sawi-taw-teeg*). Handy was no Mason but the Mohawk Terror must have been hungry too after all the bloodletting. They shared a meal. Handy remembered their conversation as if it had happened yesterday.

"Heap good vittles, eh chief?" he said, shaky but sincere.

"Bloody well right," Brant replied as he picked his teeth.

"You speak good American."

"English. You cook well. You a Nancy-boy?"

"What?"

"You cook instead of shoot."

"I ran plum out of gunpowder, not blueberries." In truth, he hadn't fired a shot.

The chief grinned. His teeth were spectacularly white except for a few blue streaks. "Good for us both. Let's bury the hatchet. What say you, you American bootlicker?"

"I ain't smart like a Philadelphia lawyer, but I'm a-likin' that idea chief."

Handy, despite the congenial talk, was not out of the woods that day. For amusement Brant brought the two prisoners together and had them fight each other. It wasn't an even fight. Brant handed his tomahawk to his fellow Mason Captain Wood but didn't allow Handy to pull his Revolutionary War knife from the scabbard attached to his waist. Handy was forced to do manly battle for the first time in his life with nothing but a wooden pudding spoon. The captain, with surprising vigor, kept waving the tomahawk at the retreating Handy. Backed up to the edge of a cliff, Hany plunged into the Delaware River. Not much of a swimmer in those days, he was fortunate to latch onto a sizable floating log and catch a ride the twenty miles back to Mahackamack. Handy had been a sitting duck in the water, yet not one musket ball or arrow had flown in his direction, let alone pierced his hide; the taste of sautauthig must have still been in the Mohawk leader's mouth, keeping him in a merciful mood.

Thinking of that earlier escape made Handy feel safer now. He would not die before his time. He dozed off on his selected branch with his head pressed against the trunk of the oak. He had never had any trouble falling asleep, whether in a bed, in a rocking chair, in a field, or on a floor, but sleeping in a tree was a first. His dream was unsettling, though. He was back to trying to outrun that angry she-bear. It was a wonder he didn't drop out of the oak like an oversized acorn. He woke up shouting, "*Sawi-taw-teeg, sawi-taw-teeg, sawi-taw-teeg,*" as if pudding could save him for a second time.

His relief at finding himself still safe in the tree only lasted a minute. When he started to climb down, he saw one of the bear cubs lumbering below, maybe thinking about climbing up. The cub must not have seen him sitting on the third branch at first because upon raising its head it let loose with a long moan, followed by a cry that sounded awfully close to *help*. Handy wasn't going to hang around waiting for the mother to answer that cry. He realized what an ignoramus he was to think he could climb a tree but a bear could not. "Get out of here!" Handy yelled. "I got a knife!" The terrified cub backed away, then ran off. Handy immediately scrambled down from the oak and ran in the opposite direction, which fortunately was the way he wanted to go.

He didn't get far before he heard a roar behind him, the kind of loud, angry roar that a cub couldn't have mastered yet. He didn't need to look back. The she-bear was on his tail again and he was positive it wasn't merely loping now. This Monster Bear was more terrifying than the Monster Brant. Handy managed to pull out his long knife while running at full speed, but he knew even if he had the mettle to use it, he was doomed. He had never once in his life wanted to be another Daniel Boone, the famed frontier hunter who would carve his name and the date in a nearby tree when he killed a bear.

The first blow was a massive paw swatting him on the rearend. Handy staggered out of the bushes onto some kind of road and tripped on a wagon rut. As he fell, he felt a second swat, which ripped a hole in the seat of his store-bought trousers. When he hit the ground, the knife flew out of his grasp. His belly took the brunt of his fall and then his chin banged so hard against the ground that it knocked his hat off. The wind shot right out of him, but he didn't lose consciousness. He was still aware of the bear hovering over him, and he closed his eyes, believing his only hope was to play dead. He expected at any moment to feel her claws dig into his back and her teeth sink into the back of his bald head. Instead, the she-bear snorted her scorn and ran off, probably back to her cubs to protect them since a great howling was now happening nearby, suggesting a pack of wolves.

A question immediately came to Handy's mind: *Is it better to be devoured by wolves than torn to shreds by an enraged bear?* When something firm touched his back, he screamed. It took him a minute to realize no paws were involved. He finally twisted his neck to look back. Hunched over him was a squat figure, like a gigantic red toad. Human grunts came from it and something close to a smile appeared on the unsightly face. Handy wasn't sure if he would ultimately end up in heaven or hell, but at least he could lie still and catch his breath knowing he hadn't been consigned to either place yet.

2
CATAWISSA MANAYUNK

"Bbbear?" Handy said, too stiff and sore to move off his belly.

"Gone," said the squatting figure.

Handy turned just enough to see the figure wore clothes, a buckskin shirt dyed red and rust-covered pantaloons. With a groan Handy twisted to see more. It was a small round old man with a large buffalo hump on his back, knotty hands as red as plums, and a wrinkled face a shade darker. His furry cap had a blue jay's feather sticking out the top and long hair, like the silver-gray feathers of a turkey vulture, flowing out the back. Handy expected a hawk-like nose but instead saw a bulbous snout sniffing as if something smelled bad. This was no noble-looking Chief Joseph Brant, who in the 1780s had posed in splendid attire for portrait painter Gilbert Stuart. But when this ugly cuss flashed a grin, he showed a good set of choppers with blue streaks, just how Chief Brant's teeth had looked in that cave when they shared sautauthig after the Battle of the Minisink.

"What about the wolves?" Handy asked.

"Me."

"Huh?"

The old man's dark eyes darted like a pair of rolling dice. He went onto his knees, pointed his rounded chin to the sky and let out an eerie howl, exactly like a wolf. Then he offered lesser howls, all fine imitations of the real thing. This one Indian—ugly, short, lumpy and humped—was all by himself a pack of wolves.

"I see," said Handy. "That she-bear had me awful streaked. Your howling sure enough caused her to pull foot. You are a good Indian."

The old man's nostrils flared. "You are a stinking white man."

Handy took no offense. "I mean you no harm. I mean to get away from stinking white men."

The Indian laughed as if he had pebbles in his mouth. "You shat pants. You shat blue-green."

Handy imagined his face reddening and squirmed onto his side.

"And you are flapping." The Indian pointed to Handy's backside.

Handy reached back to make sure it wasn't flesh that was flapping. The trouser seat was hanging down like a beaver's tail, but his fingers found minimal blood...only shit. At least he was still in one piece. The Indian grabbed a handful of ferns, bunched them, and wiped Handy's bottom as gently as one might a baby.

"Glad you happened along," said Handy, sticking his fingers into the ground so they would become coated with dirt and not stink.

"I make long walks many." The old man fetched Handy's hat, then spotted the Revolutionary War knife, which had become lodged in a wagon rut. He yanked the knife out with some difficulty, wiped the blade clean against his pantaloon leg, and touched the point with a bony finger. "Big knife."

"I reckon it's big enough." Handy rose to his hands and knees, then stood. The Indian also stood, his back cracking. Once Handy's straw hat was back on his head and his knife back in the scabbard, he forgot about the hole in the seat of his pants and felt better. He was at least two heads taller than his savior, whose head was in a constant forward-leaning position became of that hump, only partially hidden by the long silver-gray hair. "Handy Boyd is my name. I hail from Mahackamack, though I was born in Tappan, New York, some time ago—November 13, 1759, to be exact. I'm looking for a new home."

"All this my home, Big Knife." The Indian clicked the heels of his moccasins together and clapped once. His palms stayed joined as if in prayer for ten seconds before his arms shot outward from his body like a bird stretching its wings. He held the pose and bopped his head, which appeared too large and square for the rest of him. "Home of Lenni Lenape!" He reminded Handy of those arrogant Tory landowners who were forced to admit they were beat and fled to Canada. "Me born same moon as third president, Thomas Jefferson," the Indian added. "Thirteenth of April in year 1743."

Handy was impressed that the Indian could know the date of his own birth let alone that of an American president. "Go ahead and call me Handy. Everybody else does. Truth be known, though, I am hardly handy with my knife. Never killed anything with it." Handy thought his words might make his savior feel more at ease, though the man showed no sign of being intimidated by a much taller, armed white man.

The old Indian was frowning, his eyebrow like daggers. "You no bear killer. Boy know that."

"That's true enough. But it's Boyd with a d."

"Me Munsee."

"Oh, that's your name?"

"No. Munsee mean Wolf Clan of Lenni Lenape Nation." He rubbed his cap. "Wolf fur."

"Oh, I see." Handy wasn't positive what the Lenni Lenape Nation was, but he felt certain it had not survived into the 19th century, at least not in the state of New York. He began to feel sympathetic toward this Indian relic with a conspicuous hump, a nose only a mother could love, and wrinkles upon wrinkle on his ugly mug. "What should I call you?"

"Name Catawissa Manayunk. Mean 'Growing Fat Where Go to Drink.'"

Handy looked his savior over. He was round and squat but not fleshy. A stiff wind would likely knock the little fellow over and send him rolling like a ninepin ball. "I reckon you never lived up to your name."

"Starve much when white man come. Catawissa Manayunk much hard for white men say. Call me *Man*. I call you *Boy*."

Handy would have preferred Boyd or *Big Knife*. "Whatever you say," he said. "You saved my life, Man. You are my friend."

"*Elangomat* mean friend."

"*Elangomat*," Handy repeated. "You're a good *elangomat*."

He reached out to shake the old Indian's hand, but Man chose to turn to the sky and again howl like a wolf. "Wolf *elangomat*."

"Had a dog once who was friendly most of the time. I wouldn't dare get cozy with a wolf. No offense."

"You need pin, Boy," the Indian named Man said, grinning again. He pulled a pin out of his wolf-skin cap and awkwardly reached around Handy to fasten the flap in the seat of his trousers. He pricked Handy twice before getting the job done. "Hate you go bare-assed on turnpike. Happen to me. Sat on porcupine. Much long ago. Carry pin always. French give me. *Qui, qui, qui, bonjour.* French give my people much many presents. Trade fair. Want no Lenni Lenape land. Me and French brothers fight King's men. Too bad Boy no French."

"Sorry. Granddad Braxton Boyd came to this country from Scotland in 1708. But neither he nor my father, Benjamin, fought the French. And I was only four when the French and Indian War ended. In fact, my father inherited the big knife but didn't fight against the British in that war or in the American Revolution either. I did, well, only a little—that is to say I survived the Battle of the Minisink. But that's another story. Boyds are not known fighters; we like peace and quiet and being left alone. Now, what's that you said about a turnpike?"

"Newburgh and Cocheton Turnpike. Big road between Hudson and Delaware rivers."

"I heard tell about it. This is it, huh?"

"Good for wagon, not for Indian."

"This must be Ulster County."

"Sullivan County. Break from Ulster two years past. Named for bluecoat chief John Sullivan."

"Ah, yes. During the Revolution General Sullivan chased Mohawk

Chief Joseph Brant all over creation. It was at the Battle of Minisink I met the chief. We were on opposite sides but he befriended me." Handy hooked his thumb in the waist of his trousers and stuck out his chest. The Brant connection was something he felt he had a right to boast about, especially to an Indian. "I was peaceable, you see, and he was a real gentleman. We enjoyed a meal, me and the chief."

"Monster Brant big enemy," said Man, his black eyes narrowing and growing darker. "He chief but no control men with blood on tomahawk. Iroquois tell all Lenni Lenape: 'We conquer you. You women. We make women of you. Give up your old lands. Go west.' Iroquois kill Lenni Lenape."

"Sorry, Man. I had no idea. Brant wasn't really much of a friend. We just happened to share a bowl of pudding together."

Catawissa Manayunk grunted and sat on his haunches. He looked to the sky, where the first clouds of the day were moving but not in any particular hurry. Handy expected to hear another howl. Instead, the toad-like hunchback straightened the blue jay feather in his cap and prayed to someone he called Ketanëtuwit, also referred to as the Great Spirit and the Creator. Man seemed to be asking Ketanëtuwit to resurrect the true people, the Lenni Lenape. It was taking a lot of time—his praying that is.

"I better push on," Handy said. "Thanks for everything, Man."

"Where you go?"

"I'll need a home near water, and I figure they'll be plenty of water in this direction long before I reach the Hudson River. *Au revoir.*" He adjusted the seat of his pinned trousers, waved, and started down the turnpike. The old Indian did not respond; he looked to be in some kind of trance, perhaps consulting again with his Creator.

Handy walked briskly down the turnpike. He figured he could make better time without the old Indian along. He just hoped he didn't run into another bear or a pack of wolves.

"Hey, Boy! Where you go?"

Handy stopped and looked back. The old Indian, still squatting, was grinning once more. "I told you. I'm looking for the right place to settle and it must be near water."

"Water both ways. But Boy go that way, Boy go back to Delaware River."

"What? Oh, I see. I thought something was funny. I must have got turned around after my fall. I didn't see the sun because of the clouds and...anyway, I want to proceed forward, not go back the way I came."

"East that way," said Man, making a sweeping motion with his right arm, then a vigorous point. "Hudson east."

Embarrassed, Handy did an exaggerated about-face the way he imagined the British soldiers must have done after their defeat at Yorktown. As he walked quickly past the old Indian, Man rose and followed him. "What are you doing?" Handy asked. "You going my way?"

"Yes. Ketanëtuwit tell me Boy need much help"

"Help? Really?"

"He say Boy brain like brain of *mamalis,* what you call fawn deer."

That didn't sound like a compliment, but there were worse things to be compared to than a deer of any size. Handy had a fondness for whitetail, the way they munched vegetation, the way they walked on tip-toenails, the way they ran and jumped, the way they came near but were still wild and wary. He had never shot one in his life. "Deer are dear," he said.

"Yes," the old Indian said as if the white man was touched in the head. "Man show you way to where you go. Boy follow."

Handy Boyd didn't know where he was going and now welcomed the company.

3
WALK LIKE A MAN

Catawissa Manayunk walked bent forward, but his hump and a slight limp from some ancient injury didn't slow him down any. At times he hopped and reminded Handy more of a frog than a toad. Mostly the old Indian kicked up a cloud of dust with his rapid shuffling steps. Handy needed to quicken his pace to keep up. The turnpike passed with few curves through forests of hemlock and mountain laurel. They saw no signs of civilization, red or white. An occasional crow scolded them for trespassing. A blue jay flew low and whistled as if commenting on the kind of feather the old Indian wore in his wolf-skin cap. One whitetail deer fled across the road ten feet in front of them. Neither of them said a word for miles.

Man whistled while he walked. What the old Indian was thinking, Handy had no idea. Handy wanted only to think about his sweet young bride back at Mahackamack. Henrietta would be a mother sometime in the dead of winter; he needed to find her a better home. Truth was, he found himself thinking almost as much about Adam K. Caulkins, the high-handed banker of Mahackamack.

As puffed up and as bejeweled as old King George III, the banker had taken a shine to Henrietta when she was twelve and he foreclosed on her family's pig farm. Handy figured that with the husband off house hunting, Caulkins might not stop at talking. As for all those slicked-up peddlers who paid too much blame attention to Henrietta's fine form, even when she was with child, they made him plum huffy. No, you couldn't trust the men of Mahackamack, though they were probably no different than men anywhere.

Handy halted and fanned himself with his straw hat. He was sweating more than he had been when the she-bear was chasing him, and he was almost as exhausted trying to keep up with an old Indian. He blamed his condition on his thoughts—the good ones about his bride and the bad ones about what other men thought of his bride—as much as the heat of the day. His Indian companion continued another fifty feet before stopping and pointing ahead. "Soon creek cross. Drink there."

"Good."

"Belly empty?"

"I'm good."

"Boy has no gun to hunt."

"I left my musket with my bride in Mahackamack. I've never shot man nor beast but I told her to shoot any bothersome fellow—white, red, black, or yellow—who steps uninvited on the front porch of our log cabin. That would be most any man except the doctor."

"How you get meat? With big knife?"

"I don't. I'm not a meat eater."

"No eat meat? You eat like deer or sheep?"

"A deer, I guess. I don't eat grass." He hoped to make the old Indian smile, but Man frowned and held his belly as if it ached. It was hard to guess when Man would grin or grimace. Handy decided he must explain himself, especially since talking seemed less tiring than walking. "As a boy I spent too much time locked in the smokehouse, where meat was always smoking over hickory shavings. My father was a hunter, for our family and for pay. He put me in the smokehouse as punishment for refusing to hunt, refusing to be like him. I couldn't kill any animal, you see, not even a mouse. When my dog got into some spoiled meat and died, I cried for a month. Father punished me for that. All I had done was cry. My mother was no different. She saw me through Father's eyes. She was as hard as him. She insisted I eat whatever meat she put on the table—deer, rabbit squirrel, possum. Whenever I refused, I was given either a licking with a hickory switch or confinement in the smokehouse. The smokehouse was worse."

Man came back to Handy, stared at him up close for a minute, then poked him in the belly. "No kill animal for food. Strange white man. You grow food?"

"No, I don't. I'm not a farmer."

"This not farm place no how 'less you grow rocks."

"Henrietta's people were pig farmers. But neither of us eat the porkers. Now that most of her family is dead, my bride is beginning to see things my way—that fat, ugly swine have as much right to live as us, not to mention deer, rabbits, squirrels, and possums."

"How you get food to live?"

"Well, when I can't find it myself and I have a little money I buy it, and if I have no money, I trade for it."

"What Boy trade?"

"Things I can offer for food."

"Things?"

"Yes, things I can do for them." Back in Mahackamack he was a gravedigger and in times when nobody was dying, he sat on his porch ready to sharpen razors, scissors, knives, and axes with his portable grinder. Those long stretches when nobody had anything to grind or didn't trust him to do the job well, he slept in his chair or went back to bed to tend to Henrietta. There were times when he and his bride stayed hungry. He saw no reason to tell the old Indian all that after already revealing he was no hunter or farmer. It would sound as if he wasn't self-sufficient, was a poor provider, and lacked ambition—all of which were true, of course. At least he was bound and determined to find a better home for Henrietta away from so-called good citizens like Adam Caulkins and the drudgery of daily toil.

"No food to buy here," Man said. "Near Hudson more settlements. Follow turnpike."

"I won't be going that far. You see I don't want our new home to be too close to the Delaware or the Hudson or even this turnpike. The farther I am from any civilized white men, the better. I don't need their talk. Nature's perfect silence suits me."

"Everything talk—animals, birds, trees, bushes, wind, rivers, spirits, rocks."

"That so? In my new home, I'll listen to those things."

"But how Boy live in new home with no eating?"

"I'll eat. I'll gather what I can, just like I've been doing on this Great Home-Hunting Expedition—mostly berries and an occasional nut, mushroom, or wild onion. And don't forget there are roots and shoots, seeds and pods. That should do it. Henrietta eats lightly, like a sparrow. Of course, with a baby coming and Henrietta being so young and inexperienced about such matters... well, I might need to get a milk cow or goat."

"Ahh, Boy no hunter, no farmer. Boy gatherer."

"You could say that. I'd like to make a home near a small river or creek where there are plenty of things to gather."

"Your squaw gatherer, too?"

"Sure, my bride gathers. She also likes to fish. Henrietta's favorite granddaddy was a sea captain from New England, and she fishes good. Fact is I met her when she came to my porch with a dull fishing knife. We got to palavering while I was a-sharpening. I was near old enough to be her granddaddy, but her favorite granddaddy was lost at sea and she was fed up with her daddy and all them pigs. She took a shine to me straight away."

"You lucky dog. You rest. Make young squaw hunt, fish, cook, wash, shoot bad men."

Handy thought such a statement would shame some men, but not him. Besides, Henrietta didn't hunt. "What about you, Man. You ever take a wife?"

"I take much many wives, one at time. None take long. Walk away or die. Wigwam empty now."

"Too bad. I imagine it's hard to find an Indian wife around here."

"Me last of Lenni Lenape. Full blood."

"Me sorry. That is to say it must be hard being the last of anything."

"My heart beat like war drum of old. We must go now."

Man adjusted his wolf-skin cap and shuffled along so quickly that Handy ran to stay close to the heels of his moccasins. They reached an unnamed creek and sipped cool water, but Man insisted they keep moving. Handy wasn't sure what the rush was, but he obliged. He soon found out the ancient Indian could speak broken English and walk fast at the same time. Man claimed that the Lenni Lenape were the oldest tribe in the country, his hot-blooded ancestors having crossed the Bering land bridge from Siberia to populate the North American continent. Other tribes referred to them as "grandfather" or the "old people." His particular group, the Wolf Clan, built many wigwams between the Hudson and Delaware rivers where they lived fairly peacefully until Dutch miners and settlers ventured up from New Amsterdam. Then came bigger trouble—the English and the raiding Iroquois, the ones who called the Lenni Lenape "women."

"You don't walk like any woman I know," said Handy. "Won't you slow down some?"

"No woman. Me Man." He patted his buckskin shirt over his heart and chuckled while walking faster. "Soon we sleep, Boy."

It wasn't soon, but as darkness set in over the rugged country, they reached a river, which confused Handy because it was far too narrow to be the Hudson. "*Nkëchehòsi sipu,*" said Man. "Means 'crazy river.' You call 'Neversink.' No one drown here." He made camp, not in any wigwam but under the open air among the ferns and rhododendrons. They went a short way to find several handfuls of blueberries, most of which they devoured at their campsite while sitting on the ground admiring the stars and listening to the river rumble over and around its rocky bed.

"Boy belly rumble like river," Man said.

"Maybe I should have filled my hat with those berries."

Handy was nibbling on what looked like a fern but seemed satisfied. "Boy sleep now. When sun rise, I take Boy cross river to place where bushes wear color of sky."

Handy sat up as if bitten by a snake. "You mean more blueberry bushes?"

"More than see in dream. Blue Place. Now sleep."

"But how far to this Blue Place?"

"Not far as crow fly."

"But how far as man walks?"

"Not far for Man. How far for Boy cannot say."

Catawissa Manayunk suddenly flopped down on his belly; his hump must have made sleeping on his back disagreeable. Using his wolf-skin cap as a pillow, he drifted off to sleep with one eye still open. Handy couldn't sleep. He felt agitated but didn't know why. He remembered something told him long ago by his mother, who used to scrub the floors of the Reformed Church of

Tapan but knew many things because she would read books when not cleaning or serving meat. He touched Man's round shoulder. "You know, it was pretty foolish for your people to sell Manhattan Island to the Dutch for a few trinkets two-hundred years ago."

Man grunted. "No person own land. Land like ocean and stars. My people trade right to use island to Dutchman. Dutch no understand. We no sell land. No sell!"

"Seems to me that Dutchmen made one hell of a deal."

"Balls! You been to Manhattan?"

"That's not the point. Mahackamack is too big for me. I don't wish to go to Manhattan, but it is an important place for Americans. Many, many people live there and many more come there to make money. It has no interest to me but that's me. I like trees and animals more than buildings and people. You are nodding your head. Have you been to New York City?"

"One time. Ketanëtuwit tell me: 'Go there. Learn white way.' Horse wagon run me over. Leg break. Beads stolen. Ketanëtuwit say: 'Go no more. No place for Lenni Lenape.'"

"Well, at least the Dutch are long gone."

"English pay Dutch nothing for Manhattan. Dutch more fools than Lenni Lenape. Yes?"

"I wouldn't know about that. Anyway, it's American now. We defeated the British."

"And Monster Brant. Lenni Lenape gone. Old enemies gone, too."

Handy suddenly felt generous. "At least you're here with me, Man, and New York City and all those swarms of people are many, many miles away."

"Sit on porcupine better than go to Manhattan."

"Agreed."

"White man want everything. Much greedy."

"Not me. Just want a home. I haven't enough money to buy trinkets."

"Tomorrow, we see Blue Place. You find home. Free. No worry."

"Thank you. Sleep well, Man."

"Boy sleep good."

4

BLUE PLACE

Both woke up with the sun. After a breakfast of blueberries, they crossed the Neversink on stones and stumbled upon the Old Mine Road, which ran north and south for a hundred miles. Catawissa Manayunk insisted that Lenni Lenape had used this very route to travel between their hunting and fishing areas and that later the Dutch had built a road over the Indian trail to haul ore from a couple mines whose locations were known to him but few others. Handy, breathing hard, only shrugged.

"Some say mine holes full with silver and gold," the old Indian said, stopping suddenly and nudging Handy in the ribs with a sharp elbow.

Handy shrugged again. "How far now to Blue Place?"

"Strange white man. No like silver and gold?"

"I have nothing against them personally. But mining is too much work. And if you are rich, you can't enjoy life. You spend all your days trying to get richer."

"I tell truth now. No gold. No silver. Lead. Lenni Lenape know. Hear stories from old ones now in spirit world. Only lead."

"I see. So, you were only testing me. Can we please continue now?"

"Good, Boy. We go."

They traveled along a Neversink tributary, the Basha Kill, which was full of fish. Near midday, Man used Handy's big knife and a willow switch to fashion a spear. Primitive or not, it took the Indian only three tries to spear a trout the colors of the rainbow. Seeing the pierced fish wiggle on the blade didn't repulse Handy. Quite the opposite. Something about that movement caused him to long for his fifteen-year-old pregnant wife. It didn't take much. And he was hungry, too. He came to his senses, though, when Man cleaned and cooked his catch. While Man was filling his belly, Handy washed the death off the blade, then stared into the river, trying to find his own reflection. That took his mind off his hunger pains. He ate not a single bite of fish; he smelled fresh fruit on the horizon.

A village called Rome was nearby in the Mamakating valley, Man said. He had heard a story, supposedly from a white man rather than one of his own ancestors, that an optimistic fellow standing on that spot could see seven hills and decided to name the place after an ancient city with seven hills that stood across the great ocean. By mutual agreement, Man and Handy decided to bypass the tiny community. Instead, they followed old trails of the Lenni Lenape toward several of those hills—the foothills of the Shawangunk Mountains.

When they crossed a stream known by some as the Little Basha, the blueberry bushes, both high and low varieties, were thick as thieves. Handy paused under the shade of a magnificent chestnut tree to survey his surroundings, a sea of blue. "Are we there yet?" Handy asked.

Man shook his bent head and kept walking, sometimes putting a hop into his step for no apparent reason. "Come, Boy."

A half mile further on what wasn't much more than a deer trail through the brush, they came upon a red fox that stood on a flat, rectangular rock with most of its head lowered into some kind of hole. The fox was slow in reacting to human presence. Its ears twitched but the head stayed lowered. Handy listened to the silence of nature until it was disturbed by slurping sounds.

The old Indian addressed the fox: "Save some for Man and Boy, ôkwës."

The animal bolted and Man laughed.

Handy didn't know what was so funny. "Why'd you scare him off?" he asked. "It's not like he was a wolf."

"But me wolf. Remember?"

"I remember. Where are we?"

"Place where go to drink. Big spring." Man waved Handy forward. "Boy go first."

Handy stepped onto the flat rock, went to his knees, and cupped his hands in a natural basin with a continuous flow of groundwater rising out of the clay bottom to the surface like a living, breathing amphibious creature. He carefully scooped water to his blue lips and took a swallow. Then he removed his straw hat and repeated the process over and over, not caring how much water splashed on his face and neck. It was the sweetest water he had ever tasted, going smooth and easy down his throat and soothing his insides. Though not a religious man, he imagined he was at some holy alter and mumbled his thanks to somebody up there for this liquid bounty.

"Ketanëtuwit, blesses this spot," said Man as if he had read Handy's mind.

"Good medicine," Handy said. He took another long swallow, and he hummed, the hum seeming to originate from deep in his belly. He scooped a hatful and turned the hat over to put it on his head. As the water dripped over his ears, he at last relinquished his spot at the watering hole.

The old Indian squatted on the rock and said a few words in his own language before partaking. Not to appear too greedy, he withdrew to give the white man another crack at the spring. Handy gulped away, then stuck his entire head, hat and all, under water. His thirst was long gone, but he felt as if he wanted to drink until he burst.

"Water go to head," Man said. "No worries. I lie to fox. Water forever. Never die."

Handy did not reply. He excused himself and walked to where a red pine was sandwiched between two boulders suggesting the private parts of a male giant. It was downhill from the spring and seemed like a good place to relieve himself. He then returned to the spring for yet another drink. He invented a silly song: *Here I drink/Here I pee/One or the other/Endlessly.* Man wasn't listening. He had advanced up the hill and dropped into his favorite position—a toad squat. The old Indian was chanting in his own language. Handy determined Man must be blessing the water or else blessing Ketanëtuwit for creating the spring. Handy saw that as most appropriate behavior. He started up the hill to join him and noticed a new spring to his step as if he had just drunk from a northern version of the Fountain of Youth. He stepped on, over, and around scattered fieldstones as he wound his way upward through the bushes with such vigor that he soon stepped on the heels of his savior's moccasins.

"Watch it, Boy," said Man.

"Sorry," said Handy. "My feet are moving faster than usual. That spring revived me."

"Always do that."

"You have been here often, I take it?"

"Much many. We here. Watch blueness."

"You mean the sky?"

"And berries. All same. Look!" Man pointed a bony finger upward.

Ahead, Handy saw a long gentle slope that looked as if it might extend right up to the cloudless sky. This hill was layered in bushes dotted to overload with rich blues and purples. The berries and sky began to run together creating an indigo glow that temporarily blinded him. As if he didn't believe the white man had enough sense to pick the berries himself, Man plucked several small ones growing at eye level and held them out in his open palm. "For you, Boy," he said, watching instead of feeding himself.

Handy bit into one, and the blue juice gave him a jolt. Then he popped another in his mouth and it was as gratifying as the water. He gobbled up the last four from Man's hand. He again thought of Henrietta. What else could compare but her sweetness? He picked several more off the bush himself before he realized the old Indian was staring at him and tittering.

"Do they all taste like this?" Handy asked

"No. All kinds. High and low. Some better. Best near top."

"I see. Is this Blue Place?"

It had been a dumb question that needed no answer. Man clicked his tongue and meandered through the bushes, never stubbing a toe despite all the exposed stones that had been deposited on the hill by the last flow of ancient ice. Handy licked his lips and continued, unable to resist picking during his ascent to a clearing where the land flattened and a ledge cut into the hill like the blade of a giant's knife. He wasn't tired but Blue Place had left him breathless. He paused and sighed as he scanned beyond the ledge. The hill's sunny slope became steeper, but the blueberry bushes looked no less thick.

"I can't believe it," Handy said. "There's more hill ahead. We aren't even halfway up."

"Stop here," said Man, laughing. "Hill will wait for us."

"All right, if you're tuckered."

That made Man snort merrily. Handy had never imagined an Indian could be so easily amused. Man hadn't stopped on the ledge to rest. He picked up two heart-shaped rocks as if he knew where they would be and clicked them together over his head while chanting and dancing in a circle. His hump seemed alive, moving back and forth, up and down, beneath his animal skin shirt. Handy told himself it must be his imagination, but the hump wouldn't be still.

Every so often Man would raise a knee above his waist and call out the names of spirits—family members who had left this earth, Handy gathered. The white man had enough energy to dance, but he thought it might offend his friend to imitate a native ritual. Handy settled for bobbing his head and clapping his hands.

"Later use turtle-shell rattles," Man said. "More better than stones or rattlesnake rattles."

"From rattlesnakes around here?

"Rattlesnakes like old rock."

"Oh. And I've noticed many old rocks beneath these wonderful bushes."

"Much many rattlesnakes."

"I don't like to kill things. But rattlesnakes..."

"Lenni Lenape Blueberry Dance scare away."

"Good, then I'm all for it."

"Get stones. Boy dance. Follow me."

Handy found two quickly—both fit nicely into his hands, though neither was heart-shaped—and beat them together awkwardly as he joined in the dancing. He tried to do whatever the old Indian did, including calling out to an ancestor, in his case Granddad Braxton Boyd, once known for his fair Irish jig and fiddle playing. It was a relief that Man did not look back to find fault with him. There would be time enough later to learn how to do the Blueberry Dance properly.

They danced till dark on the ledge. Both exhausted, they still climbed nearly to the top of the hill before their legs gave out all at once and they collapsed. In the darkness, Handy barely made out the ghostly outline of a massive rocky outcrop on the hilltop fifty feet ahead. It was a hot night. They stretched out on a bed of moss, Man on his stomach with his nose buried in his wolf-skin cap, Handy on his back using his rolled-up shirt as a pillow.

Man whistled in his sleep, a soothing sound, and the blue jay feather quivered with his every breath but somehow stayed upright next to his open mouth. Handy fanned himself with his straw hat as he watched the old Indian. He wanted to stay awake as long as he could to stare at the stars. When they came out in full, they cast a blue light that twinkled. When the moon appeared, even it had a blue face. Handy decided that Man was the best friend he'd ever had during his half-century of life. For the next ten minutes he thought about not only the old Indian and young Henrietta and the child that was coming but also the great beyond. Not since his early boyhood living in the shadow of the Reformed Church of Tappan had he put so much faith in the belief that somewhere up in the high blueberry blue sky was a Supreme Being.

5
NEW LIFE ON THE HILL

Handy was overcome by the beauty of Blueberry Hill and to fully appreciate it in the morning he first climbed half a dozen branches up a hemlock for a bird's-eye view, then up the rocky outcrop on the hilltop for a panoramic view. Afterward, not yet fully recovered from his two-day expedition from Mahackamack, he dropped into the bushes and took up his favorite position—supine. He might have continued lying there all day, but his old-as-the-hills friend, Catawissa Manayunk, advised him against it. "Nature offer bounty but no home," he said. "Man need shelter. Boy need shelter. Time now to clear, make space in Blue Place."

"Of course," said Handy. "I'll be with you in a minute."

It was more like an hour before Handy rose from the ground to do his share. He apologized, but didn't make up for lost time. Catawissa Manayunk had already cleared dead wood and rocks from the ledge halfway up Blueberry Hill and started to build a wigwam. The slow-moving Handy only contributed a few sticks but Man didn't hold the white man's lax work habits against him.

For two months they shared the wigwam without the hint of a squabble that might jeopardize their friendship. During the second month, they worked at their different speeds nearby, digging deep into the side of the hill using animal bones and sticks sharpened with Handy's Revolutionary War knife, throwing aside stone after stone, and collecting branches, tall grass, moss, and leaves to fashion a dugout. The roof was the hill itself. The rough home was still unlivable in early November when Handy bid Man goodbye to find his way back to Mahackamack to fetch a shovel and his pregnant wife.

He made good time getting to her, but their plan for a quick return to Blue Place didn't happen. Their first born, Chester, arrived ahead of schedule and neither mother nor baby was up to traveling for weeks. There were also debts to pay, the principal one to Adam K. Caulkins. The lustful banker made an indecent proposal to Henrietta involving a hayloft and money enough to erase the debt. When Handy learned of the proposition, he stepped out of character and told his wife he was mad enough to thrash Mr. Caulkins. Henrietta assured her husband she had already taken care of the matter by striking the unprincipled man with a ham bone, making his considerable snout bleed like a stuck pig. But the debt was not forgiven.

The Boyds sold their rickety cabin and personal belongings to pay back Mr. Caulkins and avoid arrest. Handy was glad to be rid of his portable grinder but had mixed feelings about the shovel that he had promised to bring back to Man. On Blueberry Hill he had no intention to sharpen other people's axes and knives or to dig their graves for them. To him, being a free man meant being free of the demands of others, except, of course, those made by his young bride and baby Chesty. Henrietta, tired of the tiresome men and busybody women in Mahackamack, wanted to leave as much as he did. Almost all of her family, the Deckers, had passed on. She didn't care for a last look at the old pig farm that a maiden aunt was selling. When Henrietta said she was ready to go, they went…on foot.

Handy's back bore the brunt of an overloaded pack and strapped-on bundle. These held Henrietta's things: pots and pans, fish-oil lamp, carved wooden ware, salt box, candles, dresses, chemises, second pair of shoes, extra straw bonnet, combs, face powders, blankets, an unworn Bible, and a soiled quilt she had inherited from her pig-farming family. Chester rode on Henrietta's back in a wood-framed contraption that didn't quite measure up to an Indian cradleboard. "If Sacajawea did it, so can I," the young bride boldly announced, though of course they were not going up the wild Upper Missouri (only plodding north roughly parallel to the Neversink). "And you can lead the way, Handy, just like Lewis and Clark." Handy was relieved he did not have to be another Lewis or Clark; he already knew the way to Blue Place.

They met neither bear nor Indian on their journey. Handy wanted to lessen his load along the way, but Henrietta wouldn't allow him to discard a single item from the pack. They moved at whatever pace she wanted and rested only when she felt like it. Whether she walked on the road ahead of him or behind him or next to him, it always felt as if she were leading. Halfway to Blue Place, it occurred to him that, though she was unquestionably young and desirable, she was more strong-boned and headstrong than he had realized back in Mahackamack. Not that he had reason to complain. He couldn't imagine her ever striking him, her loving husband, with a ham bone. He also realized, considering his sluggish nature, he needed on occasion to be prodded. No matter how domineering she might be by day, he could live with it, for he knew each night the pig farmer's daughter would energetically wrap her splendid legs around his waist and squeeze until he squealed with pleasure. Handy anticipated he and his fervent bride producing more than a handful of sturdy children. His hope in the long run at Blue Place was to have one girl to help Henrietta with the cooking, cleaning, and organizing and at least four boys to handle whatever other household chores and outside work needed to be done.

Weary as he was and sore as his back felt, Handy still had the energy upon reaching the Hill to slap Catawissa Manayunk on his hump, hug him like a long-lost relative, and praise his thoughtfulness. The ancient Lenni Lenape had completed the dugout after acquiring a sturdy shovel from a white man living in Mamakating Hollow. Not only that, Man had made it feel homelike by covering the stone floor with thick Indian blankets; by obtaining sugar, flour, and coffee in trade for blueberries he picked, fish he caught, and the enthralling 18th-century stories he told of warfare, scalping and massacres; and by, most amazing of all, bringing in a supply of baby clothes given to him by a lady whose ten children had grown and who had a soft spot in her heart for the put-upon Indian race, especially a redskin with a huge hump and a slight limp.

"Me deal with much many pale face in Rome," Man said. "'Me no scare them. Me laugh with them, smoke peace pipe with them, tell tales with them. Me big trader."

"I never saw your peace pipe, Man," Handy said.

"No have. Smoke clay tobacco pipe of pale face."

Henrietta found the dugout cozy and warm that first winter at Blue Place, and Handy slept a lot, as did the baby. All three of them liked the ancient Lenni Lenape, who chose to stay in his wigwam but assured them he was within shouting distance if needed. Indeed, many times when Henrietta was busy and Handy was resting, Man would carry the crying Chester through the bushes and tell him the names of trees, plants, animals and spirits, great or otherwise. Man hunted and fished and scared away the large predators—bears, panthers, and, yes, wolves. So often was Man needed that Henrietta couldn't imagine surviving the winter and beyond without his able assistance. In the spring, they did the Blueberry Dance together and in the summer the Hill provided a bountiful supply of blueberries.

In 1812 the Indian was there to help Henrietta bring her second child, Elmer, into their wonderful world, and two years after that he lent a hand when Henry arrived coughing and crying his oversized head off. Ezekiel Tears, the young white doctor in Mamakating Hollow, said this sickly third baby wouldn't live out his first year, but Catawissa Manayunk—with the help of prayers to Ketanëtuwit, guidance by Man's wolf spirit, remembered advice from former wives, mysterious herbs, mashed blueberries, and doses of pure spring water—proved the better medicine man.

"He's like a woman and a man, an angel and a saint, a medicine man and a brave—all rolled into one," Henrietta told her husband five years after arriving on the Hill. "He is our savior."

"You are absolutely right, Pudding. His connections must extend to those in higher places." Handy pointed toward a sunbeam streaking between the open crowns of pyramidal-shaped hemlocks. "Here on Blueberry Hill, we are blessed with the tall trees, the berries, the spring water, three mostly healthy boys, and the last of the Lenni Lenape. He is our friend for life. He can live next to us in his wigwam as long as he likes. Wouldn't it be great, Pudding, if *our* Man proved immortal on top of everything else?"

Man was what they both called him and the boys learned to call him, too. Never *Old* Man, for while he had sixteen years on Handy, he never seemed to age. He didn't get uglier and he didn't get shorter. His hump, though, began to shrink. He claimed that, without asking for it, Ketanëtuwit was slowly lessening his burden as a reward for his being a true believer in the Lenni Lenape way.

Catawissa Manayunk kept calling Handy *Boy* and often called Henrietta *Wulinaxin*, meaning "One Who Looks Fine." Handy didn't mind. She did look fine, and he knew his friend was nothing like those scoundrels back in Mahackamack. He could trust Man around Henrietta. For more than a dozen years, Man was the main provider on Blueberry Hill. All three Boyd boys delighted in riding his hump and shaking the turtle-shell rattles he provided each of them. He showed a feminine touch when comforting their fears, healing their wounds, and telling them his stories. The boys delighted in his bedtime tales of creation (the first man came from the roots of a tree, and when the tree bent down and kissed the ground, the first woman sprang from it) and of Lenni Lenape foxlike cleverness (which allowed them to outwit the mighty Mohawk and the deceitful Dutch). The squat hunchback rose above his station in Henrietta's eyes by starting a small corn, bean, and squash garden amid the blueberries without neglecting traditional manly duties—hunting deer and even bear with a bow and arrow, trapping rabbits and squirrels, destroying poisonous snakes, shoring up the dugout, chopping wood, chasing off the occasional human trespasser, and hobnobbing in town with white men to keep up with current events and sell them venison. Handy objected to all that killing of animals, except for the rattlesnakes, because he didn't believe his family needed to eat meat. But he could look the other way to keep the peace with Henrietta. He felt that without Man around, his life as a husband and father would have become too difficult on Blueberry Hill to carry on despite his unbounded love for his Pudding and his three sons. His wife, he was convinced, felt the same.

Henrietta found her husband caring and loveable but also languid and limited in his adroitness and ambitions. The family of five (not counting Man) was dirt-poor, yet Handy thought they had all they needed—each other; a roof over their head, even if it was the Hill itself; trees that would never know the ax; the constant flow of spring water; and all the blueberries they could eat, fresh or dried, alone or mixed with cracked corn in the pudding he called sautauthig. He did not seriously attempt to build a regular, above-ground house and it wasn't just out of laziness. He didn't have the tools or the skill for such a grand endeavor and, in any case, was not out to harm living trees. He was content to contribute nothing more than wild food—hand-picked berries, nuts, seeds, and mushrooms—to the dugout table that Man had cobbled together with dead wood and fieldstones. He rarely set foot in the garden maintained by Man and Henrietta. Vegetables were less objectionable than meat to eat and he did so on occasion to please Henrietta, but he barely found them palatable and he didn't like the fact that growing them disturbed the land and diminished the soil. "I prefer not to harm plant or animal," he liked to tell his wife. "Eating blueberries doesn't harm the bushes. They come back on their own."

Henrietta didn't fully understand Handy, but she could live with such a peaceable man who never laid an angry hand on her or the children or even cursed in front of them. He patiently taught the boys how to read using Henrietta's Bible, though he told them not to believe everything they read. He also told them all he knew about the world, though he was prone to suggest that much about the world needed to be questioned if not outright rejected. Living with Handy was made easier, of course, because Catawissa Manayunk was such a damn good provider.

When the three Boyd boys were done with mother's milk, Man traded with Mamakating Hollow farmer Archibald Seybolt to bring a milk cow named Paddy and three unnamed hens to the Hill. The results were mixed at best. The milk made Henry sick, and his two brothers mostly stuck to spring water, though they would put a little milk in their coffee and considered Paddy a fine pet. The boys ate the eggs for a while, but they had to be scrambled with sugar on top. Handy ate eggs, too. He found it acceptable because there was no rooster around and no chicks would ever hatch from the eggs. But then a family of foxes came to the Hill and made off with all three hens. Handy told Man to never bring home another chicken.

The ancient Indian regularly took Henrietta fishing in the Basha Kill, and they returned with trout, largemouth bass, chain pickerel, and once a remarkable "prehistoric" bowfin. Handy was strictly a homebody, anchoring himself to the dugout. He raised his boys to respect fish and other animals too much to slaughter them, though the trio never turned down the trout their mother caught and fried or the deer meat Man roasted on a spit. None of them questioned their father's questionable eating habits except when whispering among themselves until Chester, at age eleven, spoke up in spring 1823 after seeing a live Easter bunny hop past. He and his father were sitting on the hillside roof of their dugout home digesting their dried blueberry and brown bread afternoon meal.

"I wouldn't eat a rabbit," Chester said. "Not even if it wasn't Easter time."

"Good boy," said Handy.

"But I might like a pig...you know ham. I could put some on my bread."

"I know ham. No ham in my house. We human beings should even respect pigs."

"Man respects animals like you do, Dad, but he still eats them."

"He's an Indian. Indians eat meat."

"He thanks them for giving up their lives so we can live. He blesses the slain animals and asks them to forgive him."

"And, Chesty, do they—gutted, cut into selected parts, and cooked medium rare—forgive?"

"Their spirits do. Man says animal spirits attach to human beings. Or maybe it is the other way around. Anyway, Dad, there is an attachment. His guardian spirit is the wolf."

"He told me."

"You don't believe it?"

"He can howl like a wolf and scare off a bear. He saved my life. I doubt that would have been possible without the help of a wolf spirit. Still, that doesn't explain why the wolf spirit was guarding me that day."

"Could be you have a wolf spirit, too."

"Not likely. Wolves are voracious meat eaters, and I would not trust a wolf to guard me. If I were a Lenni Lenape, my guardian spirit would be something else, say the unicorn."

"Unicorn? But they aren't real."

"And so, they could not eat me. Nor could they be eaten. Unicorns don't grow old and die."

"I suppose not, but you would still grow old and die. Not even unicorn guardian spirits can help you avoid that, Good Old Dad. It's the price we all pay for being alive."

"And that includes Man himself, smart boy. Catawissa Manayunk has occupied this Earth for a great many years. But his time will come."

"He has no fear of the next world."

"Good for him. But I see no good reason to behave like a meat-hungry wolf in this world, and I don't intend to start doing so in the spirit world either."

"You think if unicorns actually existed, they would feed only on blueberries and nuts?"

"Of course. I would expect nothing less of my guardian spirit."

Chester loved his Good Old Dad, but the man was, besides being a meat denier, a delayer, a dawdler, and an idler. Nothing emphasized that point more than where they lived—a three-room dugout—dug out of the stony hillside as a temporary living space way back when he was born. Catawissa Manayunk, defying his age, had done most of the digging even though he preferred to live alone in his wigwam. Since then, Handy, who treated most labor like the plague, had made countless promises and resolutions about building a genuine house one day. One obstacle to building any kind of house had come in 1818 when a group in Wurtsborough, the former Rome, challenged Handy's declared ownership of Blueberry Hill. The next year, though, with the help of Henrietta and Elmer, Handy was able to convince a distraught War of 1812 widow to sell him the forty acres on the west side of the Hill for almost nothing since she had never occupied it and didn't believe it was good for anything. After that the land needed to be surveyed and mapped, and a deed drawn up. All well and good. That was done by 1820, but a bigger obstacle remained to moving up from a dugout to an above-ground structure—Handy's laziness.

6
ON THE CANAL

In spring 1825 when Man finally showed signs of slowing down—as the Boyds' substance provider; he continued strong as spiritual provider— Henrietta pushed the idea of a family blueberry business. To acquire basic goods, they would begin selling their choice berries rather than eating all they picked. Handy was skeptical. "It won't work, Pudding," he told his wife. "Nobody likes blueberries better than me but when there are so many available bushes to pick from, nobody will want to buy our crop."

"Hogwash," she said. "We have the richest blueberry patch in New York state, and people are too lazy or too occupied to pick, even if they can find a place to pick."

Although not a practitioner of any established religion, Handy considered Blueberry Hill's bounties of berries a blessing to his family, and he did not wish to become a money grabber. He stopped objecting, though, when Henrietta told him he wouldn't have to sell anything himself and she herself would not appear in Wurtsborough as a tradeswoman among all those untrustworthy tradesmen. Chester, thirteen and becoming more and more free spoken every day, and Elmer, twelve and resolute, were old enough and bold enough to do the job. Husband and wife agreed that ten-year-old Henry was not mature enough to go with his two brothers. He thoughtlessly ate ten blueberries for every one he picked off the bush and couldn't resist throwing rocks at every squirrel or chipmunk he saw. Besides, he was sickly since birth and a Mama's boy who had developed his father's fear and distrust of strange people (anyone not in the family), especially crowds of them.

It was on July 13 of that year that Chester and Elmer pushed and pulled a cartful of Boyd blueberries to the valley for the first time. Their mother had given them explicit instructions: Bring the berries to Archibald Seybolt's fruit stand in Wurtsborough, haggle with Mr. Seybolt for no more than five minutes, sell him *all* the berries at whatever his best offer might be, have *only* one drink apiece of apple cider, purchase one sack of flour from the general store, and return with cart, flour, and the remaining money directly and at good speed to Blueberry Hill for more picking. They were immediately sidetracked by a great commotion taking place in a town where normally nothing much happened and the population welcomed any diversion from the routine. Against Elmer's better judgment they stashed the fully loaded cart under a grove of rhododendrons to better maneuver through the milling town folk. Neither boy had ever seen so many people gathered in one place, and they couldn't make sense of it until Chester bumped into a man too tall, wide, and bullheaded to slip past.

"No need to get a wiggle on," the man said, grabbing Chester by the collar. "Nothing's happening yet. I'll let you know when I see something."

"I want to see for myself," said Chester, breaking free and ducking under a dripping wet armpit. The fleshy man was no doubt a meat eater, could probably eat a whole chicken or pig himself.

"Excuse my brother, mister," said Elmer. "We don't come to town much and Chesty don't know how to behave in society. What is supposed to happen?"

"Where you been, sonny? The bigwig is about to break ground."

"What for?"

"Progress, my boy, progress. Today's the big day we've been waiting for—the groundbreaking ceremony of the Delaware & Hudson Canal. You must have heard about it."

Elmer shook his head. "I ain't been waiting. A canal, huh?"

"Sure," said Chester. "Man mentioned hearing of a Big Ditch coming this way. I plum forgot."

"It'll be big all right," said the fat man, "One hundred eight miles long, four feet deep, thirty-two feet wide, hundreds of locks and bridges, and passing right through our valley."

"Not nearly as big as the Erie one, I reckon," said Chester. "I heard tell that canal up state runs more than three-hundred miles."

"Three hundred sixty to be exact, from Buffalo to Albany. Our canal is big enough. The D&H will bring us prosperity. I see President Philip Hone now waving to the crowd."

"I thought John Q. Adams was president," said Elmer.

"Mr. Hone is president of the canal company. Somebody has handed him a shiny new long-handled shovel. His sleeves are rolled up. He means business. He's about to turn the first shovelful of earth."

"I can't see a damn thing,' said Chester, standing on his toes. He pushed his way between a narrow man in a Sunday go-to-a-meetin' coat and a broad-shouldered woman wearing a yellow dress with leg-of-mutton sleeves. "Follow me, Elm," he shouted as he disappeared into the crowd.

"Not me, Chesty." Elmer then addressed the fleshy man. "You mean to tell me, mister, all these people are here to see this fellow dig dirt?"

"Looks like just one shovelful from the bigwig, sonny. That's all that's needed. It's a symbol of growth and progress. I saw this very same thing happen on July 4, 1817, when work commenced on the Erie Canal on a long level stretch at Rome. Now there's a historic coincidence for you. The first dig in the Mohawk valley was at a village called Rome, and this dig eight years later in the Mamakating valley is occurring at a village formerly known as Rome. What does that tell you, sonny? I'll tell you what it tells you: It tells you and everyone else that the great progressive state of New York is more important than all of Italy. Over there, they've always had but one Rome."

Elmer grimaced. It didn't tell him why the village had changed its name from Rome to Wurtsborough. He doubted any other place anywhere had the name Wurtsborough. Even he knew Rome, Italy, was chock full of important buildings, including a Colosseum, a Forum, and a Pantheon, whatever that was, along with baths, fountains and aqueducts. He took an interest in *that* Rome because he admired grand structures built in stone. He didn't know anything about the Rome in the Mohawk valley, but the former Rome they were standing in right now didn't have much more than a few wooden houses, a general store, a tavern, a livery stable, and farmer Archibald Seybolt's fruit stand.

"Somebody else is digging now," reported the fleshy man. "That would be chief engineer John B. Jervis. He gained a world of experience working on the Erie Canal. Why, I was there when J.B. decided to..."

The clapping and cheering from the crowd drowned out Mr. Know-all. Elmer, not wanting to disappoint his mother, decided to slip away, backward, not forward, to check on the blueberry cart. But the fleshy man interrupted himself to say something that made Elmer stop in his tracks: "Good Lord! Look who has the shovel now! It was left stuck in the ground unattended and he picked it right up! I swear to God that's your pushy brother!"

Elmer reversed course and excused himself a dozen times as he worked his way to the front of the crowd. He arrived at the hole destined to be transformed into a canal in time to see a burly fellow with a corn pipe in his mouth wrench the long-handled shiny shovel out of the hands of Chester. The tool was passed around to at least four well-dressed men before it ended up with D&H President Hone, who was surprised to see it again. "Sorry, young man," said Hone, taking a gigantic step toward Chester. "No construction contract has been signed yet. But as soon as that happens, I expect to see you back here ready to get your hands dirty. Nothing Philip Hone likes better than an eager beaver." He laughed, the crowd laughed with him, and finally Chester laughed. Everyone laughed except Elmer. If he had learned anything from his Good Old Dad it was to lay low and never make a spectacle of yourself.

While still in a jolly mood, President Hone tossed the shovel to Jervis, but it bounced off the chief engineer's hands and struck the shins of the burly fellow, whose scream caused the corn pipe to go flying into the hole. Even that didn't cause Elmer to crack a smile. "What on earth got into you, Chester the

Jester?" he asked with arms crossed and eyes darting about as if he didn't want anyone to think they were related.

"Like some wise graybeard once said: When in Rome, do as the Romans do."

"It's not Rome anymore, you idiot. It's Wurtsborough!"

They left the scene fast. Chester spotted a man with a badge coming his way, and Elmer was desperate to get back to the blueberry cart. Neither brother said a word until they had reached the rhododendron grove. Then Elmer screamed. All four sacks of blueberries were missing from the cart.

"I knew this would happen," he said. 'I told you this would happen. Now we have no berries to sell Mr. Seybolt and we'll have no money to buy flour and..."

"At least they left the cart."

"Yes, to carry back nothing."

"Damn it, Elm. It was worth it."

"Perhaps if we explain to Mr. Seybolt about our misfortune, he will lend us enough money to at least buy the sack of flour."

"Forget it, Elm. Seabolt ain't no friend. He's as much a businessman as a farmer. You know what Old Dad says about businessmen. They put business ahead of men, treat women like chattel, and believe children should be seen not heard."

"Well, it's all your fault and you had better say so when we get home. Why should I get the switch from Mama?"

"Why indeed. And you never do, do you. You're such a good boy."

"And you're so bad, Chesty."

"Could be but I'm also famous."

"How do you figure?"

"I turned over the third shovelful of dirt on the D&H Canal."

"Nobody will remember the third man."

"Nevertheless, I am *that* man. I'll never forget it and neither will you."

"I'll never forget that it cost us four sacks of blueberries."

"When you get older and wiser, Elm, assuming that you do, you're gonna find out there are some things in life more important than blueberries."

Their parents hadn't learned that particular life lesson yet. That evening Handy, who loved blueberries as much as life itself but never delivered corporal punishment, nodded approvingly while Henrietta applied the hickory switch to Chester's backside. Elmer was spared.

Later that month, a contract for constructing the seventeen-mile, lock-free "Summit Level" section of the canal was signed and Chester was eager to do some serious digging, but Handy and Henrietta could not spare the boy. "Blueberry bushes are one of the finest creations of Ketanëtuwit; he dreamed of them and they were born," said Handy, who had adopted various bits of

Man's Lenni Lenape beliefs. "But they still can't pick themselves."

The rest of that summer, Elmer, Henrietta's favorite son, followed Chester around with a cowbell that he rang anytime it looked as if his older brother might stray from the blueberry patch. Elmer, though he preferred to work with stone, honed a better switch from a hickory tree so that their mother could thrash Chester more efficiently anytime he got wandering feet. So, without any help from Chester Boyd, the D&H Canal was being built in a hurry along the Old Mine Road, headed for Rondout Creek near Kingston where it would meet the mighty Hudson River.

§

In 1826 Philip Hone became mayor of New York City, which figured to benefit the most from the Pennsylvania anthracite coal that would be hauled to market on canal barges. That year, Henrietta, who had suffered two stillborn babies after Henry, gave birth to her first girl. Aida was fussy to an extreme but no matter—she was alive! The family was growing again, and to support it, Henrietta pushed the blueberry business more than ever. For Chester, 1826 was nothing but a lost year, during which he was forced to endure another long, blueberry-picking summer and a boring blueberry-drying fall on the increasingly intolerable Hill. The Blue Place, particularly the dugout, was giving him the blues.

For a while Handy gained support for his anti-house attitude from Man, who had conferred with Lenni Lenape spirits and was convinced that an above-ground white man's house was wrong. It would mean destroying too many trees and bushes on a hill sacred to the Wolf Clan of the Lenni Lenape Nation, never mind that he was the only Lenni Lenape left in the area. "This my Indian homeland," Man reminded the Boyds in June 1827. "White man house make Ketanëtuwit angry. He creator here, not Boyds. No build!" Of course, nobody had to listen to Man, an ancient Indian who theoretically was a mere squatter. Handy did.

"We do well to listen to Man," Handy told his wife. "He was here first."

"Maybe so, but didn't he build this dugout for you?" said Henrietta. "Was the land any less sacred back then?"

She had made a good point, but Handy wasn't ready to admit it. He stayed quiet while he considered the matter.

"Like *Wulinaxin* but squaw no speak of this," said Man.

"I am not a squaw and I'll speak of this and anything else I damn well want to speak about."

That was certainly true, thought Handy. But he remained silent. He preferred when she said *darn* instead of *damn*.

"Dugout no house," said Man.

"I agree with you there," said Henrietta. "I want a real house just like you want your wigwam. This dugout is not a suitable place for a white woman with three sons, a baby daughter, and likely another young-in on the way."

"Perhaps we could expand the dugout," suggested Handy. "Wait! Did I hear you right, Pudding? Are you expecting again so soon? That is wonderful news, Pudding."

"Nothing definite yet, but whether or not another one comes, no dugout will do. We are not a growing family of moles."

"*Wulinaxin* no mole," Man agreed.

"None of us are," said Chester. "I don't want to be underground forever, at least not until I'm dead!"

Henrietta looked for a minute as if she wanted to put the hickory switch to him for talking out of turn. But then she must have realized her oldest son was supporting her side. She cried out, "Yes, Yes, Yes," and shook her husband by the shoulders as if he were a naughty child. "You don't want to bury your children alive!"

The conversation had taken a shocking turn as far as Handy was concerned. His son and wife were both too young to be bringing up death. He himself avoided the painful subject. "You're darn right, Pudding, something must be done."

"Like *Wulinaxin*," Man said again. "Me go back to Ketanëtuwit."

Later that month, Catawissa Manayunk did seek further guidance from the Great Spirit, who apparently decided that the Boyds were an exception, being less destructive and less greedy than the usual white settlers, more like the true people, the Lenni Lenape. *Let them build,* the Great Spirit proclaimed. It wasn't until the end of June, with another blueberry picking season about to happen, that Man passed the word onto Handy, who then took a few more days before letting his wife know. Chester didn't hear the news until the third of July and it didn't change his thinking. Even with the permission of Ketanëtuwit and Man, he knew an above-ground house wouldn't appear for many years, if ever. Nothing happened too fast on Blueberry Hill.

That day Chester picked many berries, and Henrietta told him he would need to pick many more the next day. Meanwhile, Elmer was not expected to do anything but fetch water from Handy Spring and gather a few beans from the garden, giving him time to expand his brain with wild visions of the great stone house he intended to build some day. Meanwhile, brother Henry, now nearly twelve going on either six or sixty, was allowed to lay in bed all day nursing a summer cold. Chester figured the only reason a ball and chain hadn't yet been attached to his ankles was because it would cut down on his productivity. He was expected to be a-picking blueberries on the Hill every damn day as if he were a Negro fieldhand a-picking cotton on a plantation down South. Seized by dissatisfaction and wanderlust, Chester declared his independence while lying in bed in the middle of the night. At dawn on July 4, 1827, he planned to spring out of bed, quickly gather a few items, and abandon that dreadful dugout.

7
RUNNING AWAY

At dawn Chester packed some bread, beans, and blueberries and bolted from the dugout. He raced down the Hill as if something more than a she-bear were chasing him. While filling up with water at Handy Spring, he was surprised by Catawissa Manayunk, who popped out of the bushes like some hostile warrior of old. Man let loose with a flurry of sharp words, among them "desertion," "disobedience," and "disgracing the family." Getting pierced by arrows from ambush would have been easier to take. Chester was shamed, and though he was almost positive he could outrun Man, he bowed his head and walked back to the dugout kicking at fieldstones and hating himself for becoming obedient again. He had slept very little that night and returned to his bed. Two hours later, Henrietta woke him, gave him bread and water, and sent him outside with a pail around his neck.

It was the Fourth of July, fifty-one years after the United States had declared its independence from Great Britain and seven hours after he had declared his own independence. He paused in his blueberry picking to pick his nose, swat at the black flies attacking the back of his neck, and spit in the direction of the sunken dugout door. Then he built up more spit while circling the square garden, an insignificant patch on the thick cover of blueberry bushes. *How easily he could squash the squash.* He prepared to give it a kick but held back. The squash wasn't to blame. It was the blueberries, an entire hill of blueberries! It was his mother the slavedriver, too. And it was himself. He had failed to make his early-morning escape. Now his mother was watching him. He could feel it.

When he turned to the dugout again, Henrietta was actually there, still wearing her white nightshirt but with a black apron hiding most of it. The Queen of the Hill was shooing flies and staring directly at him. He grimaced and wanted to stick his tongue out at her. But that would be too childish—he was fifteen—so he caught himself and licked his dry lips instead. Fireworks were going off inside his head while the relentless black flies kept attacking as if they could defy his hand and certain death. It's *the Fourth of July, goddamn it*! Those words remained on the tip of his woe-wearied tongue.

"Keep at it, Chesty," Henrietta called out, rapidly clapping her hands as if that would get him picking faster.

He grabbed a handful of berries off the nearest bush and made a show of stuffing them into his mouth instead of his pail. Passive resistance was his modus operandi, a word—or was it two words?—he had learned in town from that greedy farmer and blueberry buyer Archibald Seybolt. His mother put her hands on her childbearing hips and glared with fire in her eyes but held her tongue. She finally went back inside, perhaps to fetch the hickory switch. Chester waited, but it was his father who next stepped out. Old Dad took four deep breaths as if had been suffocating inside. He had spent most of the so-called holiday morning singing "Yankee Doodle" over and over to sooth difficult Aida. The one-year-old mostly coughed and cried, ate and defecated, but she did less of all that when Old Dad sang to her.

"Fresh air, fresh air!" Handy declared as he reached up and pulled downward as if trying to get more of it down his throat. He didn't notice Chester at first.

"Come to lend me a hand, Good Old Dad?" Chester asked, though he already knew the answer.

'What? Oh, Chesty, it's you."

"Absolutely. It's always me."

"Your baby sister is handful enough, son. She needs my full intention."

"Ain't that women's work?"

"Your mother is feeling poorly. She's fretting something awful, certainly not up to the task today. She needs her rest. I got news for you. Come January, you'll be getting another brother or sister. That's right, son, after a couple of mishaps, along came Aida last year. And now the Boyd family shall continue to grow."

Chester took the news in stride as it wasn't exactly news. He wasn't blind or green as grass. A bit of a protruding belly on a skinny woman didn't lie. He knew full well his mother hadn't had much success in the birthing department for an eleven-year stretch after Henry emerged sickly but alive. There were two stillbirths that Henrietta never discussed with her children before Aida appeared, not the prettiest of babies but with strong lungs that allowed her to bawl and fuss like a bear cub. If there ever was to be a fifth Boyd baby and it was a healthy boy, the young-in wouldn't be able to help with the picking for five or six years. What's more, the dugout was already overcrowded. Chester spit in self-defense, and a wet black fly dropped off his lower lip. Talking to Handy Boyd about the foolishness of another mouth to feed or the importance of a first real house to live in was like beating a dead horse, not that the Boyds had ever owned a live one.

"Why do I got to work today?" Chester said. "It ain't fair. Why isn't Elner picking?"

"You know your mother has her reasons. You are *our* best picker. Elmer is fetching water today."

"All day? I could have done that when I was down at the spring this morning."

"What were you doing down there?"

"Just getting a drink. What else! Anything wrong with that?"

"Nope. Our spring refreshes any time of day. Elmer is down there now. I'm sure he'll bring you some water. It's a mighty hot day."

"You're telling me. And the flies are biting. It's miserable out here."

"You'd rather come inside and care for Aida? You think that is so easy? You want to trade places with your Old Dad, maybe? You want to defy your mother's wishes?" With each question, Handy's face turned redder and his words grew louder. But after stamping his foot and wiping his brow, he took three deep breaths of fresh air and became his free and easy self again. He ignored the flies. Live and let live was Handy's motto. "It's too hot to be a-fighting with each other. Pick whatever you can at your own pace, Chesty. It'll please your mother. Later on, we'll head up to the hilltop as a family, take in the view, eat some good grub, and sing the praises of the good old United States of America. You'll like that, son."

"By good grub you mean nothing but blueberries. Even the ants will be disappointed."

"Is that any way to talk? Things haven't been easy for Pudding, your poor dear Mama. A woman has more woes than you know. But things will get better, you'll see. It's only a matter of time."

"You always say that, Old Dad. Things are getting worse. Don't you realize that your Pudding has soured on that dungeon-like dugout and our never-ending poverty. She's back to longing for her family's pig farm."

"Nonsense. What poverty? Nobody is starving here. Look at all this land we own. Her Decker family is finished. Henrietta is a Boyd now. And Boyd means blueberries. God knows—and Ketanëtuwit, too—I'd be out here picking alongside you right now if I could, but I'm dealing with a demanding baby and trying to give her tired mother a moment of peace. What's more, I'm experiencing painful inflammation of the joints."

"Sick like Henry, is that it?"

"Not like Henry. He's young. I'm old. Aches and pains come with age. You just wait!"

"But what about laziness? Ain't that always been there, *Boy*?"

Handy threw his arms in the air, but when he spoke, he sounded more shocked than angry. "You speak to your Good Old Dad that way? You called me *Boy. Boy*! Only Man has a right to do that; he's older than me and saved my life. What kind of son calls his father *Boy*?"

"One who isn't as good as Elmer, I reckon. I'm awful sorry. I shouldn't have called you *lazy* either. *Idle* is a more polite word."

"Look, I'm up there in age. It isn't easy. I'm not complaining mind you. I love our life here on the Hill, but—tarnation, Chesty—I was already half a century old when I married Henrietta and you were born."

Chester couldn't register that much time in his head, which was swarming with more immediate thoughts. Fifteen was old enough to be off on his own. From inside the dugout, Aida began to screech and was soon accompanied by the mooing and groaning of Bessie, who had replaced the late Paddy as the family milk cow and was tied up downhill from the dugout. Then Elmer appeared and, as if he were Christ the only Savior, handed glasses of water to Chester and their father.

"I seen an expressman heading down the Old Mine Road," Elmer reported. "He came up to drink at the spring and we chatted. He had some news."

"No new war I'm hoping?" said Handy. "Is Great Britain acting unfriendly again?"

"Nothing like that. He told me the state of New York has officially abolished slavery."

"About time. Never saw any point to it. Suits me fine."

"Me too, Old Dad," said Chester. "Ain't it high time you took the chains off your eldest son so I too can be a free man!"

"Chester the Jester," said Elmer. "What chains?"

"That's right, what chains?" said Handy. "I don't see a one. The blueberry patch is for all Boyds now and forever. You enjoy the bounty of berries as much as I do."

"That's not the point. I'm picking on Independence Day?"

"And I'm getting our water for the day," said Elmer. "I didn't have to bring you a glass, you know?"

Chester had nothing more to say. He gulped the water, then handed the glass back to his brother.

"Thank you, Elm," said Handy between sips from his glass. I best go back inside and relieve your mother. Aida sounds worse. Before you resume your picking, Chesty, you ought to think about doing the milking. It would please your mother."

"But not Aida," Chester yelled. "Milk won't stop the brat from bawling!" If his father said one more word at all, he wouldn't apologize. But Good Old Dad said nothing. "Sorry," Chester said. "I know you didn't make me a slave."

Handy shrugged and walked slowly back into the mole hole that was their family home. Elmer followed with the two glasses, one empty, the other half full.

Chester fetched the milk bucket and went to Bessie. But after the milking was done, he went inside and set the half-full bucket in front of the frayed curtain, behind which his parents and Aida sometimes slept. He strapped on a sack containing his only change of clothes, half a bar of soap, two potatoes, one crooked carrot, johnnycake, and the lucky copper cent piece that Man had given him one early birthday. He would have slipped out of the dugout unnoticed if not for Henry, who had risen from his sick bed thinking he heard Elmer return with the jugs of water.

"Oh, it's only you," Henry said. "I thought you were out picking, big brother."

"I thought you were in bed coughing your head off, whippersnapper," replied Chester.

"I was but I got thirsty. Why are you carrying that sack?"

"I got sense. I'm heading out."

"To fill the sack with berries?"

"Nope. No damn blueberries. It's already filled. I've had my fill of this dugout and the whole Hill. I'm leaving."

"You can't do that, big brother. Mama and Old Dad won't let you. You're a Boyd. Blue Place is your home." He coughed to be heard by all in the dugout.

"Just watch me, whippersnapper. Not another sound out of you!"

"But...but it's such a big world out there, full of horrible and dangerous people and dark places and diseases."

"You've been listening to Old Dad too much. Even mother would hightail it back to her people and pigs if they were still living. I'll find plenty of new and wonderful things away from Blue Place."

"Name one?"

"Freedom."

Henry thought about that for ten seconds before he began screaming for his mother and father to come quickly. But by then Chester was already out the door. He patted Bessie the cow on the rump and told her goodbye before running the rest of the way down the Hill. There was no sign of Catawissa Manayunk this time. He was on his way at last.

The path Chester followed was only wide enough for the family pushcart, used primarily for bringing blueberries to market in Wurtsborough or on occasion to some outlying farm. He stopped thinking of blueberries and slavery long before he reached the Old Mine Road. Convinced nobody was chasing him, he slowed down. In his mind he saw canal boats carrying coal and lumber. On the generous deck of the grandest boat, he pictured himself wearing a blue wool captain's hat with a gilt band and barking orders that were immediately obeyed. For two whole years now, he had been experiencing "canal fever," but his family dismissed it as "growing pains." Well, from this day forth he would be doing his growing away from Blueberry Hill.

His long legs made great strides on the public road, but he was still glad to hitch a ride over the last stretch in a wagon full of hog carcasses. The driver, about his age, was red-bearded, redheaded, and red-faced. His name was Jeremiah Bender but his customers knew him as "Red." He was a wandering butcher, traveling from farm to farm ready to turn any livestock into fresh meat for those farmers too squeamish to slaughter their own animals.

Jeremiah said matter-of-factly that he had inherited the job, the horse, and the wagon two years earlier from his father, Raymond, who had been turned into a cripple when he fell in a pigpen and was attacked and trampled by half a dozen hungry and ornery hogs. Chester said that the same thing— only worse—had happened to his maternal grandfather; the fallen man had died from the attack in the pen and his heart had been devoured by the hogs. None of that was true, but Henreitta's father had truly been a pig farmer, and to reveal he had died of a heart attack while straining in the outhouse seemed too mundane. Chester found himself trying to impress the meaty, self-sufficient "Red" Bender, who couldn't have been much older than him but drove the wagon as if were king of the road.

"Your cargo would make my father sick," Chester said. "He was practically raised in a smokehouse. He doesn't eat meat and doesn't think the rest of the world should either. Not that I have anything against it personally."

"I don't have anything against the hogs, cows, and chickens. But I slaughter 'em good. It's a living."

"My mother and father make me pick blueberries all day long this time of year. My hands get stained, and sometimes mashed blueberries make me puke."

"Let me tell you, pal, having blue fingers beats having red ones."

"Red fingers?"

"Butchering is a bloody business. Now, I'll tell you straight out because I plain like you, Chester Boyd. I'm a bacon and beans man who enjoys a stuffed and roasted bullock's heart now and then. But I am *not* like my old man. What he'd give to stand up again and hack off the head of a hog. You need anything slaughtered where you live?"

"Like I said, Red, Boyds rarely eat meat. We live in a...It's halfway up Blueberry Hill."

"Never heard of it. Blueberry Hill, you say?"

"Also known as Blue Place. Well, I used to live up there under slave-like conditions. I freed myself. I'm looking for new opportunity."

"That so? I'm looking to get out of the butchering business. Everything must die but its none too pleasant speeding things along for the dumb beasts.

The old man will hate me for saying that, but one thing's for damn sure, he can't catch me any more to give me a serious whipping."

Jeremiah burst into raucous laughter, one hand holding his unquiet belly, his face getting redder if that was possible, his watery eyes looking every which way except at the road ahead. Chester expected the driver to fall out of his seat or crash them into a tree at any minute, but Red Bender proved he could control the reins with just one hand while the rest of him had more fun than any Boyd could ever summon up. Once that was evident, Chester laughed, too.

"I get whipped plenty," said Chester.

"That's what fathers do. They think they got to be mean to keep you under their thumb."

Chester nodded, not wanting to reveal that in the Boyd family it was the mother who did the whipping. "Mine uses a hickory switch."

"Beats being chased with a meat cleaver."

"Or a Revolutionary War knife."

"Or a shotgun."

That called for another round of laughter. Both of them resented their status quo and were looking to break away from family obligations. Chester had found his first friend as a free man.

8
DOWN AMONGST 'EM

They arrived at Wurtsborough in time to see the canal fully watered and to celebrate with the progressive folks who saw economic growth and opportunity in the canal. They learned that the canal project was conceived in 1823 by the Wurts brothers, John, Maurice, and William, who owned tracts of Pennsylvania land rich in anthracite coal deposits.

"Oh, so the village was named for them?" Chester said to his newfound friend.

"What did you think?" said Red Bender. "You thought maybe you were in *Worstborough*?"

"It's not so bad. I've seen worse." The truth was, Chester hadn't seen anything better or worse. His horizons were that limited.

"The big bugs are already shortening the name to Wurtsboro. Writing that pointless *ugh* at the end was giving them all arm fatigue."

"Whichever way it's spelled, it honors the Wurts, right?"

"You bet. They are without doubt men of vision."

"I can see that, Red. Meanwhile, Handy Boyd can't see past our blueberry patch on a hill way out where nobody goes."

"And Raymond Bender can't see past a stuck pig."

Maurice Wurts, who was in town for the Fourth of July and was the one most responsible for "watering" the canal, humbly accepted all praise and gratitude. Eager to become men of vision themselves, Chester Boyd and Jeremiah Bender went to the Tavern in the Hollow and found a table right next to Maurice and his retainers.

Maurice had ordered calf's head, and a cook was explaining to him how the windpipe had been left on because if it hung out of the pot while the head was cooking, all the froth escaped through it. The two young men ordered the same. It was a long wait but worth it. After the brains, seasoned with sifted sage, had been boiled for an hour, they were broken up with a knife, peppered, salted, and battered and served with Boston baked beans, coleslaw, and mugs of applejack. Chester felt delightfully evil to be consuming meat, on Jeremiah's coin no less.

"Sakes alive!" said Chester. "I never ate so good in all my born days."

"Brain food," said Jeremiah. "It will help us become visionaries. Let us toast our vision and good fortune."

When their glasses of applejack clanked together, Chester smiled and slurped. "If Good Old Boring Dad could only see me now. His heart would give out for sure."

"You mean the meat feast would do him in?"

"No doubt. I'm not exaggerating when I tell you he's strictly a fruit and nut man. Whenever his old Indian friend and mother bring home fish from the Basha Kill, we got to clean them outside and eat 'em away from him. The fish can never appear, headless or otherwise, on the kitchen table."

"Don't know how you stood it so long up on that hill of yours, Chester old boy. I got higher ambitions for damn sure, but butchering has never killed my appetite for animal flesh."

"I offer another toast, Red. To freedom, brains, and applejack."

They toasted everything from the Wurts brothers and the mayor of New York City to headless chickens and the pesty flies who laid eggs that hatched into tiny white maggots that fed in the inside of blueberries. "Father doesn't even care if the berries are infested," Chester said, already slurring his words. "He'll eat 'em maggots and all!"

After drinking enough applejack for courage, the two pals ventured over to Mr. Wurts' table and were generously offered chairs. They toasted the Wurts brothers and brains again, as well as canal water, coal, and the town's bright future under the fitting name *Wurtsboro* (Red Bender spelled it out without the "ugh" at the end). Next, they indicated their powerful desire to work for the visionary founder of the D&H.

"If you boys had brains, you would have come to me two years ago," Maurice told them between bites of his apple dumpling. "Canal contractors were paying laborers the exorbitant wage of fifty cents a day, sometimes more for men who knew their way around black powder. Many a man who tried to light a delayed fuse vanished from the payroll. A sad fact." He stopped working his fork and held it near the breast of his coat for a moment of silence. "Still," he continued, "the misfortune of some opened up jobs for others. Through the winter of 1825-26 we had five hundred men engaged in rock cutting and removal. One day at the end of February '26 we contracted for sixty locks of hammered stone. By late spring we had twenty-five hundred men and two hundred teams engaged on the Rondout and Summit sections."

"A grand endeavor, sir," Jeremiah said. "I'd like to be part of it. I'm done butchering hogs for sissy farmers and weak-kneed shopkeepers."

"Alas, boys, we don't need canal builders now. The canal is more or less built."

"You need boatmen, don't you, sir?" Chester asked.

"The captain steers the canal boat, the bowman is aboard to assist him, something like a first mate."

"Sure," said Jeremiah. "We could be either."

"You're awfully young boys. Have you ever even seen a flicker?"

"Well, sort of," said Jeremiah, but he caught himself scratching his head. "Sure. My bird-loving brother Nathaniel caught a yellow-shafted flicker and we…"

"I'm not talking woodpeckers, boys." Maurice Wurts smiled the way successful businessmen smile when they see stupidity that doesn't cost them money. "We call the canal boats *flickers*. They need to carry at least ten tons of cargo."

"Oh, you mean *those* flickers," said Jeremiah. "Yes, I know about them, too. Always wanted to operate one."

"Me, too," said Chester.

"We don't give away the boats, boys. They cost two-hundred dollars apiece."

Chester bit his lip. "That would be four hundred buckets of blueberries."

"We wouldn't have to pay all that money in one lump sum, would we?" asked Jeremiah.

"Some individuals buy company boats through installments, with interest. Payment is deducted from the money they make carrying the freight. The boat owners are responsible for equipping the boats, maintaining the boats, hiring personnel, and supplying the motive power."

Chester couldn't stop scratching his head, but Jeremiah now sat there nodding thoughtfully as if everything was making sense.

"Look boys, at your age, you can't expect to buy a boat, let alone run one. How are you with animals?"

Chester bit his lip, hard enough to draw blood. His brain had gone all topsy-turvy. He knew now that flickers were canal boats as well as woodpeckers. Was Mr. Wurts possibly switching the topic to woodpeckers? Chester couldn't remember ever seeing a yellow-shafted flicker. The birds that seemed to like blueberries the most were gray catbirds, towhees, grouse, robins, crows, blue jays, and bluebirds. But what did those birds or any birds besides water fowl have to do with boats and canals? There were so many other animals besides birds, but all he could do was think of birds. He felt the stare of Mr. Wurts, who was clearly staring at him, not Jeremiah.

"You look confused," said Mr. Wurts.

"Yes, sir," Chester admitted. His mother had schooled him in many things, and Old Dad had added his two cents to his education, but they hadn't taught him the things that mattered most in the vast world off the Hill—such as dealing with people, making money, enjoying expensive meals, imbibing liberally, meeting members of the opposite sex, going where you wanted without fear of the switch, and knowing about flickers that were boats.

Jeremiah shook his head. "I'm good with animals sir," he said, pounding a fist on the table for emphasis. "I've been butchering them all my life."

"Birds?" said Chester.

Jeremiah frowned at Chester for the first time. "Turkeys, hens, sure." Then he leaned closer to the canal boss, who was now patting his belly in full contentment. "Hogs, sheep, cattle...most any critter, sir. I could keep butchering for boatmen. I mean it would be an honor, sir."

"It's not our job to feed the canal boat operators," Maurice said. "You don't know what I'm talking about, do you?"

Jeremiah sat back. "I do, but my friend doesn't." He nudged Chester to let him know it was his turn to talk.

"Animals," said Chester. Now both Mr. Wurts and Jeremiah were staring at him. He struggled to come up with things he knew about other animals besides birds. He knew his father didn't like cats because they ate birds, baby bunnies, and such. He wasn't sure why his father never got him a pet dog, maybe because they couldn't afford to have another mouth to feed, especially one that consumed meat. "I know there are big cats roaming out there in the wilds, but I never seen one," Chester said, and the words began gushing out like spilled applejack. "I know there are rattlesnakes in the rocks. Haven't seen them either, but I've heard them rattling. I know you can scare most bears away from a blueberry patch by howling like a pack of wolves. I know the different kind of fishes in the Basha Kill and the Neversink. I never caught one, but I bet I could. I can milk a cow."

Maurice Wurts wore half a smile but it looked ready to expand. He was drinking his share of applejack, too. "Wildcats, bears and wolves don't often come down to the canal to drink. The boatmen and laborers know all they need to know about fish, and, let me tell you, these men don't drink milk. Nothing makes a man work harder for six days than the prospect of getting drunk on a two-gallon jug of whiskey on the seventh day." Maurice wiped his mouth with the large napkin that had been tucked into the ruffled front of his clean white shirt.

"I'm an applejack man myself," said Chester as if that might make him a little more special than the average whiskey-drinking laborer.

"I can work hard seven days a week without a drop of alcohol," said Jeremiah. "It's too risky butchering anything when you're drunk. A sober man can do any job better, Mr. Wurts. I'm one of those. Sober as a judge." He pushed aside his empty applejack glass.

"Look," Maurice Wurts said, tossing his napkin on the table and pointing at the window on the canal side of the tavern. The boys turned their heads and nodded though they had no idea what they were supposed to be seeing. "The flickers are towed by horses and mules. Those are the animals I'm talking about. Hoggees, or towboys, will be needed to walk the towpaths, guiding the animals, keeping them in line. Ten cents a day for hoggees."

"Hoggees?" Chester said, now holding his head instead of scratching it. He was dizzy. Feeling ready to topple over, he clutched the Wurts table and braced himself. He wondered if applejack went to a fellow's head quicker than whiskey.

Jeremiah started to shrug his thick, sloping shoulders but decided that being indecisive wouldn't do. While more money could be made killing dumb animals, there was no room for growth or self-improvement in the wandering butcher business. He had driven a horse-drawn wagon over most of Sullivan County. He was full of ambition. On the canal, he might own a flicker one day. "Towboy," he said. "I'll take it."

"Me, too," said Chester.

"Good boys."

It wasn't that easy, they soon found out from others after Maurice Wurts went off with two other privileged men to smoke cigars. The canal had some kinks in it. The banks were too porous to hold the necessary water for boating and several of the locks didn't work right. The D&H Canal had no immediate openings for boys or girls. Yes, there was no rule that prohibited female hoggees.

"Just as well there are no openings," Jeremiah said. "A hoggee ain't a job fit for a man."

The friends turned to plan B. Chester became an apprentice wandering butcher and hit the road with Jeremiah. But it took plenty of applejack for Chester to stomach the job. He wasn't as different from his father as he thought. He closed his eyes at killing time, held his nose most of the time, and came to hate calf's head, at least when sober. "You better learn to control your vomiting," Red Bender warned him. "A butcher who vomits is like a pastor who spews profanity."

In August 1827 Chester quit the awful bloody business and took a job washing dishes at the Tavern in the Hollow as if that was a way to cleanse himself. Red said no hard feelings, that he would remain Chester's friend for life. Chester's new job didn't work out. He kept drinking the applejack and was fired for breaking too many dishes. Finally, in mid-September, the first freight, a raft of pine lumber, was sent up to the end of the canal near Kingston. The two boys celebrated the occasion. "No applejack today," said Red, who had somehow gotten his hands on a bottle of ratafia de Champagne. "Three cheers for the D&H." He raised a glass of the sweet liqueur as he licked his lips. "There's plenty of money to be made. There's no stopping us now, pal."

In October, jobless and homeless Chester wrote a letter to Maurice Wurts, who had decided not to live in the town named after him. Maurice didn't remember Chester but he did recall enjoying brains at the tavern. One of his retainers said so in a return letter, adding that there happened to be a job open at twenty cents a day as a canal walker; he wouldn't have to deal with unfamiliar mules or horses, either. All he had to do was walk up and down the towpath each day to check for any leaks in the locks or breaks in the channel banks.

He didn't get the job, though. Jeremiah "Red" Bender learned about it from him and, by showing more spunk, was hired. "It's my first step to a long canal career," Red told Chester. "You didn't really want to do all that walking anyway. Something else is bound to come along for you, pal. Wish me luck. I'm going places." Chester obliged, handing over his lucky copper cent piece since it hadn't brought him any luck at all. Red pocketed the coin and walked away without once looking back. He stopped having anything to do with his *friend for life.*

Chester became Wurtsboro's No. 1 guttersnipe, a street Arab who roamed, drank, and often slept in the streets. Come winter, he slept in barns and other outbuildings, sometimes invited, sometimes not. He relied on the kindness of strangers, many of whom stopped being complete strangers and were kinder than his own family—at least that was what he told himself whenever he was invited to sit down for a hot meal that included meat. Red Bender became a complete and unkind stranger, forgetting him to pursue important connections, fast advancement in the business world, and the almighty dollar. Red had a younger brother named Alexander whose avarice was rumored to be unmatched, but Chester had no dealings with him, either. He was too busy trying to survive to pay any mind to the promising Bender brothers.

Chester considered migrating south like certain birds but his instincts told him he'd rather die close to home. If he had believed life on the Hill was hell, what was this? Nevertheless, returning to the dugout on Blueberry Hill with his tail between his legs was out of the question. He figured he needed minimum food, water, and shelter to keep going—but applejack aplenty. He knew applejack wasn't the answer for anything, but when he drank enough of it, he stopped asking himself questions like *What the hell am I doing here?*

9
HANDY AND HOME

Wind of Chester's sorrowful condition got back to the Hill, but it wasn't until July 1828 that his father actually came down to the valley to get him. Handy loved his eldest son but might not have made the trip to Wurtsboro had not Henrietta insisted she needed Chester's capable blueberry-picking hands and Elmer required his brute strength to move stone. While he was in town, Henrietta added, he might as well purchase additional blueberry buckets from the general store. She let him know that a failure in either part of his double mission was unacceptable.

Handy found his son in surprisingly short order. A woman at the store mentioned a young man who she often saw with a newspaper over his face lying on a public bench near the D&H Canal. He wore ragged clothes and was unkempt. He always got up, apologized, and offered her a seat. She wasn't afraid of him, but she always politely declined. Indeed, she was describing Chester, but when Handy reached the bench, his eldest son was sitting, not lying, on the bench and was knocking back and forth between his feet part of a newspaper he had crumbled into a large ball.

"We've missed you, Chesty," Handy Boyd said, setting down three new buckets before joining his son on the bench.

"Looks like you found me," Chester said, his eyes on the empty buckets, not his father.

"You've stayed away too long. I must say you're looking thin and slovenly."

It was true, of course, but Chester didn't need to hear it. Chester looked at the body next to him and rubbed his eyes as if he were having a hallucination, perhaps one brought on by excessive alcohol. He reached out and pinched a bony arm to make sure his father was really there. "As do you, Old Dad, but at least I'm *not* old."

"Living as you do, you'll be lucky to ever reach half my age."

"I'm a...a free man." Realizing he couldn't state that with conviction, Chester grew teary-eyed and had to turn his head away. When he realized he was now looking in the direction of Blueberry Hill, his tears began to fall but didn't exactly flow—mostly just stayed in place like canal water, he thought.

He wiped his entire face with the torn sleeve of a holey shirt he hadn't washed in months.

"I don't know how you could stay away so long," his father persisted. "We all feel your absence. It's not right. Your mother, bless her sweet soul, can't sleep from worry—about business, sure, but about you, too, Chesty. Man is on his deathbed in the wigwam but still asks his guardian spirits to look after you. Every time your brothers push the blueberry cart to town, they ask Mr. Seybolt if he has seen you. Neither of those boys can pick a lick, as Henrietta often complains. Elmer occupies his time building with stone, which is good and bad. You could out-pick him twice over with one arm tied behind your back. So far, he has made a stone shelter for the cow, a stone wall around the garden, a stone wall around our spring, and a stone outhouse."

"You're kidding?"

"No, Chesty. Elmer is passionate about stone structures. Each was his own idea. He says natural stone is sturdier and more long-lasting than wood, and that's why the ancient Romans had the sense to build their grand structures with it. Elm does have his mind on a bigger undertaking—one that if realized would greatly please Henrietta and make up for his slackness in the blueberry patch."

Chester didn't want to hear about it. Their mother had always liked Elmer best. Elmer was never going to lose his favorite son status. *It's set in stone,* Chester thought. "What about Henry? Still a sloth, I bet."

"I wouldn't say that exactly. His health is bad and he sleeps too much. Of course, he still eats more than he picks. But he has his active moments. He hurls rocks at inanimate and animate targets to no end. I suppose that's how he gets his exercise."

It sounded as if everybody was the same and nothing had changed on the Hill. "What about Aida?" Chester asked. "She can't possibly remember me. She still coughing and crying all the time?"

Handy smiled, showing his usual blue around the edges of his otherwise fine straight teeth. "No, son," he said, as he removed his straw hat to fan himself. Chester was surprised to see that his father had ridges and furrows on top of his bald head. "Your mother brewed some blueberry leaves and it cured the baby's cough. Aida's bouncing around the Hill as happy and playful as a kitten."

"You hate cats."

"Aida can be serious in a funny sort of way, too, telling Elmer and Henry what they should do to please her. I'm sure she would like you, Chesty, and you would enjoy seeing her."

"Right. Another person on the Hill ordering me around."

"Don't be silly. She's a two-year-old. Anyway, you aren't doing so well telling yourself what to do down here in the low lands, are you?"

"At least I'm a...free man." It didn't sound any more accurate this time.

"Not the kind of man you need to be. How much applejack have you been consuming?"

"Hard to say. Lack of spending money can limit a fellow."

"A good thing. Applejack can't do you any good."

"You'd rather I was drinking homemade blueberry wine?"

"It would be an improvement. The blueberries are waiting. Just come home, that is if you are a mind to."

"You aren't going to make me?"

"You know me better than that, son."

"Right. You take orders from Mother, too."

"That's not exactly fair. I'm three times older than my Pudding, and I'm set in my ways. She doesn't try to change me. She is a wise woman, wise beyond her years. She makes good suggestions. She wants what's best for the entire family and that includes you, son. You will always be a Boyd no matter where you are or what you're doing. So why not be a Boyd at home on the Hill rather than down here with all these strangers?"

"If I go back up there, Old Dad, it'll be more of the same—picking blueberries, storing blueberries, trimming the blueberry bushes, and eating blueberry meals. I may seem beggarly down here but I still got a deep-down ache to do something different. I don't know what. But there must be something else I can do."

"You're in luck. Elmer is now laying out fieldstones on the ledge, which makes an excellent foundation."

"You mean for a house?"

"Elmer has drawn up the plans. He's a clever boy. He says all families must have a real house and anybody with any sense would know that a stone house is better than a wood house. He has a vision. The house will have thick stone walls and be quite long, as long as the ledge to allow for many bedrooms. Man has already moved his wigwam off the ledge and set it up one hundred yards below, closer to the spring water."

"A stone house, huh? Will it have a roof?"

"Yes. Elmer is like me; he doesn't want to destroy too many trees. The roof will have clay tiles and a gentle slope. The roof will flatten out and extend over a porch supported by two stone columns. That was my idea. He has promised to build stone steps outside so I can reach the porch roof."

"What for?"

"A place where I can sit and think day or night and look out at all our beautiful blueberry bushes. I'll be closer to the sun and the moon and the stars and the Great Spirit, whether he be Man's Ketanëtuwit or Henrietta's God."

Handy closed his eyes and stretched his neck as if he were trying to stick his head into the low, slow-moving clouds. "And not just me. We will all be able to sit out there."

Chester couldn't help rolling his eyes. Elmer might have a vision and might have already made a stone outhouse but that hardly qualified him for building a genuine residence for human beings. He thought of the Boyds' longstanding home—that dismal dugout—and shuddered. "So, your big ambition in life is to be able to sit on a roof?" he said.

"It beats sitting on a bench in town."

"Maybe. All this seems too big for Elmer. I know you and Mother think the world of him but he's no genius."

"Elmer met a gentleman in town who has built two stone houses and knows about clay-tile roofs. He also owns a lime quarry and can provide all the mortar Elmer needs."

"Elmer needs mortar?" Chester wasn't sure what mortar meant.

"To fill in the cracks between the stones, as I understand it. That keeps the rain outside where it belongs and prevents damage from frost when temperatures drop. According to this Mr. Roscoe, lime mortar is essential when building the kind of house Elmer has in mind. Mr. Roscoe put Elmer's vision down on paper...actual construction drawings."

"How you going to pay this Mr. Roscoe, with blueberries?"

"In part. Henrietta has saved money from our blueberry sales. My sweet Pudding also put money aside from the sale of her family's pig farm."

"It sounds like this fellow knows what he's doing. Is there really enough money to satisfy him?"

"Yes. He likes Elmer. He's teaching him all he knows about masonry. And he likes Henrietta. She feeds him and it amuses him to flirt with her."

"Really? And that doesn't worry you Old Dad? She's so much younger than you."

"Look, I'm over my jealousy days. Men will always be men. But Pudding is a one-man woman. I trust her and she can fend for herself. Besides, Mr. Roscoe is no spring chicken himself. Don't worry about anything unsavory occurring."

"I'm not worried. It's no concern of mine."

"But the house is. You are family. The dugout will be used as a root cellar to store our blueberries and vegetables. Like I said, there will be enough room in the stone house for a growing family. We all want to grow, right? One day you'll marry and have children."

"Maybe. Right now, that seems beyond the realm of possibility."

"Never mind such despairing thoughts. You're still young. The thing to do right now is picture the beautiful house. Won't that be wonderful, son?"

"I'll believe it when I see it. There has been talk of a real house for many years."

"It's not just talk anymore. Between Elmer and Mr. Roscoe we have all the planners and know-how we need. You can help with the rest."

"Lifting and carrying stones, you mean?"

"It will be something new for you to do after the berry picking is done."

"I suppose I do make a good beast of burden."

"I'm not going to be around forever, you know, and the house will belong to you boys and Aida after I go to that great blueberry patch in the sky."

Chester looked up at gray clouds and lost himself in thought. He wasn't thinking about his father's fragility, Elmer's cleverness, Henry's illnesses, or Aida's growth. His mother was occupying his mind, and his body slumped on the bench. He felt a great weight, not exactly on his shoulders, more on his back. It was as if he had developed a hump like that of Catawissa Manayunk. Surely after Old Dad passed on, the still-young widow Henrietta would be there on the Hill, house or no house, Mr. Roscoe or no Mr. Roscoe, running the show, giving orders, criticizing her eldest son's habits, inhibiting his freedom.

"A penny for your thoughts? Handy said.

Thoughts came so cheap, Chester thought. He angrily booted away the newspaper ball and rose to his feet, accidentally kicking over one of the new blueberry buckets. His shoes were about worn out, and the big toe on his right foot throbbed. He cursed and hopped on his left foot like a crippled frog. Once he had dug his heels into the earth and steadied himself, he crossed his arms and stared at the new canal water. He was done with crying, done with wanting to please his mother and father, done with being homesick. Arriving at that decision had left him exhausted. Still, he bent down and righted the bucket. He then turned in several small circles in front of the bench as if he were a dog getting ready to lie down for the night. What he needed was money. He wondered if Good Old Dad had anything left over after buying the three buckets. It wasn't something he could just ask outright? Handy was no money man. The more Chester thought about it, the more convinced he was that Henrietta wouldn't send her husband to town with any extra cash.

Handy reached out and grabbed his son's hip, pulling on it to help himself stand. He leaned against his son and spoke in a confidential whisper. "Still not convinced the Hill is the best place for you, Chesty? Well, I've been saving for last my best reason for you to come home."

"It better not have anything to do with Mother promising to change her ways—becoming nicer, no longer ordering me around as if I were her personal slave. She won't change. You don't see it, Old Dad, but she doesn't treat me right."

"I see more than you think. Could be you need to change your ways, be more helpful and understanding of Henrietta."

"Land's sake! That's your best reason for me to come home?"

"Not exactly. But it does concern your dear mother and the growing Boyd family."

"All right. Tell me. I'm game."

"You have a baby brother now. I'm talking about a real baby brother, not like Henry. He's a cute little pea we call Blue Boy. Born last January. Healthy as a horse...a pony anyway. Wouldn't you like to meet him?"

"I had no idea. Why didn't someone tell me he was born?"

"You were out of touch, remember. Nobody knew where you were."

Chester felt agitated, ready to argue the point. Sure, he didn't have a regular residence and was often sleeping off drunks in various places, but he was always around town. Thoughts of the new brother, though, filled his head and calmed him down. New Boyd blood. Maybe that was what was needed on Blueberry Hill. Maybe he'd be an improvement over Elmer and Henry. He'd be cuter and more playful for sure. It would be like getting a dog. "Blue Boy is an unusual name," Chester said.

"Not for blueberry lovers like Pudding and me. She let me name him. After all she had named you after her father the pig farmer, Elmer after her grandfather the sea captain, and Henry after her uncle who wrote flowery poetry, never married, and died young. Anyway, Henrietta readily approved of my choice."

"How big of her. May I be the last to offer you both my congratulations."

"You can congratulate your mother in person. And that's not all."

"What do you mean *That's not all*. Haven't I heard enough—an actual house in the works, Aida learning how to be bossy at a young age, a baby born behind my back!"

"Double congratulations are in order. Your mother is expecting number six before Christmas."

"You mean...I mean, so soon?"

"I expect she'll go back to naming this one. Henrietta is dying to have a second daughter. Odds are she'll get her wish."

Chester looked his father up and down. Maybe the old man wasn't as fragile as he appeared, and those ridges and furrows on his head didn't mean he was slowing him down any. "And if she doesn't get the girl?"

Hardy grinned and poked his eldest son in the ribs. "Try, try again, I reckon," he whispered. "Either way, you'll want to be up on the Hill with your growing family, our glorious blueberries, and our cherished spring water instead of down here with unloving strangers, damaging applejack, and dirty canal water."

Chester might have argued that the canal water was still fresh, but as he stared at it now, it darkened before his eyes as if it were nothing more than a channel of waste water. He thought about how he had never landed a job in the

Big Ditch and how his onetime friend Red Bender had joined the canal crowd and left him in his wake. He separated himself from his father to move closer to the water. He was in spitting range now, but he swallowed his saliva along with the despairing words he really wanted to say. "Anyway, I hear tell that the future is in railroads, not canals," he blurted out, and that made him feel slightly better about his current lot in life. His father crept up behind him and handed him two of the blueberry buckets to carry. Chester took a deep breath and allowed Good Old Boring Dad to lead him on the long walk out of the valley.

10
BLUE ROCK HOUSE

Slowly and not always surely, Boyd brothers Elmer, Chester, and Henry worked on erecting what their mother and self-proclaimed supervisor had already named Blue Rock House. They found most of the usable building stones toward the top of Blueberry Hill and would roll them down through the bushes whenever possible. Chester ended up doing most of the heavy lifting, using muscles never needed for plucking blueberries off bushes. After each long workday he soaked his tired arms in spring water and welcomed Catawissa Manayunk's willow bark back rubs. Man realized he was too old to lift rocks, but he spiritually supported the construction after consulting with Ketanëtuwit and offered advice as if the Lenni Lenape people had for centuries dwelled in stone houses instead of wigwams. Handy frequently stood in front of the dugout watching, sometimes with Aida sitting on his shoulders, sometimes with Blue Boy in his arms, sometimes with hands free to feed himself blueberries. He lifted a finger to contribute a light stone once or twice a day but never tried to offer a single word of advice. He knew his limitations.

Schuyler Roscoe regularly rode a horse from town to bring bags of lime mortar and offer his expertise to Elmer. Each man took pride in his ability to select, stack, and fit fieldstones, and Elmer soon enough believed he had a better eye for building with stone than the trained stonemason. Mr. Roscoe also flirted with Henrietta in the dugout while he enjoyed heaping bowls of Handy's sautauthig and Henrietta's expressions of profound gratitude. "You may call me Schuyler, my dear," he told the lady of the dugout. He didn't extend the same privilege to Elmer or the others. They were instructed to call him "Mr. Roscoe" or "Master Mason," because of his fine stonework, not because he had any ties with Freemasonry. Master Mason called Elmer "Kid" or "Apprentice," never addressed Chester or Henry by anything but "You," and acted as if Handy and the two youngest Boyds didn't exist.

"Schuyler is such a generous man," Henrietta told her husband. "We are fortunate to have him around. He has so much to offer Elm."

"And to you," said Handy.

"Mr. Roscoe is full of himself."

"He has kindly brought his vital presence to the Hill? Would you say he wants you to return the favor?

"I feed him and let him carry on. He knows my limits. I am not made of stone but no man can take advantage of me."

"Of course not, Pudding. I know there are no cracks in our marriage."

"So true, my dandy Handy. We are solid as a rock. No mortar needed."

Yes, they could joke about it, but that didn't change the fact that Mr. Roscoe the stonemason reminded them in many underhanded ways of Mr. Caulkins the banker. Master Mason found it easy to carry on when alone with Henrietta and only slightly harder while right under Handy's nose. He could go only so far with Henrietta who was capable of utterances that felt like a slap to the face, and her responses were limited (she never hit him in the nose with a ham bone) because she knew Elmer couldn't make the house come true without him.

"We can't go on this way," Mr. Roscoe told his lovely young married lady during a lunch break in mid-October 1828. "The house is shaping up, but I'm ready to burst. I can't keep my volcanic feelings for you dormant any longer." But he did since he was indeed no spring chicken, had no other warm-blooded female in his life, and truly loved putting stones on top of other stones.

Bigger problems arose in the construction. A rivalry developed between Schuyler and Elmer. Each day the two men had their own unpleasant words over differences in method and form. Elmer refused to see himself as the stonemason's apprentice. Things came to a head around Thanksgiving when they each stopped being thankful for the other one and were tempted to throw stones at each other. "We can't go on this way," Mr. Roscoe said to Elmer. "You are becoming increasingly headstrong and impetuous."

"I have my way of doing things, a better way," said Elmer.

"Oh, my, you have no idea. Such brashness. Putting together a stone house is akin to doing a larger than life-size jigsaw puzzle, Kid. You can't force the pieces in places they don't belong. It takes a wise old thinking man like myself to do things right. Experience counts...years and years of it."

"Nothing about it puzzles me," said Elmer. "Stonework comes naturally to me. My fresh insight is invaluable, and I have the energy of youth on my side."

"And sometimes a rock for a brain."

"Which can be highly useful when laying stones. Each stone talks to me."

"Constant babbling, I presume. I am Master Mason. You are Apprentice Elmer."

Their relationship was broken, but not beyond repair. Mr. Roscoe missed one workday in protest of Elmer's behavior but couldn't stay away longer than that. Henrietta proved an excellent mediator because she knew it was up to her to hold things together. Mr. Roscoe was besotted with her (she reminded him of his first wife, he confessed), Elmer adored her as only a favorite son could, and both builders were needed to make a proper home for her and her growing family. The two men shook hands and apologized without looking each other in the eye, then began to work on opposite ends of the house so that it would be some time before they bumped heads again.

Handy was content to stay out of the way while Henrietta mediated and supervised and Master Mason and Elmer thrived in their divided labors of love. When in the dugout Handy tended to the babies—the demanding Aida, who no longer coughed or vomited on him but still had screaming fits when he didn't sing to her or she missed her mother; and the placid Blue Boy, who rarely cried or fussed for a diaper change and lay like a bump on Handy's knee till one or the other of them drifted off to sleep. When both babies were slumbering at the same time or Henrietta relieved him, Handy would wander through the bushes observing from different angles his sons and Mr. Roscoe in action. He liked to imagine himself climbing the future outdoor steps and sitting on the porch roof like a blue bird, singing perhaps, seeing things with eyes open or closed, and having streams of uplifting thoughts on what he figured would be higher spiritual ground, even if he'd be on clay tiles only twelve feet off the ground.

How could he protest the presence of the haughty, love-starved Mr. Roscoe day after day when he knew each night Henrietta would wrap herself around her loving husband in the dugout and would ultimately be doing so in one of Sullivan County's finest stone houses? Henrietta's late mother had produced a crop of nine children at the Mahackamack pig farm, and Henrietta openly expressed her desire to "do my Sow Lady one better." Handy didn't fully understand but he didn't question his Pudding; he was willing to go with the undertaking as long as he could.

In early December 1828, Henrietta gave birth to a striking girl with high forehead, large blue eyes, cute-as-a-berry nose, and chubby cheeks asking to be gently pinched. As expected, she, not Handy, did the naming. At four weeks and a perfect seven pounds, beautiful Blue Belle slept through the night and when awake on her stomach could already lift her head toward the sound of her mother's voice. Henrietta heard occasional cooing and detected the hint of a smile. Aida was too difficult and unattractive (she had Handy's protruding ears and some of his hair loss) at this stage to be totally loveable. Not so Blue Belle. Henrietta announced, in front of Aida no less, that Blue Belle was the perfect baby—a dainty female who wouldn't fuss or fume and would be a living symbol of gratitude, humility, and everlasting love. On New Year's Day, Blue Belle died suddenly in her crib. Doctor Ezekiel Tears from town was at a loss to say why, but Man said it was because Ketanëtuwit considered Blue Belle too perfect for Earth and had reclaimed her for the Spirit World.

Henrietta watched in silence as Chester dug a shallow grave in the frozen earth atop Blueberry Hill under the shadow of the great rock outcrop. Man lined the grave with bark that a bear had stripped from a tree with its claws, and Handy sprinkled in dried blueberries for the baby girl to taste in the afterlife. Elmer had taken time off from his house building to make a coffin, which seemed as light as a blue bird's feather when Henry lowered it into the hole with Blue Belle's head facing east. Man lay flat on his little round belly and reached down with Handy's Revolutionary War knife to cut a small notch in the coffin near the head. "Big enough for soul to come to and leave body," he declared, which caused Henrietta to begin wailing and pulling out her hair. Handy put an arm around his wife but said nothing to her and shook his head when Elmer suggested he say a few words over the grave. Man rose to his knees and spoke again, "No time for little one to prepare for life, let alone death, but Ketanëtuwit accept all innocents like her into His keeping."

Handy led Henrietta into the dugout, where she remained behind a black curtain for a week, taking spring water but little nourishment. She stopped entertaining and feeding Mr. Roscoe, who had not been allowed at Blue Belle's burial, and barely said a word to her three grown sons. She paid only slight attention to Aida and less still to her youngest surviving child, Blue Boy. When she finally emerged, she yelled: "No more! No more!" For the next year she sent Handy away each night to sleep under the stars or in the roofless shell of what the family was now calling Blue Rock House. She lost her taste for fruit of any kind but still managed the blueberry business, urging her sons indirectly to hurry up with the house so that they could become more active pickers again.

Meanwhile, Mr. Roscoe acted strangely. Instead of curtailing his Hill visits because Henrietta no longer paid him any mind, he often camped out near what the family now called Handy Spring. When he did go to Wurtsboro he brought back more lime mortar for Elmer, who had assumed full control of the construction, but also gifts for Henrietta's sweet mouth—assorted meat pies (though well aware of Handy's aversion to meat) and hard-boiled peppermint sweets he called "humbugs." He told Henrietta he could totally understand her grief because his first wife had left him when their own baby girl was born dead. He never mentioned the second wife who had also apparently left him for reasons unknown. He vowed to ask Henrietta to marry him after the house was completed and the "obstacle" was removed, namely Handy, by divorce or death. She could barely tolerate the man anymore, even if Handy could. Still, she didn't order him off the Hill because while Elmer had learned the intricacies of stonework, Mr. Roscoe's expertise was still needed to put on the roof with its clay tiles and many challenges.

Mr. Roscoe pressed her one noon hour after presenting her with a tasty deer meat pie. "I need some assurance, my dear one, that you will consent to be my wife once the roof is completed and you are free to remarry."

"My husband is a good man, Schuyler. You sit at his table and eat his sautauthig. He is here every day."

"It won't be forever. He is a dozen years older than me and does not eat well. He is nothing but skin and bones like that decrepit redskin friend of his."

"I assure you my husband is very much alive and plenty active when he wants to be."

"Surely, he cannot last, and I can outlast him. Will you marry me then, my sweet?"

"I can't make any promises," she told him. "Unexpected things happen. We can never be fully prepared for how fate treats us."

"I shall wait. A man who builds stone houses must have patience."

Henrietta was still constantly thinking of her lost child in the fall of 1830 when a roof finally graced both the long house and the two-column porch with the stone steps access that suited Handy's vision. Handy was delighted and in full good health. Henrietta thanked Mr. Roscoe for his time and effort and insisted he accept the full amount of money promised him. She then said the words that were like more than a slap to the stonemason's face. His services were no longer required and she would not welcome any further meat pies or humbugs and would not permit another of his overnight stays on Boyd property.

"I can't believe this unfair treatment," Mr. Roscoe told her. "You can't be that cruel. You can't be that two-faced. You are no different than my second wife. A wagtail! That's what you are, Henrietta. You led me on. You're nothing but an unscrupulous, deceptive wagtail who has ill-treated a good, honest man."

"Call me what you like. I have never ill-treated my husband. Handy is truly a good, honest man."

Mr. Roscoe stood his ground, even if it wasn't his ground. Handy told him he was welcome to return should he ever be invited to the house. Mr. Roscoe brought up the possibility of a duel, but Handy said he believed in restraint in all things, especially when it came to fighting and other forms of violence. Elmer and Henry showed far less restraint. Elmer's resentment had been building for more than a year and, while waving Handy's Revolutionary War knife, threatened to cut off the stonemason's favored left hand. All Mr. Roscoe had to fight with was a masonry trowel, so he dropped it and retreated. He mounted his horse and shook his fist at Blue Rock House. "I curse every stone in that house and every last one of you Boyds," he shouted. 'I curse you for a thousand years."

Henry, having one of his better days, threw a half-dozen rocks to hurry Mr. Roscoe's horse down the Hill.

11
THE GRAVE BEYOND

Once she was settled into the new house and the old dugout had become home for Bessie the cow and stored berries and vegetables, Henrietta acted practically like a newlywed, albeit like one who already had five living children. She and Handy occupied the largest of the half-dozen bedrooms in Blue Rock House, and she welcomed her husband to their bed with open arms and frequently parted legs. "I cannot bear *not* to have another sweet baby girl," she declared. Handy welcomed her change of heart, joking with his sons that all parts of his body were not deteriorating at the same alarming rate. "You bear fruit in old age," ancient Man told the old man he called *Boy.* "Many heirs carry on Boyd name. Ketanëtuwit bless you. Both."

Henrietta, however, did not feel blessed. Much to her chagrin, the girl she longed for and fully anticipated did not arrive. Noisy Jacob emerged with minor difficulty but a full head of black hair in 1831, and chubby Peter followed with a particularly painful entrance in 1832. "Enough, finally enough!" Henrietta told her equally exhausted husband after she ran out of breast milk for the insatiable baby Peter. She would make due with seven children. When she counted her two stillborn babies and short-lived Blue Belle, which she often did, that made a total of ten, outdoing her late mother's nine. Henrietta told herself she could live with that and would show six-year-old Aida her undying love. True to her word, Henrietta devoted most of her time to her only living daughter, and Aida, in turn, was fiercely intent on becoming everything her mother wanted her to be.

Henrietta was forty-four and Handy eighty in late February 1840 when "The Accident" occurred, so named at the time by the family and remembered as such by the Boyds to this day. Despite Doc Tear's best efforts at her bedside in Blue Rock House, Henrietta died giving birth to another girl, one neither longed for nor anticipated. This one lived, but her other children had no idea why. She was a tiny, blind, blue-skinned hairless female who resembled a withered blueberry. She looked more like Catawissa Manayunk than a blood relative. For a wife to die producing such a pathetic creature might have made some husbands hateful and bitter, but not so Handy. Unexpected things happened, and all he could do was to believe there were reasons for them beyond his comprehension and to carry on and let fate run its course. Henrietta would have wanted it that way. He saw this second daughter, however unsightly and damaged, as a special parting gift from the woman he loved. He was proud to revive the Blue Belle name. He often sat on the porch roof now, looking every which way but mostly up and imagining his Pudding helping to keep Heaven running smoothly.

Five days after Henrietta's death, fourteen-year-old Aida climbed the outdoor stone steps to the porch roof as if marching up to the gallows. Her father sat there, bundled in two blankets to keep off the morning chill. He liked to take the air up there early. If it had been summer, he probably would have slept on the roof. Blue Belle was in her cradle inside the front door finally sleeping, having reluctantly settled again for cow's milk instead of mother's milk. Aida approached her father with heavy heart and crossed arms already feeling defensive about what she was about to say to him. His round bald head stuck out of the blankets as if it had separated from his body and was waiting patiently to be thrown or kicked.

"How is it possible Mama could die before you?" she cried out. She was shaking.

"Henrietta hasn't really died," he said, opening his blankets to share them with his eldest daughter. "I see her in you."

Aida remained standing. "Who do you see in Blue Belle? She's a monster."

"You don't mean that."

"I do. I hate her."

"You don't really. Your sister can't be blamed for anything. If you must blame somebody, blame me. I just hope you don't hate me too much."

"I don't hate you. You are Good Old Boring Dad. That's what my big brothers call you."

"There are worse things to be called. You're cold. Please, sit."

"I won't. I want to freeze. The first Blue Belle died and, well, I don't want to see this second Blue Belle again."

"Of course, you do. Your mother raised you right. Now it's up to you to raise Blue Belle right, just as Henrietta would have done. Where is your baby sister now?"

"Sleeping. Her eyes keep rolling under the lids. She must be dreaming. What do babies dream about? When she is awake, she stares at me, but I can't look back. She's hideous."

"She will grow on you. Man says that Ketanëtuwit has blessed her with knowledge and understanding that not even he, at ninety-seven, possesses. She is a Boyd and something more. For now, her presence reminds us that we should appreciate our own lives."

"But Mama can't appreciate her life; she is *really* dead."

"Sit, Aida. You'll catch cold. Your mother is watching over you, me, Blue Belle, and your six brothers. Please, please sit. We are all counting on you."

Aida looked up at the ominous clouds rolling in from the west and scowled. It looked like snow. She wondered if the day would ever come when man—or more likely woman—learned to control the weather. Then she wondered if it ever got cold in Heaven. That thought made her squat, a favorite thinking position she had learned from Catawissa Manayunk. She hugged her knees and her head dropped between them as if her neck had been chopped with a dull, insufficient executioner's ax. Handy pulled her closer so that she sat with her head resting against his ribs and he could enclose her in his blankets. He thought he heard her weeping, something he hadn't seen her do in ten years. He stroked her hair until her head suddenly popped up and she appeared to be counting the wrinkles on his forehead and furrows on his hairless scalp.

"How is it you lived so long and fathered so many children in old age?" she asked.

"A luck of nature, I reckon. You might say my four humors are in balance."

"Four? You aren't that funny, Old Dad."

"I'm talking about blood, phlegm, yellow bile, and black bile."

"Sounds vile, disgusting."

"Look, Aida, dear daughter, all I'm saying is that my natural tendencies are to sit when others stand and lie down when others sit. Sometimes I sit and think and other times I just sit and sniff. This allows for harmony between body and spirit. By building Blue Rock House, my boys have provided me with all the comfort I need. I am surrounded by nature. All the green around me calms me and all the blue nurtures me. This wonderful fresh air we receive on the Hill is good for a body; I breathe like the trees and bushes. I avoid eating meat, which angers up the blood. My blueberry diet, even if Doc Tears is disinclined to admit it, promotes vigor and vitality."

"Vigor and vitality? You don't do anything. You are always sitting around—on the roof, under a tree, on top of a rock, in Man's wigwam."

"I don't always show off my vigor and vitality. I don't waste it. I preserve it."

"Mama said that when left to yourself, you are lazy."

"That's another way of putting it."

§

Three months after Henrietta's death, her family made the twenty-mile journey to bury her at the Mahackamack Churchyard Cemetery near the old pig farm. Nobody really wanted to go, but the ground had thawed and she had told Handy at the end that while she had spent most of her life on Blueberry Hill, she wanted her permanent resting place to be "back home" in the Decker plot, already occupied by her maternal grandmother, mother, father, and a sister too frail to survive childhood. "It is our duty to fulfill her last wish no matter how much we wish her last wish had been to remain on the Hill," Handy pronounced. "I have always tried to give Henrietta what she wanted."

Catawissa Manayunk, hobbled by age and a series of falls between his wigwam and Handy Spring, wasn't up to making the trip. "I sure die on way to *Wulinaxin* grave," he told the others. "You no want two bodies to carry and put under. I die here later. I stay and watch Chosen One." He meant Blue Belle, and the baby showed her approval by cooing and gurgling. Not even a warmhearted prevaricator would call the baby cute, but her intelligence and enthusiasm for life showed itself every day and Man recognized in her qualities that transcended humanity.

The Boyds rented a swayback mare and a wagon-cum-hearse from the Sears & Rhodes Livery, but none of them had previously dealt with a horse. This one was named Bethany but didn't answer to it. The mud season was not yet over, and the sludge on the road proved a problem for Handy's three oldest sons who took turns driving. Each inexperienced driver managed to get stuck and suffer the criticism of the other two as well as Aida, who shared the front seat the entire way. Because the mare balked at heavy loads, Handy was the only one to sit in back with the coffin and the family's only shovel. The three younger brothers—Blue Boy, twelve; Jacob, nine; and Peter, eight—walked the whole way, first as if they were going on a pleasure excursion but later as if they were on a death march. Never in their lives had they been so far from home.

They arrived at the cemetery in a mist that looked as if the ghosts of half the dead were rising at least part way toward heaven. Chester located the Decker plot after a long group search. There was one flat horizontal stone that said simply "Decker" for the entire family, but Elmer dug up a suitable local stone for a vertical marker and stuck it in the ground next to what he believed were the graves of Mr. and Mrs. Decker, the pig farmers. Handy broke the designated ground for the new grave before relinquishing the shovel to his sons. With only one Boyd working at a time, the digging was slow. It was late afternoon before the hole was deep enough for the coffin. Henry had collapsed with exhaustion, and his three younger brothers playfully danced like Indians around his prostrate body while pronouncing him "as dead as Maw." When the trio tried to bring him to the open grave, Aida told them to stop dragging Henry and to respect those who were truly dead. She ordered them to sit on the pile of removed dirt with their hands folded while their elders spoke. Henry revived long enough to sit halfway up and wail for his mother and himself.

Handy rubbed his wet eyes and circled the open grave twice before he was able to dislodge any words from his dry throat: "Well, Pudding, you made it back. It's a long way from the Hill but you got your wish. You are where you want to be with your Deckers and can finally rest in peace as long as the neighborhood hogs don't root you up." He hadn't meant it to sound frivolous, and when Aida gave him a fierce look, he quickly added: "Man says you'll only be here eleven days before your spirit soars up into the highest heaven to meet your maker. Regardless, we'll always feel your spirit on Blueberry Hill."

Elmer stepped up next and praised his mother as "an untiring frontier woman who proved sincerely earnest about motherhood and died far too early, denying her the opportunity to fully enjoy life in Blue Rock House." Henry begged off speaking, but Aida, all of fourteen, insisted he stand like a man. He tried but stumbled and seemed to faint, falling four feet short of the grave. Blue Boy, Jacob, and Peter all gasped as if Henry was really dead now, but he wasn't. As Chester stepped over him and cleared his throat, Henry mumbled: "I'll see you later, Mama, maybe sooner than you'd like." Chester spoke directly to his mother: "You wielded a mean hickory switch and exhibited slave-driving ways, but I couldn't stay away from home for long. I never doubted that you loved me deep inside and that you wanted me on the Hill as much as my brothers and Aida. Now you've left Blueberry Hill, but I'll be there remembering you. I won't leave the Hill again. I promise."

"None of us will," said Elmer, as he tossed a shovelful of dirt on the coffin.

"Hold on brother," said Aida. "I have something to say. She was my mother, too."

"And she always liked you best," said Chester. "You and Elmer."

Aida stepped in front of Elmer and positioned herself like a rock by the gravestone. When she spoke it was with a clear, unwavering voice; she sounded so much like Henrietta that Chester thought for a moment that his mother had spoken from the grave: "Listen up, gents," Aida said. "Yes, that includes you, Blue Boy; you, Jacob; and you, Peter. Mama raised me right. She raised me to follow in her footsteps. She showed me how to make meals without meat; how to make blueberry picking profitable, how to make Good Old Dad do his share of the work, how to handle my unmanageable younger brothers, how to deal with you difficult older brothers, in short how to run Blue Rock House and maintain reasonable order. Thank you, Mama. So, I say to all you gents, don't you dare think of me as *too young*. Know that I am fully ready to assume the role Mama intended for me. The Boyd family shall live on!"

Her amazing words caused Handy to cry harder and see his eldest daughter in a way he never had before. Elmer and Chester stood up straighter, speechless as they wondered how their sister could grow up so fast. Even Henry perked up and rubbed his eyes as if he were seeing Henrietta's spirit rise too early. Blue Boy, just a couple years younger than Aida, still sat quietly with his hands in his lap, perhaps waiting for Aida to give him another command. Only the two youngest, Jacob and Peter, weren't showing their sister or dead mother any respect. During Aida's speech, they had slipped behind the gravestone, then raced away. They were now lying on their bellies behind a cemetery stone wall, shooting at each other with long sticks, throwing stones to represent cannon balls, and declaring the other one dead already. While Elmer and Chester shoveled and kicked dirt to cover the coffin and fill the hole, Aida excused herself and marched behind the stone wall to disarm the two little soldiers. She threw one of their sticks aside and used the other to give them sincerely earnest swats they wouldn't forget.

The ordeal at the graveside took its toll on all of them, not just Henry. Black clouds brought darkness earlier than expected. They spent the night at the cemetery, some of them sleeping in the wagon bed, others on the ground, inside and outside the stone wall. Handy couldn't sleep and paced until the early hours next to his wife's burial pit as if standing guard against grave robbers or rooting hogs. By dawn it was raining, and a downpour lasted the first ten miles on the trip home. The rain, wind, and flashes of lightning made the swayback horse skittish. The Boyd wagon drivers had not improved overnight, and they—with Bethany's help—found every muddy rut in the road, but the wheels only got stuck twice. "When I die, I don't want any transporting or grave digging," Handy stated while standing in ankle-high mud waiting for his sons to free the wagon the second time. "Cremate me and scatter my ashes among the bushes on the Hill or I'll come back and haunt you all."

12

ON THE CANAL AGAIN

In June 1841, sixteen months after Henrietta Boyd's death, Dr. Tears sent to Blueberry Hill a curious stranger with a shaved head, deathly pale skin, catlike whiskers, enormous nostrils, and a receding chin. The man, who called himself Professor Wadsworth, was a phrenologist eager to examine the unusual female creature living at Blue Rock House. He arrived in a one-horse buggy. Man came out of his wigwam and frightened him at the spring but then volunteered to look after the horse while the visitor walked up to the house. Aida stepped forward to greet him on the porch. The way he looked her over— from head to toe and then back to the head—made her nervous. She wondered if his intentions were honorable and, remembering that her mother had married at fifteen, told him she was fourteen. But he had no interest in her.

"I am here to see Blue Belle," he said. "I assume she is your sister."

"She is and I am their father," said Handy, stepping out the front door. "Dr. Tears said we should expect you any time, but I didn't think it would be so soon."

"Sir, I couldn't get here soon enough. I have come all the way from Brooklyn. Professor Wadsworth is the name. Perhaps you have heard of me."

"No, sir, but Brooklyn is a long way from Blueberry Hill."

"I am eager to get my hands on your other daughter, the blind baby who Dr. Tears tells me is an exceptional specimen, physically distressed but mentally gifted."

"She is in *no* distress," said Handy. Somewhat reluctantly he led the stranger inside the house to wake Blue Belle from what no doubt were vivid dreams.

Professor Wadsworth lifted Blue Belle onto a table and told her to sit. Blue Belle did; she had been doing so without any support since she was six months old. She sat still, too, even when the stranger bent down and ran his fingers over her skull to read the shapes and bumps.

"Remarkable," he said. "Only a year and a half."

"Sixteen months," said Handy. "She's a very sweet baby."

"Sweet? My interest is in her brain, her capacity for learning."

Blue Belle threw her tiny arms around the professor's neck, leaned forward and planted a sloppy kiss on one cheek, then the other. Clearly stunned, he straightened quickly, breaking her hold on him. He took a lacy handkerchief out of a coat pocket and wiped his face.

"She doesn't see many strangers," Handy said. "I suppose she is affectionate to anybody."

"But she can't even see who I am," the professor said.

"No matter. Your face wasn't hard to find. Are you done?"

"Not quite." He bent again and went back to her skull for a second reading.

Blue Belle's little hands were also busy, reaching out to touch the stranger's weak chin, fingering his nostrils, tugging an ear. It was as if they were reading each other.

"More than remarkable. Incredible!" Wadsworth's hands came to rest on Blue Belle's forehead and he turned to address the father. "Sir, it is my expert opinion, both scientifically and transcendentally, that this misshapen child was no accident. She is here for a higher purpose, blessed with a rare combination of genius and kindness and the potential to become nothing less than a living saint."

It was good to hear but wasn't exactly news to Handy. His own impressions and the observations of the admittedly wiser Catawissa Manayunk had already told him of Blue Belle's innate capacity for prominence. What's more, this stranger couldn't keep his bloodless hands off the baby's head. When Handy pulled Blue Belle away and the professor lost his grip on the child, Blue Belle bawled, which was out of character. Handy kissed her and put her back on the table, where she quickly quieted and offered her head back to the professor. But he was done now.

Aida, having heard the crying, carried her sister off to the kitchen, maybe to show the baby how to set a table or make coffee. The professor waved goodbye, and Blue Belle waved back. Handy was upset. It was one thing for Blue Belle to respond more to Aida and Man than to him, but how could the child his late wife gave him as a last gift prefer the touch of a total stranger? Handy decided he would test the phrenologist's knowledge, maybe show him up to be a charlatan. He lowered his bald head and offered it to Wadsworth.

"Tell me," Handy said. "Does the child take after the father? Is my head also remarkable? Go ahead, professor. I want to hear what you have to say about me."

The phrenologist mildly protested this imposition before touching Handy's bald head. His examination lasted no more than a minute. "Not particularly interesting, I must say, since honesty is the best policy and is *always* my policy," he stated after withdrawing his fingers and wiping them with his handkerchief. "I am not one to lie to be kind, sir."

"Boyds don't like liars," said Handy. "Say your piece."

"You are a family man without doubt, Mr. Boyd, but...I hesitate to say more. My reading was not favorable."

"Stop hesitating. I can handle the truth, as you see it."

"Yes, as I see it—that is to say, as I felt it—your cranial bumps indicate stubbornness, ignorance, and nonconformism."

"Is that all?"

"No, if you must know. You have an inclination toward torpidity."

"Talk plainer than that. Remember, I'm ignorant."

"In short, all indications point to you having no more energy than the sluggish opossum except when you are mating or are looking for sustenance."

"Eight children are enough. Anyway, my mate is dead. And I need to look no farther than our many blueberry bushes for sustenance. Furthermore, I have nothing against opossums; they are smart enough to avoid people."

"Your fondness for opossums doesn't surprise me. I must be going."

"I'll show you to the door."

Out on the porch, Professor Wadsworth paused and reached out to Handy without quite touching him. "What I would like to do, sir, is to come up here periodically, say every other month, to measure the developing bumps on Blue Belle's head. This will allow me to keep a detailed record of how her exceptional mental traits show themselves through the years. She is a fascinating case study, and it will create quite a stir when I share my findings with the scientific community and, may I dare say, the world."

"Absolutely not. Blue Belle isn't a case study; she is my baby daughter. I have no wish to share her or anything else with the world. As a matter of fact, I must ask you to leave at once. Doc Tears should never have sent you here. We are a private family. We don't mix well with those who live down below." Handy was not only thinking of Professor Wadsworth the phrenologist but also Mr. Roscoe the stonemason, Archibald Seybolt the greedy farmer-cum-businessman, and Adam K. Caulkins the banker who had pursued young Henrietta back in Mahackamack.

"At Doctor Tears' request, I came all the way from Brooklyn Heights to examine this amazing child. Yes, she is a member of your family, but you must not hold her back as she develops. She belongs to the world at large. You see, sir, as young as Blue Belle is, I am convinced she is a unique creature and it would be criminal to keep her isolated on this Hill of yours."

"This is her home, Wadsworth, and it shall remain her home. I may be full of torpidity as you say, but I possess enough energy to escort you below to our property line."

"That won't be necessary, Mr. Boyd. But you shall hear from me again."

"Fine, professor, as long as it is nothing more than a letter sent in two or three years from Brooklyn Heights inquiring how Blue Belle is getting along. Now, be off with you."

The phrenologist agreed to go but first wanted to do a further, more intricate, reading of Blue Belle's skull. Handy refused and asked Chester to make sure the annoying visitor left the Hill. On the way down, Chester asked many questions, and Professor Wadsworth agreed to give his skull a quick going over. First the professor licked his fingers on both hands.

"Tell me your age," the phrenologist said as his moist fingertips surveyed the bumps on Chester's noggin.

"I'll be thirty soon. Guess you can't tell age from a head."

"I can tell you this, young man. You have no formal education but are of more than average intelligence and are far more aspiring to new heights than your father."

"Really? Tell me more, professor."

"You are restless, bored, impatient and dissatisfied with your life on this remote Hill. You deserve something more, as does your baby sister, I might add."

Catawissa Manayunk was whispering in the Lenni Lenape language, trying to calm down Professor Wadsworth's nervous horse. Chester pointed toward Man's head. "I wonder about him," Chester said. "I bet he'd be a most interesting read."

The professor gave only a passing glance at Man's globular skull, whispering to Chester that it was "primitive," before he climbed into his buggy. The learned visitor offered Chester a ride into town to "seek new opportunity," and Chester was tempted but declined. "Watch over Blue Belle, young man," Wadsworth said in parting. "Don't let your father destroy her brilliance and inner beauty or for that matter your own opportunities and ambitions in life. Good fortune to you." Chester watched the buggy until it was out of sight before he took a seat on the flat rock at Handy Spring and liberally splashed water on his bumpy head as if he could inundate his restlessness.

"Strange white man," Man said.

"Maybe I am but I can't help it. I promised my mother at her grave I would never leave the Hill and now I feel guilty. Another dreary blueberry picking season is upon us and I don't want to be here."

"Don't mean you, Chester. That skull man strange white man. Scare own horse. See only lumps and bumps, not spirits, not nature."

"I didn't see him read your skull."

"No want to touch me. No like Indian skull. He believe white man skull have better form, much many lumps and bumps in right places. I read him good. He believe Indian man no think beyond belly and staff of life." Man paused to rub his stomach and grab his crotch. "He think we savage, warlike and unwise, much slow in gaining knowledge. Him full of sheep shit."

"I don't know. He was impressed with Blue Belle's head."

"Bah. He no see Blue Belle's soul."

"He examined my head and indicated I would do better off the Hill away from all the blueberry picking."

"Better stay, Chesty. Home good. Berries taste best without lumps and bumps."

§

Chester grew more restless once the picking began. His father's lack of purpose and complete attachment to Blue Rock House and the stony, bushy unlevel land surrounding it irritated Chester more than ever. Young Aida had turned old long before her time. She was outdoing their late mother in the role of tyrant, Queen of the Hill. Blue Boy, a fine-looking young specimen, couldn't do enough in the blueberry patch or around the house to please her. She insisted that Jacob and Peter hang buckets around their necks so they had two hands free to pick berries. When the pair dumped the berries and used the buckets as helmets for their wooden sword fights, she put the switch to them. Chester once spilled his own half-full bucket while pursuing a white-tail doe out of boredom. Aida lectured him about time and waste, and he figured she would have taken the switch to him, too, if he hadn't been full grown.

"Hell, I'm twenty-nine-years-old and have no better prospects now then I had at age fifteen," he blurted out after her scolding in early July. "I've been diligently gathering berries for more than a dozen summers since returning from my 1827 escape that didn't stick. I don't feel well."

"Don't you go pulling a Henry on me," Aida said. "He's always sick. You're well. The whole family is counting on you. Nobody picks like you when you really want to pick."

She may as well have been quoting their late mother. "Stop picking on me, little sis,' he said. "I'm going inside to rest."

"You're too young to sound like Old Dad."

"People can get tired at any age. We aren't rocks."

"All right, all right, a short break will revive you. But send Blue Boy and Elmer out. Our bushes are brilliant, but they can't pick themselves."

Chester had heard that before. His sister was now quoting Handy quoting Man. She wasn't yet an original thinker, but she certainly was adept at incorporating the ideas and thoughts of others. As had been the case with his mother, he found it difficult to challenge her about anything. She was reminding him of his family obligations as he opened the front door, which creaked as always. The house that Elmer built was flawed.

Wanting a quick bite of something meatier than a blueberry, he stopped in the kitchen. Handy was in there looking livelier than usual as he showed Blue Belle how to make his favorite blueberry dish—sautauthig. The baby genius watched with an amused look, as if she had already learned how to make superior sautauthig in a previous life. Chester decided he wasn't hungry. There was no sign of Blue Boy, who liked to take "nature walks." In Henry's room he found Elmer and Henry arguing about which one of them had cheated at checkers. Chester decided not to interrupt. He peeked into the spotless master bedroom that now belonged to Aida, who shared it with Blue Belle. After Henrietta died, Handy no longer wanted to sleep in *their* bed and chose to occupy the small room off the kitchen that would be just right for a servant if they could ever afford one. Handy spent most of his waking hours on the porch roof, where the air was fresh and there was nobody to interrupt his lassitude and boring thoughts. Chester sniffed the wild flowers Aida had put in her mother's vase, sighed, and went to the room he shared with Elmer. Henry was so sickly he needed a room of his own. So did Jacob and Peter or else the excitable boys would stay awake fighting all night. Blue Boy slept outside under the stars during these warm months. When it got too cold, he would move into what was originally conceived as the guest room, though there never had been an overnight guest. They now called it a parlor.

Chester stared at his unmade bed in disgust. He had never shared it or any bed with a woman. He decided he would not rest. Instead, he posted himself at the window looking out at the many berries and spotting the place he had dropped the bucket while in hopeless pursuit of the whitetail. A sharp pain in the gut and a scratchy throat sent him to the corner of the room where Elmer usually kept a pitcher filled with water from Handy Spring. The pitcher was dry. He gagged and dropped on all fours to look under the bed. He had a powerful thirst. He was relieved to find that neither Aida nor Elmer had confiscated his bottle of homemade blueberry wine, but when he saw it was empty, he smashed the bottle against Elmer's arrowhead collection. "I hate this place," he shouted. "Elmer is so damn proud of Blue Rock House but to me it's no different than sleeping in that suffocating old dugout. Everything is different but the same. Everything is going against me." He reached up and, with aggressive fingers, tried to locate every bump on his aching head. He discovered the four most prominent protrusions and named them *Restless, Boredom, Impatience* and *Discontent.* That phrenologist, what's his name, was no charlatan.

Chester apologized to his mother, for he felt the presence of her spirit, even as he stuffed a change of raggedy clothes into a bag. He tiptoed through the kitchen and left the house by the backdoor. He ran through the bushes down to Handy Spring, where he stuck his head in the bubbling water for half a minute as if to drown himself rather than quell his thirst. He accomplished neither. When he saw the ghostly figure of Catawissa Manayunk limping toward the spring, Chester bolted without a word. Man would only tell him Indian fables and try to talk him into staying. He didn't stop running until he was in sight of Wurtsboro, now a flourishing village with more than one tavern.

What he found that same day was a temporary job sweeping one of the taverns, and that allowed him to rediscover on his second night the warm slightly sweet taste of applejack. When he left the tavern to clear his head, he walked off and kept walking. A misstep landed him in the canal water, but while he splashed about waiting for his life to flash before him, a canal boat came along. "Man overboard," cried a female voice from a passing canal boat. Next thing he knew he was clutching a pole and being rescued by the captain of the flicker. He sobered up fast looking into Jeremiah "Red" Bender's face, meatier, redder, and prouder than ever.

"Bloody hell," said Chester. "It's you. Never thought I'd see you again."

"If my wife hadn't seen you, you would be headed to bloody hell," said Jeremiah. "You are one lucky dog. We're headed up to Kingston with twenty tons of coal."

"You got this boat and a wife, too? You're the lucky dog, Red."

"You could at least thank me for fishing you out, Chester old boy."

"Thanks. I'd like to thank your wife, too."

"She's in the cabin fixing some grub. You see, Anna and I pretty much live on *Annabelle*. Named my flicker after her."

Jeremiah, once back at the tiller, said he had worked hard to find the right wife and the right profession. He admitted to getting a boost from the death of his father, the longtime butcher crippled by ornery hogs. It was at Raymond Bender's funeral that Red met Anna, the daughter of one of Raymond's oldest and best customers. This belle of Tarrytown, New York, was looking for a man who could stand head and shoulders above all the other contenders for her hand in marriage. Jeremiah Bender, who had inherited substantial "animal blood money" from his frugal father, filled the bill though he was at most an inch taller than Anna.

"I had the spondulix and the spunk to win over the lovely lass with the great ass," Red boasted.

"I'm dying to meet her," said Chester, who maybe hadn't sobered up entirely.

But it didn't happen right away. Jeremiah went on to do more boasting—not only about how well and lucratively he operated his D&H canal boat (calling himself a captain, not a mere boatman) but also about how well younger brother Alex conducted business. Alexander Bender had opened a canal boat yard and beyond that was making real estate deals across the county. "Alex buys and sells anything and always comes out on top," said Red. "He wants as many money trees as possible and has been buying up farmland the old settlers gave up on due to the rotten, rocky soil. I'm as proud of Alex as I am of myself. He hasn't landed any kind of wife yet, though. I'm one up on him in that area, way up with Anna."

Chester couldn't believe he had ever been friends with this braggart. He walked to the bow and paced like an impatient man in a waiting room. He had his eye out for the belle of Tarrytown despite knowing that seeing Red's wife would only make him feel worse. Resentment flowed through Chester as if a lock gate had opened. He marched back to Jeremiah in a foul mood.

"Reckon you no longer need the lucky copper cent piece you stole from me," Chester said as he held out his open palm in Jeremiah's face. He hadn't thought of the lucky piece in years but suddenly he felt he couldn't live without it.

"You gave it to me as a gift, old pal."

"Well, I'm taking it back. It's mine."

"Sorry Boyd. I gave the trinket to a deadhead in Kingston ages ago." Jeremiah lit up a cigar without offering one. "I saved your life. That must be worth more than any copper cent piece."

Chester was trying to figure out if he should be offended by those words when Red's buxom, auburn-haired wife stepped out of the tiny stern cabin. She caried a plate on which slices of cold boiled ham lay between thin slices of bread. Chester had never seen anything like that in his life.

"Looks good," he said, though he was now looking at Anna Bender, not what was on the plate.

"A new thing from England," she said. "They're called sandwiches."

Jeremiah introduced Chester as an old pal who was down on his luck. Chester bowed his head, too ashamed to look directly at any part of the belle of Tarrytown above her ankles. The three of them ate standing up in back. Chester mostly watched the two hired boys on the towpath leading the workhorse that was pulling the boat up the canal. The enterprising Benders were hauling not only the coal cargo but a load of hay to feed the horse. Chester wasn't sure what the towboys ate.

"First time?" Anna asked him.

"Huh?" Chester said, turning to look at her feet.

"Never been on a canal boat before?"

"No, ma'am." He raised his eyes to her stomach, then to her chest, then to her neck, then to her chin, caught her eye for a second, and kept going up to her fine auburn hair on top. He was about to tell her he had never been on any kind of boat before but thought better of it. "I...eh...like it."

"How far you going?"

"Me? I don't know. How far you going?"

"Kingston, of course," said Jeremiah. "Canal's end. We can let you off anywhere."

"Thanks. Anywhere will do."

"Oh, why don't you stay awhile to get a real feel for it," said Anna. "It's the least we can do for an old pal of Jeremy." She turned to her husband and touched his elbow. "Agreed, dear?"

Jeremiah finished chewing the last of his ham sandwich before answering: "Sure, Sugarplum, if he really wants to."

"I don't know. I mean..."

"Think about it," said Anna, staring at him as if challenging him—to what, Chester didn't know. She brushed a bread crumb off the plate and turned again to her husband. "I'll be in the cabin if you need anything," she said.

Chester watched her turn and walk away. The movement of her bottom made the movement of the boat seem insignificant. He looked as long as he could with Red Bender breathing down his neck. "I've never seen Kingston," he told his old pal.

Jeremiah acted as if it was his idea to give Chester the free ride to near where the canal met the Hudson River. Chester turned down the offer of a cigar and another ham sandwich but not a few swigs of apple brandy, which wasn't as sweet as the applejack he was familiar with but went down just as easy. He was certain he wasn't already drunk when the flicker passed through Summitville and he found himself alone in the stern cabin with Anna Bender, but he still opened his heart to her. He told her that while the Greeks had their goddess of the sea, she must be America's goddess of the canal. Instead of slapping his face, she identified the Greek goddess in question as Amphitrite, whose name Chester had not known. She told him she liked the cut of his jib. He didn't know the expression and anyway heard "rib" instead of "jib." As if having a spasm, he took her in his arms and held her tight, hoping they would be able to feel each other's ribs. She didn't attempt to separate from him until she felt both his hands land flat on her buttocks, and that was about the time Captain Bender appeared with his face already too red for anybody's comfort.

Red made him disembark at Spring Glen in Ulster County just across the Sullivan border. Chester didn't protest. He immediately made up a rhyme: *Red is right, I am blue/ For I love Anna/Her great ass, too.* He didn't remember doing anything that literary before, but more rhymes followed as he made the long walk on the towpath back to the comfort of the Wurtsboro taverns. When not rhyming he muttered how unworthy Red Bender was to have found such good fortune. As for Red dumping him off the boat, Chester knew it was deserved. That didn't keep him from picturing every minute of his solo journey the full Anna or Anna in parts—auburn hair, moist lips, full breasts, glistening ribs, splendid bottom.

Even though he hadn't recovered his lucky copper cent piece, luck was with him when he reached the first tavern and encountered Philip Hone, who had been the first D&H president and mayor of New York City and was now taking writer Washington Irving on a pleasure trip along the canal. Mr. Hone remembered the skinny bold youngster who had taken shovel in hand at the canal groundbreaking ceremony in 1825.

"You showed plenty of pluck that day," Mr. Hone said.

"I did? Sometimes I can't believe that young shaver was me."

"We all grow older."

"Age is a matter of feeling, not of years," said Washington Irving.

"Right now, Mr. Irving, I feel plum tuckered out," Chester admitted.

"A little sleep will do you good. But beware of enchanted liquor offered by mysterious men. Because he didn't, Rip Wan Winkle slept for twenty years."

"A year and a half should be enough for me."

The three of them laughed and shared a bottle of French wine. Mr. Hone and Mr. Irving were headed to the other end of the canal, Honesdale, Pennsylvania. "Named for yours truly," said Mr. Hone. "Maurice Wurts got Wurtsboro. I got Honesdale. I won't be so modest as to say I didn't deserve the honor, but the citizens no doubt saw Honesdale as an improvement on the earlier name, Dyberry Forks."

"A toast to the great town of Honesdale," said Washington Irving, raising his glass.

"A toast to America's greatest writer," said Philip Hone. "And to Rip Van Winkle, if you please."

"A toast to great French wine," said Chester. "But I'm fine with blueberry wine and applejack most of the time. They are dear to this patriotic heart of mine." He raised a fist but paused before pounding his chest. He couldn't remember which side his heart was on.

"Excellent," said Mr. Irving. "What we have here, Philip, is a poet and true American."

What they also had, after Mr. Hone's invitation, was a traveling companion. They said they would welcome Chester's buoyant (Irving's word) and congenial (Hone's word) company. Chester couldn't remember anyone calling him even *good* company before. He instantly stopped craving French wine, applejack, and homegrown blueberry wine, put down his glass, and graciously accepted their kind offer. He wasn't going to spoil this trip.

13
LIFE IN WURTSBORO

The writer was a world traveler, world famous, and almost twice as old as Chester, but they hit it off, especially when they stood on the stern of the canal boat looking back and discussing their respective homes. Washington Irving said he lived in Tarrytown, New York, where he had purchased a neglected cottage that required constant repair and renovation and was costing him a pretty penny. Chester countered with the story of how he and his brothers, with modest skill and little money, had built the labor-intensive Blue Rock House with native fieldstone and the erratic advice of a Lothario claiming to be a stonemason.

"There are problems," Chester told the famous writer because he wanted to be totally honest. "It's a great improvement over the dugout we used to live in, but the doors stick when opened or closed, walls lean and bulge, the roof leaks in three places, the floors are uneven, there are cracks in stones, cracks in bad mortar, and my room feels like an oven on hot days."

Irving offered Chester a sympathetic sigh, then looked back as if he expected to see another canal boat trying to overtake them. "To cover my escalating cottage costs, I began contributing essays and short stories last year to a magazine, *The Knickerbocker.* What do you do, my fine fellow?"

"Well, like I said, I helped build our *cottage* on Blueberry Hill, but that's done. I pick blueberries in the summer, but instead of doing that this year I left home, ran off."

"To do what?"

"Don't know. The truth is I'm at loose ends. No money, no prospects."

"A common predicament in a world in which the almighty dollar rules. Have you ever done any writing, Chester?"

"A little poetry...very little, and only in my head. Truth is I can write my own name but not much beyond that. I don't write letters—nobody to write to. You see, Mr. Irving, all my life I've been on that Hill dealing with nothing but blue shit."

"Interesting. Blue shit you say?"

"Boyd blueberries. I don't mean to sound bitter."

"Blueberries are sweet. The low blueberry has a pleasant flavor and has long been gathered and enjoyed by the American Indian."

"I know. There's a blueberry-loving Lenni Lenape named Man who's nearly one hundred years old and lives in a wigwam in the shadow of our Blue Rock House. I suspect he or his wigwam—or maybe both together—will collapse right soon."

"Interesting. An old Indian named Man. Another Rip Van Winkle, perhaps?"

"I don't think he sleeps that much, Mr. Irving."

"He must have fascinating adventure stories to tell."

"I suppose. I don't listen to him much anymore. He's quite the windbag. I never know when he's telling the truth or making things up."

"Critics have said the same about me. You do read, don't you?"

"Oh, sure. I know about your books, sir. When my mother lay in bed sick, pregnant or both, she complained about a lack of books on the Hill. She apparently had been a reader before she married. She told me about Icabod Crane and she said that your Rip Van Winkle fellow has much in common with my father, Handy Boyd."

"You mean your father *does* sleep a lot?"

"I suppose. He goes to bed early but gets up early. What she meant, though, is that my Good Old Dad can be lazy like Rip. She would nag him about that some. But she is no longer with us. There was an accident last year. She died giving birth. She was kind of young but I reckon too old for doing that sort of thing anymore."

"Sorry to hear that. But hear this young fellow: The natural effect of sorrow over the dead is to refine and elevate the mind."

Philip Hone had come within listening range, and he now threw fraternal arms over the shoulders of Irving and Boyd as if they were the Three Musketeers. "Don't be modest now, Wash," he said. "You are America's first Man of Letters. You should know, Chester, that our celebrated author also writes readable history. My favorite still is his 1809 work *A History of New York from the Beginning of the World to the End of the Dutch Dynasty, by Diedrich Knickerbocker*. You had me fooled, Wash. It didn't sink in for years that the actual writer was you, not some crusty Dutch historian."

Chester had never heard of that particular book. In fact, he wouldn't have heard of Washington Irving and his famous writings if not for Henrietta Boyd. Maybe his mother had been about something more than pigs of the past, endless demands, hickory switches, blueberries, and babies. He figured out something to say that he hoped would make him sound more knowledgeable and wittier than he was. "You may have the Headless Horseman in your Sleepy Hollow, Mr. Irving, but up on our sleepy Blueberry Hill the Boyds have the

Brainless Blueberry Picker." To explain, he hit himself a little too hard on the forehead.

Washington Irving didn't smile. He scratched his brilliant head as he studied Chester's prematurely balding head and said in all seriousness, "But I thought you told me you had run away from home."

"I suppose I have, but I'll be back some day. No matter what I say now, blue shit is in my blood."

§

The ride to Honesdale went as smoothly as possible. Chester Boyd didn't mind how all those locks slowed things down or how one stubborn mule cost them an hour by refusing to be the "engine" that pulled the boat up the canal. It gave him more time to hear about the history of the canal and New York City from Philip Hone, who had been making sophisticated, detailed observations in his diary since 1928, and to listen to the legendary tales of Washington Irving straight from the author's mouth. Chester made his own modest contributions to the conversations by satirizing the lifestyles, traits, and beliefs of Boyds, most notably his lazy father, and by mocking the selfishness, acquisitiveness, and heartlessness of the newly rich, citing one Jeremiah "Red" Bender in particular. In Honesdale, people cheered when they arrived, and Chester felt for the first time in his life that he was *somebody*.

"What a gratifying excursion," Irving told him. "I have looked up at the stupendous cliffs and forests overhead and looked down upon the Delaware, roaring and foaming below us, at the foot of an immense embankment which supports the canal. For more than ninety miles, I have traveled through a constant succession of scenery that would have been famous had it existed in any part of Europe. But it would not have been half as gratifying without the company of one such as yourself—an insightful young man with a wonderful bent for satire and a bright future in America."

Chester stared for a long while at a bigger canal boat loaded down with anthracite coal. "What?" he finally said. "Oh, you mean me." He could feel a blush coming on as if he were a naïve school girl receiving compliments from an older boy. "I...I thank you kindly." He had never gone to an actual school.

That seemingly fortuitous meeting should have led to wonderful things, Chester often said later, such as his becoming the next great American writer as soon as he learned to write, an intrepid traveler once he got in the habit, a homespun wit, and a New Yorker much admired across the country and abroad. "My lot in life, however, was differently cast," he told anyone who might have a sympathetic ear. Still, the trip had been a brush with the famous (Irving) and near famous (Hone) and he had managed to have fun while sober the entire time. It also led to a job. Chester worked for the next five years, on and off, as a canal laborer alongside a bunch of rough men, mostly Irish and German immigrants. What he mostly did was dig soil from the bed of the canal and pile it alongside the canal so more experienced laborers could raise the height and increase the strength of the embankments. By 1845 the canal held five feet of water instead of four and the D&H Canal Company built forty-ton-capacity boats to replace the flickers.

Red Bender paid four-hundred dollars for one of those forty-tonners and was making sixteen profitable canal trips a year. Red's opportunistic brother, Alexander, was also making money in buckets after opening a larger boat yard where the Masten Pond Feeder entered the canal. He maintained boats in dry dock and also sold bigger and bigger boats as the years went by and the capacity of the canal grew. The brothers acquired enough wealth to purchase property in Wurtsboro on both sides of the canal and along the Newburgh-Cochecton Turnpike. Chester saw more than he wanted of both Bender brothers. Not that they took note of him or at least never said anything to his face. He suspected if they thought of him at all, they considered him nothing more than a lowly ditch digger. Tired of canal work—digging was as dreary as picking—but not wanting to return to Blueberry Hill with his tail between his legs, he took a Wurtsboro job clerking with the Fulton & Holmes General Store. The store catered to the needs of canallers and also served as the village post office, but one day Anna Bender showed up expecting Chester to cater to her needs. It wasn't his imagination.

It was the day after December ice had ended the boating season in 1846 that she lured Chester into the storeroom. He hadn't seen her in five years, not since the time her husband fished him out of the canal and he went for that shortened ride on *Annabelle*, the flicker. He was surprised she remembered him at all. Red's wife was as fleshy and lusty as Chester remembered but her auburn hair had become prematurely silvery white and her skin had turned slightly scaly because of a medical condition she attributed to "too much exposure on the canal." She asked him if he thought her too ugly now.

"Too ugly for what?" he asked, innocently enough, and she immediately pressed her breasts against his chest so hard he staggered backward and knocked over some Fulton & Homes merchandise. It was fortunate that neither owner was present.

"Oh, I see," she told him. "That's how it is. You're like all men. I run into a little temporary bad luck in the looks department and give birth to two big babies and you stop looking."

Chester made a point of not looking away, but his eyes stayed steady on her healthy features below the neck. She didn't wait for him to put any words together. She complained about her life, saying that while she was minding the two twin boys and keeping house on her husband's latest canal boat, *Mighty Bull*, Jeremiah made a habit of carousing like a bull on land, having acquired more than a passing acquaintance with all the adventuresses and strumpets between Honesdale and Kingston. "Therefore," she said as she hiked up her skirts, "I come to you, Lester, with thirsty limbs and a hungry quim."

Her blunt words shocked Chester for a minute and excited him for two. He lacked experience with women and the only social graces he knew were learned from dealing with customers. Anna Bender certainly wasn't behaving like any customer he had previously encountered, and he didn't have a response. As a man, he felt like responding in a certain way, but how could he? He wasn't drunk. He politely told her he wasn't *Lester* and kept his trousers on. It wasn't so much a moral decision. He figured too much of her husband and the canal had rubbed off on her and besides he knew that either Mr. Fulton or Mr. Holmes could show up at any moment. He wanted to keep his job and the windowless sleeping place the bosses provided him in the store's cellar.

"I heard you have a room here," she said.

"A room? No, no. I..." He knew she knew he was lying.

"I know that door there leads to the storage room." She took hold of his right wrist and dragged him there, although she wasn't nearly as strong as he made her seem. The shelves were stacked with coffee beans, teas, spices, baking powder, medicine bottles, and canned goods. Pots and pans hung from hooks on the ceiling. On the floor were barrels of crackers, pickles, molasses and vinegar as well a pile of wool blankets, two rolled-up Venetian carpets of wool, and a half-dozen rag rugs of cotton. But there was enough open space in the middle for a body to lie down, which Chester had done on occasion when feeling exhausted. Right now, he wasn't sure what he was feeling, certainly not exhaustion as she all but threw herself against him. He did not go down. He heard the front door bells ring and the singsong voice of Mr. Holmes. Showing strength that he didn't know he had—nor did Anna, no doubt—he grabbed something off a shelf, took hold of her shoulders and guided Mrs. Bender out of the storage room. He had chosen wisely. Out in the open in front of Mr. Holmes, he handed Anna a bottle of patent medicine—Dr. Flint's Quaker Bitters.

"You need not pay now, Mrs. Bender," he told her. "I'll put it on your husband's account."

Anna's scaly flesh turned crimson. She cursed him and hurried back to the *Mighty Bull* to report the attempted assault by that "randy scalawag" Chester Boyd. For days Chester expected dire consequences but Red never made an appearance. If Anna had hoped Jeremiah would perform a knightly act of vengeance to protect her honor, she was mistaken. Jeremiah had agreed that Chester was rotten to the core but then had told his wife it was up to a woman to thwart the appetites of strange men and that in the future she might bring along their young twin boys anytime she *needed* to visit the Fulton & Holmes General Store or, for that matter, leave the safety of the boat for anyplace on dry land.

Chester was *not* totally relieved. Yes, Anna had damned him and exaggerated his sins to her husband, but in so doing she had risen in Chester's estimation. He began to have reoccurring dreams about Anna, naked and with healed skin, sensuously brushing her silvery-white hair (not auburn anymore but really not bad at all), and Red Bender in his captain's hat challenging him to a duel at ten paces with either pistols or large knives. In real life, he sometimes spotted Anna swinging her hips down the street with a son on each side of her, but he chose to watch her only from hiding. He often heard of Jeremiah's escapades on the canal and in the taverns up and down the 108-mile watery route. Red had become something of a king among the boatmen. Enterprising Alexander Bender, by contrast, had a reputation for controlling rather than cavorting. Other Wurtsboro merchants tended to bow to Alexander as if he were royalty. Those two oversized Bender heads, Chester decided, were only fit for crowns of cracked fieldstones and fool's gold. With clenched fists, Chester came out of the general store's cellar nightly to gaze at the upstairs windows of the Hocking House, where Jeremiah and his family stayed when on land and kept the candle lights burning well into the wee hours.

Only infrequently did Chester look in the direction of Blueberry Hill, though on occasion Elmer showed up at the store to buy a few items on Aida's shopping list and to tell him about the refinements he was making on Blue Rock House. Their father was still alive and, for that matter, so was Catawissa Manayunk. Chester was glad, but he wasn't dying to see either of them. It wasn't so much because of who they were but more because of who he was and the guilt he felt for abandoning the homestead.

He missed Blue Belle the most. She apparently was as undersized and homely as ever but hadn't let blindness hold her back. She was having Aida read to her every literary classic they could get their hands on, advising her big sister against favoring materialism over spirituality, talking in Lenape with Man, teaching slightly older brothers Jacob and Peter how to play nice, showing Blue Boy how to raise his knees and manipulate the turtle-shell rattles featured in the Blueberry Dance, helping Henry deal with his physical ailments and melancholia, and sharing with Handy sautauthig deserts and porch rooftop sitting.

Professor Wadsworth had twice returned to Blueberry Hill to reexamine Blue Belle's scalp but had been turned away both times by her protective father and Indian "grandfather," as she now called Man. "Our Good Old Boring Dad cares for none beyond our family circle," said Elmer. "He has no wish to mix with the rest of the world, let alone an obnoxious, swollen-headed humbug from Brooklyn Heights."

Meanwhile, Chester continued to do the necessary mixing with that tiny part of the world that shopped at Fulton & Holmes, with the notable exceptions of the Benders. He managed to stay out of the paths of Jeremiah and Alexnder, whose prosperity and greed made them revered and envied by the villagers in Wurtsboro and other residents of the Mamakating valley. As for Anna Bender, he assumed she no longer wanted him, so he told himself he hated her and made himself scarce, even those times she came shopping without her twin sons. His bosses, Fulton and Holmes, both seemed to understand and didn't hold it against him.

14
ANOTHER BENDER

In early July 1847 another male Bender became known to Chester, not that Jeremiah and Alexander weren't already two too many. Nathaniel, twenty-six, was the youngest of the late Raymond Bender's three sons. Alexander had ten years on him and Jeremiah eleven. He showed up at the Fulton & Holmes General Store with a package under his arm. He introduced himself as the "Afterthought" of the Bender family. Although he asked to be called Natty, because everyone called him that, he addressed Chester as "Mr. Boyd." Chester liked the way that sounded.

"I'm not buying anything today, Mr. Boyd," he said as if making a confession. "But I hope you will be able to help me."

Nathaniel Bender was nothing like his brothers in manner or occupation. He was a lisping, long-haired painter of birds (including yellow-shafted flickers) and flowers (mostly wild) who wanted to sell his artwork in front of the building. Chester told him that would be up to Fulton and Holmes who were at home mourning a relative who had been killed by Mexican soldiers at the Second Battle of Tabasco. Nathaniel, seemingly surprised and bothered that a war with Mexico was going on, pushed his stringy blond hair out of his eyes, and spoke with passion. "Do we Americans really need more land; we have so much already!"

"Well said, Natty," Chester said. "My family has all the land we need. We're not greedy." Just saying that made him miss Blueberry Hill. He had been away a long time but was still saying *we*.

"I love land. It's beautiful. We should share it with each other."

"I guess the Mexicans didn't want to share their land with us."

"That's too bad. We should all get along. I hate fighting."

"The way I see it, Natty, some men are fighters and some are lovers. We have soldiers who spill blood so they can claim victory and land but we also have artists, like yourself, who spill paint so they can depict woodpeckers, roses, and natural landscape."

"Sounds about right, Mr. Boyd. Which one are you, fighter or lover?"

"Well, fighting is for fools, and I haven't yet found the right woman to love. I'd say I'm halfway between. How 'bout you, Natty?"

"As an artist—not exactly a starving one but struggling nevertheless—I'm all for love and getting along with my fellow man. I see the world as a beautiful place as long as humans don't ruin nature too much. My late father, a butcher, could never understand my thinking. Same with my brothers. May I be frank with you, Mr. Boyd?"

"By all means be frank. And if you're going to do that, you might as well call me Chester like everyone else does." He recalled how most of his family shortened his name to Chesty, but he couldn't imagine ever wanting to be called that by a Bender—not even by Anna Bender, except perhaps when lustful thoughts were overwhelming him.

"It's a fact that Jeremiah and Alexander don't all the time see eye to eye with yours truly. I mean they are my brothers, and I love them dearly. But they are so unlike me. They will fight at the drop of a hat for survival, dominance, personal gain, honor, family name, and fun."

"Greedy bastards, huh?"

"I wouldn't put it that way exactly. You know my brothers?"

"To a degree. I knew Red Bender when he was himself a butcher."

"Yes, Jeremy's has come a long way, money-wise and otherwise. He has a lovely wife now and twin boys."

"I am acquainted with Anna."

"As fine a sister-in-law as I could hope for. She truly appreciates nature and my work. I sometimes wonder if Jeremy can appreciate such a woman enough."

Jeremiah hadn't fought for the so-called honor of his wife, but Chester saw no reason to bring that up with Nathaniel. Painting pictures of birds and flowers didn't seem like a manly occupation, but it sounded more interesting than being a store clerk and Natty was far more likeable than his older brothers. Anyway, Chester didn't have any other customer at the moment and decided to be friendly. "What you got under your arm, Natty? Could it be one of your fine nature paintings?"

Nathaniel beamed as he took the wrapping off his latest framed work and held it up to the light. Chester stared at the watercolor for a minute with his mouth open. "Does it leave you breathless, Mr. Boyd, or just speechless? It's no masterpiece by any means, but I consider it my best composition to date. It's an *En plein air* painting. I call it *Blueberry Field with Jays.*"

"A fitting title for sure," said Chester, "but, tell me, where were you when you painted all those jay birds and berries on that slope? It looks...well, mighty familiar."

"It might be. I know you Boyds live on Blueberry Hill's west side, which belongs to you."

"You were trespassing?"

"Not at all. Have you ever gone over the crest to the east side of the Hill?"

"Maybe five or six times when I was exploring. In the old days, my mother didn't want me to go beyond the rocky prominence on the hilltop. She considered it too far from home, too thick with laurel and Hemlock trees and too thin with blueberry bushes. I've had little occasion to cross over since. We have all the blueberries we want on our side. What's it to you?"

"Yes, but there are still many berries on the east side, as you can see in my painting. That is where early one morning I saw a band of jays flying over the bushes in this perfect beam of sunlight. You see I had lugged my canvas, brushes, and tubes of moist watercolors more than halfway up the hill in search of just the right inspiration."

"But what in the world brought you there? Those dense thickets of mountain laurel are almost impenetrable when they unite and there is no spring water on that side. I've never seen another human being over there. Not even the Lenni Lenape Indians chose to live on the backside of Blueberry Hill."

"We see it as the front side of the Hill."

"Who is we?"

"The Benders. I guess you haven't heard. Jeremiah and Alexander, of course, and sister Eunice recently purchased the large Drake Tract, including the forty acres on the east side of Blueberry Hill, from the children of the late Moses Drake."

"Who in the hell is Moses Drake?"

"A veteran of the French and Indian War who came to this area in search of a lost lead mine once worked by Lenni Lenape Indians. He had wanted to make bullets, but he never found the mine. After the Revolutionary War he became something of a hermit, living like a black-capped titmouse in and around hemlock trees on the east side of what we now call Blueberry Hill. He abandoned his wife and four children but remembered them in his will. Mrs. Drake died shortly after him as did two of his children. The other two had no use for the land but held on to it all these years while they were living in New York City. Then Eunice made them an offer they couldn't refuse. My sister, God bless her hungering heart, is more persuasive and more understanding of human nature than my brothers. Do you know her?"

Chester was stunned but managed to shake his head. *Persuasive and greedy*, he thought. He had trouble registering what Nathaniel was saying. He wondered why neither Good Old Boring Dad nor the ancient Indian Catawissa Manayunk had ever mentioned this Moses Drake, his tract, or his offspring. Handy and Henrietta had legally purchased the west side of Blueberry Hill from the 1812 War widow, but the Boyds had always assumed the other side of the Hill would stay forever wild. They certainly had no intention of taming it themselves. For one thing, they weren't that ambitious; for another, Handy considered it a natural barrier to civilization. Chester began to pace behind the store counter, all the while wringing his hands as he would the Fulton & Holmes mop.

"Is something wrong, Mr. Boyd...Chester?" Nathaniel asked. "You seem upset."

"All right you bought it. What now? My father says the vegetation over there runs wild and free like the beasts of the forest."

"I've never seen vegetation run, but all the birds certainly *fly* wild and free."

"You Benders aren't seriously considering occupying that untamed land?"

"Oh, it's a done thing. Definitely. Alexander sees the value in all those trees."

"Cutting them down and selling the lumber, you mean? Don't you like trees, Natty?"

"I do and so do the birds. Alex wouldn't cut down all the trees."

"Only the strong tall ones, I'm betting. My father planted himself among those trees back in 1811 when our Hill was total wilderness."

"Yes, the trees on your side of the Hill. Look, it's about far more than chopping down a few trees. You get firewood from trees, don't you?"

"We use trees and bushes that are dead and branches that have fallen in the wind. We are sparing with the ax. My father doesn't bother to keep our ax sharp anymore."

"My sister Eunice likes trees. She likes them around. They are scenic. But she also knows that some trees and bushes will need to be cleared to make a house and to provide better views. Some of the growth is too thick anyway."

"The beasts and the birds don't say so, do they?"

Nathaniel was still clutching his painting, but he now found a place to lay it down safely on the counter. "I only came here to see if I could sell my work in front of Fulton & Holmes. I didn't mean to start anything."

"Your brothers and sister started something by buying the backside of our Hill behind our backs."

"It's a big hill, Mr. Boyd. Eunice has always wanted to live on a hillside away from the crowds and the canal commotion. Jeremiah's wife, Anna, feels exactly the same way. It's a good place to raise her sons. And it's lovely up there, as you know. I have already counted on our property a dozen kinds of wild flowers and twice that many varieties of birds, including the jays of course and my favorite, the black-capped titmouse."

Chester realized he was still wringing his hands. He freed his fingers and closed them tight, seeing no reason to hide his fists or to continue being polite to this starry-eyed Bender or for that matter any Bender. "It's wrong to destroy the vegetation. I don't think you realize how difficult it is to build a house, especially on a hillside. I know. It's hard labor."

"You Boyds did it; we Benders can do it."

"Damn it. There's room for only one house on the Hill and we already have it. Blueberry Hill belongs to the Boyds."

"Legally, only half of it does, Mr. Boyd. Please don't get yourself worked up over this. You wouldn't even be able to see a house built on the east side. But why fuss over it. You don't live there anymore. You live right here."

"Maybe I'll go back. I'm sure I will. I won't be working at Fulton & Holmes forever."

"That's fine. Glad to have you. There is nothing to keep us from being good neighbors."

"Sure. Like the Patriots and the Tories. Like the American soldiers and the Mexican Army. Like the English and the French. Like the Lenni Lenape and the Mohawk. Like the bear and the wolf."

"I appreciate your wit, Mr. Boyd."

"I'm not trying to be the least bit clever. I'm indignant."

"Oh, well, no need to be. I'm glad to have stopped by and to have had this conversation. I'll certainly tell Jeremiah I met you."

"Don't bother. We aren't exactly friends anymore."

"Oh? I'm sure you'll be seeing a lot more of each other now that we'll be sharing the same hill. You will be able to rekindle your friendship. And get to know Alexander."

"Why would I want to do that? I don't need his business."

"Alexander isn't so awful. He might seem a little reserved at first, but he's not *only* about business. He will grow on you. And I know you'll be impressed once you meet Eunice. Everyone is! She's extremely efficient and forthright, a thoroughly modern woman who would be a great catch for any man who wants an equal partner for a wife."

"You are missing the point, Natty. My brothers Elmer and Henry aren't looking for such a wife any more than I am. We Boyds don't want *any* neighbors. If you come to the Hill you come as invaders. You heard me right—invaders! There has been enough human disturbance. We want our peace and quiet and *our* blueberries."

Chester surprised himself with those last two words. He had been secretly anti-blueberry, or at least neutral about them, his entire life. Now he was acting like a typical member of the Boyd family, and it was rather frightening. Still, being a Boyd beat being a Bender. He had an urge to bodily throw the rather slight Nathaniel Bender out of the store and then toss *Blueberry Field with Jays* after him.

"It'll all work out," Nathaniel said.

"Hogwash," said Chester, using one of his late mother's favorite words.

When he was a small boy, he used to take the word literally since Henrietta was raised on a pig farm.

"Why say such a thing, Mr. Boyd? I'm a peaceable man, as you no doubt are."

"Maybe, but what about those two brothers of yours? You said yourself that they are fighters."

"Yes, but not all the time. Allow me to be frank with you again, Chester. While I am quite different in my nature from my two brothers and even my sister, I do see eye to eye with them when it comes to this land purchase. It's entirely legal and, as I've told you, I love the land. I'm sure you'll find that Benders are reasonable people who, whether we read the Bible or not, believe in the biblical phrase 'though shalt love they neighbor as thyself.'"

"Well, fuck you and the entire Bender family! And if you aren't buying anything, Natty, get the hell out of this emporium."

15
FIRST BLOOD DRAWN

Chester started to backslide after hearing Nathaniel Bender's bad news and missed so much work time with applejack-related absences that in early 1848 Mr. Fulton fired him from the store and Mr. Holmes told him, "It's best for everybody if you left town and went home, permanently." That sounded good to Chester because he wanted to find out if the Benders were truly making plans to occupy the backside of Blueberry Hill. But first he needed a drink, so he took his last week's pay to the Tavern in the Hollow to work up the courage to face Handy, Elmer, Aida, and the rest of his family.

As soon as Chester entered the tavern, he noted two distinguished gentlemen seated close together, not eating or drinking but studying blueprint drawings spread out on the table in front of them. The tavern keeper who Chester knew quite well, identified the pair as Delaware & Hudson chief engineer R.F. Lord and German-born civil engineer John A. Roebling, hired by Lord to build some kind of bridge. Chester had already encountered Jervis, Hone, Wurts, and Washington Irving, and now, emboldened by two glasses of applejack, he approached Lord and Roebling to experience another brush with important people.

"I'm delighted with your plan to replace the rope ferry with an aqueduct to safely and quickly carry the canal above the busy Delaware River," Mr. Lord was saying as he ran a finger across one of the blueprints. "I don't doubt your suspension design will allow more room for the busy river traffic and ice floes."

"Of course," Mr. Roebling replied as he stroked his beard. "I thought this was all settled, Russ. What's the problem?"

"No problem, John—the Delaware Aqueduct is progressing nicely and should be finished on schedule and under cost. I only wonder about the necessity of an additional three aqueducts, at Lackawaxen, Neversink, and High Falls."

"Must I go over all that again." Mr. Roebling pounded a fist on the nearest blueprint. "I thought you understood."

"I do. I do. It's just that there are men more concerned with budget than you and I. They have their own notions about how much investment in extra structures is actually required for a smooth-running operation."

"*Dummkopfs*. As for their notions, I say, *Es ist mir scheißegal.* "

"I'm sorry, John, I can't quite follow your German."

"It means 'I don't give a shit!'"

Russell Lord tapped the same blueprint with an open hand. "Got it! I'll talk to them, John."

Chester tried to restrain his laughter but couldn't. John Roebling seemed like a right fine fellow. Chester apologized. "I just wanted to say I'm with Mr. Roebling all the way. We need a new strong aqueduct to carry all those cumbersome canal boats over the rocky Neversink."

Mr. Lord jumped out of his chair and stood between his fellow engineer and Chester to confront what he imaged to be a crazed man. Chester smiled but raised both his hands as if a gun instead of a finger was pointed at his chest.

"I'm good," Chester said. "I'm no engineer. But I'm a former canal man. Dug out plenty of dirt during the recent expansion. In fact, I shoveled dirt at the groundbreaking ceremony twenty-three years ago."

"*Das ist gut,*" said Mr. Roebling. "You want to work for me?"

"You bet."

"I don't know," said Mr. Lord, looking Chester over as if he were a broken-down horse for sale. "We always need willing hoggees. But you are far too old to be a towboy. What is your job now?"

"Working for Mr. Roebling, I hope."

That was too much to ask for. As it turned out, John Roebling had all the help he needed to build his four suspension aqueducts. Chester briefly suspended his belief in any kind of future and turned to applejack anonymity. But another planned enlargement of the canal, this time to a minimum of six feet, had brought out a call for laborers. Chester sobered up as best he could and went back to unsatisfactory bottom digging.

By the summer of 1849, the D&H could boast of a channel deepened to six feet and locks ninety feet by fifteen feet instead of seventy-six feet by nine feet. Four different times Chester scrambled behind trees to watch Jeremiah Bender's ninety-foot-long *Annabelle II* pass by. It could carry ninety tons of coal or whatever. Those sighting actually made Chester feel good, because if Red was on the canal, he wasn't on the backside of Blueberry Hill. He was initially disappointed not to see Anna aboard this second boat named for her. He figured she must be in town shopping with her two twin boys, but on no occasion did he go looking for her. He remembered how her hair and skin had aged before their time, how she had lied to her husband about him, and how he had vowed to hate her. At the same time, he couldn't forget how her arousing body called attention to itself whether on the stern of a boat or in the middle of a street. He convinced himself that he would be better off never laying eyes on her again, though keeping her out of his dreams was behind his powers of self-control even when sober.

His days of employment ended suddenly in early August. With the enlarged canal running smoothly, Chester lost his job, though he had done nothing wrong. It didn't matter that he knew Mr. Lord and Mr. Roebling. Bad luck was bad luck and he couldn't remember ever having had any other kind of luck. He could have returned to Blue Rock House to catch the end of blueberry picking season but instead went back to serious drinking, sometimes alone, sometimes with other unemployed D&H laborers. One afternoon he passed out near the towpath. While Chester lay flat on his back, Jeremiah "Red" Bender and a burly canal pal named George Washington Monroe splashed canal water on his face until they were certain he wasn't dead. The pair of captains had been doing their own drinking and were hardly being kind.

"Look, George, it's the Boyd bottom feeder I was telling you about," said Captain Bender. "I can't say it's unexpected to see him like this. I once had to fish him out of the canal."

"You don't say," said Captain Monroe, nudging Chester with the toe of his boot. "The Worst of Wurtsboro, right? One of the dregs of the Delaware & Hudson, right?"

"Not to mention the Black Sheep of Blueberry Hill," said Red.

"Blueberry Hill, huh? That's where you're building a house, isn't it?"

"You bet, George. Our family house is going up on the eastern slope. Eunice's fiancé, Daniel Leach, is building it. He is a jack of all trades. Chester's old man is still over there on the other side, along with a parcel of brothers and sisters. But if they are anything like our comatose friend here, they'll eradicate themselves soon enough."

Chester heard every harsh word but couldn't lift his head or even mutter a protest about the unwelcome house or his family's future. His head and eardrums pounded.

"The bastard once did wrong by my wife," Captain Bender continued.

"You don't say," said Captain Monroe. "In what way?"

"In the way you can imagine, George. But the letch was too pathetic for me to give him a whipping. I forgave him, but got no thanks for it. Anna says she can still feel him watching her from behind shutters and doors. What's more he abused my young artistic brother, Nathaniel—cursed him and threw him bodily out of the general store. You know how helpless Natty is when it comes to physical confrontations."

"Indeed. He's quite the queer sort."

"Nevertheless, Boyd had no right to manhandle him."

Chester turned onto his stomach and managed to raise up on his arms like a reptile. "I never touched your brother any more than I touched your wife," he said, and he would have said more except he felt George Washington Monroe's boot pressed against his ribs.

"Try picking on someone your own size, Boyd," said Red, whose red hair stuck up on both sides of his square head like the horns of the devil. His disciple gave Chester another swift kick.

"Go to hell," Chester said, rolling away from the kicker.

"Try to make me," said Red. "Can you even stand?"

"Can't stand you."

Red merely sneered, letting his pal's boot do the talking—another kick. The pain was excruciating, and Chester clutched his ribs and vomited. Both tormentors stepped back.

"Sickening sight," said Red.

"Don't see how Anna can stand you either," Chester said as he scrambled to his feet, holding his ribs. It was common knowledge that Jeremiah Bender now usually operated his canal boats without his wife and sons aboard and found the time and space to copulate up and down the length of the canal faster than the channel could be deepened. If the kicker came at him again, Chester was prepared to dive into the canal.

"Never mind, George," said Red, holding his pal back. "The letch is not worth the trouble. Besides, it's time I headed up to Blueberry Hill to see how much progress Daniel Leach has made on the house."

Chester grimaced. Hearing those words was worse than another kick. It was more than he could bear. But he held his ground and snarled like a wolf. It wouldn't scare a mouse, let alone a bear of a man.

"Maybe you are out of touch with the news, old pal," said Red. "Maybe nobody has told you about the Bend going up on our side of the Hill."

"The Bend?" Chester didn't want to bend over but he couldn't stay upright. It felt as if he had been punched in the gut though George Washington Monroe had only kicked so far.

"The Georgia gentleman who has come north to marry my sister happens to be a first-rate lumberman and builder, and the Bend figures to be one of the finest homes in Sullivan County. I know your brother Elmer is inordinately proud of the Boyd stone house, but I've seen the place. It's primitive, the work of amateurs. The Bend promises to be an architectural marvel, a masterpiece in wood that will dwarf Blue Rock House in size, style, and elegance. The finishing touch will be a cupula with a spire on top."

"Wood houses burn easily," Chester said, still slightly bent but with hands on hips.

"A threat, perhaps? I warn you: Daniel Leach also happens to be a first-rate shot with every sort of firearm you can name. When he marries Eunice in September, he'll be a most welcome addition to the Bender family. You should pop up to Blueberry Hill sometime when you aren't intoxicated and marvel at the Bend."

"You're nothing but dirty land-grabbers."

"Nonsense. We buy land. We're proud landowners. The Drake Tract has endless possibilities for lumbering and quarrying. It's one thousand twenty-three acres. Of course, our favorite forty acres are on the eastern slope of Blueberry Hill. Anna and my sister Eunice chose the ideal spot for the Bend. Before long, thanks to those two marvelous ladies, the house that Daniel Leach is building will be a true home and the Benders will be living under one roof. Alexander and I will still have our boats, of course, but like the Englishmen have been saying for centuries, *A Man's Home Is His Castle.* Eunice considers it her castle, too, naturally, and I have no problem with that. I am a big enough man to allow sis to call herself Queen of the Bend."

"I won't stand for it!" said Chester, remembering how his mother had called herself *Queen of the Hill.* He braced his legs to keep his knees from shaking. That worked but his upper body began to sway. He hadn't landed a finger on Nathaniel Bender earlier but he was seriously thinking about punching Jeremiah Bender now. The trouble was he had never thrown a punch in his life, and George Washington Monroe was clearly used to such rough stuff. Chester heard his brain scream, "Duck!" but the rest of him didn't cooperate. The blow landed square on his nose and Chester again landed on his back.

"You figure he needs that whipping now?" the brute Monroe asked as he stood over the fallen man.

"No, George," said Red. "He's had enough for now. Let's give bad boy Boyd the old heave-ho."

Jeremiah took hold of Chester's arms and George the legs. They swung his limp body back and forth over the towpath, then on the count of three pitched him into the canal. Chester revived and began to splash wildly while crying for help. The two canal boat captains left him to his fate. Although he had taught himself to keep his head above water in the Beaver Kill and Neversink, he was in no shape to do anything but flop about. Red Bender had once saved him from these same stinking waters and now he had condemned him to a watery death. He decided his last thoughts on Earth would be of Anna's bare breasts and splendid rear end, as if that would somehow get back at Red. With eyes closed, he did see those breasts floating on water like buoys, but he was disappointed to find that they were covered with mermaid-like scales, and then he saw a mermaid's tail.

"I am neither a lover nor a fighter!" he shouted. "I am lost in the middle. I might as well drown." His head did go under once and then a second time before a passing lock repairman fished him out with a baling hook. Chester marveled at the way history could repeat itself.

Given a reprieve, Chester decided he could be both a lover and a fighter after all. First, he would go to a tavern, not to drink but to seduce either a barmaid or a female customer of easy virtue, whichever came first. Afterward he would march back up to Blue Rock House and defend Blueberry Hill with body and soul against the onslaught of Benders. The first part of his plan didn't happen because he was intercepted on the street by Elmer, who was red-faced from running and in a panic. They hadn't seen each other in more than a year, but there were no hellos.

"You seen a ghost, Elm?" Chester said while his brother stopped to pant.

"We got to fetch Doc Tears," said Elmer between gasps for breath. "Where's his house? We got to wake him. It's bad."

"How bad? "Death in the family? Not Good Old Boring Dad?"

"No, he's breathing slowly as always."

"Poor Blue Belle?"

"No. She's livelier than ever."

"Blue Boy? He must be over twenty by now. Jacob? Peter? All too young to die."

Elmer finally caught his breath. "The young'uns are fine. Would you shut up and listen to me."

"Has Man finally kicked the bucket and gone to his ancestors hunting grounds?"

"No. He's his own medicine man. Won't let himself die. Nobody's dead. . . not yet."

"An accident? Did Man fall and break his hip doing his Blueberry Dance?"

"No. He doesn't dance much anymore. Didn't old Doc Tears move his office?"

"Don't tell me Old Dad cut himself with his Revolutionary War knife?"

"Of course not. Come on, Chesty. We need the Doc. Lead the way."

"But it was an accident, right? Who?"

"No accident. It's very bad."

"Sickness then? Henry? No, he's always sick. Aida? No, she's too tough."

"It's Henry all right, but no sickness."

"What then? Why don't you come out with it, Elm."

"Shut up, Chesty. It's terrible. Henry has been shot!"

"Shot? Is it bad?"

"What do you think? He was shot."

"Who done it?"

"Daniel Leach, a Bender defender. I didn't even know about him yesterday, but now I do. He used to hunt coons in Georgia. He's a deadly shot."

"And he's going to marry Eunice. Damn those Benders."

They found the doctor's new office at his residence, but his sleepy-eyed maid said he was out delivering a baby. Elmer, who was balding even more quickly than Chester, tore at what hair he had left around the temples. The maid's next words caused even more distress: "It was less than an hour ago that Doctor Tears hitched up the buggy and rushed off on an emergency call to somewhere far from town, way up in the hills. I believe he referred to the place as Blue Hill."

"You don't mean Blueberry Hill, do you?" asked Chester.

"Yes, yes," said the maid, covering her mouth to hide a yawn. "Blueberry Hill. That's where the doctor went."

"What are you saying, woman!" said Elmer. "That's impossible. I just came from there and the only female even remotely capable of having a baby is my sister Aida, and she wouldn't have anything of the kind."

"I'm sorry, gentlemen," continued the maid. "But I am certain the woman in a delicate position is at that Blueberry Hill, presumably experiencing her labor pain in her home."

Elmer and Chester glanced at each other and at the same time realized that this unnamed woman must be at the uncompleted Bend on the other side of the Hill laboring to send forth another Bender into the world.

"The horror!" shouted Elmer. "A Bender being born up there while Henry is dying up there, shot by one of theirs."

"Damn those Benders," Chester muttered. "Every last one."

It turned out that the wounded Henry was no longer "up there." Elmer had rushed down from Blue Rock House to get the doctor for Henry, who had taken a .54-caliber ball from a Mississippi Rifle in the groin, but the younger boys, Jacob and Peter, had soon after loaded Henry in the blueberry cart to bring their brother to the doctor.

Elmer and Chester had sent the maid back to bed and just begun the long journey back to Blueberry Hill when the cart appeared out of the darkness and rolled free straight toward them. While Jacob and Peter blamed each other for allowing the cart to get away, Chester braced himself for the impact and stopped the cart. For his trouble he received a kick in the chin from the patient, who then slipped into unconsciousness. Fortunately, Henry had arrived in town no nearer death than he had been back home. Unfortunately, Doc Tears wasn't in town.

"You idiots, you fools!" screamed Elmer. "Now you have to push him all the way back up and that will probably kill him!"

"I don't understand," said Jacob, whose ears stuck out even more than most Boyd ears did, but who otherwise was, according to Aida, "so darkly handsome, it's dangerous."

"And someone will have to go to the enemy's lair and drag out Doc," said Elmer.

"Damn Benders," Chester said twice more.

"Huh?" Jacob flattened his ears and tugged on them as if that could make him better understand what he was hearing.

"It was his idea," said Peter, who at seventeen was a year younger than Jacob but taller than him by a head and twenty pounds heavier. They hadn't outgrown their brotherly quarreling. "Aida said we should take Henry to the wigwam and let Man use his Indian magic on him. We did. Man removed the bullet and stopped the bleeding. But Jacob insisted Henry be brought to an actual doctor, a white man." Peter wagged his man-sized fist in his brother's face. "If Henry dies, it's your fault."

"Bugger!" Jacob shouted. "Man can't do everything."

"Only saved Henry's life, that's all."

"Never mind, you two," said Elmer. "We'll help with the cart, me and Chester. We'll get Henry back home. We won't let him die. Isn't that right, Chesty?"

"Sure," Chester said. He was surprisingly calm. He noticed how much Jacob and especially Peter had grown. He smiled at them.

"Howdy, Chesty," said Jacob. "Glad you're here."

"Long time no see, brother," said Peter.

Chester acknowledged them with a quick wave and brushed past them. He leaned over the cart to see for himself how bad off Henry was. He saw some blood and blue streaks on the patient's torn trouser leg and sniffed. He didn't smell death on his wounded brother, but there was a distinct odor he knew well—the musty, sour scent of blueberries mashed and otherwise gone bad.

16
THE FEUD

The wounded Henry was still alive in the cart when he reached Blueberry Hill. The combined pushing and pulling efforts of older brothers Chester and Elmer and younger brothers Jacob and Peter had gotten him back home. They stretched him out on the bearskin rug in Catawissa Manayunk's wigwam so he could once again receive whatever medicinal herbs, healing stones, feathers, potions, and blueberry concoctions Man thought best. There was debate about who would cross over the divide to fetch Doc Tears from the Bend, but Jacob and Peter were allowed to go together because Jacob knew how to smile congenially and was the fastest runner and Peter was less easily intimidated and not known to have offended any Benders yet.

Doc Tears got the message from Jacob and Peter but was a long time leaving the Bend because the laboring woman and her baby were in a life and death struggle. And he had to leave his horse and buggy behind as there was no roadway, let alone a defined path, over the crest of Blueberry Hill. When he finally arrived by foot at the wigwam in the dark, all he did for Henry was bandage his groin, pronounce him on the road to recovery, and have him drink blueberry tea. Henry said his wound was painful but not unbearably so and he could live with it. Then he fell asleep.

"But what were the results at the Bend?" Chester asked.

"The baby couldn't make it, but I saved the mother," the doctor said as he sipped Blue Belle's tea.

"Anna Bender?"

"What? No, not her. Eunice Bender. Eunice is one tough cookie. During her moments of sharp pain, she remained as stoic as a good soldier. She was upset that the baby stopped breathing, of course, but not as much as one might expect. She admitted she could do without, in her words, 'a bastard female child.'"

"That's cold," said Chester, but he was glad Anna was clear.

"Eunice is sensible," Doc Tears said. "She assured me that once she marries Daniel Leach, I would have the opportunity to help her deliver a respectable male child to carry forth the Bender name."

"Wouldn't such a boy bear the name Leach?" asked Elmer.

"Apparently not. Eunice takes great pride in the Bender name. She knows that Nathaniel has no interest in women and brother Alexander hates children. Jeremiah, of course, has had the two twin boys Maurice and Robert with Anna, but Eunice calls them namby-pambies who likely will never fulfill their manhood."

"What you're saying is that having a female child with Leach before they were married was bad. But once she is wed, Eunice will take it upon herself, with some assistance from the same loathsome Leach, to maintain the oppressive Bender line with a boy?"

"That's the gist of it. I expect the planned baby boy would be a Bender-Leach or a Leach-Bender. Eunice can be extremely persuasive and her husband is obliging. He took the loss of the female baby in stride."

"Cold," said Chester. "Colder than Eunice."

Elmer spit out his next words: "I don't believe any of us on the Boyd side will be wishing her and Leach any luck in their future fucking endeavors."

The doctor grimaced and shook his head. "There are certain medical concerns. Not that she couldn't try to have another baby, but...Why am I telling you this! You are Boyds. Must be that brandy I drank over there before having tea over here, and I'm awfully tired. That baby girl kicked hard while she could. I tried my best but..."

"We don't doubt it. And it was good of you to come to our side, Doc."

"I didn't do much over here. I hate to admit it, but Handy's old Indian friend did what was needed to keep the patient alive and out of immediate danger. He must be close to one hundred by now."

"One hundred seven," said Catawissa Manayunk, who was squatting with his back pressed against the wigwam's far wall. "Same birthday as Thomas Jefferson. Good man him. Call Indian noble race, equal in body and mind to white man. He died Fourth of July, 1826. Only eighty-three."

Doc Tears got into a long discussion with Man about medicine—Lenni Lenape kind and white man kind—and how their different cultures treated life and death of not only people but also animals and trees. Chester was more interested in learning about the Blueberry Hill shooting and what had led up to it while he was down in the valley. Aida and Elmer both spoke up at the same time, heaping most of the blame on Eunice's gun-toting fiancé. Chester cut them off to listen to Blue Boy's account, which he figured would be more objective. While Blue Boy was usually obedient to Aida, supported his brothers, and liked Handy's sautauthig and imperturbable personality, he had also befriended Nathaniel Bender. He admitted to picking wildflowers with Natty on both sides of the dividing ridge and posing for him once, though the artist usually only did pretty landscapes.

According to Blue Boy, the bickering between the two families started because Leach was cutting down hemlocks, even if they were on the east side of the hill and he was acting on orders. The verbal barbs became a torrent once Leach and two hired assistants had prepared the building site and begun forming the wooden skeleton of the Bend. Behind most of the barbs were the equally outspoken Aida Boyd and Eunice Bender, but others on both sides contributed to the nastiness. Handy was an exception, but even he quietly spoke to *his people* about "discouraging these invaders from below." Henry had decided to do some discouraging.

Leach was climbing down from the cupola-in-progress on the Bend roof when Henry, who as a boy had sharpened his aim throwing stones at squirrels, crept through the bushes and hurled a flat "skipping stone" that skidded over the roof ridge and struck Leach's forehead. Though it had been only a glancing blow, Leach had slid all the way down the roof and, after hanging onto the eaves for half a minute, dropped down into Eunice's flower garden. The fall wasn't great and Leach didn't break anything, but he suffered a concussion when his head banged against a flower pot and he developed a strong desire for revenge against any Boyd who trespassed. When he recovered enough to go back to work, he carried along with his hammer and nails a Model 1841 Mississippi Rifle. A week later, Henry made the mistake of venturing again to the wrong side of the Hill. Whether or not he intended to throw another stone at a human target was open to debate. Henry was behind the Bend urinating on timber that was steeping in a water-based mercuric chloride solution when Leach threatened to shoot him. Henry ran, showing uncharacteristic energy born of fear. With rifle in hand, Leach gave chase, bullying his way through the bushes. At the ridgetop, the panting Henry stopped and turned to see how far back his pursuer was. He found out that he was within rifle range.

The gunshot could of course be heard from Blue Rock House. Leach didn't stick around to see what damage he'd done to Henry. He was gone by the time Aida and four of her brothers rushed together to the hilltop. Elmer then took off to fetch Doc Tears from Wurtsboro. On Aida's instructions, Peter, Jacob and Blue Boy carried their wounded brother down to the wigwam. Man removed the bullet and, after renewing his connection with Ketanetuwit and the rest of the spirit world, stuffed moss into the wound to absorb blood, applied a herbal poultice using birch bark decoction and cattail pollen, and induced the patient to drink a pitcher of blueberry tea prepared by his capable assistant, Blue Belle. It was indeed Jacob's idea to transport Henry to town for further treatment from Doc Tears. But, of course, the doctor wasn't in.

As Chester listened to Blue Boy, he felt the glare of Aida. She wasn't about to make Chester's homecoming anything to celebrate. His sister didn't forgive easily. He could hardly blame her. He had deserted the family after their mother died giving birth to Blue Belle, then stayed away from the Hill all those years as if the other Boyds had the plague. He had barely gotten to know his brothers Blue Boy, Jacob, and Peter, and about all he knew about sister Blue Belle was that she had some extraordinary bumps and lumps on her misshapen head.

"You let us all down," Aida told Chester as soon as Blue Boy finished talking. Her fierce red-eyed stare burned into Chester's forehead. "Now you come back when it's too late for Henry. We are under siege from the well-armed Benders, and from what I've heard about you and Anna Bender, I don't know if you are for us or for them. You broke your word to our dear mother about sticking with the family and have proved yourself untrustworthy."

Aida was wrong about it being too late for Henry. Man had done good by him, and Doc Tears had confirmed it. Chester started a weak defense of his long absence but his sister said she didn't want to hear his "sorry excuses and lies." Chester shut up. Aida left the wigwam without saying goodnight to anybody.

Doc Tears was thanking Catawissa Manayunk for something, but Man had stretched out on his blanket and appeared to be asleep, albeit with one eye open.

"We thank you, too, Doc," said Elmer. "We appreciate you coming over the ridge to see about Henry. May we offer you a bed in Blue Rock House for the night?"

"I was hoping you'd say that. I'll go back to the Bend for my buggy in the morning."

"Great. And when you do, you can tell Eunice and whatever other Benders are over there that we won't let Daniel Leach get away with shooting a Boyd."

"Now, Elmer, I understand you are upset. But don't do anything hasty."

"Boyds don't do anything hastily."

"It is best to go to the law if you feel it is absolutely necessary. If Henry recovers, as I feel he shall, you might think twice about even reporting what happened and simply count your blessings. You must understand that your brother was trespassing when shot and I understand that your family had been warned many times to stay away."

"You've said enough, Doc. It's a matter between the Benders and us. You best go up to the house. Handy is no doubt already asleep. He's ninety now and not even a shooting can keep him up at night. But Aida will find you a bedroom—not as luxurious as an overnight stay at the Bend for sure but at least you won't be sleeping with people as coldblooded as rattlesnakes."

Nine-year-old Blue Belle, though still tiny, round, and blind, volunteered to show the doctor the way in the dark from the wigwam to Blue Rock House. She gave the sleeping Man a long hug and the sleeping Henry a long kiss, then said goodnight to Elmer, Blue Boy, Jacob, and Peter. "Oh, and I mustn't forget you," she added, raising on her tiptoes to press her blue-skinned face against

Chester's belly. "I'm glad to have you back home, eldest brother. You must tell me where you have been and what you've been doing and show me how you at an early age became the best blueberry picker in Sullivan County."

"I don't know about that."

"Good Old Dad says it is so, and he says our Mama said it was so. Aida agrees. You are the best, Chesty."

Chester lightly patted her nearly hairless, wrinkled head, fearing he would damage her brilliant brain if he pressed too hard on her special lumps and bumps. "I'm sure we'll find something more interesting to talk about." He moved away slowly, worried she might topple over if he separated his stomach from her face too suddenly. He had no experience dealing with such fragile creatures. She immediately located Doc Tear's left hand and led him out of the crowded wigwam into the night without bumping into anyone. Perhaps she was delicate, not fragile.

"My little sister is amazing," Chester said after watching her go.

"We're used to her by now," said Elmer. "I know it's late, but this is a good time for the rest of us to talk about what to do next?

"About Blue Belle?"

"No, Chester, we need not worry about our little sister. I'm talking about the Benders' hired gun, Daniel Leach. I vote for immediate retaliation. What do you all say?"

"I say the same," said Henry, suddenly awake and in pain. He groaned and attempted to raise up to look at his bandaged wound. "It hurts like hell down there. We have to make the bastard pay."

"You aren't up to throwing stones, Henry," said Blue Boy.

"Stones aren't enough," said Jacob. "Handy keeps his old Mahackamack musket somewhere in the house."

"That won't do," said Peter. "It's all rusted out, can't even be fired safely. We should put our savings together and buy a Colt Walker. It is powerful and has six shots. It's superior to a musket even at two-hundred yards."

"We can't go shooting anybody," said Blue Boy. "It's against our nature."

"We're not talking about anybody," said Jacob. "Daniel Leach deserves to be shot."

"Good Old Boring Dad won't like that," said Blue Boy, crossing his arms and knitting his brow, looking like his father but already a larger, stronger version of him with a lot more hair. "He shoos away flies instead of swatting them. He wouldn't shoot a fox or a wolf. He only wants to discourage the Benders. Shooting back won't discourage any of them, except Nathaniel, and Natty is already plenty discouraged by this family feud."

"I agree that Good Old Boring Dad speaks against the Benders but will never take action," said Peter. "None of us has ever shot anyone or anything. The proud bucks that come to the house are fearless. They lie down and stare us down. But these are different circumstances. A Colt Walker will put the fear in Leach and his Bender masters. Anyway, we should go ask Aida. She'll tell us what we should do."

Elmer stamped his foot, just missing Henry's hurting midsection. "We don't always have to go to Aida. This is man's business. Isn't that right, Chesty?"

Chester was caught off guard. He wasn't thinking about revenge; he was pondering the fragility of life—his near drowning in the D&H Canal, wounded Henry lying in pain on Man's bearskin rug, the original Blue Belle's shocking death in her cradle, those three other babies who didn't make it (two from Henrietta Boyd, one from Eunice Bender), and his mother's dying while giving birth to the second Blue Belle. Then, out of the blue, he considered the good news that Anna Bender had not been the laboring mother at the Bend and likely had no intention of ever having a third child with her beastly husband.

"Chester!" shouted Elmer. "You still with us? What about paying Leach back?"

"I don't know about that, Elm," Chester said at last. "We should get all opinions on this serious matter. It doesn't mean we have to do what Aida says."

"All right, but what's your opinion on what we should do?"

"I'll have to think on that. A lot has happened, and I just got back here. I do know one thing, brother—this business on the Hill is my business. I'm a Boyd."

"Hallelujah," called out Man. Upon awakening he had gone into a squat and was chewing an unidentified plant, perhaps for his own medicinal purposes. "All Boyds leave wigwam now, except Henry. All do what Boy, who you call Good Old Boring Dad, do best—have deep sleep in stone house and no think of this thing till morning when, no matter what else happen, sun rise."

17

EYE FOR AN EYE

Handy awoke with a start from a bad dream in which an expanding black cloud hovered over the Hill blocking the sun. The dark image suggested death. But the sun wasn't even up yet. And since he could hear his heart pounding, he was relieved he wasn't the one the Grim Reaper had visited. Then he remembered his third son in the tepee and his heart pounded harder. Had Henry made it through the night? All was quiet in Blue Rock House except for the snoring of Elmer, or perhaps it was Chester, seemingly back in the fold. No matter, he'd let them sleep. But he wasn't about to wait for the sun to rise to find out about Henry's condition.

Wearing his nightshirt but no shoes or hat on his bald head, Handy grabbed the hand-carved lion-headed walking stick Elmer had given him for his eightieth birthday—already almost a decade ago—and went out through the back door, which always screeched like a barn owl. He didn't stop to pick a single blueberry and only fell to his knees once—due to the early morning hour not age, he decided—but the walk to the wigwam still seemed to take longer than ever.

He found Henry and Man on their backs shoulder to shoulder on the bearskin rug. Henry groaned once and squirmed twice, but breathed peacefully after that. Man, though, was as still as the turtle-shell rattle that rested on his hollow stomach, and his face had turned pale as a puffball mushroom. One eye was closed, the other half open. He wasn't talking to his Lenni Lenape spirits. He only had the strength to wink at Handy and speak to his old friend in a whisper: "I go now, Boy." His right arm stirred, and he raised his hand high enough to seize the rattle off his belly and give it a vigorous shake. Then his arm dropped, but his hand continued to clutch the rattle at his still chest. Now, both eyes were closed. "I see the star berries," he said, his last breaths unlabored. "Everywhere the star berries."

Handy sat down on the bearskin rug and waited for Henry to wake up. The tears that he expected to flow—and that had come so readily when his wife died and before that when the first Blue Belle died—didn't appear. He had never seen Man cry, though his Lenni Lenape friend had suffered far more losses during his long lifetime. Man's entire tribe had virtually vanished. Anyway, Handy figured to be seeing Man again soon in a better place (well maybe not better unless there was a blueberry Heaven), and he needed to give his full attention to his wounded son and the rest of his living offspring.

Henry was still asleep and Handy was starting to doze off when the second Blue Belle appeared, leading overnight guest Doc Tears by the hand. Neither acted surprised at what they saw in the tepee. Both took knees—Blue Belle to pray that her Indian grandfather find hospitality and happiness in the spirit world and that her wounded brother rediscover health and happiness in this life; the doctor to pronounce Catawissa Manayunk stone dead and Henry out of danger. Later Aida came down and took charge. She had Elmer make a stretcher to transport Henry up to his own sick bed where she assured the patient he would feel more comfortable. She allowed the other Boyds only ten minutes each observing Man's body that morning because she expected a full day of diligent blueberry picking. That angered Chester, who had not totally lost his rebellious spirit. "How generous you are, dear sister, and we can burn the wigwam with Man inside so he can go up in smoke and leave us to concentrate on our important business—selling our berries and souls to the highest bidder."

"You know we will do nothing of the kind," Aida said, squeezing her brother's upper arm in a show of family solidarity. "We shall honor *our* Indian. Initially, I thought he might like to join the fishes in the Basha Kill, but his body would float to the surface after a few days and possibly float all the way to the Delaware at Mahackamack and create a commotion."

"You mean Port Jervis," said Chester. "You must have known, Sis, the name changed from Mahackamack to honor D&H Canal Chief Engineer John B. Jervis, who I once dug dirt with back in '25."

"Nevertheless, I feel it is best to bring Man to the Mahackamack Churchyard Cemetery and bury him next to Mama or, if that's too much for us, to find a graveyard in the valley that will accept an old redskin."

"That won't do, dear daughter," said Handy. "He must be buried on our Hill in a wooden box—dead wood is acceptable—at the site of his choosing. We owe him that much."

"We will not bury him at the top of the Hill next to my lost sister, the first Blue Belle," said Aida. "I forbid it. That space is reserved for her."

"Plenty of room up there," said Handy. "But it is a rather difficult climb getting there for some of us."

"No worries," said the living Blue Belle. "That isn't Grandfather Man's chosen resting place. He told me he wanted his body under the ground overlooking Handy Spring, close enough to quench his great thirst now and then but not so close that he would contaminate the Ketanëtuwit-blessed water."

"Near the spring it must be," said Handy.

Aida held her tongue. Man had told Blue Belle where he wanted to be buried and Handy, who made few requests, supported his longtime Indian friend. She knew it would be a losing fight to try removing him off the Hill. She wondered who would miss Catawissa Manayunk more—Handy, the widower who had lost his only friend and might have trouble living without him, or Blue Belle, who because of cruel fate could never grow into a normal woman and probably could never love a man more than her Indian grandfather. Well, they all would miss Man. He was a fixture in his wigwam on the Hill. Aida instructed Elmer to make a coffin.

While Elmer worked, Jacob and Peter escorted Doc Tears over the ridge to reclaim his horse and buggy at the Bend. Aida allowed an extended lunch break for the pickers to provide a brief service for Man. All the Boyds except Henry circled around the burial site—a moss-covered knob thirty feet from the spring. The coffin lid, which didn't quite fit right ("I'm far better working with stone," said Elmer), was lifted so the corpse could be exposed for viewing. The bearskin rug was draped on the naked body and the wolfskin hat with blue jay feather was secured on the small head. It struck Handy that his friend's death face looked remarkably similar to the face Blue Belle was born with, but he kept that to himself.

Handy had already smeared twenty blueberries on a saucer and now painted his old friend's lifeless face blue. Blue Belle, whose face was naturally blue, danced beside the coffin while shaking Man's turtle-shell rattle. When at last tired out, she placed the rattle on top of the body, threw herself onto the ground, and began pulling out what little hair she had on her berry-like head. Aida found this alarming and made her stop. Although he doubted it was a traditional Lenni Lenape burial practice, Handy placed at his dead friend's feet several heart-shaped stones that Man had collected through the years. Before Elmer could work the lid shut, Blue Boy tossed into the coffin the gourd that Man had long used for carrying spring water. Handy had made sure the gourd was full.

Man couldn't have weighed much in the end. His hump, which at one time seemed to be shrinking, now appeared larger than ever and, as Peter noted, "must account for most of his weight." The coffin felt heavy, as if it held a giant. It took a group effort to lower it into the six-foot-deep hole. All the Boyds helped fill the grave with soil, pieces of bark, moss, ferns, and blueberry branches. Then, without discussion, the family collected large stones and small stones to create a three-foot-high memorial cairn nearby. They all contributed, but Elmer rearranged most of the stones to make it more symmetrical.

"That takes care of the body the way he wished it," said Blue Belle from her knees. "His spirit will take care of itself." Handy helped his second daughter, not even ten years old yet, to her feet and smoothed her remaining hair.

"As some of you already know, Man told me that his spirit would separate from his body at the moment of death but wouldn't leave Blueberry Hill right away," Handy said. "It will stick around for eleven days subsisting on berries from the bushes and sautauthig from the house."

"Come on, Old Dad," said Jacob. "How can a spirit eat when it doesn't have a mouth or teeth or tongue?"

"Nobody knows but the Lenni Lenape. I imagine no visual eating is involved. The spirit must extract nourishment from the blueberries and such the same way a tree drinks water."

"It is so," said Blue Belle.

"Makes sense to me," said Peter. "God works in mysterious ways, and I assume Ketanëtuwit does, too."

"Anyway," continued Handy, "after eleven days his spirit will travel to the home of the Creator and reside in the Happy Picking Ground, where it will connect with the kindred spirits of those who met their maker previously, such as Henrietta. Yes, my friend Man, like my dear Pudding, shall be enjoying a pain-free spiritual feast for eternity."

"It is so," said Blue Belle.

"Excellent," said Aida. "Now let's all get back to picking to please Man's hungry spirit and to keep the rest of us alive."

§

The picking was good and so was the selling for a week. Boyd blueberries were recognized as the cream of the crop in the region, and the demand was such that Aida approved the purchase of a second cart to haul what clever little Blue Belle called "our berry special cargo." Aida was all about profit without loss, and under her strict supervision, the family business flourished while talks about retaliation against Leach and the Benders withered. Chester, though only half trying as he dealt with his internal confusion about his place in the world, reestablished himself as the best of the Boyd pickers. Even Henry, healing fast from his gunshot wound, would sit on a wicker stool under a productive high bush and pluck every berry within reach for hours without once contemplating revenge. The bumper crop excited them all.

Eight days after the death of Catawissa Manayunk, the Boyds arose for another work day under sunny blue skies, Aida called for an all-family breakfast. "I couldn't have asked for a better month for the Boyds," she said, standing at the head of the table. "It has been an unprecedented harvest, surely our most venerable, majestic, magnificent, and noble month. I salute you all on this fine August morning for your *august* performance in our fruitful blueberry patch." She smiled at them all and said, "Thanks little Sis" to Blue Belle, who had suggested using august and August in the same positive sentence and had reminded Aida they were not pronounced the same way.

Handy sat at the other end of the table looking downcast. Yes, Aida had developed quite a way with words, thanks to all her recent reading with Blue Belle, including the two-volume second edition of Noah Webster's *An American Dictionary of the English Language* that Aida got in trade for three quarts of blueberries. Handy was now reasonably pleased his family could make a modest living off this blueberry haven showed to him by Catawissa Manayunk way back in the summer of 1811. But he was missing Man, and how could August 1849 be so wonderful when Man had died that month.

Aida took a long sip from her glass of homemade blueberry juice and ended her morning talk with a family nudge: "This doesn't mean you should rest on your laurels, everybody. There's only a short summer window of opportunity in the blueberry world, though I'm hoping and praying that the slim picking time won't begin on the Hill this year until at least mid-September. Now finish up your morning meals, people, and go to picking while the pickin' is good!"

The Boyds were prepared to do their best, but the sun disappeared at noon and a sudden summer storm struck that afternoon, producing heavy rain, strong winds, and blueberry-sized hail that undermined their efforts. The weather calmed during the night but by dawn the hard rain had returned in a gale. Storms raged for the next two days. Wind gusts knocked berries to the ground. Too much water caused hanging berries to grow so plump that they split, and one bursting berry often spoiled the whole bunch. Another round of hail broke and bent twigs and bruised berries to the extend the public would reject them on appearance alone. Sales would plummet. Aida took nature's nasty turn personally. Still, she kept her self-command and preserved as many blueberries as she could for winter use. Some were kept fresh by stashing them three miles away in a secret ice cave (ice stayed there even in summer) whose location Man had revealed before his death. Some were dried by laying them on pans in the oven while it was cooling and leaving the fruit overnight. Still others were packed in heavy syrup using a preservation technique called "sugaring."

Nevertheless, any Boyd optimism Aida might have inspired with her breakfast talk was shattered. The Benders were back on Boyd minds, as if their Hill neighbors were to blame for the storms that ruined the end of the blueberry season. On the eleventh day since Catawissa Manayunk's death, Blue Belle remembered that this was the day his spirit was supposed to leave home. Handy remembered, too, but he decided to stay in bed all day anyway because he wasn't feeling up to going outside to possibly face another teary-eyed goodbye.

"I understand, Good Old Dad," Blue Belle told him. "Man will, too. You rest up. I'll send your warmest regards and wish his spirit a safe journey."

That afternoon, Blue Belle talked Chester and Elmer into taking her up the outdoor stone steps to the porch roof. The three of them sat there for an hour looking to the west in the direction of Man's memorial cairn. When the wind whipped up, as if to show them they shouldn't expect quiet, peaceful days ahead, Elmer was past ready to give up on the notion that anybody's spirit could rise, and Chester was trying to convince Blue Belle to leave. Both older brothers became protective, taking hold of their tiny blind sister so she wouldn't blow off the roof.

"I feel it," Blue Belle said, trembling like a leaf but not one ready to fall.

"It's only the blasted wind," said Elmer. "Another storm is brewing. Haven't we had enough weather! Look at all those blueberry bushes dancing over there."

"It's him," said Blue Belle.

"I don't see anything," said Chester.

"I don't mean all of him. I mean his spirit. It's rising."

"Leaves are swirling high in the air, that's all," said Elmer.

"No, no. Look, brothers! See him. There he goes."

Elmer and Chester weren't sure what a spirit looked like, but they humored their sister by telling her they might have seen a wisp of vapor reaching the clouds somewhere above Handy Spring.

"Bon voyage, Man," called out Blue Belle.

"Adios," said Elmer.

"So long, see you later," said Chester.

At least in the backs of their minds, the two brothers suspected their blind little sister saw more than they did. Blue Belle kissed each brother on the cheek, rose to her feet and went back down the steps on her own. Slow to react, Chester and Elm finally gave chase, too late to catch up with her until she had gone inside the house to their father's bed. She hovered over the gently snoring Handy, whispering in his ear until he awoke. He rubbed his eyes as he looked up at her.

"His spirit has gone to the lofty land of Ketanётuwit," she said, grasping his shoulder. "All is well, Good Old Dad. I saw him rise."

"Of course, you did," he said, freeing his shoulder and patting her on the head. "That's wonderful, my darling little one, and now we can all get some rest." He rolled over onto his right side and resumed snoring. Maybe he had already seen the old Leni Lenape rising in his dreams and wanted to get back to them. Blue Belle returned the favor, patting her father's bald head before leaving the room with a brother on each of her arms.

Blue Belle was uplifted by the spirit of Man rising but nobody else in Blue Rock House was. Handy didn't wake up until noon the next day. He hadn't slept that long since boyhood when he often preferred slumber to facing the smokehouse or the switch as punishment for things he did or didn't do while awake. Neither Man nor Boy was in the dream he woke up remembering. What he had seen were unrooted trees flying through the hail and rain while under fire from a sneering marksman below with the face of a bear, the body of Hercules, and a name tattooed on his superhuman chest—Daniel Leach.

The empty wigwam near Handy Spring, Henry's cries of pain over his gunshot wound, and the stretch of stormy weather—put every Boyd except Blue Belle in a bad mood. The youngest family member tried to bring cheer by pointing out Man had lived the long peaceful life of tortoises, Henry was a little sore but was over the worst of it, and the sun was out today and would be out tomorrow. She could feel it. The next day, though, the ground shook as Leach and other sawyers trimmed and fell trees near the ridgeline, too close to the Boyd side of the Hill for comfort. "Every tree that hits the ground sounds like a cannon going off in my head," said Handy.

Two days later the chopping and crashing stopped but a new noise replaced it—not cannon fire but gunfire. The Benders and their friends were hunting wild turkeys and ruffed grouse. That was just the beginning. There would be other animals to hunt all through the fall. In Henry's bedroom on the final day of summer, Handy named the ones he could think of—whitetail deer, black bears, cottontail rabbits, ducks, quail, pigeons, raccoons, squirrels, porcupines, bobcats, foxes and wolves (if any were still around).

"And us!" Henry shouted. "Leach has already hunted me down. Who will be next?"

"Are any of us really safe?" asked Aida, who like the others was there to see how Henry felt. "As far as I can tell the whole crowd on the other side hunts."

"Damn Benders," said Chester.

"I'm sure it's not all of them," said Blue Boy. "The shooting of birds bothers Natty Bender as much as it does any of us."

"We don't care a lick what bothers your sensitive artist," said Elmer. "A Bender is a Bender. So why don't you shut your trap."

Blue Boy closed his mouth and turned away. But Blue Belle spoke out: "I have much sympathy for the animals and a sense of sisterhood with them. I don't think any creature should be shot. But not every person thinks like me, like us. Boyds don't shoot anything. Some Benders do. I know Natty does not. We must learn to live together."

It was hard to argue with anything she said but nobody patted her on the back or said how right she was or how thoughtful she was at such a tender age. Blue Rock House grew still—so quiet, thought Chester, that you could have heard a yellow-shafted flicker feather drop. The impromptu end-of-summer gathering in Henry's room broke up quickly. In the hallway, Blue Boy gave Blue Belle a brief hug without saying a word. It was understood that they understood each other, at least when it came to animals and Nathaniel Bender.

"Where you all going?" Henry called out from his bed. "I'm horribly wounded! Nobody said a word about revenge. You all just left. Revenge! Revenge! I'd do it myself if I wasn't lying here in pain. Live together! That's little girl talk. Revenge is what men should be talking about."

Out in the hallway, Jacob and Peter heard the outcry. They hadn't said a word while in Henry's room and were often at odds with each other, but now they shared a knowing glance and exclaimed at the same time, "Let's do it." One was eighteen and the other seventeen but it went without saying that boys with the right grit didn't have to wait until they were twenty-one to become men.

What they did was put their savings together and borrow money from Elmer to buy a Colt Walker, then took turns patrolling at the top of the Hill as if they were posted on the Mexican border. They couldn't resist firing their powerful weapon on occasion and seeing those .44-caliber balls penetrate tree stumps on the other side.

With Elmer's blessing, Peter and Jacob kept their Colt Walker ownership a secret from the rest of the family as long as they could. Blue Belle, though, somehow recognized the shots as coming from the Boyd side rather than from the Bender hunters. She protested, but Aida declared it good that not every Boyd was "gun shy." Henry approved whole-heartedly. Elmer pointed to the necessity of a strong defense in a world full of belligerent people. Chester advised his two youngest brothers to be careful and never point the large revolver at any other human being unless absolutely necessary. Handy didn't want to dig up the old Mahackamack musket he had never actually fired at a living creature, but he started to sleep with his Revolutionary War knife under his pillow in case the Benders broke through Jacob and Peter's position at the top of the Hill.

On October 3, 1849, Peter and Jacob couldn't agree on whose turn it was to patrol with the Colt Walker, so they passed the gun back and forth as they walked the ridgeline. At dusk, a rustling in the bushes on their side of the Hill brought them to a halt. They saw movement from west to east, from Boyd property to Bender property, but couldn't identify the large figure. They considered the dangerous possibilities. A panther, suggested Jacob, though he had never seen one of those secretive killer cats and had only heard about them in the wild tales of Man. A bear, suggested Peter, who well knew the oft-repeated story of how Man had saved their father from a she-bear while Handy was on his expedition to find a home in Sullivan County. They then recalled how Man had belonged to the Wolf clan of the Lenni Lenape Nation and wondered if the animal in the bushes could be him, come back to life as a wolf.

"We can't shoot a wolf that might be Man," said Jacob.

"Well, give me the gun just in case," said Peter. 'He wouldn't return as a panther or a bear."

Whatever creature was out there decided to halt as if it knew that trying to run from these steadfast young men was futile. They inched closer, Jacob slightly out in front to act as locator while Peter held the Walker at chest level. They heard clucking that seemed to come from somewhere off the ground. Jacob pointed, and through the branches and needles of a pine tree, Peter saw an indistinct figure.

"Betcha it's only a wild turkey," Peter said. "Wonder if they make good eating."

"Good Old Boring Dad wouldn't want us to shoot a turkey."

"We won't tell him. Let's do it, Jacob. We'll gut it and cook it ourselves. I'm hungry...for meat!"

"You can't shoot it from here. Better give me the gun."

Peter didn't want to argue about it. Instead of handing the Colt to his brother, he pointed it and pulled the trigger. Whatever was in the tree didn't cry out as it fell out and landed in the bushes with a thud that made them both shudder. The Hill became dead silent, but only for a few seconds.

"Idiot!" Jacob shouted. "That was no turkey. I saw flapping arms instead of wings."

"Gadzooks! A wild Indian?"

"No. A trespasser. You shot a trespasser, Peter."

Peter tried to hand the gun to his brother, but Jacob wanted no part of it.

"You think I killed him?" Peter asked, freezing with the gun pointed straight up.

"I don't know. You should have fired a warning shot first, like the sheriff does."

"How would you know what a sheriff does? I wasn't warning the turkey. I was shooting it to eat it."

"It was no turkey."

"I know that now. You'd better go look, Jacob. I don't want to see."

"If the trespasser was a Bender, that wouldn't be so bad."

"No? I never even shot a wild animal before this."

"Now you have. How do you feel?"

"Like a murderer. I hope he isn't dead, even if he is a Bender."

"You were within your rights. Daniel Leach shot Henry on Bender property. You shot one of them trespassing on our property. An eye for an eye!"

"Leach didn't shoot Henry in the eye."

"I'm not saying you shot the trespasser in the eye, either. Or, for that matter, the groin. Are you going to look or are you chicken?"

"You go ahead. I don't want to see where I shot him."

"All right, chicken." Jacob grabbed the Walker and held it out in front of him as he approached the fallen man who, if only wounded, could very well be armed and dangerous.

Jacob managed only four steps. He dropped the gun when he heard a scream, an all-too human scream. The trespasser was alive. The scream was coming from the bushes directly in front of him and was answered by another scream, coming from the chicken behind him.

18
ACCIDENTAL MEETING

Nathaniel Bender was the innocent victim of Peter Boyd's shot. With sketchpad in hand, he had left the Bend on the cloudy afternoon of October 3 looking for inspiration on his family's land. Upon seeing a murder of crows flying west, he had given chase, sketching as he plowed uphill through the underbrush and continuing to do so as he crossed the crest near the large rock outcrop. He was too focused to know where he was until his stumbling feet told him he was going downhill. He reversed course, and came again to the outcrop. He found the rock formation intimidating. His landscapes didn't include mountains or rocky protrusions. The Hill was enough. With pad still in hand he had climbed into a tree to study the gentler landscape and locate the crows from a supportive lower branch. He was fully absorbed in the creative process and heard no human voices nor the warning calls of the crows. He did hear the shot that scattered the crows and felled him.

As he later told Daniel Leach, who had found him crawling in the woods, and repeated to his family and to various lawmen, he "simply got carried away by those alluring winged figures in the clouds and the treetops and all around him." He further explained that since his painting *Blueberry Field with Jays* had sold for twenty-five dollars to blueberry-loving farmer and businessman Archibald Seybolt, he believed he could make an even bigger sale with one called *Blueberry Field with Crows*. "Not that I am in it for the money," he assured everybody.

His gunshot wound, though painful, was hardly life threatening. The .44-caliber ball that struck him did no internal damage, seeming to miraculously bounce off his backside. After Doc Tears patched up the wound and said Nathaniel was fine but wouldn't be able to sit comfortably for a week, his relieved brothers changed his nickname from "Nature Boy Natty" to "Iron Butt Bender." Not that they found anything funny about who did the shooting. No gun was found at the scene of the crime, but under interrogation, Jacob admitted that the Colt Walker was stashed under his mattress. At the same time, he fingered Peter as the one who pulled the trigger. Peter called his brother a "dirty snitcher" before admitting that the weapon was "too much gun" for novice shooters like himself and especially Jacob. "I thought Nathaniel was a turkey," Peter insisted when questioned by the sheriff. "I will never fire a gun again at a beast, let alone a man. I have made that vow to my Old Dad, who believes guns and hunting are the devil's work."

Nathaniel's older brothers, Jeremiah and Alexander, wanted to see the shooter prosecuted, and Peter spent one night in the Wurtsboro lockup. But Nathaniel wasn't so sure, since no real harm was done, and he had indeed crossed the imaginary dividing line atop the Hill. Eunice Bender, who prided herself in being fair-minded, stepped in and told her brothers: "Those deficient people didn't press charges when my Daniel plugged Henry in the groin region, so how can we make a big to-do about Nathaniel getting it in the bum? Natty will live to paint tomorrow." Eunice told the authorities the shooting had been an unfortunate hunting accident, though it was common knowledge that the Boyds were fruit and vegetable eaters and nobody had hunted on their side of Blueberry Nill since their late Indian companion had employed a bow and arrow. Shortly thereafter, Eunice and Aida crossed paths on the road to town. After a few awkward moments over what to say to a sworn enemy, they came to an understanding when Aida revealed she sold the Colt Walker to buy flour and sugar and Eunice replied with conviction, "The way I see it, Miss Boyd, what happens on the Hill, stays on the Hill."

And it stayed that way all through the next decade. Nobody was shot on either side during the 1850s, but nobody forgot the two earlier shootings. Although not actively feuding, the two Hill families were well aware of their ideological differences over land usage and expected treachery by the enemy could dismantle the shaky peace at any time. Blueberry Hill was as full of tension as the nation as a whole. On the Boyd side, the blueberry business was up and down, largely depending on the fickleness of nature rather than human nature. Aida conceded that no matter how much planning she did or how much work her people put in, bad berry seasons still sometimes happened, even on the high-yielding Hill.

Like her late mother, she found that controlling family members could be as difficult as controlling the weather. The only one Aida didn't need to keep a close watch on was Blue Belle, who never acted as helpless as she should have been considering her most unfortunate condition—miniscule body, misshaped head, blindness, failure to accept that nature was indifferent to mankind. She had never seemed like a needy child. Blue Belle not only took care of herself but also helped her brothers whenever she could. Sometimes Aida wondered if her poor little sister was too good for this world. She did not dwell on that notion, though. The rest of the family needed too much of Aida's attention.

A big worry was their father. In his nineties, Hardy became steadily more unsteady. His obstinance grew at the same rate as his fragility. When he required two walking sticks to keep from falling, he insisted on going to the bushes with nothing but his Revolutionary War knife to fend off bears, wolves, panthers, and the Bender crowd. He had numerous falls but broke nothing. His favorite occupation, at all hours and even on rainy days, was to shuffle outdoors and climb the treacherous stone steps so he could sit on the low-pitch porch roof to enjoy his sautauthig and watch for trespassers (Benders), spirits (Man, Henrietta), harbingers of bad luck (owls, crows), and comets (after regretting how he had somehow slept through the Great Comet of 1843).

Henry eventually acknowledged, half in jest, that he would put his gunshot wound behind him the way Nathaniel Bender had done, but he kept finding mysterious sicknesses and minor injuries that laid him up more often than not. That aggravated Aida to no end, but Doc Tears, becoming increasingly feeble himself, was always on Henry's side, and Handy said that Henry couldn't change his spots any more than a measles victim could. Meanwhile, against Aida's wishes, Blue Boy met twice with Nathaniel Bender in town hoping the artist, who held no grudge against the Boyds or anyone else, would teach him some brush strokes. There was no third meeting. Blue Boy realized that every tree, bird, or rock he painted looked like a glob and that he didn't really want his long brown hair stroked by the sympathetic, nimble-fingered Natty. Besides, fraternizing with a Bender made Blue Boy feel practically like an outcast in his own home.

Peter and Jacob, at separate times, followed the earlier example of Chester and left Blue Rock House to seek their fortunes elsewhere. Peter, breaking his vow to his father, tried to open a gun shop in Wurtsboro but didn't have enough money or backing and came home after finding a series of odd jobs less tolerable than picking and selling blueberries. Jacob hitched a ride to Port Jervis to revisit his mother's grave and stayed on to help bring the New York & Erie Railroad to town. He became lonely and later hurt when he fought with a tracklayer over the affections of a redhaired girl and lost. After the tracklayer, twice his size, knocked him silly with a railroad tie, Jacob came home to rest under the care of Blue Belle, who tended his head wound and mended his broken heart by reciting memorized love poems and teaching him to put his faith in family, even Peter.

Elmer, on the other hand, found love. If not "true love," it was certainly "unconditional love," for he stuck by a woman as flawed as a badly bruised blueberry or a cracked building stone. On an 1855 blueberry cart trip to town, Elmer met Mary Turner, a laundress fifteen years his junior who had "graduated" from the New York State Lunatic Asylum at Utica. The hospital's director had believed in "labor as the most essential of our curative means," and Mary produced so much honest sweat in the garden, in the laundry, and in the stable that he judged her to be "cured" and released her from the asylum. After Elmer brought Mary to Blue Rock House, Aida questioned her brother's sanity. Mary, haunted by parents who treated her like a slave and an uncle who treated her like a harlot, could not look anyone in the eye, frequently had minor "accidents" with knives, and was observed eating dirt. But the odd newcomer proved herself a hard worker, eagerly dealing with the family's blueberry- and dirt-stained clothes and the weeds in the family's neglected vegetable garden. Aida could not object when Elmer chose to marry Mary, especially when the woman announced she was with child. It turned out to be a false pregnancy, which disappointed everyone because the Boyd family wasn't growing while the Benders were prolificating. Mary decided it was cleaner to be childless, and Elmer accepted her decision. "Mary and I are rocks," he said. Aida, who wanted a child but only with the perfect man (if such a creature even existed), wasn't sure exactly what Elmer meant but it didn't sound good.

Aida was more worried about Chester than her father or anyone else, for her oldest brother was still in his forties, far too young to be habitually passive and despondent. She wished he would find a wife, bring her to the Hill, and add to the stagnant Boyd family. The trouble was he had eyes and thoughts for only a woman who was an impossible catch—Jeremiah Bender's allegedly faithful wife, Anna. Aida rarely spoke to Chester about his foolish lovesickness, though, because she didn't want to upset the blueberry cart. Even when in the doldrums Chesty always out-picked his brothers.

On the Bender side, new life appeared. Alexander had never cared for children but in 1851 he married Daniel Leach's visiting Georgia cousin Delilah, a Southern belle who decided she wanted children and riches more than an immediate return to the South. Alexander, who possessed money, land, and a fondness for her accent, white skin, and colorful bonnets, obliged her. She named their offspring, who came in quick succession, Cal (for South Carolina statesman John Calhoun), James (for James Edward Oglethorpe, founder of the colony of Georgia) and Georgia (for her beloved home state). Like most Benders, Alexander occasionally popped a blueberry in his mouth but never appreciated the berries. Delilah avoided eating them all together because they caused the inside of her mouth and lips to swell and her throat to itch. Like most Southern belles, she wanted to look her best not only for her man but for all gentlemen and fashionable women.

Eunice never cared much for the taste of blueberries until she became pregnant again and married in 1852 and began to crave them. During her uneventful second pregnancy she changed her mind about wanting a boy instead of a girl. With her new appreciation for the small blue fruit, she chose the name "Berri" for the precious female baby who instantly became the "apple of her eye." Husband Daniel Leach, the invaluable handyman, lumberman, and defender of Bender property rights, had nothing to do with the selected name. He still wanted the son Eunice had once promised him and had an aversion for blueberries because their scent made him vomit and because of what they represented to him—the lowdown abolitionist Yankee trash who thought everybody could get by picking blueberries instead of cotton, who loafed under trees instead of logging them, and who dabbled with stones instead of quarrying them.

"Of course, I realize no cotton is grown in the North," he said in one of his frequent debates with brother-in-law Nathaniel. "That's beside the point. People who don't strive for anything more than subsistence living are little more than animals! It is up to upstanding men like us to force nature's agreement with our designs and construction."

"The Boyds contend that nature allows no master over itself."

"The drivel of lazy savages. They want us and all our progressive ways to disappear. You dare stand up for their kind, Nathaniel?"

"Of course not, Dan. I'm a Bender. We have every right to our side of the Hill and all our other properties. We paid for them. That's the American way."

"So, what are we arguing about?"

"No argument. I'm a simple painter. I enjoy the freedom to be natural."

"Neither Eunice nor I can understand you. Your brothers certainly cannot. What you don't seem to realize, Nathaniel, is that nature is an opponent that must be subdued for the sake of civilization."

Under Leach's supervision, countless bushes and trees were removed to build three wagon roads—the widest one shortening the distance from the Bend to town, the longest one making more accessible the family sawmill on the lower section of the former Drake Tract, the scenic third one winding up to the highest point on the Hill where the outcrop of rock provided a view of the snaking Delaware & Hudson Canal and across the valley to the hills west of Wurtsboro. Anna Bender named the impressive outcrop the Castle in 1852 and got in the habit of taking walks up there with her twelve-year-old twins—Maurice (named for canal man Maurice Wurts) and Robert (named for Robert Fulton, the man who had come up with the first commercially successful steamboat)—those times when Jeremiah was off captaining his favorite canalboat, *Annabelle II,* without her.

While standing on one of the two natural "turrets" on the castle, Anna didn't look only at the far-off scenery. From there she also could see a small section of the Blue Rock House's roof, though not the part where Chester sometimes sat to keep his father company if not safe. Not quite being able to see Chester on the porch roof didn't keep her from often picturing him there. Chester was a Boyd and over forty, but she pictured him the way she wanted him to be—a young, dashing, virile white knight rather than an aging, balding, slovenly black one. She went so far as to imagine that the turret was actually a tower where she was being held prisoner by the evil King Red and waited for her good knight to come rescue her. She knew it was a silly thing for a thirty-eight-year-old woman to do but it was harmless for she never intended to tell anyone about her fairy tale dream.

"I'm spotting wildlife for our hunters," she told her twin sons on one such walk to the hilltop in November 1852. "It goes without saying that the deer and the bears have to cross over the crest for us to target them on our side, but they will eventually."

"When they do, I'll be here to shoot them," said Maurice. "Papa is giving me my own rifle as an early Christmas present."

"Me, too," said Robert. "And if a Boyd crosses over, I'll shoot him, too."

Anna allowed such talk to go on. She knew that if she said anything supportive of the Boyds, word would get back to her husband. Jeremiah would be mightily offended, as would Daniel Leach, Eunice, Alexander, and probably Delilah. Only Nathaniel might understand what she really thought, but he was so different from the rest of the family. Jeremiah told his wife that same month that only a Bender who hunted could be considered a real man. "Does that mean Eunice is a real man?" Anna asked him. "Hasn't she already shot a buck and a doe this year?" That made Jeremiah angry for a long time because he didn't allow her to say anything negative about his sister any more than he did *his* canal. The Bend was a gorgeous house but there were days she needed her Castle awfully bad.

In a visit to the Castle with her sons in September 1853, Aida saw something from one of the turrets that was far more interesting than wildlife. Blue Belle Boyd and Chester were walking right toward the rock outcrop, with the amazing little blind girl doing the leading. Anna quickly climbed down from her high point as not to be seen. She didn't tell her sons what she saw. Instead, she pulled them toward the Bend and anxiously advised them to hurry home so they wouldn't miss the chance to go to town with Uncle Natty and be treated by him to black licorice and chewing gum at the general store. The twins raced off, and Anna sighed twice while brushing her hair, auburn again, from her eyes. She then checked the grounds to see if Chester and Blue Belle had come all the way up to the Castle, which Daniel Leach had determined was at least eighty percent on Bender property.

Anna found the pair exploring a shallow cave that she hadn't discovered because it was almost certainly on the Boyd side of the Hill. Blue Belle was all the way inside while Chester was on all fours, halfway in and halfway out. She approached as silently as she could. She couldn't help herself. His derrière stuck in the air inviting a smack, but Anna resisted the urge and instead grabbed him by an ankle. "Got you!" she said. "You are under arrest, mister." Chester kicked his leg free, and the heel of his shoe thumped her in the chin. She didn't lose consciousness but she lay on her back as still as a log while Chester raised her legs onto a convenient rock, then bunched his jacket and slipped it behind her head for support. She half opened her eyes and saw him staring at her chest, beneath which her heart was pounding too hard. She was sure he could hear it. She held her breath as if that could calm her down and ease the pain that ran from chin to brain. She stirred only when Blue Belle rubbed cool cave lichen on her bruised chin.

"Thank you, deary," Anna said to Blue Belle while looking up at Chester. She forgot for a moment that it was he who had nearly knocked her cold. He was kneeling beside her as a white knight might do for a respected wounded enemy.

"That was a damn crazy thing for you to do," said Chester, not at all like a gallant knight.

"Me? You kicked me in the face?"

"It was an involuntary action. Why'd you grab my ankle?"

"It was there."

"On our side of this rock formation. It's the dividing line, you should know. You're the one trespassing, Anna.

"So, shoot me."

"No need to be overly dramatic. I'm like my father—I have never fired a gun in all my born days. I'm simply saying this cave is on Boyd property."

"That's debatable. Anyway, I suppose it's better you kicked me than shot me."

"Oh, really, you two, stop this silly talk," said Blue Belle, now twelve but no less wise than she was in her early years. "We all know you don't hate each other, not really. It was an accidental meeting, but it could be a fortunate one. We can all be friends. It's what Chesty wants. It's what Anna wants. And it is what Blue Belle wants. Am I wrong?"

"Of course not," said Anna. "You truly are a dear." She dramatically planted a kiss on the blind girl's forehead, wrinkled since birth. "I can't believe you are the same age as my Maurice and Robert."

"I understand. I am tiny for my age."

"It's not that. You can't measure a person by how big she or he is. You have a big heart."

Chester couldn't help looking at Anna up and down, from head to toe. Living on the Hill had been good to her. She no longer had the scaly look he had seen down at the canal. Her hair was back to its original color. She appeared younger, slimmer, and curvier than ever in her fan-front dress. He might have pounced on her had Blue Belle not been there. Instead, he helped Anna to her feet. He brushed the prominent backside of her dress though he couldn't actually spot any dirt, then removed a bit of lichen from her chin.

"Thank you, Mr. Boyd," Anna said. "Come up here often?"

"Blue Belle does, sometimes with me, sometimes with one of her other brothers."

"I adore the cave," Blue Belle said. "It's a perfect fit for me."

"I imagine so. I come here from time to time with my sons. That is to say

I come to the rocks that tower over your little cave. I call it the Castle. I like to stand on top, sniff the air, breathe deep, and look out at the wonderful land."

"That would be Boyd land." said Chester.

"I don't only look in your direction."

"You may as well stop looking our way. We'll never sell it to you Benders or anyone else. You can tell Jeremiah that."

"He's not looking to buy, not at this time. None of us are."

"How do you figure to get rid of us?"

"I don't want to get rid of you. I..." Anna turned away. She sensed she was blushing, something she couldn't remember doing in years. "I had better get back home before I'm missed."

"By Jeremiah, I suppose."

"Yes, I mean no. He's on the canal."

"Good for him. He can have it."

"You love to be in your Cave. I love to be in my Castle. Jeremy loves to be in the D&H Canal."

"Right. Commanding *Annabelle,* I mean *Annabelle II.*"

Anna frowned and put her hands on her hips. "It was so nice to see you again, Blue Belle, but I had better go."

"It was nice to see you, too," said Blue Belle. "We should get together like this more often."

"Yes, well, it could happen. Goodbye." Anna didn't move. She seemed to be debating whether or not to pat Blue Belle on the head.

"Come on, Blue Belle," said Chester. "We got to go, too. Aida will miss you." He walked away, waving for his little sister to follow, but stopped after five steps to glance back. "See you later, wife of Jeremiah. Give the captain my warmest regards."

He knew she knew he was being sarcastic. He wished she was his, that he was with her in a marital bed, not necessarily commanding the flesh-and-blood belle Anna but going along with whatever notion she might have in mind.

19

THE KIDNAPPING

In 1858 many people, North and South, feared that the United States was so divided over slavery that a civil war was likely to break out. At a campaign speech that year at the Illinois Republican State Convention, Abraham Lincon said, "A house divided against itself cannot stand." Aida Boyd had mixed feelings about that line. While she disapproved of slavery, she didn't believe the North should go to war over that objectionable Southern institution. "Fortunately, here on Blueberry Hill, slavery is a foreign concept and Blue Rock House isn't divided against itself," she told everyone at one of her monthly family breakfasts. "We Boyds have had our differences through the years, but we are now united and standing strong in the face of all adversity. We are working diligently for the common good of the family, even Henry does so in his own way."

Henry grumbled but assured the family it was because of indigestion, not his sister's words. Chester, who as a young man had several times compared his forced blueberry picking to slavery, clapped his hands before anyone else. He knew he was free to leave or stay, and he had chosen to stay. It was about his newfound love for blueberries, for his nearly one-hundred-year-old father, and for his family in general, of course—but *not only* about those things. On and off for five years he had been secretly rendezvousing with Anna in and out of her Castle and the Boyd Cave below. Blue Belle had figured it out and Aida no doubt suspected something unsavory was up between her big single brother and a married Bender woman, but the Boyd sisters were content to remain quiet and not force the issue. Now, Blue Belle joined Chester in applauding Aida's words, followed by Handy, despite the arthritis in his dominant right hand, and Mary, who became animated upon hearing those two magic words—"working diligently." Elmer clapped next, perhaps more for his wife than for his sister. Blue Boy showed his approval by whistling, while Jacob and Peter raised their blueberry juice glasses and each offered a toast to the speaker.

Aida wiped away a tear of happiness while she waited for things to quiet down at the merry table. Then she cleared her throat and resumed her speech, projecting her voice as if she wanted it to be heard as far away as the Bend. "We all agree then that our house is not divided and shall never be divided. The same cannot be said of the Hill. With us on one side and the Benders on the other we are, for the most part, as divided as Heaven from Hell." She glanced at Chester, who bowed his head. "Will it ever come to doing battle again? I cannot say it won't. As Lincoln said about the country, but which also applies to Blueberry Hill, there can be no compromise. You've got to be on one side or the other. I'm certainly not endorsing fighting at this point. I can safely say that though this glorious Hill is divided against itself, it stands now and shall stand forever. The Boyds shall never give up!" The applause was deafening. The nearly deaf Handy had to stop clapping to cover his sensitive ears.

All was not quiet on the eastern side of the divided Hill. Eunice could match Aida when it came to family pride, though Eunice reserved most of her praise for husband Daniel Leach, who was making the Benders prosperous with his land operations. Delilah, the cousin of Daniel and wife of Alexander, lauded the first more than the second but no man as much as she did the Old South with its cotton plantations, spiritual Negro fieldhands, fertile soil, aristocratic gentry, warm nights, and hominy grits.

While Jeremiah and to a lesser extent Alexander were still committed to canal boats and reasonable returns for their D&H involvement and investments, Daniel Leach had turned the old Drake Tract into a commercial hotbed. On the north side of a stream named "Around the Bend," less than a mile from the Bender home, the sawmill operated eighteen hours a day, and on the south side a tannery flourished. He cut down white pine to make lumber and hemlock trees to get tannin. The Bender side of Blueberry Hill was stripped of its big trees except for a few that shaded the house. At his tannery, workers processed animal hides and made leather, which was preserved by the tannin. Most of the hemlock wood was left to rot because there was little demand for it. The way the Boyds viewed it, Leach had no concern for them, trees, blueberry bushes, common laborers (when two of his sawyers were crushed, he didn't attend their funerals) or the nation (his loyalty was to the state of Georgia), only for making money. To Eunice and the other Benders, though, the man was a God-sent. With his grandiose additions, the two-story Bend became three times the size of Blue Rock House, and the members of the household never had to worry for a second about living beyond their means.

In 1859 the nation came closer to a civil war when John Brown and his band of abolitionists assaulted the federal armory at Harpers Ferry, Virginia. At the same time, an event occurred on Blueberry Hill that made the Boyds and Benders fighting mad. The incident became ever after known to the Boyds as "The Kidnapping" and involved the same family member associated with "The Accident" of 1840—Blue Belle. She had been born during the so-called

Accident (Henrietta's dying giving birth to her), and she was now nineteen, still small, ugly, blind, brilliant, and kind, but now too adventurous for her own good.

Like Chester, Blue Belle made many trips up to the Cave, but they didn't go together. Chester went for heart-to-heart and loin-to-loin assignations (as Elmer put it when he finally realized what was going on) with Anna Bender. Blue Belle, now without escort, went for the womblike comfort of that small chamber in the rock outcrop. It was on a cold mid-October morning that Blue Belle heard movement in her Cave. She imagined the occupant to be an adolescent bear (a big one wouldn't fit) or a family of foxes, but her powerful nose told her differently. She picked up the scent of lavender, indicating a human presence, but she knew it wasn't the agreeable Anna Bender, whose heavy use of eau de cologne gave her the fragrance of citrus fruit. The Boyd family was wary of strangers, but Blue Belle fearlessly investigated anyway and found Nathaniel Bender in the fetal position, curled up around his blank sketchpad.

Nathaniel was despondent because he was in an artistic rut. Archibald Seybolt had bought two of his landscapes with birds but was presently only interested in portraits of women at half length. The artist found no buyer for his *Blueberry Field with Bluebirds* or his *Blueberry Field with Yellow-rumped Warblers* and had himself grown weary of blueberry fields if not birds.

"I know I won't find inspiration in a dark cave in a cramped position, but it fits my mood and disposition," he told her. "I think things started to go downhill for me when your brother Peter shot me here." Nathaniel slapped his rump. "Not that I hold any bitterness or anything, certainly not against a harmless sprite like yourself. I blame only myself for being holed up here. As an artist I am unrecognized by the public and I'm beginning to recognize why. I simply lack talent."

"That's hogwash, as my Good Old Dad and my brothers like to say because it was a favorite expression of my mother, who was raised on a pig farm and died *when* I was born. You have your health, live in a mansion on this beautiful Hill, and are part of a prosperous family. All I'm saying, Natty, is things could be a whole lot worse."

"No doubt, but it doesn't matter how well off I am if I have no talent."

"Everybody has a talent for something. Look at me. I have been told by outsiders that I am a dwarf, ugly as a stump, and unwelcome, but I don't see that, and not just because I am blind. I have a talent for believing in myself, my family, and the United States of America. I also believe in you. My brother Blue Boy says you have a great talent for art, just not for teaching it to clods like himself. Of course, he really isn't a clod. He has a talent for self-depredation."

"Nice of him to be so kind. Is it also his talent to be kind? I believe you have that same talent."

"It doesn't take talent to be kind. It takes compassion. Is there room for me in there? It is my Cave, you know."

"You also have a talent for speaking your mind. I'd rather you not come in here. It wouldn't be, you know, proper."

"Very well. Then you come out and come out with your chin up. Could be what you need is to switch to a different subject matter. You could sketch people and paint their portraits."

"I suppose I could. But I happen to like birds and flowers better. People always want you to portray them in their best light even when they don't have a best light. It's dishonest."

"Hardly any person is as ugly as me."

"Hogwash, as you say. You aren't so bad. Besides you have inner beauty."

"Does inner beauty show up in a portrait.?"

'Well, it should if an artist is halfway decent."

"Fine. I would like you to paint me sometime. Don't you dare say no. You are more than halfway decent, and if you paint me in a bad light, I wouldn't know. What's more, my portrait wouldn't have to be a woman at half length. I'm so short you could do me at full length."

It was agreed. Two days later, they met at the Cave before moving up to the Castle where there was more room and better light. Nathaniel sketched Blue Belle holding a blue blanket from his bed at the Bend and with a turret towering behind her. This was just the beginning. He had a new vision, thanks to her. Instead of depicting the rich and famous, as most portrait artists did, he would allow only the poor and forgotten to pose for him. His naturalist portraits would be so true to life they would transcend realism and confound the critics. If his subjects couldn't pay him, no matter. If the rich didn't want to buy pictures of unfortunate people, so be it. It was his intent to turn the art world on its head with his "Genuine People" series. He would no longer worry about making money. He'd be just fine as long as his brothers, Eunice, and Daniel Leach didn't boot him out of the Bend for not pulling his weight in family matters or for refusing to do their portraits.

Twice more the artist and his willing subject met on the top of the Hill for more posing and sketching. The next step for Nathaniel was to line up his sketches and set up his canvas in his north-lit studio far from the children's nursery and from nosey brothers and the fussy females of the Bend. There, he would lock the door and create in peace and privacy. "I have my title already for the first in my Genuine People series," he told Blue Belle the last time. *"Blue Belle with Blue Blanket on Blue Hill.* Sound like a groundbreaking masterpiece to you?"

"It's Blueberry Hill, not Blue Hill," she said.

"Three blues are better. I don't want this one to have anything to do with blueberries."

"Oh, I see. But doesn't *blue* alone mean sad?"

"It won't be a sad picture. It will capture your inner beauty."

"Sounds wonderful, Natty. But does this mean I won't be posing for you anymore?"

"Won't be necessary."

"I'll miss it, the posing I mean. And meeting you here."

"I'll get word to you if I need you again."

"What if I need you?"

"Look, little one, I can't have you showing up at the Bend. You know how my family feels about your family. Besides, I don't want anyone to know what I'm painting. Not yet. It could be weeks or a couple months or more before I'm finished. I'm not a fast painter. And I'm used to painting nature, not people. Masterpieces aren't created in a day. But you'll be the first to see it when it's done. Well, you know what I mean."

Blue Belle knew what he meant and tried to understand how an artist, now one with renewed belief in himself, needed time and space to produce his best work. Anyway, she had been warned by her big sister and brothers to never cross over the imaginary line atop the Hill, let alone venture all the way down to the Bend, where the so-called enemy dwelled in indecent luxury. But when she didn't hear from Nathaniel the rest of October and most of November, she took it upon herself to visit her artistic friend. She didn't do so to make trouble. In fact, she believed that her tiny presence at the Bend could help make the Benders realize that to continue to feud made no sense. How could they hate, let alone fight, such a harmless human being who looked like a bruised blueberry but was loaded with compassion and believed in the innate goodness of mankind? At the same time, she was mighty curious about how her portrait was shaping up.

Bundled in an oversized coat that had once belonged to Aida, Blue Belle set out without giving notice to her sister or anyone else. It was no problem reaching the top of the Hill and crossing over near her perfect-sized cave. Once on the Bender side her sensitive feet had no trouble locating the new scenic road built by Daniel Leach. On the way down, though, she faced a cold wind that gave her the shivers, then, even worse, she heard a growling animal in front of her. Immediately she thought of a hungry wolf. Catawissa Manayunk, her dearly departed spiritual grandfather, had possessed an affinity for wolves, but she had never encountered one and didn't believe he would come back as a four-legged beast of any kind. If anything, Man would return as a songbird or wise owl.

She could not interpret the growling. Was the mysterious beast vicious or only frightened? It mattered not at the moment. She did not trust it could see either her gentle nature or her inner beauty. She darted into the damaged woods and beat through the brush, managing to miss the stumps and stones with what must have been a sixth sense. She heard the animal following her but she did not scream. She went far and feared she had run around in circles. When at last exhausted, she heard panting close by and used the last of her strength to climb a tree too small to interest Daniel Leach and his sawyers. She reached only the first branch. One of her moccasins fell off, and she felt a rough tongue licking her dangling bare foot.

"What is your intention?" she asked. "Do you mean to eat me?"

She heard a sharp bark in response. She remembered hearing that sound before and that it had been associated with guns fired from the Bender side of the Hill. What followed wasn't so much barking as baying. Little did she know that Daniel Leach and Delila Bender had arranged to have a redbone coonhound brought up from Georgia, where its specialty was hunting down and treeing red foxes. Blue Belle figured any dog would be smart enough to tell she was only a small human being who shouldn't be torn apart, yet if the dog belonged to the Benders, she couldn't be absolutely sure. Why did it keep baying as if it had cornered a raccoon?

"Nice doggie," she said, and the dog barked once more before it did nothing but pant. "Where you from fellow?" The dog nudged her foot with its cold nose. "That tickles," she said. "I don't believe you want to bite me, so I'm coming down." Once she was on the ground, the dog rubbed against her leg. She petted its head, then scratched its neck. It offered a soft moan of pleasure so she continued to pet and scratch. Further investigation told her the dog was two-feet high, lean, deep-chested, and muscular. As she stroked its warm coat, she could somehow feel that it was neither black nor white nor brown and had no spots. She guessed with surprising accuracy that the coat was a rich crimson. She finally took her hands away and felt around the ground around her. "I seem to have lost a moccasin. My friend Man made them for me and I'd hate to lose one." The dog moved away a short distance but soon presented to her in its drooling mouth the missing footwear.

"Thank you so much," she said as she slipped on the moccasin, not caring that it was wet. "My name is Blue Belle. I'm from the other side of the Hill. Are you from around here? I don't know your name but I'll call you 'Big Red' for now. Dog or doggie seems too impersonal. I've gotten myself all turned around and I'm afraid I'm lost. I'm also very cold. You want to show me the way home, to your home of course?"

The dog barked its answer, then raced off continually barking. She followed the sound as best she could. When she hadn't reached the scenic road after fifteen minutes, she suspected Red had gone after a wild animal. She was prodigiously tuckered out and knew if she kept walking, she'd likely get deeper into woods she didn't know. She lay on the ground, tightened the coat collar, and hugged herself. The wind was howling through the trees. If the temperature dropped much lower, she supposed she would freeze to death. She rarely cried but now couldn't help it. She prayed first to the white man's God, then, to play it safe, to the Lenni Lenape's Ketanĕtuwit. She was determined not to die with frozen tears on her face.

The worst scenario didn't happen. Big Red returned and curled up on the ground next to her. She pressed against the dog and hugged him dearly. She warmed up fast and felt as safe and comfortable as she did in her Cave. She slept through the night. In the morning she filled up on Bender blueberries, not as good as Boyd berries but they would do.

§

Back at Blue Rock House, Handy was the first to notice his youngest daughter missing, and his sons searched with lanterns most of the night all the way from the top of the Hill to Handy Spring and as far south as the public road.

Mary, who had started to do some mindless wandering herself once the gardening season ended, claimed to have seen a blue elf go beyond the "big fairytale rocks," meaning Anna's Castle. Nobody took her seriously except her husband, and before dawn Elmer ventured to the east side of the Hill. Daniel Leach, who was fortunately unarmed at the time, came upon Elmer hiding behind the grand gazebo that the handyman par excellence had recently built for cousin Delilah, whose pale skin was highly sensitive to direct sunlight.

"What the hell are you doing here?" Daniel Leach said, grabbing the intruder by the collar. "I know you aren't here to admire my additions to the Bend. You trying to spy on us or are you some kind of peeping Tom?"

"I won't dignify that with an answer," said Elmer. "I'm a happily married man."

"Congratulations. So am I." Leach let go of the Boyd enemy and wiped his hand on a pant leg. "Eunice informs me your wife is touched in the head."

"Eunice should keep her bone box closed. What are all these tiny footprints I see in the mud?" Elmer squatted low and pointed at the disturbed ground. "They're suspicious."

"What are you Boyds doing now, tracking children instead of game? My four-year-old daughter, Berri, loves to come sit in the gazebo and play with her dolls. Cal, James and Georgia are always running around here like darling savages. They belong to Delilah and Alexander in case you didn't know."

"I don't give a lick about Bender and Leach children."

"No? I thought you might, considering the fact you and crazy Mary haven't managed to produce one of your own."

"You best shut your trap about my wife. Where is she?"

"How the hell should I know. Did your old lady go wandering off on you again?"

"I'm not talking about Mary. I want to know about Blue Belle. I got a hunch you are keeping her here."

"That makes no sense."

"You deny it?"

"Why would I want a young gal as ugly as sin and blind as a bat when I have Eunice?"

"I won't stand for any more of your insults, lumberman."

"I'm talking straight. She is ugly and blind, isn't she?"

"These footprints aren't large, but some are too big to belong to children. Maybe you haven't taken Blue Belle yourself, but I'm thinking one of you is holding her prisoner this very minute in that oversized wooden crate." He pointed with disgust at the enormous structure, which might have seemed impressive to most people but to him was overblown and vastly inferior to his masterpiece in stone, Blue Rock House.

"You must be as crazy as your wife. We don't have any use for her or any Boyds here."

Elmer stood up and raised onto his toes to see eye to eye with Daniel Leach. "One more word about Mary and I'll..."

"You'll do what? Don't try to get tough with me, Elmer. It doesn't become any of you Boyds. You are superfluous people, no longer useful to society, if you ever were that."

"I don't have time to waste with you, Leach. I'll just take a look inside."

"The hell you will. Nobody has invited you to the Bend."

Elmer kicked mud on his adversary's shoes, then tried to walk around him. Daniel Leach caught him around the waist with a burly arm and spun him around. When Leach got him in a firm headlock, Elmer tried to bite his adversary's arm. Nobody threw a punch but they tumbled in the mud, wiping out most of the little footprints. They were still at it when Eunice came running out the Bend's back door yelling for them to stop acting like children. Daughter Berri followed, also on the run, and flapping her arms as if they were wings. She seemed to think her father and the stranger were playing. Delilah was next, marching not running to see what the fuss was about. Her boys, Cal and James, forged ahead of her while Georgia held back, hiding behind her mother's skirts.

Finally, Nathaniel emerged, looking sheepish as he led Blue Belle by the hand. She looked none the worse for wear after a night in the forest with the coonhound Big Red, whose actual name was Dred (as in the 1857 Dred Scot decision that denied the legality of Negro citizenship in America). After her blueberry breakfast in the forest, Blue Belle had easily convinced the hungry dog to take her to its home at the Bend. Natty was as surprised to see her as the rest of the Benders. Delilah scolded Dred, probably for staying out all night and causing her worry. Or possibly she was angry to see the coonhound bring home a Boyd.

Although Blue Belle hadn't really been kidnapped that was what the Boyd family chose to label the event. Nathaniel took most of the blame from both his family and Blue Belle's family, though he had never asked Blue Belle to visit and had never done anything to her but sketch her. He did tell her that he had almost completed her portrait but wasn't satisfied with it because he had made her look too much like an elf. At some point that very week the painting ended up in a Bender bonfire made to burn waste wood and bothersome brush. Natty never told Blue Belle that her portrait was destroyed, and he never revealed to any Boyd or other outsider whether he or another family member had done the burning.

The kidnapping that wasn't did fuel the tension on Blueberry Hill. Mistrust, if not hatred, reached an all-time high. Handy Boyd, for one, broke out his large Revolutionary War knife once again and insisted on standing watch (though he could barely stand on his own) from his familiar perch on the Blue Rock House porch roof. Daniel Leach did considerably more. With the help of laborers willing to work with rock instead of wood, he began to build a wall of stone across the crest of the Hill except where the castle-like rock outcrop formed a natural barrier to any Boyd crossing. Although not a trained mason, he was proud of his work, not exactly the Great Wall of China but more impressive than any of the many stone walls built by early Sullivan County settlers. Elmer grudgingly admitted to his family that the dreadful Leach's stonework was exemplary. He could not blame the noble silent stones for what wrongful purpose evil men made them serve.

The American Civil War began, as many had predicted, in April 1861. No fighting occurred on Blueberry Hill, but early returns from the battlefields elsewhere pleased some of the Benders and shocked most of the Boyds. June 1861 saw a stunning Confederate victory in the First Battle of Bull Run (called First Manassas by the Benders) as well as the completion of the Hill's stone wall, which Delilah predictably dubbed "Jackson."

20
NURSES BLUE BELLE AND WALT

In the heat of July 1863, when news reached the Hill about the Battle of Gettysburg, Chester Boyd was drunk. That was no aberration. His choice of beverage was homemade blueberry wine (applejack from town being too expensive), and he had overindulged in it for more than two years. He said it was to get through the war, as the South was winning most of the early battles, but Anna Bender's wartime decision to break off all relations with him and stick by her sumptuously rich swaggering spouse was Chester's secret reason for his relentless pursuit of intoxication. At fifty-two he was seven years too old to be drafted into the Union Army, and no amount of drinking could convince him to volunteer. After all, he was a man of peace like his Good Old Dad. That didn't mean he couldn't become "fiery" about who was right and who was dead wrong in the Civil War.

"Let them Rebel Benders bring it on and we'll knock 'em to Kingdom Come; Blueberry Hill will be another Little Round Top!" Chester made that drunken declaration (echoing the sentiments of his father) while standing atop the Hill where he used to rendezvous with Anna but now went to kick and throw rocks at the massive wall named after Confederate General Thomas "Stonewall" Jackson, who thankfully had died in May. Henry Boyd, four years younger but an experienced rock thrower, was with him all the way to do his part. Henry was also overage for the draft, but he told everyone he would have joined the 124th New York Regiment if Doc Tears hadn't confirmed his exemption for "decided feebleness of constitution."

It was hard to miss "Jackson" at thirty feet, but Chester managed to overthrow or underthrow the wall most of the time. Henry, despite his delicate constitution, never missed, though his "hits" did no damage to the wall. They moved in stealthily to finish off the enemy. Realizing they couldn't capture such a formidable enemy, they kicked the wall simultaneously, imagining they were giving the boot to wall-builder and Southern sympathizer Daniel Leach. Pain shot up through their legs, but only Henry screamed. It was a wonder they hadn't broken their toes. They limped to Blue Rock House to lick their wounds and perhaps come to their senses. They struggled up Elmer's outdoor steps to the porch roof where their 104-year-old father had called for a family conference. They were on time, relieved they wouldn't have to make excuses for being late.

Not all the family was up there. Mary was busy in the backyard scrubbing a pair of Elmer's trousers that had become blood stained when her husband misdirected his ax while splitting wood for the cook stove ("I'm so much better with stone," he had declared while clutching his wounded foot). Jacob, thirty-two, and Peter, thirty-one, had always handled that daily chore, but they had enlisted not long after Congress passed the first conscription act in April. Elmer's foot was bandaged but his limp wasn't much worse than the limps of Chester and Henry. The three limping brothers all sat behind Handy, oldest to youngest from left to right.

Thirty-five-year-old Blue Boy sat in the rear, in part because he was the youngest of the brothers present but more so because he felt guilty about being there. Acting on a sudden impulse in August 1862 to honor the country and his family, not necessarily in that order, he had hooked up with Company E of the newly formed 143rd Infantry, the so-called Sullivan County Regiment. That October he left the state to serve with the Third Brigade in the defenses of Washington DC but almost immediately drank dirty water (contaminated by excreta) and nearly died from typhoid. Sent home, he loaded up on Handy Spring water and recovered, but he had lost his will to fight, not from seeing anyone get shot but from seeing too many men die of disease in unsanitary conditions. He still would have been required to return to his regiment had it not been for Doc Tears's testimony that he was suffering from old and ulcerated internal hemorrhoids. And so Blue Boy sat uncomfortably behind his brothers on the clay tiles.

That Jacob and Peter were risking their lives down South was not even the primary reason that Blue Boy felt guilty about his abbreviated time in the service. Blue Belle, of all people, was also missing from the roof that day in July 1863. Incredibly, the twenty-three-year-old undersized blind woman was serving her country, not as a soldier of course but as a volunteer nurse in one of the makeshift Army hospitals in Washington. What had inspired her, besides her natural empathy and caregiver personality, was her admiration for Walt Whitman and his poetry collection *Leaves of Grass*.

Her favorite poet had gone south on an errand of mercy after a brother was wounded at the Battle of Fredericksburg in December 1862. The wound turned out to be slight, but Walt was so affected by "a heap of feet, legs, arms, and human fragments, cut bloody, black and blue, swelled and sickening" that he decided to become a nurse.

"If such a man of infinite virtue and wisdom can bear the horrors of war, why can't I?" Blue Belle had told her father. "I am naturally blue, swelled, and sickening in the eyes of the world, but I share Mr. Whitman's vision. I am blind but I have compassion. I am small but I can deal with disabled full-sized men. Haven't I nursed Henry through the years? Haven't I lifted you out of bed and let you lean on me when you became too feeble to stand on your own?"

"No need to remind me, my darling little one. I agree you can do some nursing and possess wonderful sentiments. But how in tarnation are you going to get to Washington D.C., let alone pay for your food and lodging? It's not possible, child. I know you mean well, but it's absolutely impossible."

"Catawissa Manayunk says that nothing is impossible. He says that the Lenni Lenape believe that all things came from the tortoise. It brought forth the world and from the middle of its back sprang up a tree, upon whose branches men grew."

"Man has been dead a long time."

"He still talks to me. If I can hear the dead, I can nurse the living. If spirits can travel and find nourishment, so can I."

Handy couldn't disagree. He realized he couldn't tell his youngest daughter that anything was impossible. Blue Belle enlisted the help of Chester and began a correspondence with Horace Greeley, founder and editor of the *New-York Tribune,* who was already planning to send a reporter south to find Whitman and tell his story. Having Blue Belle tag along was bound to sell even more papers. The big city newspaperman was moved when she proposed a future headline: *Blind Nurse Teaches Famous Poet How to Deal with Death and the Grotesque.*

"So, you happen to be blind as a bat," he wrote her on May 1, 1863. "If you can make it to the *Tribune*'s Gotham office by the fifteenth, you can go the whole hog—I'll send you down to the nation's capital by railroad express with Hester Norris. She is no Margaret Fuller, but she's better than three-quarters of the male reporters I now have. If Whitman's still down there, she will sniff him out. No need to add that Hesty has the added advantage of being able to see, as long as she stays off the spirits. Safe journey. Yours, Horace. P.S. All expenses paid (one-month limit). Hope this is hunky-dory."

Nathaniel Bender, feeling bad about the so-called "Kidnapping" episode and how *Blue Belle with Blue Blanket on Blue Hill* and his "Genuine People" series of paintings never came to fruition, made it possible for Blue Belle to keep her date with Horace Greeley. After convincing Jeremiah and Alexander that they owed something to the poor girl who was so unlike all the other Boyds, Blue Belle received free passage on a canal boat to the Hudson River port of Rondout, near Kingston, and from there to New York City by passenger steamer.

Mr. Greeley was impressed by Blue Belle's "gumption," and took both her and the rapid-talking Hester Norris to the Bull's Head hotel for drinks. Since nothing with blueberry flavoring was served there, Blue Belle settled for mineral water, which didn't taste half as good as Handy Spring water. Mr. Greeley, who as a boy had vowed never to drink distilled liquors again, had the same. Hester Norris, on the other hand, consumed four glasses of a recently invented drink comprised of gin and vermouth and called a Martinez, or a martini.

During the long trip by rail from New York to Washington, Hester Norris found other things to drink and said many shocking things. She insisted that President Lincoln's Emancipation Proclamation was upsetting many white workers who were not abolitionists and feared the job-stealing Negroes certain to head north. Mostly, though, she talked about her radical views, such as how marriage and procreation between blacks and whites had the potential to ultimately unite and strengthen the nation and eliminate the need for civil war.

Once in Washington, Blue Belle soon found her poet turned nurse without any help from the elegant and witty reporter, who was drinking with newfound friends in a Georgetown tavern. A one-legged veteran showed Blue Belle to Armory Square Hospital, across from the grounds of the Smithsonian Institute and just beyond a canal. Walt Whitman stood with his head bowed over an empty cot on which a wounded man had just died of an overdose of opium pills and laudanum. Blue Belle tried to comfort him as they strolled outside and found a bench overlooking the canal—the Chesapeake & Ohio, he said. Blue Belle thought it smelled just like the Delaware & Hudson.

Blue Belle found her first conversation with Mr. Whitman so fascinating that she memorized it and had Hester Norris put it down in a letter addressed to "Handy Boyd, Blueberry Hill, Wurtsboro, New York." Handy clutched that letter in his arthritic hands as he sat on the porch roof clearing his throat before opening the post-Gettysburg family conference in July 1863.

"Welcome everybody, everybody who is here," he said, waving the letter over his head with his better hand, the not-so-arthritic left one. "Glad you could all make it, but especially glad I could make it up those crooked steps at my age."

"The steps aren't crooked," said Elmer, much too loudly.

"Meaning I am?" said Handy.

"I'm not saying that at all, Good Old Dad. I'm just staying that not every flat stone is perfectly smooth and straight. I never heard of anyone making stairs to a roof. I did my level best."

"The best man I ever knew was crooked. I'm talking about Man and his hump!"

"Can we please get on with it," said Aida, who sat close to her father to help keep him propped up. "There are blueberries to be picked."

Handy cleared his throat again. "As I was about to say before I was disrespectfully interrupted..." He paused, no doubt to recall what he was about to say. "Blueberries are good like bluecoats," he shouted, then paused again.

"Yes, yes, we know, Old Dad," said Aida. "We're all for the bluecoats here. Anything else?"

"What? Of course, *anything else.* What we must do is cut down the graycoats here, there, and wherever they may be. We must save our Blueberry Hill, every berry, every leaf. We must draw our swords and fight to save it." He reached down to pull his large Revolutionary War knife from its sheath, but neither knife nor sheath were there. Aida had hidden them after her father accidentally cut his ear during one of his rabid anti-Rebel, anti-Bender rants. The lifetime passive peace-lover had turned wild man since turning one-hundred.

"Relax, Good Old Dad," said Chester. "The Rebs were turned back at Gettysburg. They won't be visiting our Hill anytime soon."

"What's that you say? I don't need any backtalk out of you, boy."

Aida repeated Chester's words directly into Handy's best ear. "Chester supports the blue. We all do."

"Amen," said Blue Boy from the back row.

"What? Who spoke?" When Handy tried to turn his stiff neck, the letter flew out of his hand and would have likely blown off the roof had it not caught on the ornamental tortoiseshell comb tucked into the hair at the back of Aida's head.

"Blue Boy said *Amen,* Dad," she said as she secured the letter.

"Why ain't he down South teaching them Rebs a lesson?"

"You know why."

"Don't tell me what I know, daughter. I know what I know."

"Hemorrhoids," volunteered Elmer.

"What was that?"

"Elmer said *hemorrhoids,* Dad. Blue Boy is finished fighting. Jacob and Peter are down there now doing their duty and surely representing our family well."

"Ah, yes, Peter shot that bastard Daniel Leach."

"That was before the war, Dad. And it was Nathaniel Bender he shot."

"Peter and Jacob. Fine boys. They'll be home soon. They whipped Robert Fucking E. Lee at Harrisonburg."

"Gettysburg," corrected Aida. "I don't believe my brothers were there."

"What? Don't tell me. Peter and Jacob are fine boys. Not like those sissy sons of Jeremiah Bender who paid three-hundred dollars each to exempt them from serving the Union."

"Delilah wanted nephews Maurice and Robert to fight for the

Confederacy, but their mother was against them doing that, of course. We can be thankful for that at least."

"Traitors!"

"Delilah said her own two sons, Cal and James, would surely have joined the Confederate Army if they were only a few years older."

"Hogwash. All Benders are pampered babies. Peter and Jacob are real men, not backing down from their duties.

"It's not *only* those sons of yours who are serving the Union, Dad. You should be as proud of your youngest daughter as I am. You mustn't forget what she's doing"

"Damnation! Of course, I haven't forgotten Blue Belle. Isn't that the reason I called his meeting. Hell, I brought this here letter so I could read part of it to her kin." He looked at his better hand but there was nothing in it. The other hand was twitching as if trying to touch air.

"I have the letter, Dad."

"Well hand it over, daughter. She wrote it to me."

"She wrote it to all of us. We'll read the part about her conversation with Walt Whitman, just as we practiced together. You read what the great poet says, and I'll read what Blue Belle says."

"Who's a great poet? Who's this Whitman character? Not a Reb, I hope."

Handy started singing "John Brown's Body," a song honoring the abolitionist who died fighting against slavery. Aida gently quieted her father down.

"I don't wish to be Whitman," Handy said. "I never wrote a poem in my life. Poetry is for namby-pambies, not fighting men."

Aida held onto the letter and handled the duty herself. She read aloud in a clear voice, which she deepened whenever the words belonged to Whitman:

Whitman: Every one of these cots in the hospital has its history. Every case is a tragic poem, an epic, a romance, a pensive and absorbing book if it were only written.

Blue Belle: You wrote Leaves of Grass. *I found it pensive and absorbing. That's something.*

Whitman: Ah, yes, THE BOOK! It isn't finished you know. Not really. I don't think it will ever be finished, certainly not as long as America is at war with itself.

Blue Belle: America needs more men like you, Mr. Whitman. Tell me, do you actually nurse the wounded soldiers?

Whitman: I go around among these sights, among the crowded hospitals doing what I can, yet it is a mere drop in the bucket. The path I follow, I suppose I may say, is my own.

> *Blue Belle: I also follow my own path. But sometimes paths cross and even merge for a time.*

> *Whitman: I see too much—the refuse pail, soon to be filled with clotted rags and blood, emptied and filled again, the gnawing and putrid gangrene, so sickening, so offensive.*

> *Blue Belle: So grotesque. Some say I am grotesque.*

> *Whitman: No, no, my child. You are a beautiful soul. If I, too, were blind, would I still see the horror?*

> *Blue Belle: Oh, yes. I see the horror and the grotesque in my mind. But I also see the humanity. Even in war.*

> *Whitman: There was a time I only saw myself. I only understood "Song of Myself."*

> *Blue Belle: But now you see war and death and certain truths about the human condition.*

> *Whitman: Yes, yes, my child. Exactly. We shall nourish the wounded and soothe the dying together. You are wise between your ears, beyond your years. Would you mind so much, Miss Boyd, if I hugged you all to pieces.*

> *Blue Belle: Do. I know you won't squeeze me to death.*

> *Whitman: Long was I hugged long—long and long. Blue Belle, you said?*

> *Blue Belle: Yes, my Good Old Dad named me that under sad conditions. You see my mother died giving me life.*

> *Whitman: "Death" is merely another word for former life. It is not an end, only a transition. As to you Death, and you bitter hug of mortality, it is idle to try to alarm me.*

> *Blue Belle: Sounds good.*

> *Whitman: As does "Blue Belle," my child. The perfect name. It rings true. And not a belle from the South?*

> *Blue Belle: No, sir. No belle. I'm from your state, Mr. Whitman. To the west of Gotham, near a place called Wurtsboro. Blueberry Hill is the name. Do you like blueberries, Mr. Whitman?*

> *Whitman: Better than leaves of grass. Much tastier. Call me, Walt... please."*

Handy had read over that detailed conversation a dozen times, but he was still moved to tears by Aida's reading. "We Boyds have never been much on praying in front of other people," he said. "But we're only family here. Let's all pray to ourselves for the safe return of Blue Belle, Jacob, and Peter, even that Whitman fellow if some of you are a mind to. It's the least we can do."

Nobody disagreed. He was making sense. All heads bowed and some lips moved without any words coming out. Silence reigned on the roof for a minute until Mary Boyd appeared at the top of the stone stairs waving a pair of trousers. "Clean as a whistle, Elm," she said as she stepped onto the roof, then over Henry to get to her husband. As she lay the neatly folded trousers across her husband's lap, she accidentally bumped his bandaged foot. Elmer yelped, and as Mary backed away, she stepped on Henry's foot, which was still hurting from his kicking the stone wall Jackson. Henry screamed and, in his pain, accidentally kicked Aida in the back.

"Henry!" shouted Aida, who flinched and accidentally elbowed her father. "Do we all have to suffer just because you're suffering?"

"Are we under attack?" Handy asked.

"Why the uproar?" asked Mary

"It's all right," said Elmer. "Thank you for doing my trousers. No sign of the blood. But you are interrupting something here, dear. We are trying to pray."

"You pray, husband? I never heard such a thing."

"Nevertheless, that's what I'm doing, what we are all doing...silently."

"I pray all day." She lifted her cross necklace and it sparkled in the sunlight.

"Fine. You are welcome to pray now if you wish, but quietly."

Mary dropped to her knees and asked for God to please help and keep safe a long list of people, naming her husband and most of the other members of the Boyd family but also all the Benders and Leaches she could recall.

"That will do, dear," said Elmer. "That isn't acceptable behavior. We don't pray for Benders and Leaches. I'll have to ask you to leave the roof."

"Well, I never. I'll descend to pray. Forgive me for living. I only came up here to ask if any of you filthy, dirt-poor, degenerate Yankees wish to have your house slave wash any other articles of clothing."

Besides being rude, it was a strange thing for Elmer's peculiar wife to say since she was paler than cow milk, wore a soiled apron, was known to whistle merrily while doing laundry, and had absolutely no ties with the South. All the family members present stared at her in stunned silence, then inspected their own clothing. None of them owned new garments but for the most part their old clothes were kept washed, brushed, pressed, and polished thanks to Mary.

Handy, in a delayed reaction, raised a fist. "Traitorous bitch," he yelled.

Aida gently lowered her father's hand and dropped it onto his lap. "Mary isn't a Bender or a Leach, Dad. She is one of us."

"Since when?"

"Never mind. Be nice." Aida addressed Mary: "You are *not* a house slave. This is New York state. There is no slavery here. You are in the North."

"I know where I am, Master! I am not stupid."

"Neither your husband nor I can mistreat you. You are your own master, Mary. We know you love to pray. Stay and pray if you wish. But know we are praying for the Boyd bluecoats."

"I shall do no such thing, Miss Bossy Boyd. War is ugly as sin, much too messy. Messy, messy, messy! I must scrub the kitchen floor. I must wash my own garments. Cleanliness is next to godliness. It is wash day and I will pray that ugly messes go away." She stepped on Henry's good foot on her way back to the steps.

"God, that hurts!" cried Henry. "Ouch, ouch, ouch!"

"Traitorous bitch!" Handy repeated.

"I'm sorry for the interruption," said Elmer to nobody in particular. "Mary can't help it."

"Neither can Good Old Dad," said Chester.

"Amen," said Blue Boy.

21
A GRAVE SITUATION

Blue Belle continued to write letters home regularly but instead of writing about the dead and dying in the dirty hospitals, she penned words of hope, inspiration, eternal life, and the promise of America. Her stay in Washington would last three times longer than Horace Greeley's one-month limit. Walt Whitman always made sure she had a place to sleep and enough to eat. Hester Norris, on the other hand, sent back only one story about Blue Belle that made it into print and never bothered to write about Whitman. She soon met a recently freed slave named Brookings and high-tailed it back to her beloved New York City with him in tow. She wrote two stranger-than-fiction stories about this larger-than-life man and Horace Greeley published them in the *Tribune* before "the pervasive mood of disenchantment among our Irish readers" convinced him to discontinue the series. Hesty wrote Blue Belle one letter saying she was giving up drink, quitting the paper, and marrying her "black Colossus." But it never happened. Mr. Brookings was killed in the New York City Draft Riots.

Jacob and Peter never wrote home, so the other Boyds didn't know if they had been killed, wounded in battle, or simply negligent. Handy's prediction had misfired, namely that the Rebels would soon give up after the Yankee triumph at Gettysburg and he would have his entire family around him again. While the Rebels had left the North after Pickett's Charge proved a monumental disaster for them, they still had plenty of fight left. He likened them to the blueberry stem borer and maggots that were plaguing the Boyds' blueberry crop that summer of 1863. "It ain't over by a long shot," Handy often muttered, but it was never clear if he was talking about the War Between the States or the War Between the Boyds and Benders.

The blueberry stem borer, a slender long-horned beetle with a yellowish brown head and thorax, was the first culprit. The leaves of the bushes turned from green to yellow and dropped off; the first berries of the season wilted and died. The best solution was to remove the damaged leaf tips and burn them, an operation that Aida excelled at. But no sooner was the stem borer problem stemmed than the blueberry maggots began attacking the fruit. Adult flies laid eggs in ripe berries, and the maggots ate the pulp of the fruit, causing berries to drop or spoil. Handy blamed the Benders for sending the stem borers and maggots over the wall to the Boyd side of the Hill. "I wouldn't put anything past those Bushwhackers," Handy told Chester from the cane seat of the wooden wheelchair Elmer had built for him.

To blame the enemy for the insect pests was of course nonsense, but Chester agreed to go to the top of the Hill to check on how the blueberries on the Bender side were faring. In the back of his wine-muddled mind he was hoping to see Anna. Instead, he found Alexander and Delilah's two young sons, Cal and James, climbing the now seven-foot wall like a pair of monkeys.

Chester, crouched and unseen, spoke to the boys in his deepest, gruffest voice: "Get off me! How would you like someone climbing all over you? I am the ghost of Stonewall Jackson and I devour bad little boys who disobey my orders. Retreat or be eaten alive!"

The boys dropped to the ground and ran, while Delilah, who thought it unladylike to climb a wall, scolded the disembodied voice as she retreated. Later, she would demand to know which member of the "decayed Yankee family" had terrorized her "little graycoats." Chester never confessed.

After he was sure Delilah was gone from the hilltop, Chester climbed the wall with the help of a well-placed boulder for a peek at the other side. He was able to bring back to Blue Rock House news that the Bender blueberry crop was also suffering. Handy still didn't believe it, and Aida said it was of no consequence because the Benders didn't rely on blueberries for their breakfasts or their livelihoods. To them, she told her father, stem borers and maggots were as easily disregarded as worms and ants.

With the maggots, both human and insect, going strong and his health continuing to deteriorate, Handy told his family he wanted to take them to Henrietta's grave, which none of them had visited in twenty-three years. "We must go now," he said in the second week of August 1863. "I can't wait for our two soldiers to show themselves or at least let us know if they are casualties of war. It is an unknown whether they are dead or alive. What's known is that Pudding left us more than two decades ago and we have been selfishly neglecting my wife, your mother. It's high time we paid her our deepest respects before it's too late."

He meant too late for him. He couldn't wait for Blue Belle to get back from Washington either. Since the pickings were slim on the Hill, Aida gave her full approval to the undertaking. The family still didn't own a horse or wagon. Her centenarian father couldn't walk to the top of the Hill anymore, let alone trek twenty miles to his and Henrietta's old home town. Aida decided it wouldn't be dignified to have Handy transported to the cemetery in a blueberry cart, so renting a horse-and-wagon again was the only alternative. "We can make a family outing out of it," she said, as if the Boyds did such things regularly. "Maybe we'll have a picnic and stay an extra day or two." Actually, such an outing would be a first. She sent Elmer to the Sears & Rhodes Livery in Wurtsboro. He brought just enough of the family's blueberry money to cover the outlandish rental fee, but Jesse Sears still was reluctant to hand over the reins to a man no more familiar with horses than he was with African lions or Indian tigers.

"I know one end from the other," Elmer said as they stood outside the stable with a four-legged beast trying to make a deal. "It's not the first time I've done this. We had a no-count swayback pulling the wagon when we buried my mother."

"I remember. The swayback's name was Bethany. She died the day after you brought her back. You ran the old girl into the ground."

"Not our fault. Like you said, she was old. This animal isn't much to look at either, but she seems young and sturdy. I'll just point her in the right direction and tell her to follow her nose down the road. Simple. What's her name?"

"Salty. Not a she."

"Oh, right. The horse looks capable enough. Most of us will walk to play it safe. Only Good Old Dad needs conveying."

"Salty is capable all right, but only part horse. He's a gelded male, and he's a mule. That is to say he is the offspring of a male donkey and female horse."

"Of course. I've seen plenty of mules plowing around these parts."

"No doubt. But you Boyds have never done any plowing on Blueberry Hill."

"It's rocky up there and, anyway, we aren't farmers, Mr. Sears. We disturb the land as little as possible. We collect things when they're ready—berries, seeds, nuts, mushrooms, herbs, corn, squash, fallen wood for firewood. It's a good honest life." Elmer paused when the livery man turned his head to spit tobacco juice into the wind. The spray came back and left a yellow gob on Elmer's right shoe.

"Beg pardon," Mr. Sears said but he didn't try to hide his imperious look.

He believes he can spit on any Boyd as if our family is dirt. Elmer thought that but couldn't say it; he needed the damn horse, or mule, whatever it was. Still, he felt an overpowering need to defend the Boyd way of life. It was nothing to be ashamed of, nothing to be criticized for by lowly merchants like Sears, haughty tycoons like the Benders, the farmers of Sullivan County, or all the other conformists in American society. "We don't exercise power over natural processes, Mr. Sears," Elmer said. The livery man cocked his head to the side like a dog who couldn't understand the simplest commands. Elmer suddenly felt superior to other people, not to mention dogs. "You see, we cut down as few trees as possible, let the bushes grow, let the water flow, let the earth breathe. It's not that we don't know how to work. I built our house of stone, you know. Blue Rock House! That takes incredibly hard work, the right kind of work. Stones don't die. I stack them and rearrange them when necessary but the stones don't mind. I do right by them."

"Seems you aren't the only one," said Sears. "I heard about that stone wall atop Blueberry Hill. Eunice Bender says her husband built it without your help."

"If my family had wanted a wall up there, I'd have built it after I was done with the house. We don't want a wall up there. Blueberry Hill is ours, all of it. Leach had no right to..." Elmer stopped talking because he knew the Benders had legal right to half the Hill and the livery man wouldn't understand the Boyds' position. He pretended to look over the mule more closely and was stunned to see the beast had what must have been a full erection. "I didn't come here to talk about stone walls or farming or what my family does with our land," he said. "Are you sure nothing is wrong with this gelding?"

"Not if you handle Salty right. He can be more aggressive than most geldings. You have to be firm but not too firm."

"I'm not going to handle the mule. I only need him to pull the damned wagon."

"He's all yours. Salty doesn't know that you don't know your ass from a donkey."

Elmer was in too much of a hurry to take offense at the insult. "I'll take the mule for two days for ten dollars less than your quoted price, Mr. Sears. I was expecting a horse."

"Price is set, Mr. Boyd. Salty has his mulish pride. Don't want to offend him."

"All right, but he better behave. I don't want Mary to see him like this." Elmer, humbled, dropped to one knee, grabbed a handful of straw, and cleaned the mess off his shoe.

He didn't get his discount and had a devil of a time getting Salty to pull the empty wagon up the cart path within thirty feet of Blue Rock House. Salty was somewhat better going downhill even with Handy and Aida in the wagon bed. Elmer manned the driver's seat but nobody sat beside him. The passenger seat had been designated for Mary, but she refused to go because she thought it impious to visit a Christian cemetery with people who weren't God-fearing and, anyway, the house was a mess and she needed to give it a thorough sweeping. Chester, Henry, and Blue Boy walked behind the wagon as devout followers of their mother's memory.

Salty wasn't stubborn, just plain uncooperative, and the frustrated Elmer turned the reins over to Henry, but Henry complained of a stomachache and joined his father and sister in the wagon bed after requesting that Chester take over. Excessive drink and inexperience made Chester a poor driver. He couldn't keep Salty going in a straight line. Blue Boy ended up doing most of the driving, though Aida moved up onto the passenger seat and made so many commands that Blue Boy felt like a middle man. Somehow, they arrived at their destination, but everything looked different than it had two decades earlier at the old Mahackamack Churchyard Cemetery. The Decker family's horizontal stone was hidden by ferns, leaves, and a thorny plant. The unfinished headstone that Elmer had put up for Henrietta was still stuck in the ground but it was bent backward within inches of the ground and consumed by weeds.

§

Port Jervis was now a railroad town as well as a canal town. Many new businesses had opened up to support those two industries and the growing population. The Laurel Grove Cemetery was created in the late 1850s ("Just in time for the war," said Elmer), and the earlier cemetery looked all but forgotten. The shock of seeing the poorly maintained grounds agitated Handy, who tried to stand in protest. He would have tumbled out of the wagon into the weeds if Aida hadn't used all her strength to pull him back down. "Goddamn it!" Handy yelled. "Henrietta shouldn't be in a defiled place like this. We need to dig her up and take her back to Blueberry Hill where we can keep an eye on her."

Aida told her father that digging up a grave was not only illegal but also contrary to Henrietta's final wishes. Instead, she would organize a clean-up campaign. "Too bad Mary isn't here to help," said Elmer. "She can't stand messes. I should have made her come. I just hope she keeps to her sweeping and washing and doesn't wander off." Only Henry stayed out of it since his stomach still ached—from eating bad blueberries, he claimed, though none of the others believed that was possible. Elmer, Chester, and Blue Boy busied themselves clearing away the invasive weeds and overgrown shrubbery that threatened to swallow up the Decker plot. Aida searched the area for black-eyed Susans and goldenrods that she placed on her mother's grave. Handy hadn't been allowed to bring his Revolutionary War knife, so he used Elmer's pocketknife to carefully scratch the word "Pudding" on the headstone. Nobody had prepared to say any words this time. None of them had become familiar enough with the Bible through the years to quote anything from it.

Aida took charge, though she had no quotes, uplifting or not, to offer. She wished that Blue Belle was present since her little sister had memorized so many appropriate words from Walt Whitman, her nursing partner in Washington, and Henry David Thoreau, who had died of tuberculosis the previous year. Then, Aida addressed Henrietta: "I do want you to know, Mama, that I am running Blue Rock House the way you would have run it.

You can be proud of me. Maybe I'm not Queen of Blueberry Hill quite yet, but I'm getting close. Everyone else is doing well except that Blue Belle is down in the nation's capital surrounded by wounded men; Jacob and Peter are off fighting battles against Rebels in the South because, you see, there is this Civil War going on; Henry is in the wagon with a bellyache, though we think he is likely malingering; Chester is drinking too much, in part because he can't have Anna Bender; Elmer had been caught trespassing on Bender property when he thought Blue Belle had been kidnapped, and he now has a wife named Mary who has a tendency to wander off by herself and wouldn't come with us today because she doubts we are Christians; Blue Boy is always around to help out with the berries and such, but he seems lost and wishes he could paint pretty pictures like Nathaniel Bender; and of course Good Old Dad is finally *really* acting old and has trouble getting around, though he curses more than he ever did in your presence and seems eager to fight the hated Benders, who built a monstrous stone wall that divides Blueberry Hill in two. That's about it, Mama, except I want you to know I miss you as much as ever, we all do."

Handy stumbled onto the grave, smashing flowers and several chestnut burrs with his unsure feet, cleared his throat for nearly a minute while maintaining his balance and observing a medium-sized bird perched on a chestnut tree branch that extended over Henrietta's headstone. He rambled on about how the evil and noisy Benders and Leaches were trying to destroy Blueberry Hill before his anger turned to sadness and he told Henrietta over and over how much he missed her. Chester rushed in to make sure his father stayed upright. When Handy's words drowned in tears, Anna began singing "Amazing Grace," but she only knew the first stanza and again wished Blue Belle was there so her little blind sister could sing the rest of it. The only one besides Aida to sing was Handy. He sounded like a distressed crow and, knowing few of the correct words, kept inserting "Glory, glory Hallelujah" and "Her soul goes marching on" into the mix.

To the relief of the others, Handy stopped singing on his own. He pointed up at the chestnut tree branch and cried: "Look, children. It's her!"

Aida ended her singing and stared at the bird on the branch. The others did the same. They were all silent as they listened to the bird repeat its call over and over—a soft, low-pitched *tu-a-wee*.

"She has been there the whole time," whispered Handy. "She just sits there motionless, so lovely with her blue wings and blue tail and orange-brown breast."

"A female bluebird perhaps," said Blue Boy.

"My Pudding!" declared Handy. "She is watching over us."

"Oh, Dad," said Aida, shaking her head. "Good Old Dad."

"I doubt it is Henrietta," said Chester. "She would surely come back as something more substantial, say a kingfisher or a pileated woodpecker."

"I don't see any orange, only blue," said Elmer. "It must be something else."

"You may be right," said Blue Boy. "It could be a male indigo bunting. I met a bird man when I was defending Washington with the 143rd Infantry. One time he pointed out to me an indigo bunting that was sitting in a tree in front of the Capitol. We'll have to ask the bird expert back on the Hill."

"Mary doesn't know a tufted titmouse from a turkey vulture," said Elmer.

"I meant Natty Bender on the other side of the Hill," said Blue Boy. "He has studied so many kinds of birds for his colorful paintings."

"Fuck Natty!" shouted Handy to the shock of everyone. It was hard for the others to get used to their foul-mouthed centenarian. Even the bird perched above flew off as if offended. "All Benders are bird-witted and no more welcome than bird shit! Damn those encroachers! Not one of their names deserves to be mentioned during this sequential gathering"

"I think you mean *reverential,* Old Dad," said Aida.

"And fuck you, too, daughter. You are so damned proud of yourself. Take a closer look! Henrietta is likely turning over in her grave as we speak. She would have expected you to be a mother yourself by now with a houseful of whippersnappers. We need new Boyd blood. Who is going to carry on the Blueberry picking after we are all gone?"

Aida had no immediate answer. His bluntness had her slightly dazed. There was some truth to what he was saying, but it made her entire body shudder. She needed to hold back her anger on account of his age. She wanted to claw Good Old Dad's eyes out.

"A woman has a place outside of marriage and motherhood," said Chester. "Her first loyalty should be to herself."

"Where did that come from?' asked Elmer. "You must be thinking of Anna Bender again."

"Maybe so, but why should anyone blame Aida. What about Mary and you? You two are married, yet no baby Boyd there."

"Blame us, why don't you, you...you drunk! We tried. Mary had that false alarm and...well, it's not Mary's fault. No call to disrespect her just because she isn't here. You might as well blame Peter and Jacob, too, and Blue Belle! None of them are here."

"Leave Blue Belle out of this!" shouted Aida, finding it much easier to redirect her anger. "She will never give birth. Not that she is afraid she'll die like Mama but...but she...she just can't."

"I share the blame with Peter and Jacob," said Blue Boy. "For that matter, with Chester and Henry, too. We are all bachelors and the chances are good we'll remain that way for life and never produce a progeny."

"Speak for yourself," Henry called out as he rose up from the wagon bed.

"I . . l...I don't think mother's grave is the proper place to discuss this family matter. We mustn't bicker. Weren't we talking about that beautiful bluebird."

"Indigo bunting," said Blue Boy.

"Henrietta," shouted Handy. "It was her. It was her."

The eldest Boyd had the last word. A light rain fell, and they all looked up to the threatening sky with their private thoughts about the weather, their dead mother, and descendants they might never have. Despite the drizzle, they decided to spend the night in the cemetery as planned; after all, Elmer had paid two day's rent on Salty the mule. Chester, Elmer, and Blue Boy were hardly speaking to each other, but they first went by foot to a Port Jervis tavern by the canal where applejack was poured in libation. Aida paid no attention to the rain as she walked through the forlorn cemetery hoping to see the "spiritual bird" again, but it never reappeared. Henry and Handy waited for darkness under a blanket in the wagon bed. When the rain stopped, Handy moved under the chestnut tree to sleep by himself. Aida spent the night with Henry in the wagon bed, stretched out head to toe, toe to head. The others lay along the cemetery's back wall, which served as some protection against the wind and dampness. They all missed their beds at Blue Rock House but nobody said so. There would be no more bickering until the ride home.

Handy left the gravesite reluctantly in the morning, claiming his wife's spirit had visited him during the night and asked him to stay. When reminded that no blueberries grew in the cemetery, though, he was ready to move out. Nobody wanted to walk behind the wagon, so they all piled in and immediately complained about others intruding on their space. The long night of imbibing in the tavern had made Chester, Elmer, and Blue Boy irritable; they argued the whole way about who should drive and who shouldn't. Salty surprised them all by hitting every rut in the road at a too rapid pace as if the mule wanted to get back to Sears & Rhodes Livery as fast as possible. The rain started up again and followed them. It was a wet and bumpy ride home. Handy exhibited his new fascination with swearing. Henry vomited twice. Aida, forgetting for a moment why they had made the trip, said they never should have come. Blue Boy hummed "Amazing Grace" and thought of Nathaniel Bender's paintings to help him block out his family's bickering and carping.

Salty refused to budge any further when they reached Handy Spring. Handy was brought closer to the house on a blueberry cart and carried inside by three of his sons. Elmer couldn't help because he was busy searching for Mary, who he assumed had wandered off again. After Handy was put to bed, he was forgotten because Mary was discovered on her back on the porch roof. She was either bleeding or showing dried blood from various cuts—on both wrists, her upper chest, her forehead, and one ankle. Near one hand was Handy's bloody Revolutionary War knife that she had found hidden in the old dugout turned root cellar. Near the other hand was a broom, which made them wonder if she had tried to sweep pine needles off the roof tiles. Next to her right ear were sewing needles and thread. On a table just inside the house was a neat stack of trousers, shirts, and socks that she must have finished mending before taking to the roof.

Mary's cuts all turned out to be minor. It was raining harder than ever and nobody wanted to answer the questions of outsiders, so Elmer bandaged her up as best he could and put her to bed in their room instead of taking her in the wagon to Doc Tears' office. She wouldn't let go of her broom, which she held to her chest as a little girl might a ragdoll.

"Why, Mary, why?" Elmer asked her as she lay in bed seemingly content.

"Why what?" she replied. "I didn't wander off, did I?"

"No, but you...Tell me, did you want to be alone in the house so you could do this?"

"Do what?" she said. "I always sleep here. Are you coming to bed, husband?"

"Soon. But what made you climb up onto the roof?"

"Oh, I needed to do something. I heard voices, ghosts whispering, and strange noises. You should know, Blue Rock House is cursed...haunted. I feared the house would split in two and collapse, like the House of Usher in Edgar Alan Poe's tale. I thought I'd be safer on the roof. I brought Handy's big knife for protection and the broom to stay busy and keep my mind off the ghosts. I have no idea why I brought the needles and thread. Ghosts don't wear clothes, do they, at least not holey garments that need mending?"

"Forget the ghosts. They won't harm you. But what about all those cuts on you? Explain them, Mary, if you can."

"Certainly, I can. I'm not stupid. I wanted to make sure I was dead so I wouldn't be buried alive under the falling rocks—you know, when the whole house collapsed. I realized that even the porch roof was not a safe place to be."

"You wanted to kill yourself? I never imagined it would go that far."

"Well, you left me here alone, husband. I couldn't bring myself to slit my throat or anything like that—far too messy. So, I cut a little here, there, and everywhere and I must have passed out though I don't really mind the sight of blood as long as I am allowed to clean it up."

Elmer stopped looking at his wife's cuts. He studied the four walls of their room, the lone window, the door, the ceiling, the hard stone floor. He had proved himself an excellent stonemason and a good husband. Mary had no right to do herself in. "It's a wonderful room, a wonderful home," he told her, as he continued to survey the room with a critical eye. "I built this house, Mary. I mean others helped but when you get right down to it, Blue Rock House is *my house*. The foundation is rock solid, perfectly sound. The interior may have a higgledy-piggledy look with uneven floors, window frames slightly out of line, disproportionate wall spaces, and irregular doorways, but it is highly livable. And you can't beat the fieldstone exterior, which is designed to last for generations. The roof doesn't leak much. I continue to maintain it. I even stopped the doors from creaking. To think it could collapse is preposterous. Simply preposterous! I won't have it! Have a little faith in the man you consented to marry."

She held the broom handle against her belly with one hand and with the other rubbed the silver cross she wore around her neck. "I was afraid the Lord had forsaken me for my sins and your sins and the sins of all the Boyds and Benders on Blueberry Hill. Those loud outside noises were coming from the other side. It sounded as if the Bend had fallen first because it was only made of wood."

"No such luck, I'm sure. What you probably heard was Daniel Leach cutting down more trees. The Benders are always wanting him to fell trees, burn bushes, and make walls and gazebos, and such. In any case, it is no reason for you to cut yourself up."

"What cuts? Oh, yes, I nearly forgot. I was desperate, husband. You do understand. I'm fine now. I'm glad our house is sound and I am positive that the great, merciful Lord shall forgive all of us."

Elmer kissed each of her bandaged wrists and laid his head against her wounded chest until his wife fell asleep. Aida came into the room to check on Mary. Elmer said Mary was recovering nicely and was getting much needed rest, then asked Aida if she believed the Boyds were as horrible sinners as the Leaches and the Benders.

"I should say not," Aida replied. "They are all about making money and defacing the Hill with the notable exception of Nathaniel, of course. People like them are never wealthy enough and are embarrassed by nature. They want to contain, consume, and exhaust nature, and in so doing control us, who are poor but who appreciate what we have and don't demand more."

"I'm not so sure about us anymore. We say the whole Hill should be ours and demand they leave. You want us to sell more blueberries. I built a beautiful two-story stone house but you say you want me to add to it the way Leach made additions to the Bend for the Benders."

"I'm thinking of the future. We'll need more rooms when there are more Boyds."

"If there ever are any more of us. We should be content with this house as is. Mary said it is cursed, but I know better." His face felt as if it were made of stone and had started to crack. "I don't want to talk about it."

"I am content, Elm, truly I am. Building a house was necessary and you did a good job. I believe Blue Belle would tell you if she were here that even Daved Henry Thoreau, who could never get enough of nature, built a house. It's the natural thing for man to do. We all need shelter. It's just that sometimes bigger houses are necessary to provide proper shelter for all the people involved—the women and children. What we Boyds don't do is build unnecessary things or destroy wild animals, trees, bushes, and soil. We pick a lot and plant some but don't plow. We have an old milk cow but no horses or mules. We have two simple carts but no wagons. We don't tear up the land with modern machinery. We take only blueberries, and they grow back. We leave only small footprints. Leach and the Benders shoot, hunt, cut, clear, dig, destroy, design, build, and build some more as if that is absolutely necessary to make the Earth fit to live on."

"We are in total agreement then. All the stone structures I built were necessary."

"You are a good man, Elm. What would we do without you?"

"Yes, I am good, aren't I? On the other side of Blueberry Hill are the sinners; on our side are the saints. Thank you, sis." More and more, he was appreciating her as he had their mother. Elmer managed a smile and patted Aida on the head, something he had often done with the caring and loving but extremely short and innocent Blue Belle. Blueberry Hill, he realized, needed a Queen of the Hill, and nobody but Aida could fill that bill. "I didn't mean to become so...so animated. I was terribly worried about Mary, but she will get well and I feel much better. She has faith in God and I...Anyway, thanks again. Goodnight and sweet dreams."

"May the dreams of Mary and you be equally sweet. All is good."

In the morning Mary didn't remember whispering ghosts, curses, falling houses, or how she got all those cuts, and was eager to do the laundry. Elmer was so relieved he brought her breakfast in bed. But all was not good. When Chester went to awake Handy, his Dear Old Boring Dad's bed was empty. Chester woke others but nobody knew where the Boyd patriarch could be. In a panic, Chester raced out the front door and found his father on all fours with his mouth hanging open, as still as a pagan statue.

"You shouldn't be out here," Chester said. "Where do you think you're going?"

Handy managed to move only his mouth. "To grave," he said.

Chester was certain his father had lost his mind. "You were planning to crawl all the way back to Henrietta's grave in Port Jervis?"

"To grave of Man."

"Oh, you mean down near Handy Spring. That's still too far for you to go without help."

"First, I eat. I'm hungry as a bear." He opened his mouth as if to howl or growl but nothing came out. His hands stayed planted on the ground. His arms were trembling. "Can't pick."

"All right. I'll pick for you, but you aren't going anywhere." Chester checked the exhausted, drooping bushes in the immediate area and struggled to find three blueberries that looked whole and almost healthy. "Pretty slim pickings this year," he said as he fed them one by one to his father. "Maybe our worst ever, Aida says. But the Hill will bounce back. It always does."

Handy chewed and panted. When he tried to swallow, he met with some difficulty, as if he were consuming pebbles. Chester didn't know what to do, help his father to his feet and lead him back to bed or have him lie down to rest in the bushes. But as Chester froze with indecision, Handy collapsed onto his unfulfilled belly. He no longer chewed. He no longer panted.

Chester knelt, took off his shirt, and placed it under his father's chin.

"Is that better?" he asked, but he got no answer. "What do you want? What can I do for you?" He turned Handy onto his back, thinking that was best, and rolled up the shirt to make a pillow out of it. He felt a rigid wrist for a pulse. Nothing. He realized he wouldn't get any kind of answer ever again. "I know you can't speak, but can you still hear me? I hope you can. Maybe I never said this to you plain. I got to say it now before...I love you, Good Old Dad, I love you. There, I've said it."

"Me Boy," Handy said, quite distinctly. Those were his last words.

22
DEATH AND MARRIAGE

The death of the first white pioneer of Blueberry Hill at age one-hundred four could hardly be called a surprise, but that's what his family called it. His death, naturally, was a topic of family conversation for days. Henry, with so many sick days under his belt, admitted to having wondered if Good Old Boring Dad might outlive him. Aida said that Handy had been so spirited at his wife's grave in Port Jervis it was almost as if he were reborn. Chester, for one, believed his sister was trying to make herself feel better after sanctioning the grueling trip. Elmer said that while the death shocked him, in retrospect he should have expected the end was near because their father, so serene and undemanding most of his life, had become impatient and easily roused (to the extent of uttering profanities).

"A remarkable metamorphosis; you could see it in his face," Elmer concluded. 'He was like a sedimentary rock who under the heat and pressure of the Benders and Leaches became metamorphic."

"What the devil are you talking about," said Henry. "How can you have rocks on your mind at a time like this?"

"I don't imagine the change in personality did him any good," said Blue Boy. "I suspect Elm is right. Good Old Dad's hatred for the Benders overwhelmed his entire system. The poor blueberry picking season didn't help. His mind plum gave out."

"Doc Tears said it was his heart," said Henry.

"Of course, it was his heart," said Elmer. "It stopped."

"Yes, I know. His poor heart. I have the same blighted heart as him."

"How sad, Henry. You might only live to be one hundred."

"His last words were *Me Boy*," said Chester, the last one to see Handy alive. "It was as if he were speaking to Man, you know, Catawissa Manayunk."

"Maybe he was, or is doing so as we speak," said Aida. "Who knows? Maybe Blue Belle knows. I wish she were here at a time like this. She understands such things. We need her."

"It was God's will," said Mary.

"Leave the Lord out of this," said Henry. "Old Dad always did."

"As you like it, you...you infidel."

"Stop that, Mary," said Aida. "This isn't the time for name calling."

"As you wish. But I tell you all, there is a curse on this house. Those who do not believe must pay for their sins. It was the curse that killed him."

"Mary!" cried Elmer. "I thought you were over all that. The only curse around here is the Bender family. Good Old Dad went through every kind of blueberry season and lived nearly as long as Catawissa Manayunk. He cursed the Benders, but Old Dad wasn't cursed. The curse is on them, the evil people occupying the other side of our Hill."

Blue Belle, who had never cursed anyone in her life, got the news in a letter from her sister and knew she must head north immediately. She said her goodbyes to the doctors, nurses, and wounded soldiers in Washington D.C., and rushed back home by horse-drawn streetcar and railroad with the help of government officials, train presidents, and Horace Greeley. She wanted to be there for the family funeral service, and Aida insisted the Boyds would not proceed without their little sister who had loved their father almost as much as Man and by all indications had connections with the spiritual world beyond. Nobody was eager to put him under ground. Handy had never been in a rush to go anywhere, and the family saw no reason to rush him now. Besides, it wasn't certain where Good Old Boring Dad should be buried—in the Port Jervis plot next to his wife, Pudding, or above Handy Spring next to his best friend, Man.

"My vote is for here on the Hill," said Henry, between wheezes and coughs. "I can't urge it enough. That perilous journey to the shabby old cemetery in Port Jervis all but killed our father, and, by God, it's liable to do the same to me!"

"The love a man holds for the woman he chooses to be his life partner takes precedence over the love the man has for any other man, Indian or not," argued Elmer, while gripping Mary's hand. "A happily married couple should rest together for eternity. When we stand at their feet in the cemetery, the husband should be buried to the left and the wife on the right. That's the right way to have it done."

"God bless you, husband," said Mary.

"Handy and Man founded Blueberry Hill together," Chester reminded the family. "They spent most of the rest of their lives here, rarely going even to the valley below. Just because Old Dad died doesn't mean we have the right to make him leave. Henrietta left after her death because she wished to go back to where she was raised among the Deckers. She never loved the Hill as much as he did. That's a fact, like it or not. I say keep Old Dad right here where he belongs under the blueberry bushes."

"I respect your opinion, big brother," said Blue Boy, "but I must disagree with you. I was only twelve years old when Mama died, but I could see that, in her own way, she loved Blueberry Hill as much as Dad did. She kept everything running. She was Queen of the Hill. Dad couldn't have lasted here without her in those early years. He needed her then, and he needs her now."

"We know what Mama wanted for herself because she said so many times," Aida said. "And we know she never requested that Dad be buried next to her. What Handy wanted, none of us can be sure."

The debate continued until just two days before Blue Belle arrived back home. While Aida was going through Handy's clothes to see what could be handed down to his sons, she happened upon a note in her father's handwriting that communicated his final wishes for internment. Nobody knew for sure if he had written the note before or after the August visit to Henrietta's grave, but the message was straightforward and didn't indicate his mind had deteriorated to any great extent. She read it to the others:

Family—

I am dead or will be shortly. I have placed this dying message in a safe place (the pocket of my only vest) and feel certain you will read it in time. I'm sure Mary will find my note first as she always checks the pockets before she does the wash. No need for me to tell you to honor my legacy by protecting Blue Rock House and our blueberry bushes from Bender bastards and any other foul invaders that come along. Hopefully one day, if Ketanëtuwit and the spirits are willing, our descendants shall acquire the whole Blueberry Hill that rightfully should be ours and ours alone. Pass this on to your children, if you ever have any! I can't believe none of you dunces ever gave me a grandchild! Get a move on! But I digress.

My main reason for this message is to instruct you on what to do with my remains. It may surprise some of you that I do NOT wish to be buried next to my wife in that rotten cemetery in what is now called Port Jervis. I never liked that town or the people in it, which is why I sought out a new home and found Blueberry Hill with the help of Man. Henrietta told me in a dream that she understood, that our spirits shall reunite even if our decayed bodies don't. Nor do I wish to be buried in a cemetery anywhere. I want to stay on the Hill. Please note, though, that I have changed my mind about being cremated and scattered among the blueberry bushes. As much as I love the blueberries, I feel my ashes would blow away in time. It can get pretty windy on the Hill. Also please note, if I still have your attention, while I want to be buried on the Hill, I DO NOT want it to be in a freshly dug grave. Why mar our land any further? That's not the Boyd way. Just stick me in the same hole as Man, who guided me to this wonderful Blue Place and doesn't take up too much room. I don't mind his hump. Listen well, my children. Honor my last request and I won't reappear as one of those ghosts who can't bear

leaving this earth. I can bear it. I'll miss you all, but it won't be forever. Like it or not, Ketanëtuwit promises we shall meet again somewhere, somehow. Peace and happy picking to all of you. See you later.
–Your Good Old Boring Dad

Blue Belle was true to form upon returning, not at all downcast. She told the others that grief should be tempered by faith, according not to the Bible but to Walt Whitman: "As Walt says, nothing collapses. Death is the beginning of new life, since the body dies but the soul is immortal."

Dutifully, Chester and Blue Boy dug up Catawissa Manayunk's grave, opened the already rotting casket, and laid their father inside on top of the Lenni Lenape's remains. Elmer did minor repairs on the casket. Before he nailed it shut, Aida and Blue Belle threw handfuls of blueberries inside along with his straw hat. Henry joined his brothers in putting the dirt back over it. Mary stood in the background crossing herself repeatedly and mumbling about how everything taking place was unchristian and morbid. Elmer pleaded with her to let his father rest in peace and to allow his children to experience a minute or two of silence. Mary ran off and Elmer didn't try to stop her. The silence lasted three minutes. Blue Belle nudged Chester to say something as he was the eldest and arguably Handy's closest son toward the end.

"We didn't call you Good Old Boring Dad for nothing," Chester said. "You were all those things—old without doubt, boring with tongue in cheek, and good in that you didn't want to hurt man nor beast except in your last years, but then it was only the Benders, so we forgive you. You loved family and you loved blueberries. Which you loved more, I cannot say. I can say we loved you, too, and we will miss you. Rest in peace. You did that plenty during your long life and nothing should stop you from doing that now."

The others spoke in brief. Elmer thanked Handy for finally accepting the building of Blue Rock House to replace the dugout, Henry said he appreciated the way Handy accepted a son with delicate health, Blue Boy said he was glad Handy and Henrietta decided to have more children after Henry, Aida commended Handy for not being a controlling husband or a tyrannical father; and Blue Belle chose to paraphrase the late Henry David Thoreau instead of quote the still very much alive Walt Whitman: "Mr. Thoreau advised us to go confidently in the direction of our dreams and to live life as we imagined it. Good Old Not Really So Boring Dad did that. He simplified his life on this Hill and, in so doing, made the laws of the universe simpler for him and his family. He lived for each moment. Nothing complicated. Call it simple. Call it primitive. But call it honest and gentle. He touched the land and all of us. He didn't ask for more. I expect he shall, like Mr. Thoreau, live much the same way in the afterlife. We are blessed to have shared Earth time with Mr. Handy Boyd, our dear father." The family, with only Elmer dissenting, agreed that the memorial cairn built for Man would also represent Handy. "We honor them for eternity as they chose to live their lives—together, friends forever," said Blue Belle, who wasn't quoting either Whitman or Thoreau. Elmer was for a second cairn, at least as tall as the first, but only Mary supported him so he didn't make a fuss.

Handy had died during what seemed like the last days of the worst blueberry season of his long life. That's why the family proclaimed what occurred on Labor Day 1863 and for the rest of September a miracle. Mary credited God. Elmer went along with her but only with nods to the heavens. Everyone else in Blue Rock House leaned toward crediting the spirits of Handy and Man, as well as Lenni Lenape creator Ketanëtuwit. The blueberries ruined by beetles, maggots, and possibly Bender curses were all but forgotten. New berries appeared, later than ever but bursting with life. They showed up night after night, sometimes in great bunches, sometimes as lone sentinels. No bush was bare, and the entire hillside soon twinkled as if covered with blue stars. It was exactly as Handy had seen the place the day Catawissa Manayunk first showed it to him, according to a message Blue Belle received eleven days after Handy's burial as his spirit rose from the double grave to the Happy Picking Ground in the sky.

§

The Boyds could eat well again and sell again in town. Chester used some of the sales money to purchase a pair of used binoculars. By standing on the porch roof he could see part of stone wall Jackson through the trees. He said he could now spot "Bender bastards and any other foul invaders" who might want to breach the dividing line. "Daniel Leach built the wall to keep us out, not to keep his people from crossing over whenever they want to," Chester said, sounding much like his late father. The rest of the family didn't buy that entirely. They knew those binoculars were most often focused on the rock formation known as the Castle that was still visited semiregularly by Anna Bender.

When family tragedy struck down South in 1864 none of the Boyds at Blue Rock House blamed God, Ketanëtuwit, or any friendly spirits. Fingers were still pointed at the Benders because none of them had fought in the Civil War and some of them had Southern leanings. It was in January that the newspaper in Ellenville, New York, printed a letter from a doctor with the 143rd Regiment, which was camped in Lookout Valley, Tennessee. "Day after day the destroying Angel continues to visit our already thinned ranks, and one after another our bravest and once most robust boys are numbered among the dead. Chronic diarrhea is the prevailing disease. We have had since we came into this Department, upwards of seventy deaths from this direful malady, and probably before this article reached your paper, there may be added to this number ten or fifteen more of our bravest and best boys, who are now tottering on the verge of the grave." Private Jacob Boyd, recently turned thirty-three, was among the New York soldiers tottering in that far off valley, and on January 15 he succumbed to "consumption of the bowels." Not enough blueberries in his wartime diet, Handy Boyd might have said had he not died four and a half months earlier. The 143rd's assistant surgeon made no mention of fruit but attributed Jacob's death to the hundreds of dead and putrefying horses and mules left unburied in the area as well as the soldier's diet lacking in milk and vegetables.

Private Peter Boyd, one year younger than Jacob, lost whatever fighting spirit he possessed after his brother's death but still resisted the malady as well as Rebel bullets. He was considered "bewildered with shock" and shot nobody during the Atlanta campaign. On August 14, 1864, a fellow Union private, Mortimer Loomis from Monticello, New York, accidentally shot him in the right arm while Peter was foraging (for berries, he said later) outside Georgia's capital city. His wound caused him to miss General Sherman's March to the Sea. Totally dispirited, he cried out: "Why such pain, why such torture. The only cure is death. Bully for you, Jacob, my brother, you lucky devil. You are beyond human suffering."

At a hospital in Washington, D.C., Peter was provided anesthesia by a volunteer nurse named Ellen, who had befriended Blue Belle the previous year. When Peter returned to Blueberry Hill that same month, he had only one arm but he did have Ellen, who was considered lovely despite pox scars on her forehead and left cheek—"beauty marks for a beautiful soul," said Blue Belle. Ellen, without doubt a sympathetic soul and an excellent healer, had formed an attachment to Peter because of his two reoccurring nightmares—one about being a one-armed blueberry picker and the other about seeing Jacob, "a haunting, grotesquely distorted brownish ghost" standing on an enormous mound of diarrhea that passed as Lookout Mountain, Tennessee. Ellen had also wanted to see Blue Belle again. "No matter how badly you feel or how scarred I am, we can always look to your dear blind sister for hope and inspiration," she told Peter.

The return of Peter to the Hill at the tail-end of a good blueberry season could not wipe out the sorrow over Jacob's fate. But when Ellen consented to be Peter's wife at the end of September, the rest of the family was overjoyed. They had visions of a baby Boyd appearing, which would be a far greater blessing than the marriage. But first the wedding in October. Held outdoors at Handy Spring with a well-paid minister from town presiding, things got off to a bad start when a distressed Mary told Ellen that the family would treat her like a slave and she would be forced to produce a new Boyd baby every year. Ellen, though, could not be frightened off; and in fact, she took Mary aside and gently calmed her down as a nurse would a difficult patient.

The minister, as if to justify his large fee, spoke too long—first about how the wedding ceremony symbolized a bride's triumph in finding a man to meet all her needs as long as he lived, then about how a monogamous marriage in which sexual relations were limited to producing children was desirable but anything else was unacceptable. Thus, he stressed that a woman of proper upbringing should feign sleepiness, headaches, and illness or resort to arguments and scolding rather than submit to the daily urges of selfish, lustful husbands. His words caused Peter to blush, grow weak in the knees, and come close to fainting, but Ellen splashed spring water on the groom's face and squeezed his only arm to keep him standing erect. Only Mary seemed to appreciate what the minister was saying; she began clapping halfway through and shouted, "You tell 'em, Parson!" Elmer put a hand over his wife's mouth, but three more muffled words came out: "Don't touch me."

When at last the minister stopped lecturing and called for the bride and groom to speak their wedding vows, shotgun blasts nearly drowned out their voices. It turned out that on the other side of the dividing wall, the Benders were having a "pigeon shoot," in which live pigeons were held in a trap until the shooter "called for the bird" and one was released into the air.

"You both do, but I don't have to stand for this," said Elmer to the bride and groom. "Where's the Springfield rifle you brought home from the war, Peter? I aim to teach those Benders a lesson they'll never forget."

"Me, too," said Blue Boy, who was the best man in the absence of Jacob. "The war is on!"

"You don't have to ask me twice," said Henry, though nobody asked him. "Shooting off guns at our wedding! Such total disrespect!"

"You with us, Chesty?" Elmer asked.

"Maybe," said Chester. "But no rifle, no shooting. How soon we forget that before he went to war, Peter shot Nathaniel Bender in the buttocks. That didn't do us any good. Handy didn't teach his sons to shoot guns."

"Good Old Dad was proud that I went off to fight the Rebs," said Peter. "At times, shooting is necessary."

"And sometimes unnecessary and horrible," said Aida. "That careless shot by Mortimer Loomis, one of the men in your own company, cost you your right arm, little brother."

"Thanks, Sis. If you hadn't reminded me, I would have forgotten. What did you do with my Springfield rifle anyway?"

"The shame," said the minister. "Talking of guns! I haven't even pronounced you man and wife yet."

"Do it," said Aida. "We need to at least look into those shotgun blasts."

The minister made his pronouncement, then crossed his arms as if saying another word would be futile.

"I'd rather you not take up your rifle again, Peter," said Ellen. "It would be near impossible to do in any case."

"Right. You married a cripple."

"Oh, Peter. I don't think of you like that. Now, isn't this about the time you should be kissing the bride. Me! Or does the clergyman object?"

"A first brief chaste kiss is appropriate," the minister said. "The kiss symbolizes the exchange of souls between the bride and groom. It seals the marital contract for life."

Ellen held a wet marital kiss and the groom's one arm so long that Peter couldn't leave with his brothers. The Springfield could not be located because Aida and Blue Belle had hidden it behind Blue Belle's book shelf next to the Revolutionary War knife that had once belonged to Handy and had been used by Mary to cut herself. Despite all being unarmed, Elmer raced uphill, followed by Blue Boy, Henry, and Chester. Henry stopped to pick up three hand-sized throwing rocks, then decided he was too exhausted to continue running. He walked on, holding his heaving chest. By the time he reached the Jackson wall, Chester stood atop it, having been boosted up by Blue Boy and Elmer. Chester raised his arms to show he wasn't carrying a gun and gazed out at a dozen men with shotguns. He was ready to demand an explanation and perhaps shake an angry fist when a passenger pigeon landed on his left shoulder. The bird clucked, its voice loud, harsh, and unmusical. The shooters held their fire. Chester froze.

"Hey, you old goat, what the hell you doing up there with that bird?" asked Jeremiah Bender, who was cradling his shotgun.

"Stopping what you're about to do to it," Chester yelled. "I'm protecting him or her."

"Yeah? What about the other five billion passenger pigeons?"

"I don't know about them. You won't kill this one." The pigeon cocked its head but otherwise seemed content with its human perch. Chester avoided looking directly at the bird for fear of frightening it off.

"We're having a contest here. It's sport, neighbor."

Chester surveyed the crowd of evil-looking men. Some he didn't recognize, Bender guests no doubt. Daniel Leach stood out because he was taller than the rest and was the only one wearing a coonskin cap. Chester didn't see Nathaniel Bender, the bird-loving artist, but that was no surprise. He spotted Alexander Bender caressing his shotgun as if it were one of the thighs of his Rebel-loving wife, Delilah. That got Chester's blood boiling but not nearly as much as when he noticed Jeremiah's shirker twin sons, Maurice and Robert, laughing their haughty heads off.

The pair, at twenty-four, were the managers of the Bender Lumbering Company and the Bender Tannery, respectively, but that didn't hold any weight with Chester. He still saw them as callow boys tailing after their mother, Anna, like two lambs. Because they had the means and no pluck, they had paid substitutes to enlist in their stead; meanwhile Jacob Boyd had died and Peter Boyd had lost an arm while honorably serving the Union. Chester would have yelled an insult at Maurice and Robert but he didn't want to raise his voice and disturb the friendly bird. Instead, he looked down at Jeremiah and spoke in a low but firm voice, "You disrupted a wedding ceremony with all your shooting."

"No fooling? I had no idea. Who's the unlucky bride? Or is Aida finally tying the knot? She must be close to forty by now and can't be too choosey."

"It's none of your damn business."

"And nothing we're doing over here is any of your business. You mind stepping down from Jackson? On your side if you please."

"Or what? You going to shoot me off, Red Bender? Go ahead. I'd love them to throw you in prison or hang you for murder." The pigeon apparently had heard enough. It suddenly took flight, heading south fast, as if it were trying to catch up with its missing flock.

"You amuse me, Chester. A dead man can't love anything."

Chester had plenty more to get off his chest, but a familiar figure stepped out of the shadows and stood at Jeremiah's side. Yes, a lady was present, and not just any lady. Her auburn hair was fastened in a bun. Her arms were crossed over her full bosom at first, but she frowned and put her hands on her hips. Chester thought of the large bone structure that was her pelvis. Robert and Maurice were hers—hers and Red Bender's. At least she was unarmed.

Chester was speechless. He tottered, then staggered, nearly losing his balance atop the great dividing wall.

"I'm only watching," Anna Boyd said, as if she owed him an answer to the question he hadn't asked out loud: *What the hell are you doing here?*

"Not exactly true, Sugarplum," said Jeremiah. "That one time you actually did pull the cord to open the trap and let the pigeon out."

"I was freeing it. I hoped you'd miss."

"You know I can't miss at this range."

Anna suddenly put a hand over her heart as if she had taken a bullet. But she said nothing more. She wouldn't look Chester in the eye.

Chester wanted to stand tough, but for some reason those ominous words of Jeremiah Bender caused him to cover his own heart with one hand and his crotch with the other. Then he stumbled backward and, with Blue Boy and Elmer tugging on his ankles, he went over the side—the Boyd side. It was a rough landing. He took Elmer to the ground with him but the nimbler Blue Boy danced out of the way in time. Henry was safely behind a tree but held a testicle-shaped stone in his throwing hand, ready if absolutely necessary to defend himself and the honor of his late father. The sound of laughter from the Bender side passed through the stone wall with a vengeance.

"Anybody get shot over there?" Henry asked as he cautiously approached Chester, who lay on his back either unable or unready to move.

"Only the pigeons," said Chester.

"Too bad. I was hoping the Benders were fighting among themselves, having their own little civil war as it were."

That comment might have been Henry's idea of a joke. But his brothers weren't laughing.

23
WAR WOUNDS

When Confederate General Robert E. Lee surrendered in April 1865 but escaped severe punishment, the Boyds didn't think justice had been served. "I don't give a damn whether he was a good general or not," Chester told his family at a late April breakfast featuring blueberry pancakes. Only Mary was missing; she was pulling weeds in the garden. "How many more of our boys died because that son of a bitch wouldn't give up a fight that the South could never hope to win." Nobody disagreed, though Blue Belle pointed out that "boys" died on both sides in the heinous conflict and that families North and South suffered. She quoted from a letter she had received and memorized from her friend Walt Whitman: "Future years will never know the seething hell and the black infernal background of countless minor scenes and interiors (not the official surface-courteousness of the Generals, not the few great battles) of the Secession War; and it is best they should not—the real war will never get in the books."

Blue Boy said it wasn't fair that more Union soldiers fell (about 360,000) than Confederates (about 258,000) when the North was in the right and had won the war. Peter, with his brother Jacob in mind, told everyone of the 620,000 total deaths, 417,000 were from diseases, and only 203,000 from combat wounds. Nobody disputed the numbers put forth by either brother. "We lost Jacob and Peter lost his right arm," Chester reminded his family, though they needed no reminder. "The Benders lost nothing. They made money." This more personal statement hit the family harder. Henry cursed the Gods of War. Elmer merely muttered "Goddamn." Mary came in from the garden in time to defend the one and only true God and point her wagging finger at "the North, the South, the Middle and all of unfaithful, fickle man unkind." Her husband excused her but also apologized. Everything had become more confusing for him since his marriage.

"The weeds have made a mess of things; they are out of control," Mary said. "It's not God's doing. God is great. God is kind. God created us. But God can't control everything." She left to return to the garden. Nobody tried to stop her.

Aida thoroughly chewed every last bit of pancake on her plate, then banged her blue-streaked fork on the table to get everyone's attention. "We cannot bury ourselves or dwell in misery," she said. "We can start making good money again. The damn senseless war is over, and people want our blueberries. We need to move on, which first means going back to the way things were here before the war and second means working harder than ever to make everything better."

"And forget about Jacob and this?" said Peter, pointing to his empty shirtsleeve. His wife immediately leaned against his armless side and reached awkwardly across him to give his hand a long, tender squeeze. Ellen couldn't bring herself to let go. She never missed a chance to show her support.

"The living must go on living, like it or not, little brother," said Aida. "I refuse to let maudlin fixation keep me from doing what is best for the Boyds' collective future."

"I'll never forget," said Blue Boy, but he said no more. He lay down his fork and crossed his arms, holding himself to quell his shivering. He was riddled with self-pity for not dying or losing a limb during that Secession War but knew he didn't deserve to feel that way. Still, he wished he had a wife like Ellen to comfort him in his time of need.

"Jacob's body isn't here on the Hill, but his spirit is," said Blue Belle. "It would be fitting to put up a second cairn down by Handy Spring near the cairn we have for Man and Good Old Dad. Jacob never passed over a chance to drink our blessed water."

"Yes, another cairn," said Elmer. "I have all the rocks ready, just need to relocate them. In fact, I'm willing to build as many cairns as we'll need...as long as I am able."

"Jacob will never see it," said Peter. "When I kick the blueberry bucket no need to put up a cairn for me."

"Don't talk of such things my love," said Ellen. She finally released his hand, sat back in her chair, and patted his broad right shoulder, beneath which was emptiness. "We are just beginning our new life together."

"I don't want a cairn either," said Blue Boy. "I don't deserve..." He stuffed half a pancake into his mouth to keep from saying more.

"Me neither," said Henry. "And my health being the way it is, I could very well be on my way out soon."

"Nonsense," Ellen said. "I won't let you."

"Hey, you boys are young," said Chester. "I'm next on the list, and I want big round wet stones on my cairn."

"We know you aren't serious, Chesty," said Elmer. "You prefer to be inconspicuous."

"Not when I'm dead."

"We don't seem to have a consensus about cairns," Blue Belle said. "I have another suggestion, a compromise. We already have the one cairn for Man and Handy. I suggest we build no new cairns but add stones to the one we already have and keep adding stones whenever we feel like it for dear Jacob or whomever. This grand cairn will keep growing and will represent every Boyd, including mother in her Port Jervis plot and the original Blue Belle buried at the top of the Hill."

"Excellent," said Aida. "That's much more practical. We don't want cairns all over the place. Thank you for the suggestion, Blue Belle."

"Sounds monumental to me," said Peter. "Nobody puts up a monument for a soldier who was a mere private, never shot anybody, and died of diarrhea."

"I told you I'd build one for Jacob," said Elmer.

"Not necessary, Elm," said Henry. "We are all capable of putting a stone on top of another stone. Say, Peter, if you aren't going to eat your pancakes, pass them over to me."

"Why?" shouted Peter. "Eating any more of them will only make you sick, brother, like everything else does. As for me, I'm already sick and have no appetite. Thinking of Jacob dying so far from home sickens me. Eating with only one arm sickens me. Thinking of the Benders sickens me. Remembering those words of that self-righteous minister at my wedding sicken me. Everything sickens me."

"Oh, you poor dear," said Ellen. She pressed against her husband and raised off her chair as she made the long reach to pat his hand. Peter reacted as if she had stuck a fork in his knuckles. Ellen smiled at the others, sat back in her chair, folded her hands, and addressed them. "Please forgive, Petey. He woke up on the wrong side of the bed this morning."

"Like every morning," said Henry, laughing. "My little brother is sicker than me."

Nobody else laughed. To change the subject, Blue Belle mentioned having seen two lovely bluebirds feeding earlier that morning and noted that these birds symbolized hope, love, positivity, and renewal. Elmer pointed out that, despite the bluebirds' presence, it looked like another dreary all-day rain was in store for the Hill. Aida quickly brought up the fact that heavy spring rains did wonders for the blueberry crop.

"Having our whole world revolve around a blueberry crop sickens me," said Peter.

Blue Boy suddenly forgot his own self-pity issues. He felt an urge to slap Peter. The guy might only have one arm, but he had a devoted wife reassuring him all the time—at meals, in the blueberry fields, in the bedroom (Blue Boy was certain)—yet couldn't rid himself of his gloom and doom outlook. While others suspected Ellen, like Elmer's Mary, was to blame for not conceiving a child, Blue Boy knew the real reason—Peter's melancholia had made him a no-show in the marital bed. Ellen could talk to her dear friend Blue Belle about most everything else, but *not* that. One night, though, Ellen and Blue Boy happened to be on the porch roof together looking at the stars and she had confided in him. Blue Boy knew he was wrong to think that he could accomplish with his sister-in-law what Peter could not, and he could not tell her that, of course, which added to his own self-pity. He had suggested that she wish upon a star and hurried off to bed.

Everybody ate in silence for two minutes except for Peter, who had not passed his plate down to Henry and was staring at his blueberry pancakes as if they contained rat poison. Elmer finally decided to speak his peace. "No casualty numbers tell of the mental scars left by the war," he said, pausing to pound a fist on the table. "Not only those left on the soldiers, mind you, but on their families as well." The others all knew Elmer wasn't thinking about Peter or the rest of them but about his sensitive Mary weeding the garden alone. Nobody really wanted him to continue, but he did. "Mary has felt the stings and arrows of war as surely as if she had been on Little Round Top instead of Blueberry Hill; she is as much a casualty of war as Jacob and Peter."

"Oh, hell with your bunkum, Elm," said Peter. "We all know the bloody truth. She was crazy as a loon even before those Confederate troops fired on Fort Sumpter."

Elmer lunged across the breakfast table as if to take a swing at Peter but pulled back suddenly when his brother's empty sleeve came into focus. Peter raised his fork as if to defend himself, but Ellen touched his wrist and he let the fork clank against his plate.

"The war is over," said Aida. "No more fighting. No more brother against brother."

"They should have hung Lee," said Chester, bringing the conversation back full circle. "And they should hang Jefferson Fucking Davis when they capture that traitor."

Both Elmer and Peter murmured their assent. Chester was sounding so much like their late father these days. Peter passed his loaded plate to Henry. Peace came to the breakfast table.

§

As much as the Boyds condemned Robert E. Lee and President of the Confederate States Jefferson Davis, they reserved most of their bitterness for the Benders and Daniel Leach. Neither Leach nor his flamboyant cousin Delilah Boyd could be forgiven for supporting the South to the end of the war and beyond. That pair of Georgia-born Confederate souls were not known to have ever said a single kind word about Abe Lincoln, U.S. Grant, or any member of the Union-supporting Boyds. While Aida focused her hatred on that hellish Southern belle whose treachery matched her namesake from the

Old Testament, the Boyd men lambasted Leach, calling the lumberman a cut lower than a Copperhead, referring to both the Southern sympathizers and the poisonous snakes that sometimes joined the rattlesnakes on the Hill.

After winning the first annual Bender pigeon shoot the year before, Leach had further cleared bushes and trees in the same area to build a rifle range, with paper targets attached to the wall and bottle targets lined up on top of it. The Boyds frequently found shattered glass on their side, and Mary, who often wandered barefooted and in a dream state from Blue Rock House, cut both her soles during the 1865 blueberry picking season. Mary didn't mind as she had deliberately cut herself on many occasions during the war while managing to neglect her feet. Husband Elmer, though, was never angrier. Worry about his wife had left him unsettled. He walked all the way around the wall carrying Peter's Springfield rifle, loaded with seven metallic rimfire cartridges. He had never fired a gun, in anger or not, in his life, but he didn't figure there was much to it. He wasn't headed to the Bend to shatter Bender lives, just Bender glass. Once he reached the hated wood mansion, he emptied the magazine, firing one shot each into seven different second-story windows since he wasn't sure which bedroom belonged to Leach.

The novice but accurate shootist would have escaped the Bender side of the Hill had it not been for that Southern dog Dred. The redbone coonhound ran down Elmer, latched on to the seat of his trousers, and held on for a good five minutes until Daniel Leach caught up with them. Elmer had tried to fend off the dog with the butt of the empty Springfield but had only succeeded in bashing himself on the head so hard that he dropped the rifle and saw stars. Elmer now sat on the bare ground fifty yards from the back door of the Bend. Leach made sure Elmer was seeing straight before threatening him with a .42-caliber Lemat revolver, a handgun once used by a Confederate soldier during the war but now only by Leach at his shooting range

"You deserve to be shot, Boyd," Leach said, even as Dred licked Elmer's face, perhaps apologetically. "You're a two-time offender. The first time you trespassed on Bender land you were let off with a warning, but this time..."

"What first time!" shouted Elmer, able to be defiant in face of the Lemat because he was still thinking of Mary's bleeding feet. He pushed Dred's head away.

Leach was only too happy to remind Elmer of the time he came all the way to the grand gazebo and falsely accused the Benders of kidnapping the pathetic little blind girl.

"So, go ahead and shoot me," said Elmer, remembering how Chester had challenged Jeremiah Bender from atop the stone wall during the 1864 pigeon shoot. "That will land you in prison where you belong."

Leach wasn't amused, but he didn't shoot. He hauled Elmer back to the Bend, hogtied him, loaded him in a large wagon pulled by two fine horses, and raced to town hitting every bump along the way. Elmer spent only one night in the Wurtsboro Jail. He couldn't pay his bail money but all charges were dropped when Aida swore on her Old Dad's grave that the Boyds would repay for every broken window and never complain about the shooting range or the shooting of any living creature except themselves.

Shattered glass bottles continued to fall onto the Boyd side of the wall, and the family used up most of the blueberry sales money it made that summer paying off the Benders. Civil War veteran Peter, who despite his gloom picked with one hand faster than Henry did with two, twice accused Elmer of being as crazy as Mary for shooting out those windows. Blue Boy agreed, saying somebody in the Bend could have been killed; he was thinking of Nathaniel. Elmer took it calmly. It didn't matter anymore what anyone said about him or Mary because he knew no amount of criticism would ever cause him to love her less. Furthermore, he figured, if he himself was crazy that would make it easier for his beloved Mary to love him back.

§

Blueberry picking season was long over when a man rode a horse right up to the Boyd front door after dark and entered without knocking, as if Blue Rock House were his own home. He was well dressed, wearing a woolen black over-frock coat and tall top hat like the kind the late President Lincoln often wore. "I'm here, Peter Boyd," he called out. "I told you I'd show up at your door some day and make amends. Well, my friend, that day is today, and it's your lucky day." But Peter didn't appear. Aida did, and she carried Mary's prize broom as a weapon since she and Blue Belle had recently buried the Springfield rifle next to the garden.

"I don't know you," said Aida, ready to swing the broom.

"I know you," the man replied, tipping his top hat to her. "Aida, right? You are just as I pictured—a smart, serious woman who can take care of herself, with or without a broom. In fact, I know about your entire family, or most of it anyway. Have there been any recent Boyd additions I should know about?"

"That's no business of yours, mister," Aida snapped, but she lowered her broom while thinking how neither of the married women, Mary and Ellen, had produced a Boyd child. "Who do you think you are?"

"I *know* who I am, Miss Boyd."

"What's your name?"

"Mortimer Loomis. You can call me Mort."

"What do you want here?"

"Like I said, to make amends."

"For what? You do something to us?"

"Not to all of you. You don't recognize my name? Mort Loomis from Monticello, New York. I once did time with your brother Peter, that is as a Yankee private, not a prisoner."

"Oh. Loomis, of course. As I live and breathe, Mortimer Loomis!"

"That's me all right."

"You're the one. You shot Peter's arm off! Jumpin' Jehosaphat!"

"Actually, a field doctor chopped the arm off a few days later. I suppose it was necessary—to prevent gangrene, you know—but I was darn sorry to hear about it."

"I never expected to see you in person."

"Sorry to intrude on your privacy this way, but an intelligent woman like yourself can surely understand my desire to make amends."

"Of course. You were his friend during the war."

"Not for most of the war. We were just a couple of common soldiers doing the best we could for our country and our own survival. I hardly knew him at all before the accident. You see, Miss Boyd, your brother was harvesting Georgia rabbiteye blueberries in bushes where Rebel snipers were known to be situated. I saw movement that wasn't blue and fired my musket. First time I hit anything I was aiming at in my entire life. I of course am delighted that I only got Peter in the arm instead of the brain or heart or some other vital organ."

"We all are, Mr. Loomis." Aida wanted to raise the broom and drive Mortimer Loomis back out the door, slam it shut, and bolt it. But she realized she couldn't be that inhospitable. He wasn't a Bender. He was apologetic, polite, tall, darkly handsome, neatly dressed, clean, and smiled at her the same way her father had once smiled at her mother. She led him into the seldom used little room off the kitchen that Elmer had designated the parlor. She had him sit in the most comfortable of the three identical armless chairs. She told him that Peter was asleep upstairs with his wife.

"Ah, could her name be Ellen?" Loomis said.

"Goodness! You knew her, too?"

"Only of her. I knew Peter was taking her home to his Blueberry Hill home. He had lost an arm yes, but now he was getting, in a manner of speaking, two new arms. I'm pleased to learn Peter went ahead and married his nurse. Ellen must be a right fine woman."

"We think so." Aida considered herself an excellent judge of character and, despite her preconceived notions, she had no doubt that this Mr. Loomis was serious about making amends. "I'll wake Peter and bring him down to you."

"If you would be so kind. I thank you kindly, Aida. May I call you Aida?"

Her face lit up for a second but she didn't smile. "Perhaps you shall, Mr. Loomis."

It took a long while for Aida to return with her younger brother. She quickly excused herself and left the parlor to the two Civil War veterans. Peter wore loose trousers but no shoes, and his white shirt was unbuttoned at top and either stained or discolored at waist level. One sleeve was rolled up to the right shoulder, leaving no doubt there was nothing under it. He stood in front of the man who shot him and stared in disbelief as if he might still be dreaming. In fact, as he would later admit to Mortimer Loomis, he had not been asleep but had been trying with the loving help of his wife to make a baby. At the moment, though, he couldn't speak. He had never expected to see the man who shot him ever again, certainly not inside Blue Rock House.

From the kitchen, Aida heard the uninvited guest address Peter in a most unusual fashion. Instead of greeting him with a hearty hello, expressing how wonderful it was to see him again, and inquiring about his health, Mort Loomis threw all seriousness aside and sang out, "Peter, Peter, blueberry eater, where's your wife so I can meet her?"

24
LOOMIS LOOMS LARGE

Mortimer Loomis, who asked everyone to call him Mort, saw himself as a good man and as handsome and distinguished as he was good. He had come to Blue Rock House believing his goodwill would be reciprocated by a friendly "let bygones be bygones" Peter and his beautiful, bountiful spouse. Instead, he was taken aback by Peter's gloom and less than forgiving nature and by Ellen's smallpox scars and fidelity to her uncouth one-armed mate. Through Ellen's scars, Mort saw inner beauty, and besides that he was beguiled by nurses. For his first two weeks at Blue Rock House, he tried to get Peter to accept money from him and Ellen to regret having wed the wrong man. Neither of them had asked him to stay, of course. It was all Aida's doing. She became his third project, which he continued to work on after he had given up on Peter and Ellen, who simply wouldn't allow him to make amends. Aida, on the other hand, seemed to want something more from him. It was nothing she said outright. He sensed it. Besides, he had no desire to return to his family home in Monticello. His family could hardly be considered strange as the Boyds most definitely were, but the Loomis crowd was too prosaic, too God fearing, too hardworking, too rigid, too ready to dismiss a dashing young man with a young man's needs.

Mort admired the way Aida ran the peculiar household and how she couldn't quite hide her sensuality behind her conservative dress and methodical manner. It took him another month and a half to break the ice with her—three times longer than expected. For most of that time he slept in the late Jacob's room and was bothered by snoring and moaning sounds not his own. He didn't believe in ghosts like crazy Mary, so he attributed the noise to a malformed house and unsettling dreams. It was the fall, a largely dormant time for the Boyd family, except for Mary who did most of the household chores while Aida supervised. The others, in the absence of any blueberry picking, went around the house and the grounds by day as if in a trance. At night, Aida retired too early, Elmore usually snored, Chester often talked in his sleep, Blue Boy occasionally walked in his sleep, and Henry let out a cry of pain now and then.

Mort found himself talking to Blue Belle more than Aida or anyone else. She had the qualities of a good nurse all right, but she was blind and far uglier than Ellen or Aida and all she wanted to do was talk about three famous men—Walt Whitman, Henry David Thoreau, and, increasingly, Ralph Waldo Emerson. On Halloween day, Blue Belle recited from memory much of Emerson's essay "Self-Reliance," and when she caught him drifting off, she felt the need to explain what Ralph Waldo was saying. "You see, Mr. Loomis, for a man to truly be a man, he must follow his own conscience and do what he believes is right instead of blindly following society."

Those words of the malformed blind woman or Emerson, whatever, stuck with him. On Halloween night he lured Aida out onto the porch roof to look at the glorious moon, though it was only in its waning crescent phase. He put it to her directly since to that point he had been unable to warm anything but her hands: "I know what you want, Aida, and you know it, too. You wouldn't have wanted me to stay this long otherwise. I have put up with a lot of laziness and craziness in this household. Now, I tell you, I'm fed up with doing nothing. I've suffered enough. Have mercy, woman." He took her in his arms but when he attempted to kiss her, their heads collided. He got the worst of it and had to release her to tend to his sore, frustrated noggin.

"I detect a high degree of self-pity," she said with something close to disgust. "In that regard you are not so different from the male members of my family."

"Impossible. None of them wants to kiss you the way I want to kiss you."

"Each has his own reason for self-pity. Peter, mainly because of something missing, as you very well know; Blue Boy, mainly for the hemorrhoids that limited his war service; Chester, for not possessing his married woman from the other side; Henry, for his illnesses, imagined or otherwise; and Elmer, for always defending a wife that is barely capable of returning his affection and is incapable of giving him a son."

"What about you? You must pity yourself for not having been able to land a husband."

"Not at all. I am certain I could not tolerate one of them. I would detest the ineffectual sort and bump heads with the overbearing sort. No, Mr. Loomis. I have not obtained a husband for good reason."

"Then why in the heck did you want me to stay? I do nothing of consequence around here like everyone else, with the notable exception of crazy Mary, who does everything nobody else wants to do. I can't take another day of this. It's torture. You want me to up and leave for Monticello?"

"Are you trying in your own way to propose to me, Mr. Loomis?"

"What? Marriage? I wouldn't say that. I've gotten nowhere with you. You still call me Mr. Loomis!"

"Is it safe to say that you are as opposed to marriage as I am, Mr. Loomis?"

"I wouldn't say that exactly either. I never suggested marriage to you."

"Thank you. You just want to kiss me."

"I did a minute ago. Okay, I still do. That would be a start."

'Do you want children, Mr. Loomis?"

"No. I mean what kind of question is that? Maybe I will one of these days if I ever get married."

"But not now, correct?"

"Certainly not now. May I kiss you now?"

"Certainly, Mr. Loomis. A woman has her needs, too. Why wait for a full moon."

Mort tilted his head and moved in cautiously with his face but not his arms. When Aida puckered her lips, he made the connection he was longing for, and soon his arms and her arms went into action, hands and feet and torsos, too. They didn't notice when the waning moon went behind shapeless clouds. Upon finally leaving the roof a half hour later, she allowed him to bypass Jacob's old room and enter her room where candles were already lit and the bed displayed fluffed pillows and soft sheets recently washed by Mary Boyd.

What happened behind closed doors that night was never revealed. Aida was tight-lipped when she emerged from the bedroom late the next morning. Mort Loomis did not emerge for three days because of incessant attacks of vomiting. Nobody knew the cause—not even old Doc. Tears, summoned from town on the third day by Aida. She was not embarrassed about bringing a man into her chambers strictly for the purpose of reproduction but that it might lead to death instead was more than a little disturbing. The doctor suggested that vomit was a vehicle by which the internal world of the body was presented to the outside world but otherwise made no diagnosis. He recommended rest and no dried blueberries. Mort's suffering elicited the most sympathy from Blue Belle, who thought he was a delayed casualty of the Civil War. Peter thought the man who had shot him was faking it to receive the full attention of Ellen, the former nurse. Ellen was too much of a caregiver to ignore the sick man entirely but she accused him of "trickery of the stomach." Mary, who cleaned up vomit right and left, stated that the house guest was paying for his past sins. Chester was not helpful when he suggested that Loomis was suffering from morning sickness.

Perhaps the rest did help the patient or more likely it was his hourly sipping of healing water from Handy Spring. By the fourth day he felt well enough to travel the fourteen miles to his parents' home in Monticello. "I know I still haven't made amends," he told his hosts, "but I won't be that far away if you need me, Peter, and I promise to return next summer to help with the blueberry picking, Aida." Peter had trouble forgetting Mort, mainly because he believed Ellen had showed the man too much attention. "If he had been the one to lose an arm, you'd have married him," he told her one night after turning his back on her attempts at intimacy. Aida, though, easily put Mort Loomis out of her mind. She was not pregnant. "There are other fish in the sea," she told Blue Belle. "And far better to hook a buck bass than a vomiting shark." Mort did not return the next blueberry season. He was not missed. Nor the season after that.

No buck bass came along, though, and by the summer of 1868 Aida, now forty-two, put aside the notion of bringing a baby Boyd into the world, not that Ellen and Peter were making any progress in that department. But the future would have to take care of itself. She concentrated on the blueberry business to keep the family going. The only other money coming in was Peter's six dollars a month pension (he was denied the eight dollars for full disability) and the monthly four dollars Chester received as head of a household after losing the services of his late brother Jacob.

Aida also looked for new money-making opportunities, something that came naturally to the Benders but was a foreign concept to the male Boyds from her late father to all five of her brothers. She often went to Wurtsboro to sell the berries herself because she could make better deals with experienced traders like Archibald Seybolt. One of her frequent customers was Nathaniel Bender, who spent much of his time in town trying to establish an artistic fraternity called the Basha Kill School, an alternative to the Hudson River School. "We offer a more intimate take on the American landscape," he explained with unbridled enthusiasm. "Instead of depicting grandiose mountains full of cragged ledges and points, the Basha Kill painters focus on more comforting, smoother hills. We might show a single bird or blueberry bush on a hillside." Eunice Bender and her brothers Jeremiah and Alexander, let alone Daniel Leach and Delilah, wouldn't give her the time of day, but Natty was different. She made a practice of asking him about art to make him comfortable before peppering him with questions about his family. It was more than just curiosity. She believed that to defeat an enemy you must know them.

Delaware & Hudson Canal business was in decline, and Jeremiah Bender, known these days as the "Admiral of the Canal Boat Captains," took it personally. The Erie Railroad was now supplying much of the Pennsylvania coal to the New Jersey docks across from New York City. The railroad not only could move faster but could also do something the D&H Canal could not—make coal deliveries during the winter months. Jeremiah had been smart enough to invest in land and the family companies, Bender Lumbering and the Bender Tannery. He and Alexander were also ready to launch the Bender Bluestone Quarry, which Nathaniel assured Aida would be two miles from Blueberry Hill, though he wasn't so sure the sound of blasting with black powder would not be heard at Blue Rock House.

Aida was confused. The Boyds lived in Blue Rock House but it had nothing to do with the Benders' bluestone. Nathaniel explained that this fine-grained sandstone, which mostly came in blue-gray but in rare instances appeared purplish or even yellow, was considered superior to other sandstones and was used primarily for making sidewalks, curbs and outdoor steps in New York, Kingston and other cities. While the bluestone industry was well established north in Ulster County, he added, his family was intent on making the Bender Bluestone Quarry the place to go in Sullivan County for obtaining this classic natural and durable stone.

"I'll have to tell Elmer," Aida said. "He built Blue Rock House with just rocks lying about and none of them were actually blue. Our rocks exist scattered among the blueberry bushes. We call them fieldstones. On the other hand, maybe it won't do to mention bluestones to my brother. Elmer might want to dig up a bunch of the material and rebuild, replacing Blue Rock House with Bluestone House. He is that crazy about making stone structures."

"You and Elmer are certainly welcome to visit Bender Bluestone Querry once it is established."

"I don't think we could afford to. Fieldstone is for Boyds. Bluestone is for Benders."

On one of Aida's blueberry selling days in August 1868, Nathaniel revealed how Alexander had a better vision than Jeremiah when it came to transportation. Alexander had sold his boat dock yard in Wurtsboro and bought much D&H stock that year after New York state authorized the D&H to construct, own, and maintain railroads. According to Natty, Alexander told Jeremiah: "I'm betting on the future, Jeremy. I'll give you ten-to-one odds for any amount you name that railroads will win out over canals in the long run." Jeremiah's response suggested a rift between the two oldest Bender brothers: "Neither you nor I will live to see the end of canal operations, Alex. The canal is good as gold and most of these track speculators will go broke!"

"I, of course, have no dog in that fight, since the fledging Basha Kill School is dependent on neither the canal nor the rails," Nathaniel told Aida. "But my guess is the railroads will win the day. Another company, the New York & Oswego Midland Railroad, is already pushing forward a line that will cross the canal and have a station one mile east of town."

Aida gave it some thought. Chester had long ago taken a low-paying canal job of some kind but it hadn't worked out, and neither he nor his brothers had ever done so much as work on a railroad. She detested the Benders but sometimes secretly admired their enterprising natures. Suddenly she had a vision—Boyd blueberries traveling by rail to the end of the line, Weehawken, New Jersey, right across from Manhattan, where people would pay plenty for fresh wild blueberries. It wasn't exactly a grand money-making opportunity, but it was something when her family had so little.

"Thanks for the information," Aida said. "You Benders are always terribly busy."

"Oh, yes. Canals, railroads, lumbering, tanning, quarrying, and of course art." Nathaniel winked and opened the large brown folder he had been carrying close to his chest. He pulled out a canvas. "I am back to birds. My latest, *The Flight of the Hummingbird from Blueberry Hill.* Do you think Blue Belle would like to see it? I was thinking of giving it to her as a gift. I owe her."

"Her eyesight hasn't improved, you know. That would take a miracle."

"I realize that, but she appreciates art anyway. It touches her. If I tell her the title, she'll see the hummer and the Hill in all their glory."

"I don't doubt it. She sees spirits and angels and is touched by them. And, I assure you, it is not like Mary Boyd, who only thinks she sees ghosts. Blue Belle isn't crazy. The spirits and angels are really there, but they are invisible to ordinary people. I admit I can't see them. I suppose I must admit to being quite ordinary."

"I don't see that, Miss Boyd. I don't think the rest of my family realizes what a special lady you truly are. You are an excellent woman of no-nonsense business and, what's more, you are decent."

"Thank you, Natty. And you are no ordinary Bender. You are different."

"That I am. I'm having a nice chat with a Boyd."

"Indeed. Visualizing your painting in her mind won't be a problem for my little sister. Climb over the wall and bring it to her sometime."

"Yes, I will, if you think nobody will shoot me."

"We aren't like you Benders. We don't go around firing guns." She recalled how Peter had shot Nathaniel in the seat of his pants with a Colt Walker revolver and how Elmer had shot out those seven windows at the Bend with a Springfield rifle. "Not anymore."

"And nobody will throw rocks at me?"

"Henry hasn't felt up to throwing anything lately. You'd be safe."

"All right. Is there a certain time I should come calling on Blue Belle?"

"It doesn't matter. Any time. She's always there trying to brighten things up. I read things to her and she memorizes everything. She is never sad or lonely, but she will be glad to see you, I'm sure. Nevertheless, Natty, you still have to pay me for that box of blueberries. We Boyds can't afford to be as generous as you."

"Understood." He took out a small purse from under his belt and handed her the necessary coins. "I must say, Miss Boyd, that while we have berries on our side, too, yours always taste ever so much better. I'll never admit that to my sister or brothers, of course."

"Because you are so different."

"Exactly."

Aida patted Nathaniel's soft white hand. For just a second, she imagined him fathering a child—half Bender, half Boyd. It was really unthinkable even if he were somehow interested and capable, but it did cross her mind in passing. When it came to the other Benders, she couldn't imagine touching any of them or one of them touching her with a ten-foot pole or any other product produced by Bender Lumbering.

25
ACCIDENT ON THE PUBLIC ROAD

A dark shadow still hung over the Boyd side of Blueberry Hill seven years after the Civil War. The United States technically wasn't divided anymore but the Hill was more divided than ever. President Grant had invited Robert E. Lee to the White House in 1869, causing Chester Boyd to comment, "I'd sooner invite Jeremiah 'Red Shit' Bender over for a leg of lamb than entertain Marse Robert in Blue Rock House." It pleased the household that the old fighting Rebel died the next year while Grant was going strong as the chief of state and figured to win handily in the upcoming 1872 presidential election. On July 3, 1872, sixty-one-year-old Chester and brother Elmer, a year younger, brought horsehair cushions up onto the porch roof, by then a Boyd tradition, to reflect on their post-war world. The outdoor steps had cracks in them, but Elmer said he would not replace the damaged fieldstones with flatter, sturdier bluestones even if he could find them somewhere other than the Benders' quarry.

"Do you realize it's been nine whole years since Gettysburg," said Chester. "I thought that would be the end of it, but no, Marse Robert had to return to Virginia and go back to killing Yankees."

"And chronic diarrhea killed Jacob. I bet if he had lived, he would have come home and married a local girl and raised a fine crop of Boyds by now. Aida always said Jacob was handsomer than the rest of us."

"His ears stuck out. But I tell you, Jacob and anybody couldn't have done any worse than Peter and Ellen. Not that I have anything against Ellen. She's a dear. I reckon they just weren't meant to give us nephews and nieces, Elm."

"I suppose you're thinking the same about Mary and me?"

"Naw. I gave up on you two long ago, on Blue Boy, too. As far as I know, he has misfired with two tavern maids and has never considered marriage. I believe he is infatuated with Nathaniel Bender. Blue Boy has never painted as much as a door in his life but he has been accepted into Natty's Basha Kill School."

"Now there's an unsavory and unproductive match for you—Blue Boy and Natty, man and man, if you will."

"Not to mention Boyd and Bender."

"Perhaps in name only. What about you, Chesty? You've been remarkably unproductive with the opposite sex and of course nonreproductive. Have you ever thought about a mate—I mean besides the long-married Anna Bender, who is too old to do any good?"

"I haven't considered Natty Bender, if that's what you mean. When has a single woman, young or old, ever ventured onto our side of the Hill? Aida and Blue Belle don't count."

"I should think not. I hate to say it, and I don't mean to sound unkind, but what man would want either of our sisters? Aida is too overbearing and Blue Belle is too, you know, unusual."

"Walt Whitman might have wanted Blue Belle at one time, but he was too old for her and not exactly the marrying kind. But what about that Mortimer Loomis who stayed here too long five or six years ago? There was something going on between him and Aida."

"Don't like to think about that. We all want a Boyd boy on the Hill to carry on our blueberry traditions and such. But who would want a Loomis boy?"

"We better change the subject, Elm. All this kind of loose talk has got me longing for Anna again."

"For land's sake, Chesty. Your fascination for that Bender woman has turned you into a raving maniac!"

"Says the man who married crazy Mary, if you'll pardon the adjective."

Elmer glared at Chester, but Chester only looked to the stars. He made out the bowl of the Big Dipper, which he imagined was emptying celestial water (not quite as good as Handy Spring water) onto the Bender side of the stone wall called Jackson. Then he recalled how his father's Lenni Lenape friend, Man, had described the four bright stars in the bowl as a bear and the stars in the handle as the hunters chasing it. He figured that was the way Jeremiah Bender, Alexander Bender, Daniel Leach, Eunice Bender Leach and maybe even Anna saw the Big Dipper, if they ever bothered to notice it.

"You can be a real bastard at times, you know?" said Elmer, half raising himself off his cushion but going no farther. It occurred to him that he and his older brother had disagreed about plenty of things through the years but had never struck one another.

"I know, I know. Just ask Jeremiah Bender. But sit tight, brother. It's too nice a night to argue. We Boyds have our own minds, but we need to stick together. Am I right?"

"That's what Henrietta used to tell us boys, and what Aida tells us men now. What else do you have on your mind, Chesty, besides sex, I mean?"

"Me? Nothing. I thrive on mindless nothingness. Just look at the stars. They'll tell you all you need to know about the insignificance of us human beings and all our deep thoughts while we occupy this minor planet Earth for a short while."

Elmer closed his eyes and made an effort not to think. It was impossible. He always had something on his mind whether it be his commitment to Mary, his hatred for the Benders, his association with blueberries, or his undeniable love for putting stones on top of other stones. "The blasted blasting ruined my nap today," he finally said, yawning for emphasis. "I was proud to build this stone house beyond anyone's expectations and to put our monumental family cairn on a better foundation, but between that despicable dividing wall on top of the Hill and that contemptable bluestone quarry too close for comfort, I suffer daily and have come to detest rocks in all shapes and sizes...well, almost."

"You hate Bender rocks, not our rocks. Like Aida says, business is business."

"Our only business is blueberries."

"True. What a difference. That big Bender business—cutting down trees, quarrying that bluestone rock—devastates the land and allows their family to grow richer. We celebrate the land and can barely keep our heads above water. At least our blueberries keep growing. We haven't had a bad picking season since Handy died. He must have told the blueberry guardian spirits to quit laying down on the job."

"Blueberries never made anyone rich, and that won't change just because trains have started transporting boxes of Boyd berries to the hungry hordes in Gotham."

"Money isn't everything, Elm. Isn't that what we Boyds have always believed? We are rich in berries, and our invigorating spring water is invaluable; it keeps us alive."

"You have something there. Drinking the curative waters of Handy Spring three times a day all these years has left me feeling half my age."

"Drinking applejack and blueberry wine has the same effect on me."

"Oh, I know you don't mean that. We all know Handy Spring water is the best. Last week, my Mary immersed herself in it to baptize herself."

"Are you sure she wasn't trying to drown herself?"

"I'm sure. I don't believe she is suicidal anymore...well, not too much. She works harder than anyone else around here and has gotten over calling herself a Boyd slave."

"If I had to work as hard as she does, I'd want to do myself in. We may be poor but none of us are going to starve and we definitely won't be working ourselves to death."

"We'll always have this great stone house, if I don't say so myself, and

I'll have you know I aim to put new clay tiles on this roof as soon as I can get my hands on some."

"Thanks. It's still a little hard. We need these cushions."

"Blame it on our old bony asses. Once the new tiles are in place the rain won't be getting inside anymore. Mary has gotten plum tired of cleaning up the puddles on the bedroom floor. Don't say I don't work, Chesty. I do things. If not for me we wouldn't even have a decent place to hang our hats. Remember that God-awful dugout."

Chester patted his brother once on the back, which was all the energy he wanted to expend. "You do good work, Elm, far more than me. I'm no handyman, only handy at picking blueberries. At least I haven't run away from the Hill in years. I've been numbing the old brain so I hardly mind anymore picking my fingers to the bone under Aida's whip."

"Not getting any thoughts about independence again, are you, Chesty?"

"Of course not. I'm too old for that. Too mature, I should say."

"Right. At over sixty. But tomorrow is the Fourth of July and we'll all be headed down to the valley for Wurtsboro's biggest celebration since the canal opened. I thought you might be getting ideas."

"Me? Hell, no. That takes too much damned work. Mindless nothingness, remember? That's all I need to get by."

They said nothing more. In silence they walked carefully down the cracked steps and dragged their feet getting inside the house that needed a new roof. They found Aida and Blue Belle finishing up their preparations for the Independence Day celebration but said nothing to their sisters either.

§

Like everyone else in Blue Rock House, Chester and Elmer arose early and dressed in various degrees of red, white, and blue—mostly blue. Two years earlier Congress had passed a law that made Independence Day an unpaid holiday for federal employees, and now on July 4, 1872, every worker and non-worker in and around Wurtsboro was set to celebrate. With a newfound spring in his step, Elmer led the Boyd procession to the valley, which made him feel as if he were in charge. Mary followed close behind; they were connected by a short rope tied to their waists. It was a precautionary measure because Mary's tendency to wander off was stronger than ever and Elmer suspected she might bolt when surrounded by all those strangers in town. Her behavior had become more unstable. Because of her inclination to spill her own blood when the mood struck her, the family knives, axes, and scissors had to be kept out of her reach. Several days after her full-emersion baptism in Handy Spring she had set a blueberry bush on fire trying to re-create the burning bush seen by Moses in the Book of Exodus. Luckily, Blue Boy had doused the flames with a bucket of Handy Spring water, but clearly Mary could no longer be left alone for long on the Hill or anywhere else.

Aida, who was actually in charge, and Blue Belle both were riding to town in the blueberry cart with Henry and Blue Boy doing the pulling and pushing. The family was still reluctant to take the plunge and purchase a horse and wagon. Peter and Ellen, sometimes hand in hand or hip to hip thanks to Ellen's diligence, were next in line. Chester, who as the oldest family member might be expected to lead the procession, was happy to bring up the rear and, though on foot, pretend he was riding drag on a cattle drive taking Texas longhorns to the railhead head in Wichita, Kansas. The Wild West was much in his daydreams lately even though he was sixty-one, didn't ride horses, didn't shoot guns, and had never drunk redeye in a rowdy shoot-'em-up saloon. Maybe, like Elmer had suggested, he really was thinking about going off on his own again. Anyway, he wasn't mindless. Still, the West was far away, even if the transcontinental railroad could take you there in record time. "I'm just restless," he muttered to himself. Being last allowed for more freedom to stumble, mutter, spit, and fart. Then, just like that, he saw himself *not* on a cattle trail north but westbound on the Oregon Trail. He was an emigrant, not a cowboy, driving the covered wagon, and he was not alone. Sitting really close next to him in her floral calico dress and blue sunbonnet and with her appreciative eyes wide open was a fine-looking widow woman with long auburn hair, Anna Bender.

Chester's dreamy mood was broken when they were on the public road and he heard singing. It was no cowboy or emigrant song. The voices were young and old and loud:

> *Out of the way*
> *All you women and men*
> *For we are the people*
> *From the great Bend.*
> *Hurry, hurry, hurry*
> *Scurry, scurry, scurry*
> *Or you'll be crushed*
> *In our Bender fury.*

Chester looked over his shoulder and saw coming up the road at good speed an actual wagon decked out with red, white, and blue bunting that featured stars and stripes. He stepped to the side as the patriotic wagon sped past, pulled by two white horses, each with an American flag draped on its rump. Jeremiah, the Bender in charge, was the singing driver, and Daniel Leach, the stern-faced Georgian, rode shotgun, almost literally. He had a .44-caliber Henry repeating rifle on his lap instead of a twelve-gauge. The wagon was loaded with picnic supplies, not gold, but, in any case, no desperate road agent would have had an easy time of it. "Stand aside, peasant," called out Jeremiah, but he didn't slow down and immediately went back to singing.

A second two-horse wagon followed, with Alexander Bender driving as if it were imperative to keep close behind his older brother. He appeared unable to sing and drive at the same time. Next to him was a woman who wasn't his wife. She was much too young and demure. She turned her head slightly toward Chester and moved her hand in his direction without actually pointing at him. "Yes, Georgia," said Alexander, "that's one of the bumpkins, the fornicator, my brother's nemesis." The young woman blushed. In the wagon bed was an animated young man and a growling dog. Chester identified the dog as Dred, the coonhound who knew all too well the scent of a Boyd. "Hi, neighbor, I'm James Bender," called out the young man, waving wildly. "I finally get a look at the Boyd we're all supposed to avoid. I thought you'd be much bigger and have horns and a tail."

A third wagon, this one pulled by one plump chestnut horse, passed a minute later. James Bender's brother, Cal, was the driver. He was the oldest of Alexander and Delilah's three children and had already grown a bushy beard to hide his skinny neck. He never took his eyes off the road, but the woman beside him shook her fist at Chester. She wore a black veil and black dress as if she were going to a funeral, but her wide-brimmed white hat was decorated with red ribbons and roses as if she wanted to be belle of a ball, too. Although her face was hidden, Chester had no doubt that this was Delilah, who he suspected was the greatest advocate of the Lost Cause north of the Mason-Dixon Line and was more of a Boyd hater than her husband. Perhaps she was celebrating Independence Day reluctantly; the South hadn't gotten its independence. In the wagon bed wearing a dress more pink than red and a blue flower in her hair was Berri, the seventeen-year-old daughter of Daniel Leach and Eunice Bender Leach. She was playfully scolding her uncles Maurice and Robert, who were passing a jug back and forth and still singing that rude Bender road song. Chester couldn't help but glance at the sweet-looking Berri, but he made a point of showing no interest in the antics of the two sons of Jeremiah and Anna. *Damn her for ever giving birth to those two,* he thought or said; he wasn't sure which.

That was the end of the wagons, but lagging far behind was a black carriage with two rows of seating and a tasseled red roof. When the carriage finally reached Chester, it slowed noticeably but didn't stop. Chester didn't break stride but he found himself drawing closer to the vehicle as if pulled by a magnet. Sitting alone up front was the driver, Nathaniel Bender, who never had reason to use the whip on the lone horse. In back Eunice Bender Leach wore a sleek silver dress to match her silver hair that flowed over one shoulder. She carried in her left hand a small American flag, which Chester first thought might be a Confederate flag, and held on her lap a shield with the word "LIBERTY" printed on it. Chester was slightly acquainted with the "Seated Liberty" silver dollar, and Eunice could have served as the model for it. The effect so stunned Chester that he didn't initially take notice of the plainly dressed womanly figure sitting on the far side of Eunice until the woman leaned across the Liberty shield and waved at him. When he observed that her hair was mostly auburn, he began to tingle all over, and when the breeze made that hair flutter, he gasped. Of course, she would be there with the Bender procession, but it was as if he were seeing her for the first time, a female cardinal amid a committee of vultures.

"Anna," he called out, like a beggar pleading to a rich woman. "Where you going?"

Chester didn't have time to reflect on how stupid his question was because the nervous horse became unmanageable when it possibly heard or saw a rattlesnake. Or it could have been that Nathaniel was as little skilled at controlling a horse as any Boyd. In any case, the horse swerved suddenly, right into Chester's path, knocking him down with its hind quarters before one of the carriage wheels passed inches from his head. He made an agonizing roll into a roadside ditch that was only partially dry. Nathaniel either jumped or was pitched from his seat when the horse decided to leap into the same ditch. The carriage followed of course but somehow didn't tip over or spill out its two female passengers. The horse tore loose from the carriage and found its way back to the road where it ran so fast it not only passed the rest of the Boyds but also two of the three Bender wagons. The lead wagon, driven by Jeremiah, never stopped until it had entered Wurtsboro and pulled up on the crowded street in front of the Fulton & Holmes General Store.

The carriage horse had suffered only a slight scratch on the front leg that didn't slow it down. Eunice and Anna bumped heads when the out-of-control vehicle landed in the ditch but only showed minor bruises and never lost consciousness. The women staggered out of the carriage on their own power. Eunice remained surprisingly calm, only saying that she wished her husband Daniel had elected to drive her instead of choosing to ride up front with Jeremiah. Anna admitted she was scared out of her wits. Driver Nathaniel was rendered unconscious when he landed on his head twelve feet from the ditch. Chester was badly bruised about the face and hands, had a deep cut on the right knee, suffered a dislocated shoulder, and his clothes were torn and covered with mud.

Nathaniel was transported to Doc Tears' office in one of the two wagons that returned to the scene of the accident. The carriage was damaged but still operational after an uncoordinated group effort by various Bender and Boyd men finally extricated it from the ditch. Cal and James Bender unharnessed one of the horses from the second wagon and hitched it to the buggy. Since her husband hadn't returned, Eunice lay down her flag and Liberty shield and insisted on driving the carriage the rest of the way to town. She didn't trust anyone to do the job as well as she could. Anna's husband hadn't returned either and Anna was no longer shaking, so she agreed to climb back into the carriage.

Meanwhile, Chester was trying to walk on, but the cut on his knee hurt so much that he sat down on the edge of the ditch. Ellen was so busy keeping Peter's spirits up that she didn't realize Chester was injured. But Blue Belle located her big brother and tended to his cuts and bruises with a clean cloth and ditch water. Elmer, with Mary still attached to him by rope, and Henry both accused the Benders of intentionally running Chester over and were almost fighting mad. Blue Boy saw things differently, pointing out that Nathaniel would never do anything so vicious, so it must have truly been an accident. Delilah Bender accused Chester of being too drunk to walk in a straight line though he hadn't had a single sip of applejack yet, but she was soon gone in the wagons with most of the other Benders, none of whom was in a fighting mood on the Fourth of July. Aida had to step in and break up the argument Blue Boy was having with Elmer and Henry, but while doing so Mary tried to scratch Aida's eyes out. It was another crazy act by Elmer's wife, but Elmer was proud of her anyway for standing up for him. Nothing more was said about it and the Boyd group resumed its march down the road to town. Chester was forgotten, but Aida realized Blue Belle was missing from the blueberry cart, and they had to go back for her.

They found Blue Belle still tending to Chester's wounds, but now Anna Bender was helping, wiping the blood off her onetime lover's knee. Anna had asked Eunice not to drive off just yet, telling her sister-in law, "We have never been so cold-hearted as to leave a wounded beast on the side of the road, and, though he may be a Boyd, he is still a human being." Eunice not only had obliged but also had popped Chester's dislocated shoulder into place with a satisfying grunt. The Boyd party resumed its journey, and, for several minutes, Eunice stared at the ditch shaking her head trying to make sense of the accident. It was a hell of a beginning for a Fourth of July celebration. When Eunice finally did get back into the carriage to drive on, Anna was waiting for her on the front seat, while in the back seat Blue Belle continued her nursing of Chester.

26
THE FOURTH OF JULY CELEBRATION

By the time Elmer led his slow-moving group into Wurtsboro, the large Bender contingent had already spread out their meat and potatoes, Saratoga chips, and teacakes on tables set up adjacent to the towpath, which was lined with streamers, flags, and balloons. Missing were Nathaniel Bender, who was conscious but still woozy in Doc Tears' office, and Blue Belle, who was at his bedside reciting from memory lines from Walt Whitman's poem "The Wound-Dresser": *Bearing the bandages, water and sponge,/Straight and swift to my wounded I go,/Where they lie on the ground after the battle brought in,/Where their priceless blood reddens the grass, the ground.*

"You don't need to do this, sweet girl," said Nathaniel. "After all I wasn't in a battle, I was never a soldier, I'm lying on a comfortable bed instead of the grass or ground, I'm not bleeding, and my artist blood is hardly considered priceless."

"The hurt and wounded I pacify with soothing hand," said Blue Belle.

"Are you still quoting Whitman?"

"Yes, but maybe you'd rather hear something more fitting on this day. In his "I Hear America Singing," Walt celebrates the varied carols he hears from a variety of people, including the carpenter, the mason, the boatman, the woodcutter, the mother, the girl who sews and washes."

"What about from the artist, particularly ones belonging to the Basha Kill School?" Nathaniel laughed so hard it made his head hurt. But he kept laughing anyway, holding his head at the same time that Blue Belle caressed his brow.

Right on cue Blue Boy walked in; he being the only other confirmed member of the Basha Kill School. "Glad to see you wide awake, Natty," he said. "How you feeling?"

"Like I shouldn't get out of bed. How is Chester?"

"Looks a little beat up, but he's fine. Drinking like a fish."

"How's he taking it.? I hope he understands that I didn't mean to run into him with the carriage. I had trouble controlling that horse. Jeremiah named him Devil because he's a chestnut, but the name fits his disposition, too. He's plain mean. Tell Chester how sorry I am."

"Chester knows how sorry you are. That doesn't sound right. You know what I mean. I'm just sorry you can't be out there celebrating the holiday with the rest of us. The festivities have started."

"Tell me about it, Blue Boy. Have you seen my family?"

"Couldn't miss them if I tried. The boatmen are the most celebrated ones today. You should see all the colorful canal boats, rafts, and floats. Nobody has attracted as much attention as your sister Eunice, Miss Liberty herself, who is positioned at the bow of your brother Jeremiah's *Annabelle III.* They are bound to win the top prize for most patriotic waterborne vessel. Jeremiah has been singing the praises of the canal with abandon. Too bad Walt Whitman isn't there to hear him!"

"So nice of you to drop by, Blue Boy," Nathaniel said, trying to sit up in bed. "Funny that two of you Boyds are with me but no member of my own family. For that matter Doc Tears has left me to my own devices. He was eager to get at the free patriotic punch."

"Can't stay long. Better show you where we're all sitting, Blue Belle. The family's been asking about you. And you don't want to miss seeing all the floats and decorated boats."

Blue Belle smiled. Sometimes members of her own family forgot that she was blind. She could already picture the colorful vessels parading down the canal. "Whatever you say, brother."

"When you smile like that, I want to paint you again," said Nathaniel. "You're beautiful."

"You are clearly still foggy from the accident, Natty. But your lie is so sweet."

Blue Boy and Blue Belle said their goodbyes to Nathaniel, promising to check on him again later. They located the rest of the Boyd family, all watching the canal parade from in front of the Seaside Supply Store. Chester, who had felt well enough to walk away from the doctor's office without receiving any treatment from "the old quack," was feeling a little too free from all the free patriotic punch and straight applejack he was consuming. He was yelling insults at Jeremiah and Miss Liberty. Both were proudly waving to the crowd, Jeremiah from the bow and Eunice while posing next to the twenty-foot flagpole on the deck of the spanking new ninety-foot *Annabelle III.* Even the two mules pulling the canal boat were decked out in red, white, and blue blankets. The two towboys wore brown.

The actual Anna, who had showed such tenderness toward Chester in the carriage, was not aboard because, upon arriving in town, she had quarreled with Jeremiah. It was all because the wounded Boyd had showed up in the same vehicle as the boatman's wife. Anna was now seated with the rest of the Bender contingent on the lawn of Harding House, across the Newburgh-Cochecton Turnpike from the Seaside Supply Store. Her eyes were closed and her arms crossed, as if pouting was her only alternative to being totally miserable. Her twin sons, still able to stand despite their constant quaffing, acted as guards, not that they believed their mother would go running to Chester. But Jeremiah had convinced them that Chester Boyd was dangerous and capable of most any uncivilized act especially when he was three sheets to the wind.

"You sure you got the right flag up!" Chester called out, his latest bit of mockery. "I heard you Benders and Leaches favor one with fifteen white stars representing the slave-holding states."

Jeremiah definitely heard, but he only flinched and kept waving to the crowd. Miss Liberty kept smiling as she braced herself against the flagpole.

Chester offered a mock Rebel yell. "May you sink like the so-called Confederacy!"

"Hey, Muttonhead," yelled a stranger who was also imbibing on land and had his blurry eyes on Chester. "Where you been? The war's been over for seven years. Ain't you heard of Reconstruction? We're all united again."

"Not all of us. That Reconstruction business is all down South. Up here there's only *destructive construction* from the likes of the evil people of the Bend."

"What bend, mister? You got something against *our canal*?"

"Nope. Only against some of your diehard canal men."

"You must be a railroader. Either that or your mind is bent!"

"Bender brains are bent. Boyd brains are void."

"What are you, mister?"

"*Berry* much a Boyd and that ain't much." Chester broke into a fit of laughter and spilled his precious drink, which was intensifying his self-deprecating tendencies as much as it loosened his tongue.

The stranger had no sense of humor. And he was loud. He claimed to have helped build and expand the canal and that anyone who didn't appreciate and support the canal was unpatriotic. "You must be the real no-account rebel around here, Muttonhead," he added. "You think different? Fine. You get your ass over here and say different and we'll settle the matter man to man. It's the bloody Fourth of July, by God! Time for all of us, North and South, to stand up for the United States of America."

Chester's wounded right knee was acting up and, in any case, he felt shaky and wasn't about to get into a fight with anyone. He didn't mind being called a rebel, as long as it wasn't a Southern Rebel. And being called a *muttonhead* didn't sound too bad. He wasn't acquainted with any sheep but he had nothing against them and had never eaten one. Besides, when Jeremiah had caught him in the same carriage as Anna that morning, the boatman had called him things considerably worse—an *asshead*, an *abominable libertine*, and an *outworn anomaly*.

"Nothing against you, patriot," Chester called out cheerfully to his loud challenger. "You can drink and bathe and piss in the canal for all I care. It's only Jeremiah Bender, the onetime butcher and now Admiral of the Canal Boat Captains, who I wish to see drown in it."

That ended their conversation, because *Annabelle III* had moved on, and three large mules had pulled an impressive barge-cum-float in front of them. Brought down from Masten Pond, which fed water to the canal, the float carried clay replicas of the Colosseum, the Pantheon, and the Circus Maximus in honor of Wurtsboro's original name, Rome. The mules looked silly in their red-white-and-blue hats, but the cheering drowned out any laughter when the crowd noticed a sign on one of the mules that read, "BE A CANAL DEFENDER. SUPPORT EDSALL, LORD & BENDER." Henry Edsall was supervisor of the Town of Mamakating in which Wurtsboro was the most important village, Jacob Lord was supervisor of the "ponds" (actually reservoirs) that brought water down to the D&H Canal, and Jeremiah Bender represented the dozen experienced so-called captains who made Wurtsboro their home port.

"Who can compete with that monstrosity," Chester said to nobody in particular. "One or the other of Jeremiah's vessels is bound to win top prize and the other one will take second. The whole thing is rigged."

"It sickens me," said Peter who was lying on a blanket with his head in the lap of Ellen. She was quietly singing the sea shanty "Blow the Man Down."

Undaunted by the ostentatious display by Jeremiah and friends, Elmer insisted that the Boyd family would still be represented in the boat parade. He undid the rope that kept him attached to his wife and handed the loose end to Aida. Mary clapped her hands and danced what was more or less a jig as Irish fiddlers passed slowly by. "Free!" she screamed, but when she attempted to dance away from her family, Aida tugged on the rope and brought the wandering wife all the way to her knees.

"You stay with Aida," Elmer told his wife. "Need to find our boat. Keep your eyes on the canal and we'll wave to you. Come along Blue Belle. You, too, Henry. Today you work."

"But it's a holiday," said Henry, "and I ate some bad potato salad that must have been out in the sun too long."

"You can't worm your way out of this, brother. Peter is preoccupied, Blue Boy seems to have gone off somewhere, and Chester is still recovering or degenerating, whatever. You've been elected."

The Boyds did not own a boat, but Elmer had talked a canal night watchman into lending him a rowboat. The rowboat was brown and the owner said it could not be painted or otherwise marred. That didn't matter because Elmer was doing this for the blind Blue Belle, who wore a straw hat with a small paper American flag pinned to it and carried a red, white, and blue basket full of blueberries, mostly blue ones but a few were still pink. The night watchmen helped Elmer lower the rowboat into the canal, and they both helped Blue Belle onto the small bow seat. Elmer removed the oars and left them behind with the amused watchman. After taking his position on the middle seat between the empty oarlocks, Elmer tossed the line to Henry on the towpath. Since the Boyds didn't own a genuine mule, what Henry had been elected to do was pull the rowboat as a human mule.

"Okay, pull, Henry, pull," shouted Elmer.

Henry yanked the line as if he were in a tug of war with his brother.

"Not so hard, Henry!'

Once the rowboat was moving almost smoothly up the canal, Elmer told Blue Belle it was time to do her part. She stood up in front, showing excellent balance, and began tossing blueberries toward the crowd on shore. A dozen children scampered to the edge of the canal and held out their hands as if expecting lemon drops and peppermint sticks. The few blueberries that reached shore led to moans of disappointment. Blue Belle's tiny right arm wasn't strong, and she was throwing against a powerful wind that had just kicked up. Most of the Boyd berries plopped into the canal water like summer hail. Then the wind knocked Blue Belle down onto her seat, and she gave up the throwing. The rowboat banged against the side of the canal once, twice, and the third time was the hardest. Henry felt as if his hands had blistered and he let go of the line; this was a job for the healthy Blue Boy, not him. Mary suddenly appeared, indeed free, running the wrong way on the towpath. If she noticed her husband and Blue Belle in the boat, she didn't acknowledge them. "The sky is falling, the sky is falling," she screamed and kept running. "It is the end of the world!" was the last thing Elmer heard from his wife before he decided he better abandon ship and run her down. It was left to Henry to pull Blue Belle out of the rowboat, and to the night watchman to recover his boat.

How had Mary gotten loose? Elmer didn't get the story from Mary when he caught up with her trying to steal a bread knife from some picnickers, but later Blue Boy had the unpleasant task of trying to explain to his married brother what had happened.

It turned out that one of the Irish fiddlers was a non-Irishman who really didn't play any instrument—Mortimer Loomis. He had joined the musical group to more easily work his way through the crowd. He was specifically looking for the Boyd family to tell them he was now an important railroad man and had it in his power to give a free railroad pass not only to Aida but also to

Peter, the man he accidentally shot, and Ellen, the woman he wanted most. He had not forgotten his vow to make amends.

Mortimer had broken away from the real musicians as soon as he spotted Aida pulling on a rope to keep Mary seated. She asked him to help her control the restless wife of Elmer. Mortimer obliged. Peter and Ellen at this point were lying on their sides facing each other, gnawing on slices of watermelon and spitting seeds at each other. Peter was actually grinning, something Mortimer had never seen before, and Ellen was giggling too hard to even say hello. Mort found no opening to deliver his news about becoming something of a big shot with the New York & Oswego Midland Railroad. He redirected his attention back to Aida, telling her that Peter and Ellen were behaving like undisciplined children. She agreed and remarked how wonderful it would be if there were actual bona fide Boyd children around next year to celebrate the birth of the nation. One thing led to another. Blue Boy had found a seat on the ground next to Chester and was patiently waiting for the Boyd rowboat to join the canal parade. Before he knew it, Aida had handed Mary off to him and walked away with Mr. Loomis. Blue Boy told Elmer he had only let go of Mary's rope for a second to tie the shoe of the inebriated Chester when she took off "like a bat out of hell."

And so it was that Aida was missing and Mary was again joined by rope to her husband when the parade of water vessels ended. It was no surprise that Jeremiah's dressed-up *Annabelle III* won the token prize money for "Best in Show," barely beating out *Tribute to Rome*. Either way, the Admiral of the Canal Boat Captains couldn't lose. The railroads were forgotten. At least for a day, the canallers and canal lovers could believe they still ruled.

A speech followed. Town of Mamakating Supervisor Henry Edsall stepped up to the outdoor podium and proclaimed that Independence Day was already the most important secular holiday on the Sullivan County calendar. He belittled the kings of England beginning with George III and invited Queen Victoria to visit the United States, specifically Wurtsboro. Next, he called to the podium Eunice Bender Leach in the guise of Miss Liberty. He placed a bejeweled crown on her head and had her hold a stuffed bald eagle as the crowd roared. Miss Liberty curtseyed to husband Daniel Leach and many other admiring men in the crowd. The happy couple then coaxed their unpretentiously beautiful daughter Berri to join them up front, which caused several intoxicated men to hoot and most everyone to gawk. "Why ain't she Miss Liberty!" called out one reckless celebrator. "She beats the other one hands down. What I'd give to take liberties with this one!" Another unsteady stranger, who was more than just mouth, laid a hand on Berri, seemingly trying to remove the blue flower from her hair. For his trouble, he received a sock in the jaw from Leach. The crowd seemed to approve, though several ladies gasped and one lady fainted.

A ten-piece band, not the Irish fiddlers, began to play. Supervisor Edsall asked everyone to sing "America," the words of which he said were written by Samuel Francis Smith for a July 4, 1831, celebration in Boston. Scattered boos greeted his mention of "Boston" but soon the New Yorkers were singing en masse. Chester claimed he could hear Jeremiah's voice rise above all others and could see Anna next to him mouthing only some of the words while wincing. Of course, it could have been only his alcohol-fueled imagination. Nobody saw Delilah Bender, who already stood out because she was the only woman in a black dress, make any attempt to sing. The unrepentant Southern belle made a point of buttoning her lip and scowling when she heard daughter Georgia's sweet voice. Sons James and Cal weren't singing either despite nudges from their father, Alexander, but perhaps they did not know the words.

"Nobody go off now, you hear," said Supervisor Edsall when the singing was done. "I haven't forgotten the fireworks, but we'll have to wait until dark for what I promise will be a brilliant display of color in the sky, reflected in all its glory in the canal waters below. In the meantime, and I know many of you are looking forward to this treat because it has become a local tradition since the War of the Rebellion, we have an event that when it comes to sheer noise puts any fireworks display to shame. Yes, ladies and gents, boys and girls, patriots one and all, I'm talking about the Wurtsboro Firing of the Anvil."

The crowd was receptive, cheering and clapping and jokingly covering their ears. The supervisor quickly introduced the trio selected to fire this year's anvil—David Gumaer, the son of the stagecoach proprietor, and Maurice and Robert Bender, the enterprising twin sons of the highly successful canaller and businessman Jeremiah Bender and his lovely wife, Anna. "Stand back unless you like hot feet," shouted Supervisor Edsall, "The powerful explosion you are about to hear will knock your socks off." A space was cleared, and special items were brought in for this unique local event. The supervisor explained what was involved for any newcomers: An iron band of a wagon hub was placed on an anvil, packed with gunpowder, and topped off with another anvil before the powder was ignited. "It's more than a big noise," he added. "It's a heartfelt salute from all of us to our country, our state, our town, our canal, our forefathers, our fathers, and our mothers too, and let's not forget Miss Liberty who has delighted us with her charming presence."

The chosen trio worked diligently, though all three had been steadily drinking. Maurice and Robert Bender packed more powder on the iron band than David Gumaer wanted and far more than would have been deemed safe by anyone who had fired the anvil in the past. The excessive charge created an explosion that tore the iron band to pieces and caused Mary Boyd to cry out, "I knew it—the end of the world!" One four-pound piece struck Gumaer in the breast, passed clear through him and out the other side; the gaping wound was four inches wide. The death of the young man, according to one newspaper account, "cast a gloom over the whole neighborhood, and what was a scene of celebration was in an instant changed to one of profound mourning."

Overlooked by many witnesses to the tragedy, but not by the Bender family, was the fact that smaller pieces of the iron band struck two members of the Boyd family. Henry suffered a severe cut in his thigh and was knocked to the ground. Peter, who had flattened out on the ground as soon as he heard the explosion, received a series of cuts on his back, as if it had been scraped by a razor. Ellen, who had been standing by Peter as usual but escaped unscathed, tended to her husband and Henry until old Doc Tears arrived on the scene. He was slightly sloshed but was able to keep his pen hand steady enough to complete a death report on David Gumaer. Under mild questioning from the local authorities, Maurice pointed out that the dead man had been in charge and that brother Robert and himself had simply been following orders. Robert reminded everyone that David Gumaer had a reputation for carelessness, well-earned from his many near crashes while driving his father's stagecoach. Jeremiah and other Benders expressed sympathy for young Gumaer, but also noted the lad was done in by his own rashness. They also contended that the injured Henry and Peter had ignored numerous warnings and had stood too close to the firing of the anvil. In the end, nobody blamed the Bender twins except the Boyds.

After much discussion, the powers that be decided that despite the unfortunate death of Gumaer, the fireworks display would go on as scheduled. "He would have wanted it that way," said Supervisor Edsall. "David wasn't old enough to serve his country in the War of the Rebellion, but he has now made the ultimate sacrifice for freedom as many have done before him." The Boyd family was debating whether to stay for the fireworks display or make the long journey back to Blue Rock House before dark when Blue Belle called attention to the fact that Aida wasn't present. Blue Boy had been the last to see her; she had walked off with Mortimer Loomis and left her brother in charge of Mary, who was now acting as if she were the last living person on Earth.

"Loomis!" shouted Peter while Ellen was still applying a wet cloth to his scraped back. "I thought we'd seen the last of that son of a bitch."

It turned out they had—at least none of them saw Mort Loomis alive again. A desperate search through the crowd didn't give the Boyds a clue about Aida's disappearance, but she showed up on her own at dusk. She kept dabbing her eyes with a handkerchief, although no tears were visible at that point. She led Chester and Blue Boy, along with the sheriff and his deputy, to the New York & Oswego Midland Railroad station where Mort's body was found stretched out on the platform. He wasn't bleeding and there was no sign of foul play. A train certainly hadn't come down the tracks and smashed him to bits. In fact, he had a partial grin on his face and looked as if he would rise off the platform if somebody gave his shoulder the slightest shake.

"His heart gave out," Aida said. "Just like that."

"While waiting for a train?" asked the sheriff. "He isn't wearing a shirt."

"No train was due. He worked for the New York & Oswego Midland, you know? He was very proud to be an assistant station master. He wanted to show me *his* station."

"And his heart gave out while he was showing it to you?"

"Actually, he was done showing it to me. We were in an embrace, you might say, when that loud boom came from the canal. It must have shocked him, at least his heart. He stopped moving. He became dead weight on top of me. There's no other way to put it. I had a hard time getting him off me. I mean, it wasn't easy. It shocked me, too."

"The firing of the anvil?"

"Oh, is that what it was? I knew it couldn't be the fireworks yet."

27
FAMILY MATTERS

It seemed like a blessing to Aida when she realized at age forty-five she was with child and that the father didn't have to be dealt with, not that she had anticipated Mortimer Loomis's heart giving out during consensual coitus. She was not without sympathy for the man, even if he had admitted that she was his second choice, since it was Ellen Boyd, smallpox scars and all, who had made his mouth water among other things. Aida was just being practical. It would have been hard convincing Loomis *not* to marry her and to let the baby take the name Boyd instead of Loomis. Mortimer had been a healthy specimen and she fully expected the child to become a strapping boy who would be worth his weight in gold in the blueberry patch.

When she gave birth to a girl in April 1873, she could not hide her disappointment, nor could her brothers, who were as eager as her to see the Boyd blueberry dynasty continue. Within weeks, as the baby demanded breast milk and raised her head to get the lay of the land, Aida saw something she liked and changed her tune. Her maternal instincts flowed to the surface the way Handy Spring water had been doing since at least the time of the Lenni Lenape. She named the child Handa in honor of her late father. She was determined to raise Handa to be self-confident, smart, tough and highly motivated; in short, to be her successor as boss of Blue Rock House just as she herself had been raised to be the successor to Henrietta. Aida figured if she played her mother cards right, Handa would grow into the same kind of woman as her—one who would make sure, one way or another, to keep the Boyd name alive and the family property secure.

Her brothers weren't willing to bet on that possibility. They conspired to create a male heir behind Aida's back. Actually, it was done behind brother Peter's back, too. Although there had been two deaths (Mortimer Loomis and David Gumaer) at the 1872 Fourth of July celebration in Wurtsboro, Peter had snapped out of his blue mood (nothing to do with blueberries) and returned to his lively pre-war nature. That allowed for a return to action in the marital bed. Nevertheless, it became clear in due time that while the effort was extraordinary if not admirable, the results were abysmal. As Henry put it to Chester, Elmer, and Blue Boy, "Poor Pete is shooting nothing but blanks."

It is unclear whose idea it was for Ellen to sacrifice her body and have a baby anyway for the sake of Peter and the entire family. Most likely Elmer put it to her, the idea that is. His Mary was no longer under consideration because she had become, in her own mind, a virgin again and she intended to stay that way. If a virgin birth happened, she would not fight it, but under no other conditions. Elmer accepted this and though he was left out in the cold, he would forever be true to his and Mary's marital vows. "It's fact we need a Boyd boy, but none of you sons of a gun better so much as lay a hand on my wife or you'll have to answer to me," he told his three single brothers. "You know I'll never touch another woman while I'm among the living Boyds. You boys do what you think best, as long as it doesn't have anything to do with Mary or me."

Ellen, not yet forty, wanted no part of the shocking plan at first and resisted adamantly for a number of weeks. But Blue Belle, of all people, talked her into it. "It has to be you because you have a good heart and a complete mind, unlike Mary, to go along with a full-sized body that warrants attention, unlike me. Furthermore, you aren't a *sister.* Only you can make it happen. You are a born nurse; think of the Boyd brothers as patients. Peter must never know about it. Losing the arm was enough for him. He is only just now starting to believe he is not half a man. In saying this, you understand, I'm not suggesting you have no choice in the matter. Of course, you do. It is your body! All I'm saying is if you agree that furthering the Boyd line is important, it must be you, Ellen, who starts the ball rolling."

Beginning in May 1873, Ellen began to submit to her true love's single brothers. Chester, with his 62nd birthday on the horizon and knowing that Anna Bender could never have a child with anyone again, volunteered to give it a shot. When they had their pre-dawn meeting in the blueberry patch, Ellen insisted that Chester wear a blindfold as she couldn't bear to see his penetrating stare or balding head. Chester thought he would benefit also from not being able to see her, but alas he was made nearly miserable thinking how Ellen was a disconsolate nurse and his brother's wife while Anna was an appealing lover and his archenemy's wife. There would be no repeat performance. Next up was Henry, who felt up to the task a couple times. Before the first entanglement, on the floor of the late Jacob Boyd's bedroom, he tried to reassure her by pulling out a worn copy of Dr. George H. Napheys' *The Transmission of Life,* which provided counsels on the nature and hygiene of the masculine functions. Things went reasonably well, but the second time it was rather rough because Peter always seemed to be lurking about. The non-romantic encounter took place in the family's second blueberry cart. Afterward, they both became sick and agreed it was dangerous to risk another uncomfortable tryst.

Blue Boy stepped up to the family cause. Ellen wasn't nearly as intimidating as those bold tavern maids he had known, and he had a certain amount of frustration to overcome. In the back of his mind, though he had not consulted any doctor, he suspected that his dedication to onanistic practices could leave him as blind as Blue Belle. When Peter took the train for the first time since the war to drum up Boyd blueberry business in New York City that June, Blue Boy and Ellen copulated five times in two days. The first time was a bust but the next four were successful because Ellen had Blue Boy operate with one hand tied behind his back so she could pretend that Peter was the man on top of her. In truth, though, the way Blue Boy rode her like a horse was nothing like how her husband tried to do it.

Everything worked out fine. Ellen gave birth on March 15, 1874, to a boy, which pleased the entire household. When Peter saw his newborn son for the first time, he cried out, "Gadzooks!" and named him Gad without consulting Ellen. She didn't mind, though, because she was so relieved the ordeal was over with. When others suggested the name be changed to Chad, Glad or even Vlad, she told them that Peter had every right to name his first son. Handa was about to turn one at the time. She was already putting words together under her mother's guidance and was big-boned, blonde, and bold like the father she had never known. By age two she was as dictatorial as her mother. At age three Handa declared that her cousin Gad had the same, big nose, big eyes and scarce hair as Uncle Chester and was just as sluggish. Blue Boy thought the baby boy had his own strong chin and shoulders but said nothing. Henry mentioned that Gad had the same cough, swollen neck glands, and rashes he did as an infant. Blue Belle said all that mattered was that Gad was normal; he could see and was not shaped like a withered blueberry. Aida might have had her suspicions about what was behind this unexpected Boyd birth, but she didn't want to spoil a good thing and kept silent about something she noticed about Gad—he bore no resemblance whatsoever to Peter.

The Boyds had purchased the second blueberry cart because business was good. Peter was not only a proud father but also a delighted businessman for having made important contacts with fruit sellers in Manhattan. On several occasions, Aida cleaned a cart, bundled inside her girl and Ellen's boy, and took them into Wurtsboro so she could show them off. If the dividing stone wall hadn't been such an obstacle, she might have even carried the pair to the enemy side to show the Benders that Boyds would be on Blueberry Hill for the long haul.

§

Before the 1878 blueberry-picking season was underway, Aida was still showing off five-year-old Handa and four-year-old Gad in town. On the first of June she ran into Eunice and her daughter, Berri, who had arrived in a horse and buggy. Eunice was shopping and twenty-three-year-old Berri, more beautiful than ever, was still looking for a husband who could meet with the approval of her mother and father. Part of the way to town, Handa had helped push the cart, but she had exhausted herself and was now in the cart fighting for space with Gad.

"Five already?" said, Eunice, peering into the cart as if judging fruit. "A belated congratulations, but we are never quite sure what you Boyds are up to on the other side of the Hill. Handa, you say? A most unusual name, but I have to hand it you, Aida, you finally did it. But with whom? The child doesn't look like you. Does she resemble the father? Is his identity a secret? I assume you never married the man or I would have heard about it."

"He wanted to marry me, but unfortunately, he died before Handa was born. His name was Mr. Loomis."

"I see. You called him Mr. Loomis?"

"Of course not. His name was Mort. He was a railroad man."

"I believe you, Aida. What railroad?"

"The New York & Oswego Midland Railroad."

"I see. I never heard the name Loomis connected to it. My brother Alexander wisely sold his stock in that railroad. It went bankrupt after the Panic of eighteen seventy-three hit. A new railroad company will be inheriting the New York & Oswego Midland line in the next couple years and you can bet Alexander will be involved."

"Oh, I didn't know the railroad was failing. Nobody told me."

"Two bad. You sound worried."

"I suppose I am, if you must know. We count on the train to carry our crates of blueberries to reach the big markets in Manhattan and Brooklyn."

"Yes, well, you needn't be alarmed, Miss Boyd—or are you calling yourself Mrs. Boyd these days? Anyway, the new railroad company will still be able to transport your precious berries."

Aida was somewhat reassured but she still frowned. The Queen of the Bend said the word *precious* as if it meant the complete opposite, something *paltry.*

"I'm sure using the railroad is a tremendous step up for you Boyds," continued Eunice. "Your family has always embraced primitive simplicity."

Aida knew that was no compliment. Still, Mrs. Bender-Leach had provided some good information. "We do all right," Aida said. She might have defended her family further but wasn't up to saying more. She believed that manual work was enabling, but other Boyds didn't always agree. Picking blueberries and shipping them off barely kept the collective Boyd head above water. She had always wished her brothers could be more productive. She propped up Handa in the cart, then did the same for Gad, trying to redirect the conversation back to the children. Her daughter and Ellen's son could both walk on their own just fine but neither was ready to show off that skill. Aida wondered if Eunice would think they were slow-witted or lazy.

"He's as cute as a bug's ear," said Berri, leaning forward to touch first Gad's ears, then his nose, and finally tickling his already strong chin. She appeared to be the kind of young woman who was ready to embrace whatever life should offer, including having a child of her own one day. At the moment she could admire little Gad, who smiled up at her as if he were seeing the face of a beautiful angel. The boy could talk fairly well, too, but was speechless.

"Thank you, dear," said Aida, though disappointed Berri was all but ignoring the not-as-adorable Handa. "My brother Peter and his wife Ellen are very proud of Gad Boyd. We are all counting on him. We..." She cut herself off. She was counting on him to uphold the Boyd traditions and at least maintain the family hold on half of Blueberry Hill. She at times went so far as to envision him one day driving the Benders off the other side of the Hill. She was counting on her daughter even more, though, knowing all too well how the Boyd males had turned out so far. But it served no purpose to share such visions with any Bender.

Eunice seemed to read her mind. "I hope, Aida, you don't find me and my family as objectionable as your brothers do. Peter was the one who shot our Nathaniel. Chester, Elmer and that sickly one who throws rocks—Henry, isn't it?—are always so rude on those rare occasions when we cross paths on the road or in town. Natty, who fancies himself an aesthetic and is tenderhearted to a fault, does have good things to say about Blue Boy and Blue Belle, of course. He appreciates Blue Boy's handsome demeanor and desire to become a real artist. And he recognizes Blue Belle as the unfortunate, helpless creature she has always been. I don't wish for you or your family to look upon us as some kind of invading enemy."

Eunice was way off when it came to sizing up Blue Belle, but she was certainly right about how objectionable the Boyds found her and most of the other Benders. "The thing is, you did invade *our* Hill," Aida said. "You destroyed our peace and security. Your God-awful wall is there to always remind us what your husband has done to Blueberry Hill, our precious sanctuary ruined! You may be the Queen of the Bend, but you are looking at the Queen of the Hill."

Aida's outburst set Eunice off. "You are no such thing, you...you peasant!" Eunice shouted. She was no taller than Aida but she rose onto her toes to better look down her long nose at the Blue Rock House peasant. "How dare you talk to me that way! I have tried my best to be civil with you. A waste of my precious time! And your young daughter, if you want to know the honest truth, is homely to the extreme."

"You're a mean lady," said Handa, "a very mean lady."

Eunice looked stunned, as if she hadn't realized Boyd children could speak.

"It figures you Benders are so superficial you judge a person by her looks," said Aida.

"I...I think the little girl has a nice appearance," said Berri hesitantly, apparently afraid to contradict her mother.

"That's nice coming from you, Berri." Aida noticed how every man and woman passing them on the street gave the statuesque twenty-two-year-old a long second look. "I don't doubt you must have been a beautiful baby. You must feel fortunate not to have taken too much after your mother or father."

Berri was about to reply, perhaps even politely, but became too flustered. Eunice, however, spoke right up: "I never met your mother but from what I've heard, she was raised on a pig farm and you take after her. Heard she was a witch...a peasant witch who put a spell on your sluggard of a father, a man more than twice her age!"

Aida tried to stay calm. "My mother was a good, resolute lady who was happily married to my dad, a good man who..." She could say no more. She felt angry enough to slap Mrs. Bender-Leach in the face, but she didn't want to do so in front of the children. Besides, she wanted to drop the whole subject. Whenever she compared herself to her mother, the real Queen of the Hill, she never felt quite adequate. Henrietta was a happily married woman when she gave birth to her many children. In that regard, Aida knew she had not followed in her mother's footsteps. Handa was all she had. Not even a husband! "Come children," she said, but then remembered she had to push the two-kid cart herself.

Eunice stepped in her path. She had more to say. "You Boyds have no legitimate grievance against us. We gained half of Blueberry Hill by acquiring the Drake Tract. That is where we live. My husband built our wonderful house there. It was well within our rights to do so. When our Berri marries, Daniel will build a house for her and her husband farther up the Hill from the Bend. You can't stop him. Berri wants a home of her own to raise her children. It's only natural."

"But, mother," Berri blurted out. "I need a husband first...a live one!"

Aida didn't take that as an insult. Berri seemed so innocent, with the face of a porcelain doll, cheeks red, eyes blue, two perfect dimples, not a strand of blonde hair out of place. Her hands were fluttering as she apologized to her mother, though she had nothing to be sorry about. It was perfectly clear to Aida: This beautiful young woman wanted to escape from her mother's thumb (and no doubt her father's thumb, too) and avoid becoming an old maid. Aida smiled and gently placed a hand on Berri's shoulder—the first time she had touched a member of the enemy family.

"Come along, Berri," said Eunice, yanking her daughter away by the wrist as if she believed Aida would try to run them both over with the cart. "You need to help me with the shopping. We have spent enough time trying to be courteous to this wanton woman by pretending to admire those two Boyd brats."

"You can go directly to hell, Eunice, your husband, too." Aida pushed the blueberry cart so hard that both Handa and Gad toppled over inside it. The two children began elbowing and shoving each other. "Stop!" she yelled, but she kept pushing another few yards. Then she stopped herself, looked back, and addressed Berri: "As for you, pretty girl, I suggest you find the man you love, rich or poor, and go off to live with him, far, far away from the Bend."

Aida pushed on, right past the general store in case that was where Eunice and Berri were headed. She felt angry after the encounter but mostly frustrated because she hadn't unleashed enough hate at Eunice and Daniel Leach, Handa hadn't been appreciated, and the Benders were prospering more than ever. The dream house lumberman Leach intended to construct for his daughter was in the future, but he would do it all right, as surely as Berri would marry. Along with the Bend, Leach had already built on the Hill a rustic cabin full of gun racks and cots, a shooting range, two gazebos, a double-decker outhouse, and at least a half-dozen deer blinds.

"You two get out and walk awhile," Aida told the children.

"Don't you be mean, too, Mumsy," said Handa, giving Gad one last push before exiting the cart. "Are we poor?"

"What? Of course not. Don't we live in a big house? Aren't we in town buying things?"

"Uncle Chesty said we are poor and the Benders are bloody rich."

"Did he? Well, never mind that." But that started Aida thinking about how the Boyd blueberry business was mighty small potatoes compared to all the Bender/Leach commercial enterprises. "We are good people. The Benders are greedy and mean."

"They have lots and lots of horseys," said Gad as he finally stepped out of the cart. "We don't have any."

"We have a cow," said Handa. "That's almost as good."

"That's right," Aida said. "And we have much better blueberries."

§

Still in town that afternoon, Aida ran into another of the so-called enemy, literally. The two children were back in the cart and she was pushing them across the Sullivan Street Bridge when the blast on a conch shell from a canal boat distracted her and she rammed into Nathaniel's backside. Somehow it made her feel better. Not that Nathaniel was a bad fellow, but he was Eunice

Bender's brother and had once practically run over Chester with a horse and carriage. Nathaniel stayed on his feet, pirouetted, and fluttered his fingers. "Oh, Miss Boyd, it's you."

"Mrs. Boyd now," Aida said. "Think of me as a widow with child. That will be best." Still in a bad mood from the morning confrontation, she decided not to apologize. "I didn't see you standing there."

"I'm okay. It beats getting shot in the butt. Excuse me...derrière."

Aida didn't want Handa to hear about a Boyd shooting a Bender. It didn't make the family look so good. "You have left the Bend and are living in town now?" she asked.

"I have a room here but the Bend is still my home. When you hit me with your cart, I thought you were one of my brothers having a little fun. They love to sneak up on me when they're in town."

"Jeremiah and Alexander never struck me as being in the least bit playful. They're strictly business."

"Not all the time, though lately it might seem that way." He leaned over the cart and made cooing sounds at both Handa and Gad. "Adorable children. She has your eyes. And the boy has...Peter's...eh...handsome features."

"You aren't so mean," Handa said.

"Thank you,' Nathaniel said. "I like you, too, little darling."

Aida was impressed. A Bender who could admire Boyd children with some degree of sincerity must have plenty of good in him. "I'm glad there's one of you from the other side who is *not* all business." She gave his head a perfunctory pat—the second time she had touched a Bender.

Nathaniel pulled back as if she had poked him with a stick. He stood straight as a washboard, rubbed his chin thoughtfully, and became a grown-up again. "Right now, the businesses—you know, the canal, the railroad, the quarries, the sawmill, the tannery—keep my brothers and sister from thinking about less pleasant things."

"Such as?"

"I probably shouldn't be telling you this, Mrs. Boyd, but we've had some family problems on the Hill."

"You don't say. When I saw your sister, she didn't mention anything of the sort."

"She wouldn't talk about it with...you know."

"Marital problems perhaps? You and me have never had to deal with those, have we?"

"No, miss...ma'am. Things are fine between Eunice and Daniel, not so much so between them and Berri, their unfortunate naïve child."

"I saw Berri, hardly a child and nothing about her looks unfortunate."

"Nothing noticeable. But you see, her parents want to control her every movement. They hardly ever let her out of the house alone."

"They don't trust her?"

"They know she is easily deceived. They don't trust men. She's so gorgeous, yet so unsophisticated. They think every man out there wants to pluck her."

"Pluck? You did say *pluck*?"

"Like the choicest berry on a bush."

"And does Berri want to be plucked?"

"Let's just say she is keen on marriage for the sake of marriage. None of the countless men pursing her are good enough, according to Eunice and Dan. Naturally I myself would advise my niece to think twice about jumping into matrimony. It doesn't end one's problems as my brothers have found out, particularly Alexander."

Aida nodded but she was thinking of Boyds, not Benders. She was glad she had Handa and hadn't needed to marry to get her. Crazy Mary wasn't acting anything like a wife, and everybody except husband Elmer believed she should be placed in either the Hudson River State Asylum in Poughkeepsie or the State Homeopathic Asylum at Middletown. Peter, with his deep-seated melancholia surfacing at times, and Ellen, with her moral guilt, were still having problems, though both were glad to have Gad. Marriage was not in the picture for obstinate old Chester or fragile, self-absorbed Henry, let alone for unsightly, angelic Blue Belle. Blue Boy was a strange case. He seemed infatuated with the graceful, artistic Nathaniel, yet his several days of unrestrained passion with Ellen had left him longing for more of the same if not for another secret child.

"I understand," Aida said.

She didn't inquire further about any marital problems Alexander and Jeremiah might be having, but Nathaniel acted as if she had.

"I shan't go on," he said. "My family would not wish me to go around town discussing personal problems they might have, especially to, if you'll pardon me, a member of the Boyd family. I'll only add that it's hard for my brothers to be *playful* under some trying circumstances. Now then, let me look closer at what we have here in your cart. They don't look like blueberries to me. I bet these two snippets are playful as all get-out." Nathaniel leaned over again and gently pinched the cheek of Gad, who looked more frightened than anything.

"Leave my baby brother alone," shouted Handa, who had trouble leaving Gad alone herself, but she was family. "I thought you were nice."

Nathaniel scrunched his handsome face so that his upper lip touched his nose, and wiggled his ears without touching them. Handa scowled ferociously, but Gad laughed so hard he had to wipe his dripping mouth and nose with the back of his hand.

"It's all right, Handa," her mother said. "This is the best Bender. Blue Belle and Blue Boy like him. And he doesn't hate us."

"*Au contraire*," said Nathaniel. "I think you are good people. I am pleased to report that Blue Boy's painting is coming along splendidly, Mrs. Boyd. He did a blueberry still life that shows how far he has advanced since I took him under my wing. He has loads of promise. Really, he does. And now Blue Belle wants to join our Basha Kill School. So glad to have her aboard; she's as sweet as a cupcake."

"That isn't necessary. A blind person can't be expected to paint a picture."

"Don't underestimate Blue Belle. She can feel her way around bright colors and a canvas that has a rougher texture. She is an incredible human being."

Aida knew it was true but somehow it seemed insincere coming from a Bender, even the best of that bunch. Blue Belle could also nurse wounds and mental scars, walk the Boyd side of the Hill without help, consult with the spirits of their father and Catawissa Manayunk, avoid self-pity and melancholia, behave like a saint without pretense, sing like a songbird, and memorize with feeling the words of Whitman, Emerson, and Thoreau. If she indeed did have the ability to paint, it hardly would be something out of the ordinary for her.

"We all adore her," said Aida, which was true enough, but saying it didn't improve Aida's mood. She thought she herself sounded insincere. At times she was jealous of her ugly, blind, elf of a sister. Blue Belle had so much hidden power. Still, somebody in the family had to deal with mundane but essential day-to-day responsibilities instead of speaking to spirits and dwelling on ethereal matters. "I must go. Goodbye, Nathaniel."

Aida tried to move on, but Nathaniel took hold of a cart handle. He offered to push the two-kid cart to the general store, and before she could stay no, he was pushing merrily. She followed along wanting to protest, but saying nothing—this Bender was trying to be helpful.

On the next block, Nathaniel stopped on his own. His two brothers, Jeremiah and Alexander, and Jeremiah's thirty-eight-year-old twins, Maurice and Robert, had poured out of the swinging doors of Lord's Tavern. The two older Benders were arguing about the worth of canals vs. railroads, and the two younger ones had taken sides—Robert with his father, Maurice with Uncle Alexander.

"I tell you, brother, America runs on railroads—some might even say railroads run America," Alexander was saying. His words were clear but his short steps were unsteady.

"Look what's happening with the New York & Oswego Midland," said Jeremiah, whose words were slurred. "About to fold like a napkin!"

"A mere hiccup in the rail system. The new company will be up and running soon. The future of railroads is as bright as the sun."

"It's cloudy today. By God, brother, the canal still has life. You won't see me ever shed my boat captain's hat." He raised an unsteady hand over his head but nothing was there. "Shit. What did you do with it, Salamander Alexander?

"Nothing. I wouldn't touch your ridiculous hat. You must have left it in the tavern."

"I'll get it." Jeremiah tried to spin around too fast and became dizzy. "Later."

"It's only a matter of time, Jeremiah the Denier, before the railroads take over and the canal goes the way of the dinosaur. You'd better get aboard with the steam-powered iron horse before it's too late."

"Uncle is right as rain," said Maurice. "Railroads rule the roost. We'd be behind the times and lose half our business if we had to rely on sluggish canal boats to carry our bluestone and lumber."

"No runaway canal boat ever killed anyone," said Robert, who accidentally hit himself in the head while waving both fists. "It was a near disaster for my Trudy and five-year-old Stevie last week at the railroad crossing in Summitville. That fully manned speeding westbound locomotive didn't even blow its whistle before it shot past, missed by a foot sending them both to kingdom come."

Aida did not consider the pros and cons of the drunken Benders' loud argument going on outside Lord's Tavern. She told Handa and Gad to stay put in the cart. She hadn't known that Robert had gotten married and had a son (the same age as Handa, no less) and said so to Nathaniel, as if she had expected the Benders to keep her better informed.

"Actually, twin sons, Stevie and Nickey," whispered Nathaniel. "Robert married Trudy. Maurice married Trudy's sister, Judy, and they have just the one girl, Betty. Maurice couldn't quite keep up with his own twin brother."

"I hope that's all," Aida said, not hiding her disappointment. There were only the two new Boyds, and already at least three new Benders to deal with in the future.

"For your information, Mrs. Boyd, as much as I adore children, I don't wish to be burdened with them, let alone a wife. Unlike you, if you don't mind me being frank, I wouldn't want one without the other, but I don't want either."

He reached into the cart and patted Gad. "No offense, little shaver, but my art and my Bash Kill School come first. Look what a mess marriage and children have made for my brothers."

Gad was puzzled but smiled anyway. Sometimes grown-ups had to be humored.

"You never told me," said Aida. "Wives and kids drove them to drink?"

"You might say that. I suppose there is no point keeping it a secret. Jeremiah wasn't satisfied with Maurice and Robert having managed to produce three grandchildren in total. He wanted more Benders, male heirs to be specific. He blamed Anna for never cooperating and now she was too old. He told her to talk to her sons and their wives as only a woman could and insist that they be more productive before time ran out. She refused to interfere in their lives. They fought over that and then over his dalliances with D&H dames, as she put it, and, I believe, her own liaison with...well, someone you know well. Have I shocked you, Mrs. Boyd? If so, I am most sorry. Perhaps I talk too much."

"Perhaps. But I am hardly shocked. I know you are talking about my brother Chester and that there is turmoil of one kind or another in any marriage."

"Thank you for being so understanding about these matters, Mrs. Boyd. We see eye to eye on this subject. None of us is perfect."

"Perfectly said, Natty."

"The upshoot is we have a most unhappy couple at the Bend. Actually, Anna is not there at this time. She left the Bend to visit her sick mother in Tarrytown. Jeremiah was suspicious. He actually believed Anna had turned to your brother Chester for love and support and was stashed away in the bowels of Blue Rock House."

"I almost wish she was with us. Chester might not be so miserable in his old age."

"I understand completely. You think of your family first. Anyway, Jeremiah made a personal visit downstate and confirmed that his wife is in fact at her old home in Tarrytown, but she wouldn't return with him to the Bend."

"I could commend her on that, if I may be equally frank with you, Nathaniel."

"You may. I know full well what little regard you hold for my brother Jeremiah. I also realize everyone has his or her own opinion about everyone else. Jeremiah does have his good side; he's a first-rate provider and, in his own way, loves his boys. Anyway, my brother Alexander has suffered far worse."

"With Delilah?"

"Yes, with Delilah. So charming, so insincere. Now without Deliah. She got fed up with the North and headed back home to Georgia. She took Georgia, the daughter, with her but her two sons stayed on. After all, they are big boys now, in their twenties. James is quite the ladies' man and manages our second quarry. Cal loves to hunt and otherwise shoot off guns with his Uncle Daniel but is smart as a whip and would be a catch for any local girl."

"It hardly surprises me, about Delilah that is. The woman was born and bred in the South. The pull of her southern roots overpowered her love for the northern luxury Alexander could provide her."

"Something like that. I don't like to speak ill of anyone. I suppose she thought she loved Alexander in the beginning."

"I wouldn't know, but Alexander never has struck me as being any more loveable than he is playful."

"He has his good side like Jeremiah. While he is all business now, I know her leaving and taking their daughter with her broke his heart. Still, I do feel Delilah belongs down there amid the magnolias and cotton fields, and Georgia in Georgia sounds fitting."

Aida did some more calculating. Delilah and Georgia were two losses on the Bender side. She could only wish that Delilah's cousin, Daniel Leach, had gone south with them. But she didn't say so. Too much was going on in front of her. She wondered if she should take the children away immediately or wait to see if the arguing Benders came to blows.

"We most certainly have become frank with each other today, Mrs. Boyd. I know my older brothers wouldn't approve any more than your older brothers would. They are so set in their ways. Still, I'm glad to have bumped into you today."

"Me, too, Natty, but it was me who bumped into you. I'm so glad you are different."

Nathaniel acknowledged the difference with a smile, but it disappeared in a flash. He gasped as he looked past her toward the scene in front of Lord's Tavern. "Oh, my!" he cried. "They are still at it. Jeremiah didn't go back inside after his hat. My brothers are about to engage in fisticuffs Could it all be because of their disparity over canals and railroads? They shouldn't drink so much."

"I understand," Aida said, thinking of brother Chester, but he wasn't one to look to fight anyone even when intoxicated. She turned away from Nathaniel to better watch the two oldest Benders confront each other. She was neither alarmed nor displeased. She thought it would serve Boyd wants and needs if Jeremiah and Alexander shot each other dead, though neither appeared to be armed. She wasn't going to say anything that frank to Nathaniel, but she did step closer to better hear the argumentative Benders.

Alexander's words, only slightly slurred now, reached her first. He was right in his brother's face but spoke loud enough to wake the dead. "If you weren't spending half your time on the canal, Anna never would have packed up and gone back to a mother she never liked in the first place. It's your own damn fault. You drove her away."

"What an absolute blunderbuss!' replied Jeremiah, jamming a finger into his brother's chest. "You railroaded that Southern belle bitch into marrying you and now you're paying the price. Losing her might be a blessing, but you lost a daughter, too."

"Worry about your own affairs. Keep out of mine. I didn't drive them away. Delilah turned on me despite all I've done for her. Georgia, bless her little heart, had no choice in the matter. She couldn't very well cross her own mother. Still, Delilah could come to her senses and return to the Bend once she sees for herself it's not the Antebellum South anymore."

"You know as well as I do that Delilah is gone forever."

"Why don't you mind your own damn business. You lost your wife, too."

"Big difference. Anna will be back once the old lady breathes her last in Tarrytown."

"Maybe so. But I'll find me a better woman."

"Better than Delilah, you mean? I don't doubt that. Good riddance to her. Still, I reckon that we'll both miss the way Georgia pranced around the Bend morning, noon and night in her scanty white chemise. She's more than halfway there to becoming a full-fledged, teasing Southern belle bitch."

At that last unkind brotherly remark, Alexander raised a fist, but he never got the chance to throw a punch if that was indeed his intention. He stumbled backward as if affected by Jeremiah's heavy alcohol breath and tripped over the foot of Robert, who fell against Maurice, who pushed back. After more stumbling and pushing, Alexander, Robert, and Maurice all ended up sprawled out on the street in a cloud of dust. Jeremiah shrugged and turned away from them. He walked, slowly but steadily with chin held high, back to Lord's Tavern and, like a victorious bull exiting the arena, passed proudly through the paneled double door.

28
THE PANTHER HUNT

By age six, Handa Boyd was not only picking blueberries like a veteran but also showing five-year-old cousin Gad how to put berries in a bucket instead of his mouth. Aida was well pleased at the way her daughter was developing, especially since the manpower was running low on their side of Blueberry Hill in 1878. Blue Belle did more than her share, and even crazy Mary had streaks of picking fever, but one-armed Peter, in defiance of his melancholia, was the only consistently motivated picker among the Boyd men. Elmer only picked when Mary was at it, otherwise he was busy making sure she wasn't running off or getting into sharp objects. Henry had taken a fall off the Blue Rock House porch roof, nothing too serious, but had become a "self-imposed invalid" in the words of ancient Doc Tears. Ellen rarely picked alongside Peter for she spent most of her time as a nurse for Henry, who did have some legitimate health problems besides feigned back spasms, and for Chester, who had "picked himself out," in his own words, and possessed a "tired heart," a self-diagnosis. At sixty-five, Chester had gone into semiretirement from the blueberry patch, even though Aida kept reminding him that their father, Handy, had kept on picking after turning one-hundred. Blue Belle counseled the oldest of the living Boyds about his "mental, heart, and spirit depression," which she attributed in large part to the fact Anna Bender was keeping herself at far more than arm's length from not only Chester but also Blueberry Hill. Anna was apparently still at her mother's home in Tarrytown, playing nurse. That role had never really fit her, Chester told himself. She was no Ellen or Blue Belle.

Three times Chester dreamed about the distant Anna residing not in her mother's Tarrytown house but nearby in Washinton Irving's old cottage. Mr. Irving was not there (he in fact had died of a heart attack in 1859 and was buried in Sleepy Hollow Cemetery), but in each of the dreams Chester could see another man lying in Irving's four-poster bed next to Anna. Her auburn hair was so long and bountiful it covered most of her nakedness. The man was not touching Anna; he was clutching his detached head—the Headless Horseman at rest! In the third such dream Chester also saw another bed in the Irving cottage. An old man with a foot-long gray beard and a nightcap on his bald head lay there snoring. He was alone. Chester could tell instantly that the old man had an aversion to profitable labor and was lazy those times he was awake. It could only be Rip Vam Winkle.

Blue Boy, the sturdiest of the brothers, had left the Hill to reside in town in a room he took over the Fulton & Holmes General Store. He did some clerking—a job that Chester had held many years earlier—but spent most of his time painting or at least lolling in the company of Nathaniel Bender, director of the still developing Basha Kill School. Blue Boy confessed to Henry that he couldn't live in Blue Rock House because of his feelings for Ellen. He admitted that no night or day passed without him recalling in intimate detail his two days of bedroom bliss with her. Peter, the husband who had not actually fathered his son, wasn't the one Blue Boy was most jealous of, though; what he couldn't bear was the continuous attention that Ellen heaped on Henry and Chester, her patients.

"I was considering getting hold of a gun so I could shoot myself in the foot and become one of her patients, too," he further confessed one August day when he and Henry both showed up at Handy Spring from opposite directions.

"Now, Blue, would that be fair to those of us who are really suffering," replied Henry as he took a second sip from the tin cup. "Besides, I thought you felt a powerful physical attraction to the effete Natty?" He took a third gulp before handing the cup to his brother and complaining about his back.

Blue Boy was not bothered by Henry's words; putting a handle on feelings was like trying to tame a wild horse. And it was no secret that he and his brothers had trouble enough controlling a broken horse or balky mule made for wagon pulling. "Don't know," he admitted. "Natty thinks more highly of my abilities than I do or my family does. He shows me respect. But he's a Bender."

"A Bender who lives with you in town."

"I'm not gone completely. As tiring as it is, I'll keep coming back to the Hill to push the loaded blueberry carts to the train station. Peter has only that one arm. I just wish Aida wouldn't be so...you know, so much like Napoleon III. She treats me like a mule, but I take it. We must be making enough blueberry money by now to finally buy a horse and wagon."

"The Queen of the Bend has talked about maybe getting a mule and a day laborer from town to help with the hauling. It always comes down to lack of currency, and none of the Wurtsboro grocers are willing to barter with her anymore. Chester says what Aida needs is a full-time slave or at least Gad to grow up fast."

"You're off your chump, Henry. We fought a whole bloody war to eliminate slavery—at least some of us did."

"I didn't say it. Chester did. And can I help it if I was too afflicted by illness to take up a gun and fight the Confederacy."

"You could have thrown stones at the Rebs."

"And what about you, Blue? You gave up the good fight because of hemorrhoids."

"True, Henry. But at least I never was an idler like yourself."

"Fiddlesticks. Enough of this jabbering. Why don't you go off and paint a blueberry with Natty or something. My back is acting up something awful. And Ellen will be coming around any minute to give me my daily sponge bath."

Blue Boy tossed the tin cup to Henry, who dropped it. Henry groaned as he bent down to pick the cup off the ground and whined like a baby raccoon as he wiped the dirt off the rim. Blue Boy headed in the direction from which he came.

"Where you going?" called out Henry.

"Back to town," said Blue Boy. "I've had my fill."

§

During the next decade, the Boyds got no horse, no mule, no wagon, and no common laborer. They continued on with their limited picking power and the pair of hand-operated carts. Gad was thirteen before he could pick like an adult male but he wasn't inclined to do so. He said he liked to pick with one hand so he wouldn't make his one-armed father look bad. It was a lame excuse. Handa proved more productive even though she spent half her blueberry patch time directing or criticizing her cousin. Still the Boyds managed in season to bring crates of blueberries to the New York, Ontario and Western Railway, which in 1880 inherited the New York and Oswego Midland line, for delivery to the two million fruit lovers who lived in New York City.

The Boyd-Bender feuding was mostly low key for much of the 1880s. The Boyds would periodically complain about the noise from the target shooters and hunters on the other side of the Hill or the blasting taking place on the next hill over, Quarry Hill. Then came the felling of more trees, hammering, sawing, digging, and such when Daniel Leach began building, much too close to Jackson the dividing wall, a so-called cottage (four bedrooms planned) and digging a well for daughter Berri, her new husband, and the future children. Daniel and Eunice had finally selected the *right* man for their striking daughter before she turned thirty. Jonas Gadebusch, fifteen years her senior and so massive his presence filled any room, had recently been a vice president at the Bank of the Metropolis in New York City until he moved to Sullivan County for undisclosed health reasons and now advised the Benders and Leaches on money matters. Jeremiah Bender's rude answer to Boyd complaints about the noise: "Stuff blueberries in your rabbit ears."

It wasn't only the Bender elders who bothered the Boyds. When Robert

Bender's twin sons, Stevie and Nickey, turned thirteen in fall 1886 they began painting their faces red, climbing over Jackson, and attacking Boyds the way fierce warriors once raided unwanted settlers. They carried bows and arrows as they whooped and hollered, but they never fired their weapons at Boyds. Their method was to touch the enemy with a bow or a hand-held arrow and quickly retreat as if they were Plains Indians counting coup. Each coup meant another feather in a cap.

Stevie had the most feathers in his cap, which looked like a war bonnet. Once when Henry had a rare trip outside in the wooden wheelchair Elmer had originally built for Handy, Stevie poked the invalid in the knee with the point of an arrow. That inspired Henry to revert to his form of the old days, and he threw rocks at the Bender savage. None hit the mark, and Stevie, feeling he was invincible, climbed the wall again the next day and touched Handa, prematurely top heavy at thirteen, twice on the chest. Nickey conceded that this double coup was worth two feathers. The twins' usual targeted victim, though, was twelve-year-old Gad, a coward in their view but still a challenge because he ran so fast.

Handa wanted revenge for what was done to her, and on a hot summer day in 1887 she gave Gad a stick sharpened with the family's Revolutionary War knife, followed by a boost to get him over the wall. Her instructions to her cousin were to poke Stevie with the stick, preferably in his private parts, but to leave Nickey alone if possible because he was the nice one and so much cuter.

"How can I tell them apart?" asked Gad from atop Jackson. "They look the same to me."

"The one with the sensitive eyes is Nickey."

"You expect me to look into their eyes, too? Anyway, I have no idea what sensitive eyes look like. Are they blue or brown?"

"The one with the most feathers is Stevie. He's the one you want."

His mission was unsuccessful. The twins had transformed from Indians into cowboys. He only saw one of them at first, and since this twin wore a "Boss of the Plains" Stetson hat, Gad had no idea which one it was. Next thing he knew he was roped by the other twin and soon was being held down by one while the other poked him in the ribs with Handa's stick, drawing blood. Neither twin's eyes looked remotely sensitive. Gad felt as if he were a steer being branded. In fact, they called him a steer and didn't exactly leave his private parts alone, though no permanent damage was done. When their mother, Trudy Bender, rang the bell for the noon meal, they untied him, but only because they wanted to reclaim their ropes, and raced to the Bend as not to miss out on the grub.

When Gad got back to Blue Rock House, he took out his frustrations on Handa, pinching her arms and calling her a blueberry maggot fly among other things. That got him the switch from Aunt Aida and no sympathy from his own mother, Ellen, who told him that gentlemen should be chivalrous toward ladies, not harm them. "She's no lady, she's my ugly cousin," Gad shouted. "When I tried to avenge the wrong done to her, I got ambushed by the Bender boys and they massacred me. Besides, Handa called me a yellow-bellied sapsucker." All that complaining got him were two hard hickory switch strikes on his seat from his one-armed father and a few words of ungentlemanly advice: "Don't be such a Boyd baby. Leave your cousin alone. Get your revenge against those Bender bullies, one way or another."

Instead of looking for revenge, Gad ran away from home the next day and ended up three miles away inside the secret ice cave trying to cool off. He spent hours there pretending he was a woolly mammoth too big and powerful to be mistreated by any female of that ancient species or any current species. When he started to shiver, he defiantly crossed his arms and told himself he'd rather go extinct than go back home. Still, he was glad when the Bender twins showed up, Nickey carrying a bow and on his back a quiver of arrows, Stevie toting a Model 1876 lever-action Winchester rifle he had learned to master on the Bender shooting range. The secret cave wasn't so secret. They had followed tracks, not his but those of a large animal. They had counted four toes on the front feet and four on the hind feet. No claws showed in the prints, but a cat's claws were retractable. They were convinced the creature was much larger than a bobcat.

"A saber-tooth tiger?" suggested Gad who associated those cats with the wooly mammoth and thought that the twins were pretending like him.

They weren't. "You nincompoop," shouted Stevie, clutching the Winchester as he peered for signs of any other life form in the ice cave. "They were all killed. No plain tiger here, either, or lion, or cheetah, or jaguar, or leopard. I know all the cats from Great-Uncle Dan. The biggest cat we got here in Sullivan County is the panther."

"Right," said Gad, looking around nervously. "Do they like caves?"

"Tracks led right here," said Nickey. "You were plenty brave to come into this cave. Would never have expected it of you, Boyd. Panthers can weigh over two hundred pounds, and do they ever have teeth!" He bared his own teeth, some of which were strikingly yellow and pointed.

"The nincompoop ain't brave," said Stevie. "He's plumb foolish. He don't even know what a panther is. They go by lots of names, Featherbrain— mountain lions, cougars, pumas, catamounts, painters, and mountain screamers. By any name they are more sinister than gray wolves and harder to hunt than black bears."

"Sure," said Gad. He remembered Uncle Chester talking about the old days when there were fearsome catamounts, pusillanimous polecats, and wild

Indians on Blueberry Hill. "We better head home before it starts getting dark."

"Listen to the fraidy-cat," said Stevie. "There's no turning back for us. We're big-game hunters, hunting for panthers!"

Gad couldn't back down from the challenge or maybe he just didn't want to be left alone. Stevie was running the show and chose to be out in front with the only gun at the ready. Every so often he would point the Winchester at a squirrel or bird and say, "Pow, you're dead," but he assured his brother and Gad that he wouldn't waste a shot because it might take all nine cartridges in his rife to dispatch a full-grown panther. Nickey claimed to be a dead shot with his bow, but he had only four arrows, and Gad doubted that would be enough to do the job. Gad found himself wishing he was carrying his grandfather's Revolutionary War knife, not that it could do much good in his unskilled hand. He picked up a hickory stick, which he knew would be useless, but he couldn't spot a good throwing stone. Not that he wanted to kill a panther or anything else. Like it or not, he had to count on the Bender boys should they encounter the formidable beast.

The panther tracks faded away by a rocky ledge, but Stevie took a moment "to think like a panther," and decided the cat must have gone down into Long Swamp, where few men ever ventured. The summer hadn't been an especially wet one, but nobody had told that to the swamp. They all tried to stay on the small grassy hillocks, but most of these "islands" were unstable and even sure-footed Stevie sometimes saw a boot slip into the mud. The oozy black sucked at Gad's old shoes and found every hole in his socks, making every step a miserable uncertainty. The mosquitoes formed a cloud over his head and his sweaty shirt stuck to his skin. His misery extended from head to toe. He wished he was back at Blueberry Hill, wiggling his sun-dried naked toes on the flat rock at Handy Spring or even helping Handa make a blueberry pie. Long Swamp was well named. It meandered endlessly and had many equally uninviting offshoots.

They came across only deer and fox tracks, but Stevie was not easily discouraged. He jumped from hillock to hillock as if making a series of brilliant moves on a checkerboard. Nickey more or less followed the same unmarked path; Gad had trouble keeping up, then lost a shoe in the mud. Nickey, the nicer twin, retrieved it for him. Strong-legged Stevie pressed on and came upon ten yards of dry land. He carefully approached a pile of leaves and twigs and suddenly dropped to his knees as if he had discovered a gold nugget.

"You find a big track?" Nickey asked.

"Better than that,' Stevie said, feeling around the ground. "I found a big scat."

"That's shit to you," Nickey told Gad. They kneeled, too, for a better look.

"The beast has marked its territory," Stevie said. "I knew it. Long Swamp is his home."

Nickey was squeezing his bow so hard that it bruised his hand. "Couldn't it be a bobcat?" he asked.

"No way. See these rounded edges and one-inch segments. It's panther scat. Great Uncle Dan told me all about it. He told me how this panther named Scar munched on a woman settler and her baby. When the men folk went after the killer cat in this very swamp, one of them got separated from the others and was never seen again. That's how Long Swamp got its other name: The Swamp of No Return."

"Just a wild tale told around Sullivan County campfires," Nickey said to Gad but it was as if he were trying to reassure himself.

"Sullivan County history," corrected his brother. "Would you look at this." He picked several white slivers out of the scat. 'This son of Scar must have munched on a rabbit this morning."

"Good," said Gad. "Maybe he's not hungry."

"Don't worry, girls," said Stevie, standing up. "I'll protect you." He held his Winchester out in front of him and found some new hillocks to conquer. But he was moving more slowly now and wiggling his rifle like a dowser with a divining rod. Trying to stay as close to his brother as possible, Nickey twice bumped into him with the bow. But when they reached the end of the swamp and came alongside a group of boulders, they heard growling from above and he dropped the bow.

"It's him!" shouted Nickey, pointing to the top of the largest boulder where the panther with teeth bared stood over his meal—a good-sized whitetail doe. The rabbit must not have been enough for the enormous cat. Instead of picking up his bow, Nickey shed his quiver of arrows and ran back the way they had come, not caring how wet his feet got and only once turning his head to see if he was being followed.

The panther yowled and screamed—the most horrendous sound Gad had ever heard. He froze—all but his pounding heart—but then moved without thinking. He threw the stick aside, bent down, and nocked an arrow, something he had never done before. Meanwhile, Stevie fired one shot from the multi-shot Winchester but didn't get off another. He had allowed the muzzle to drop into the mud. Half the rifle was sucked under. This son of Scar bled from the shoulder but didn't lick his wound. He grew more ferocious.

The cat abandoned its deer kill. But instead of running away, it sprang. Gad let fly with an arrow that grazed the beast as it landed with claws out on Stevie's head. Gad heard a very human scream. He saw the panther's teeth clearly, the same teeth that had sunk into the deer carcass. The other arrows were too far away to reach quickly. He cracked the bow against his knee, hoping it would snap loudly and sound like another gunshot. Maybe it did, but

Scar was twice wounded and had nothing to lose. The beast seemed intent on tearing Stevie's head off. Once Gad saw Stevie's head hanging off his shoulder at a strange angle and blood spurting from the neck, he finally turned and ran, leaving this son of Scar to command the bloody ground.

It surprised Gad to see how quickly he got clear of the dismal Long Swamp. He didn't stop running until he was back at the ice cave. He chose not to go inside, though—that was no place to hide. He thought about climbing a tree, but a panther could surely climb better than him. He ran on. His mind was becoming numb, but his feet didn't want to stop. There was no sign of the fleeing Nickey, who would surely get back to Blueberry Hill before him. Would the surviving twin try to explain to his family what had happened? Would the Bender men bother to notify the Boyds before rushing to Long Swamp to see if Nickey was exaggerating or if Stevie had somehow survived? How could anyone from either side of the dividing wall understand this tragedy? The family feud had heated up at times—rock-throwing Henry had been shot in the groin by Daniel Leach and Nathaniel had been shot in the buttocks by Peter—but nobody on either side had come close to being killed.

The crazed wounded panther was to blame, of course, but Gad figured that somehow much of the blame would fall on himself. Maybe Nickey would lie and tell everyone that the nincompoop Boyd, like all members of his family, was against shooting poor harmless creatures and had thrown Stevie's Winchester into the mud. Anything was possible. The sheriff would be notified and ask many difficult questions. Hadn't the revenge-minded Gad been out to get the Bender twins because they had trespassed and counted improper coup on Handa? How had he made it home unscathed while Stevie Bender was lying headless and chewed to bits in the Long Swamp?

As Gad ran with abandon through the woods screaming and reliving the unspeakable horror of that day, he could no longer think. He could taste swamp water in his mouth, then his mouth went totally dry, his throat sore from the screaming, his trousers torn by the mountain laurel and thorny bushes that reached out to grab him. He passed by Handy Spring and the double grave of Grandad Handy and the legendary Indian named Man without stopping. It was too close to the house. His feet, still not dry, took him to the water trough at the New York, Ontario & Western station. He drank his fill there. A few people were milling around the station, but none of them seemed to notice him. That was fine with Gad. Invisibility was what he wanted. He hid behind an outbuilding waiting, though he had no idea what the O&W schedule was, he had never ridden on a train in his life, and he had no money in his pocket. That didn't matter. His family didn't own a horse and he wasn't about to steal one. He could try to hitch a ride on a canal boat, but they were far too slow. He had no choice; he would hop the first train to anywhere.

29

STILL DIVIDED AFTER ALL THESE YEARS

On behalf of the entire Boyd family, Aida sent a sympathy card to the Bender family. Actually, she attached the card to a stone and had Handa hurl it over Jackson while men were shooting off guns on the other side of the wall. The Benders were having a Stevie Bender Memorial Rifle Shoot to honor the gun-loving boy two days after the funeral service at the Bend, which was attended by half the population of Wurtsboro but no Boyd (none were invited). At the conclusion of that shoot, Nickey Bender climbed over the wall, not to conduct any mischief this time. He would never count coup on Boyds again. He knew that Gad wasn't at Blue Rock House because the distressed Boyd family had reported him missing and the sheriff's thorough search of the house and grounds had confirmed that fact. Nickey wanted to assure the so-called enemy, Handa in particular, that Gad was no more responsible for Stevie's death than he was. "A panther is an unpredictable wild animal," he told them in his well-rehearsed speech on the Blue Rock House porch. "The three of us all wanted to kill the beast, but he turned the tables on us when we interrupted his deer meal. I'm sorry that Gad has disappeared, but at least he can come back some day, unlike my brother. I wish I could bring them both back to Blueberry Hill this instant. Life will never be the same without my twin." Handa thought the handsome boy was sincere, but Peter, backed by Chester and Elmer, soon ran him off the property anyway. They somehow blamed the Benders for Gad's having gone missing, just as most of the Benders somehow blamed Gad for the death of one of their own.

The Boyds did everything in their power to find Gad. His parents, Peter and Ellen, sent out fliers to every village in Sullivan Cunty and as far west as Honesdale, Pennsylvania, as far north as Kingston, New York, as far east as New York City, and as far south as Washington, D.C., where Ellen grew up. Since Gad had never been photographed, Blue Belle and Blue Boy both drew his face from memory, and both images were used on the fliers though they looked like two different boys with, according to the rest of the family, only passing resemblances to Gad. Blue Belle had a good excuse; she was blind. Blue Boy, though, had made a too-mature face that more closely resembled his own. The authorities in Honesdale mistakenly held a suspicious orphan boy for several days, and the police in Washinton D.C. believed that a young petty thief looked exactly like one of the drawings. But the real Gad remained lost.

Blue Boy regularly scoured the woods between Handy Spring and the ice cave in case Gad was holding up in more familiar territory. On these search missions, Blue Boy carried the Revolutionary War knife with him and kept one eye out for panthers. He saw no signs of either Gad or panther. Mary prayed to God for Gad's return because she believed he must be dead and only the Savior could resurrect him, and Elmer joined his wife in prayer because he believed it couldn't hurt if the boy was actually alive. Blue Belle summoned the spirits of Handy and Man for any help they could provide. All Blue Belle heard from Handy was *OhW, OhW, OhW*, which she interpreted as meaning the missing boy was Oh so close in Wurtsboro. But increased Boyd visits to town turned up nothing. A week later, Man gave his own mysterious clue: *Iron Horse Steam North*. Blue Belle couldn't made sense of it at first, but she knew his spirit wasn't talking nonsense. Eventually, she, Aida, and Handa put their heads together and figured out that Gad must have hopped onto one of the steam-belching northbound trains of the New York, Ontario & Western, which was usually abbreviated as the O&W rather than the NYO&W.

The northern end of the line for the O&W was Oswego, a port city on Lake Ontario. Aida, Peter, Ellen, and Blue Belle, with no mention of the extravagant expense, all went there as passengers and found Gad working hard. He had lied about his age and was laboring at one of the seven flour mills operating on the banks of the Oswego River. He was living with a prominent lumberman and his wife who couldn't have a child of their own and was on the verge of switching his employment from flour-milling to lumber shipping. The contingent from the Hill told Gad that lumbering wasn't any fit occupation for a Boyd and worked hard to convince him it was in his best interest to take a train back south with them.

Aida and Peter assured the boy that nobody held him responsible for Stevie Bender's death and promised to stop punishing him with the traditional hickory switch for perceived transgressions. Blue Belle took a less direct approach, telling him it was his decision because, as Ralph Waldo Emerson stressed, a young man must trust in himself and find self-acceptance rather than act cowardly by relying on the judgment of others. Gad, displaying stubbornness (a common Boyd trait) and spunk (an uncommon characteristic of Boyd males) wasn't easily swayed to pack up and go home. Yet, he was too young for self-reliance, and his mother finally won him over by posing three questions: "Is flour and wood easier to work with than blueberries, Sonny? Is it better to work for the profit of rich families like the Benders than for the salvation of our poor family? Is it better to be patted on the back by strangers than embraced by two loving parents and two appreciative aunts?

While the return of young Gad lifted the spirits on the Boyd side of Blueberry Hill and made them thankful for the helpful spirits of Handy and Man, gloom lingered on the other side. Nickey, as he predicted, found that life was neither as fun nor as interesting without his more adventurous twin around. His family was still blaming Gad in large part for Stevie's death, but at the same time they treated Nickey differently, as if he had let them and his twin down by surviving and not taking revenge against the killer panther. Without Stevie around, he felt incomplete as a human being, and he wasn't sure what could make him feel whole again. He thought befriending Gad might help; hadn't they both been equally timid and run from the scene of the panther attack? He sat atop Jackson day after day waiting for Gad to come along.

Finally, they met again, but Gad saw him as the real coward for having been the first to run that fateful day and immediately threatened to thrash his "sorry behind," which he never would have dared say if Stevie were alive. Thinking he might get more understanding from Handa, Nickey continued wall sitting in the hope of laying eyes on the Boyd girl, who wasn't exactly pretty but seemed capable of giving him what he needed—a self-confident human being his age who could replace his brother as a constant, dominant companion. She met him at the wall soon enough, but it was a disaster. She gave no indication she saw anything in him worth seeing. She called him a yellow-bellied sapsucker like her cousin, a good-for-nothing, a savage, an invader, and, worst of all, a bloodthirsty Bender. If he dared jump down onto the Boyd side, she promised to use a family heirloom—a large Revolutionary War knife—to cut off his tallywags.

With the death of one of their twin boys, Robert and Trudy Bender began to argue about many things, including guns. She contended that if Stevie hadn't been permitted to carry his beloved Winchester rifle, he wouldn't have gone hunting for a panther and wouldn't have died. He told her that Stevie was an excellent gun handler and marksmen and that the panther would be dead instead of him if only that misguided Boyd boy hadn't seized the Winchester. Robert also argued with twin brother Maurice over how the various Bender businesses were being run; Robert, Maurice contended, was neglecting his management duties. Robert didn't argue with Nickey, he only neglected his surviving son, failing to recognize that a brother's loss of a brother could be as devastating as a father's loss of a son.

Jeremiah Bender was "hurting as if struck by a runaway train" over the loss of his favorite grandson on top of the absence of his wife, who was holding out in Tarrytown refusing to return to the Bend despite her mother's renewed health. Anna was making demands in letters to Jeremiah, specifically insisting he stay home more to work on their marriage instead of constantly "playing captain" and cavorting with "wenches and weathered reprobates" along the D&H Canal.

Instead of reaching out to his wife again, Jeremiah took a stubborn stand to maintain his self-image. He had too much at stake, physically and especially psychologically, to turn his back on his canal life. He took satisfaction in having *other* women at his beck and call and even more so in heading a collection of successful family enterprises. He considered himself and Alexander (No. 1 and No. 1-A) the top two businessmen in Sullivan County, yet it was his canal connection that was at the core of who he was, just as Alexander's railroad relationship defined his brother. Most recently, Alexander was instrumental in getting the Port Jervis, Monticello & New York Railroad to complete a seventeen-mile stretch of track from Huguenot in Orange County, thus connecting with the New York, Ontario & Western Railway at Summitville, just north of Wurtsboro. Jeremiah occasionally had a nightmare about a steam engine roaring right through his bedroom at the Bend, but he no long begrudged Alexander for being a railroad advocate.

Both had broken marriages, though Jeremiah still figured Anna would come crawling and wiggling back to him once her money ran out in Tarrytown while Alexander's Delilah had already filed for divorce and reestablished herself as a Southern belle in the heart of Georgia. What mattered more than wives were sons. Alexander had Cal and James, who stuck with their father rather than their mother and were doing outstanding work at the quarries. Jeremiah had Maurice and Robert, the twins who had never quite gotten over being tied to their mother's apron strings though they held prominent positions in the family's commercial operations. Jeremiah agreed with Maurice that Robert was slacking off, and such behavior was unacceptable for a Bender even one who had lost a son and was crossing swords with his wife.

"We need to do something about it, Robby my boy," Jermiah said after buying his lackadaisical son several stiff drinks at the Tavern in the Hollow on a rainy night in February 1887.

"The rain?" Robert replied. "Not even you can stop the rain, Father."

"Nice to hear the raindrops enhancing the canal water. Makes you believe the Lord is on our side?"

"What side is that?"

"The side of the canal men…you and me Robby."

"You brought me here to listen to the rain?"

"I brought you here to pull you out of your rut. You've been in the dumps long enough. It's not the rain that needs stopping. It's your state of mind, which frankly stinks to high heaven."

"Forgive me for breathing. Everything has gone sour. Stevie gone. Mother gone. Aunt Delilah and cousin Georgia gone. Trudy half gone."

"Anna will be back. Your mother will come to her senses."

"Maybe so. But my wife isn't there even when she is with me. Trudy hasn't acted like herself since Stevie left us. Life won't be the same again at the Bend."

"I heard the same thing from Nickey. You do have that other twin son, you know."

"Sure, I know, but like you know, Father, just because he looks like Stevie doesn't mean he...forget it. I don't want to talk about it."

"Your way of thinking stinks. You sound like you've given up. You sound like a goddamned Boyd."

"You know what else stinks, Father? The old, rotten D&H canal, that's what! Sure, I used to support the canal like you, but look at it now; it's hanging on like some water-loving dinosaur that doesn't know it is about to become extinct. Let's face it, Father, there isn't much life left in the Old Ditch."

"Horse manure!" Jeremiah grabbed Robert by the shirt collar, started to shake him but thought better of it. Manhandling someone you loved was never the answer. Anna had attacked the canal many times in the past but for different reasons, and he remembered trying to shake the insolence out of her a couple times. And now she was in Tarrytown. "I got me an idea sure to boost the spirits of both you and me and the canal. You and me are going on a father-son outing."

"What do you mean?" Robert asked, sounding so much like his mother that Jeremiah cringed.

Jeremiah recovered quickly, though. "Yes, Robby, my boy, an outing. Just me and you. And it won't be anything ordinary; it'll attract attention from Honesdale to Kingston and beyond."

"I don't want attention. That panther tearing Stevie apart was in all the papers. That's the kind of attention newspapers give you."

"It won't be like that. Newspapers report bad news, yes. They also like good news, like when men set records. That's what we'll be doing. I promise you it will put bigger smiles on our faces than my Anna or your Trudy could do with all their feminine wiles."

True to his word it happened the next month on Jeremiah's seventy-seventh birthday. In fully loaded, powerful but sleek *Annabelle III*, Jeremiah and Robert set out on the canal from Sparrowbush, along the Delaware River north of Port Jervis. With Jeremiah at the tiller steering and Robert on the towpath guiding the two finest Bender workhorses as he had done in his youth, they managed to cover the thirty-nine miles to Lock 49 beyond Wurtsboro in a record twenty-five hours. "You bet I wanted to prove something to the skeptics," Jeremiah told the alerted newspaper reporters. "It was the quickest time ever between those two places, proving there is still plenty of life left in what all you skeptics call the Old Ditch. Canal boats like *Annabelle III* are *not* relics of another age. They are *not* dinosaurs and neither am I."

Robert was as tired as the two horses and collapsed at Lock 49 to spend the night under the stars, but not before he told the three reporters what had made the record run possible: no closed locks at night on the Neversink Section from Port Jervis to Cuddebackville and a lock-free Summit Section. Meanwhile, a gathering of old canallers in Wurtsboro gave his proud father several champagne toasts and reassurance that they were all still relevant.

Jeremiah's newfound glory along the canal was short-lived. Another creaky captain of canal boats named McCardle noted the *Annabelle III* record that night but never joined in a toast. It seemed that Captain McCardle still resented three right-of-way violations in the canal made by Jeremiah at least thirty years earlier. McCardle was a tired, jealous, and bitter man who was looking for a chance at revenge against the "Admiral of the Canal Captains" but wasn't sure how he'd ever get it until he heard from Chester Boyd. One day in May Chester offered to give McCardle three buckets of blueberries if he could break Jeremiah's record. McCardle said he didn't even like blueberries but would shatter his rival's time anyway for free. And he did, going from Sparrowbush to Lock 49 in just under twenty-four hours with Chester aboard keeping him awake by poking him with a stick and Wurtsboro's best towboy leading the finest pair of pulling mules anyone had ever seen in Sullivan County. Chester, who had never owned a canal boat or any kind of business and had been unable to take Anna away from Jeremiah, considered it his first victory of any kind over his bitter enemy.

Jeremiah had not considered the possibility anyone would ever break his record or even attempt it. He took the news hard, cursing the miserable McCardle for days. When he learned that Chester Boyd was behind "McCardle's Miracle," as the write-up in the Kingston *Freeman* called it, he ranted and raved to such an extent that he suffered his first stroke. The stroke was a mild one, but Chester still felt a touch of annoying guilt. Much worse for Chester, Jeremiah's condition (droopy mouth and eyes, numbness in left arm, weakness in right) caused Anna to feel guilty for staying away from her husband so long. She left Tarrytown immediately and made herself at home again at the Bend to help Jeremiah recover and feel like a whole man again.

His canal victory came to feel insignificant to Chester since it really hadn't changed anything for him; he was still the loser in the game of life. Age had slowed him down in the blueberry field and, even worse, he didn't have his heart in picking all that summer or the next summer either. Tired of listening to Aida boss him and tell everyone what a brilliant brain Handa had, he suggested his sister and her big-headed daughter invent a blueberry-picking machine that didn't require rest or human kindness, only a little oiling and minimum maintenance. Aida called her brother's lethargy an "extended old age depression."

The Boyd blueberry business fell off dramatically because of market conditions but also the poor picking that Aida attributed to Chester's mental state, Henry's never-ending illnesses, Gad's continued restlessness, Blue Boy's new artistic life with Nathaniel Bender in Wurtsboro, Elmer's full-time job of watching over his increasingly unstable wife Mary, and Peter's never-ending jealousy over wife Ellen's time-consuming concern for his selfish brothers. It was a sorry state, Aida complained to the menfolk, when blind Blue Belle and young Handa proved to be top Boyd pickers most days.

Meanwhile things were looking up again on the other side of the Hill in the late 1880s. Jeremiah Bender not only had Anna back in the fold but was also honored as "Wurtsboro Man of the Year" in 1888. Alexander Bender had more reason than ever to boast over his railroad investments and had also found a second wife, Wilma, the daughter of a railroad baron. Robert and Trudy Bender had a second son, Oman, to replace the late Stevie, and Nickey was coming into his own as not just a man but a Bender man. Maurice Bender opened yet another quarry and his daughter Betty was already winning blue ribbons for her pies and other baked goods. Daniel Leach's lumber production had doubled. Daughter Berri was pregnant and her husband Jonas Gadebusch, who did the Bender books, was all the family could ask for when it came to integrity and confidentiality. Eunice Bender Leach was working with the top lawyers in Sullivan County to get hold of the other half of Blueberry Hill after learning the Boyds were arrears in paying their property taxes.

"We can't give up Blue Rock House and Blueberry Hill," Chester told his family at a family breakfast after the mediocre 1889 blueberry picking season was over. It had become clear that even though he had picked again at almost his pre-depression rate, blueberry sales alone weren't enough to keep the Benders at bay. "It's all I...we have."

"We might have no choice," said Aida. "Let's be realistic. Eunice hates us. She is one determined vicious lady and has the law on her side. We have no steady income. We are tax evaders."

"Mother is right," said Handa, who was now keeping the Boyd Berry sales records. "We have to find a way to turn things around fast."

"We don't do anything fast," said Henry, who had become the slowest mover of all.

"Damn every last Bender," said Chester.

"Anna included?" asked Elmer.

"Shut up, Elm. If anything needs to be said about her, I'll say it. Do I ever say anything about your crazy wife?"

"You just said she's crazy *again*, you mindless bastard."

"Let's not bicker anymore among ourselves, gang," said Blue Belle. "We're on the same side."

"Some of us on our side have been lazy sons of bitches for too long," said Peter. "We need to go out and find work like Blue Boy has done."

"He barely makes enough sweeping and mopping in town to support himself," said Aida. "He spends half his earnings on art supplies and he can hardly be called a real artist. Has he sold a single painting?"

"There must be something some of us can do?" said Elmer. "I have my hands full with Mary so I wouldn't be able to go out and get work even if some outsider wanted me to build a stone structure for them and I wanted to do it."

"Poor Elm," said Chester. "All that natural born talent wasted."

"What have you ever done, Chesty? And now you can't go out and do anything productive anyway. You're too old."

"Only one year older than you, Elm."

"Henry is too Henry," continued Elmer. "Handa is too young. Gad is too flighty. Blue Belle is too limited, no fault of her own. Aida is too busy keeping our house in order. Who is left? Ah, Peter. I appoint you, Peter Boyd, to go out amongst them in the valley and make some money to help us pay those ridiculous taxes. It was your idea."

"I remind you, brother, I have but one arm," Peter said.

"Ellen can help, too, by nursing outsiders who pay her. All she does is tend to our freeloading family, not that we don't appreciate her loving care. But we need money."

"My wife isn't leaving my side," said Peter, but he gave no explanation. "We all know, Elmer, you could get a job building stone walls or monuments or something and make decent money if you would only put Crazy Mary in an institution where she belongs."

Mary couldn't hear any of this; she was at the stove, trying to clean it without burning her fingers. Elmer took offense, though, and he raised a fork, threatening Peter. Ellen screamed but was prepared to get bandages if needed. Aida screamed at Gad, who had gotten up from the table and started to wander off because he hated family breakfasts, especially when there was bickering. She called him inconsiderate and lazy. Chester then screamed at his sister for trying to run all their lives, and Handa screamed because her mother had screamed. Blue Belle stood up and climbed onto her chair to show herself better. She did not scream.

"I would like to quote Walt Whitman if you'll allow me a minute," Blue Belle said, holding her autographed copy of the 1888 seventh edition of *Leaves of Grass* to her forehead. The author had sent it to her a month earlier with the inscription "To the visionary B.B. Boyd from her great friend and author," and she had already memorized many lines as if by osmosis, though Aida and Handa had helped. Her family quickly grew quiet. She was the only visionary on the Hill. She recited: *Love the earth and sun and animals. Despite riches, give alms to everyone that asks. Stand up for the stupid and crazy. Devote your income and labor to others...And your very flesh shall be a great poem.*

"I like the standing up part in part, though Mary is by no means stupid," said Elmer. "But what riches do we have? We are rich only in blueberries, which are not universally loved and, anyway, are done for the season."

"I'm afraid Elmer is right, my dear sister," said Aida. "I remind you what I said earlier. We have no income to speak of. That should be the main concern of all of us, including you, Gad. Now, sit still and sit up straight."

"I can't do both," said Gad.

"Do try your best, Sonny," said Ellen.

"We must not give up hope," Blue Belle said, lifting her hands as if in worship before sitting back down. "Walt also mentions his *Isle of sweet brooks of drinking water*. He is talking about Long Island, but those words can also be applied to Blueberry Hill. Is this not our own wonderful little island in the mysterious and confusing world the human race is occupying for the time being?"

"An island we are forced to share with the Benders," said Chester. "And now it looks as if they may get the entire Hill for themselves to dig up more earth, cut down more trees, kill more animals, run roughshod over more people."

"Do not despair family." As if by magic, Blue Belle seemed to rise up in her chair without using her scrawny arms. "We do not have sweet brooks, but we have a spring that provides continuous sweet drinking water. I woke up before dawn this morning and said words aloud that came to me in a dream."

"More Whitman?" asked Ellen.

"No. This time it was a proverb. It may have come from the ancient Lenni Lenape or perhaps the even more ancient Chinese. I do not know for sure where it came from except it came to me while I slept. I do know what it means. It is a good sign for us."

"Well, what is it, sister?" said Aida.

"It is brilliant in its simplicity," said Blue Belle. "*When drinking water, remember its source.* I'll repeat that: *When drinking water, remember its source.*"

"What does that mean?" asked Henry.

"Think Handy Spring, Brother."

"Okay. But I feel a little nauseous right now. I'm not really thirsty."

"But you will be again. Everybody gets thirsty. Everybody needs water. Think about it some more, and believe! Handy Spring may be the answer to our prayers. Believe!"

"Amen," said Mary, who had just walked in from the kitchen with two burnt fingers.

30
WATER AND FIRE

The conversation about the importance of water, specifically drinking water and nothing to do with canal water or the Neversink or the Basha Kill, extended well past breakfast. While Mary cleared the table and washed dishes, the rest of the family continued the talk on the Blue Rock House porch roof, where the Boyds believed they could think with clearer heads and talk more openly. Besides Mary in the kitchen, the only family member missing was Blue Boy, in town to help Nathaniel Bender set up the first Basha Kill School art show.

"We've always said that we have the best tasting water in the world at our doorstop," Blue Belle reminded everyone. She sat on a cushion situated on the clay tiles between protective Chester and Elmer, who wouldn't let her stand for fear the gusty west wind would sweep her from the roof. "Now is the time to let the world know."

"None of us has tasted water from another country, French mineral water for example," said Peter, who sat behind those three, clutching the arm of his wife as if he feared she would slide off the roof or too close to Henry, who had brought a pillow and a blanket.

"Who cares about France," said Henry, fluffing his pillow. "It's clear across the Atlantic Ocean."

"That's true," said Aida, who sat with Handa on one side of her and Gad on the other, to keep close to her darling daughter but also to keep an eye on her fidgety, unpredictable nephew. "I'm sure our water is good, but there is plenty of good water other places."

"On this side of the ocean nobody wants to drink the water in Mexico," said Elmer. "Canada no doubt has refreshing cold water but who wants to bring it all the way down here. The United States of America doesn't need to import water. We are top water dog."

"All right," said Peter. "The USA has plenty of good drinking water. Is our Handy Spring so special? When I was wounded and had a limb hacked off during the War of the Rebellion, I could hardly stomach the water I was forced to drink in Washington D.C. But that's swamp land. What about all those clean mountain streams in the West? And there's the entire South to think about, even if there isn't really a Fountain of Youth in Florida. During the Atlanta campaign when Mortimer Lomas shot me in the arm I no longer possess, I was drinking gallons of Georgia water. And it tasted damn good to me."

"That's my father, right, Mumsy?" asked Handa.

"Yes, yes," said Aida, stroking her daughter's slightly tangled hair and wishing she had brought a comb onto the roof. "Mort, may he rest in peace, did not intend to shoot your Uncle Peter. It was an unfortunate accident. They were on the same side. But never mind that now. I want to hear more about the water. What thoughts are floating inside your head, Blue Belle?"

Before Blue Belle could speak, Chester stamped his foot so hard he loosened a tile. "We are in New York state, goddamn it! To hell with the water in Georgia, France, and everywhere else."

"That's what I've been saying," said Elmer. "All of it is alien water." But he was staring at the loose tile.

"Right," said Henry. "Let's' talk about water closer to home. We all know that nothing people drink in the valley tastes half as good as the exquisite aqua from Handy Spring. It has kept me alive. Certainly, the water from the well they dug on the other side of the Hill is inferior; it has been known to make Benders sick."

"That's a good thing," said Chester. "The Benders are considered superior to us in everything but *their* blueberries and water."

"My Mary once saw the face of Jesus Christ at the bottom of Handy Spring. I'd better go inside and see how she is faring in the kitchen." Elmer started to rise.

"Best not bring her out here," said Peter. "She's liable to think she's a tufted titmouse and try to fly off the roof."

Elmer settled back down on his cushion but gritted his teeth and scratched his head. "We were talking about water."

"We all can agree on one thing," said Aida. "We have a ready source of decent drinking water at our fingertips."

"Decent?" said Henry. "Handy knew he had something extra special here. Our spring water is more than decent. It's downright delicious."

"Downright delicious," repeated Blue Belle. "I like that. Honesty is the best policy, but there is room for a little exaggeration in advertising. Light, soft, clear, crisp, sweet, and rolls off the tongue with no aftertaste. As refreshing as a summer breeze. In a word, sensational!"

"You want to advertise our drinking water?" asked Aida.

"Maybe just a little. After that people will start talking about it."

"You've lost me, little sis. None of us want outsiders coming to Blueberry Hill to steal our water!"

"I should say not," said Chester. "Isn't it bad enough already that Benders sneak around from the other side to fill their jugs and families from the valley make illegal pilgrimages to Handy Spring."

"That shows you what kind of water we have," said Blue Belle. "The people wouldn't do that if our water wasn't downright delicious, refreshing, and sensational."

"I get it," said Elmer. "What we do is sell our water. Isn't that what you're driving at, Blue Belle? I never realized a spiritual being like yourself would be so interested in commerce and filthy lucre."

"I am thinking of our unfortunate financial situation."

"Yes," said Aida. "We are in big trouble. But will people buy water?"

"I can answer that," said Elmer. "People and animals can't live without water."

"There's no water shortage in New York state," said Peter.

"Wait, Peter," said Aida. "It's starting to make sense to me. Why didn't I think of this before! I see the possibilities. There are many blueberries, but people will still pay for the best blueberries. There is plenty of water, but people will still pay for the best water. And we have the best of both."

"Yes, Mumsy" said Handa. "You're brilliant. We shall prosper!"

"I agree, but it was Blue Belle's idea," said Elmer.

"Of course, it was, Elm," said Aida. "What matters is that this could help all of us."

"It will. What we have here in Handy Spring is a goldmine! You're a genius, Blue Belle. I'll put a gate in the stone wall around the spring, and I'll make the wall higher. We can't make access too easy. We can charge by the cup full or the jug full. We'll need someone down there all the time to collect."

"So true, Elm," said Aida. "We can't trust the likes of the greedy Benders to adhere to an honor system."

"Outsiders aren't allowed to come to our Hill and pick our berries," said Chester. "I don't want them coming to our spring and drinking our water, even if they do pay for the privilege."

"They'll contaminate it," said Henry.

"I understand your concerns," said Blue Belle. "But we won't be inviting outsiders to our blessed water unless they are dying of thirst, of course. Then it would be the only decent thing to do."

"I'm all for decency," said Aida "But now that I have a clearer picture, I must say that to make money we'll have to allow considerably more indecent people to come to Handy Spring."

"There's an alternative," said Blue Belle. "What we can do is send our water to them!"

"How do you send water to someone?" Handa asked.

"You dig another enormous ditch, dunderhead," said Gad.

"Gad!" yelled Aida. "It's wrong to call your cousin names, and you know very well she is smart as a whip."

"Sure, if you say so. I was only trying to do what you keep telling me to do, Aunt Aida—you know, contribute to family conversations. Forgive me for opening my stupid mouth."

"Now, Sonny, we all know you aren't stupid," said Ellen. "But sometimes it is best to just sit still and listen to your elders."

"Wait a second," said Chester. "Gad might have something there—build a canal for moving water for drinking instead of water for boats."

"The water would get dirty," said Henry. "Everybody would get sick."

"Who would do all that digging?" Peter said. "Not me with my one arm. Not you, for sure, Chester. Not Henry. Not Elmer. Not Blue Boy. Not any of us. And think of the cost? Who would supply the capital—the Benders?"

"Hush your mouth," said Aida. "This enterprise will have nothing whatsoever to do with the Bender family."

Elmer clapped his hands. "I got it! Something besides a canal would work—a railroad!"

"You mean we would need to build a branch line to the Hill?" Peter asked. "That would be hard to do and even more expensive than Gad's ditch!"

"Of course, it would, but there's already a train that comes to Wurtsboro." Elmer struggled to his feet, accidentally kicking Blue Belle in the process. She ignored the pain in her shin, so Elmer didn't apologize. "Don't we cart blueberries to the train station and have them sent to New Jersey and New York City? No reason we can't do the same with Handy Spring water."

"But how do you send water?" Handa persisted.

"I believe what we would have to do is bottle it, dear," her mother said. "That would be a lot of bottles for our two little carts. We would need to buy a horse and wagon at last. But I can see it happening. We can make this come true. We can make money. We can save our home!"

"Hurrah, hurrah," cried Handa, jumping up.

"That's the spirit!" shouted Blue Belle. She also stood, losing her balance and knocking against Chester. She quickly apologized and braced herself against the wind. "Like Walt Whitman, we should all reach out to each other with unmitigated hope."

"Still sounds like a hell of a lot of work," said Peter. "But I suppose it is possible if we would all get off our derrières."

"That'll be the day," said Chester.

"Don't listen to gloomy Chester," said Aida. "We can do it. We *must* do it. It's our only hope!"

"Mumsy is right," said Handa, stamping her right foot for emphasis. Another tile broke loose.

Chester pictured profit and loss numbers spinning around in both of those female heads.

"Let us pray!" shouted Mary, who had climbed to the top outdoor step. In one hand she carried a plate that she had cracked somewhere along the way from the kitchen; in the other a Bible. "Water purifies and provides deliverance. It is a blessing."

"So true, Mary," said Blue Belle, who raised her hands to the sky in praise of Ketanëtuwit, the spirits of Man and Handy, and Walt Whitman.

When Elmer tried to help Mary onto the roof, the broken plate dropped to the bottom step and shattered. Mary instantly changed her tone. "A bad, bad sign," she said. "I'd better clean up the mess." She clutched the Bible to her bosom as she descended.

"Watch that second to last step, dear," said Elmer. "It's tricky. The stone has deteriorated."

Too late. Mary tripped and fell to the ground She landed flat on her back but the Bible heaved on her chest as she panted. "She's breathing," said Elmer, looking down at her from the edge of the roof. He seemed frozen.

Others rushed to his side to see for themselves. "I'll check on her," said Ellen, scrambling down the dangerous steps. In the rush, Blue Belle was accidentally bumped by one or more of her family members and stumbled helplessly. The wind was against her, too, pounding against her tiny back. She was now propelled forward and couldn't seem to stop though she knew she was headed for the front edge of the porch roof and a long fall sure to be more damaging than the one Mary had just taken. She figured she needed spiritual intervention to stop her momentum and cried out: "Help! Good Old Dad. I'm falling." But she wasn't really. Somebody had bounced after her on the seat of his pants, grabbed her by the ankle, and pulled her back to safety. Her undersized body landed on his lap.

"That was too close." said Blue Belle, her heart pounding. Mostly by smell, she believed she knew who had grabbed her. "Thank you so much, Peter. You saved me."

"You're welcome, but I'm not Peter. I'm his son."

Blue Belle wrapped her arms around her nephew and pressed her face to his chest. "Thank you, Gad, thank you. I'm so glad you are here listening to your elders and chose *not* to sit still."

"Sure," said Gad. He hadn't felt this good in a long time, like some time before that panther made a meal of Stevie Bender.

§

In the weeks that followed, Chester and Gad helped Elmer install an iron pipe that carried water on the downslope from Handy Spring to a large storage tank beside the public wagon road. "Let's let gravity work for us," said Elmer. "It's free." The work did him good because he now had plenty of time on his hands and needed to stay busy on the project to keep from thinking too much about Mary, who was no longer at Blue Rock House. Under the care of Ellen and Blue Belle, she had recovered nicely from her fall on the steps but then did something far worse on purpose—she stuck her entire head into the blessed water of Handy Spring. It would have been a successful suicide attempt had not her husband come along to see why the water wasn't flowing through the pipe. She had left a neatly printed one-sentence note: THE WATER SHALL PURIFY ME AND DELIVER ME FROM SIN. That was too much for Elmer. The good people at the Middletown Homeopathic Asylum for the Insane were now keeping Mary safe.

Chester, to the surprise of most of the other Boyds, was keeping himself as busy at Elmer. Like his father before him, Chester had come to think of Handy Spring as the closest thing on earth to an actual Fountain of Youth. He also got the late-in-life notion that he could finally become an enterprising all-season businessman like Jeremiah and the other supercilious Benders. Gad, who had true youth on his side, now believed that his best chance for a better future was by making as much money as possible at home rather than running away again. He figured he could always do that later when he had pockets full of coin and the concept of self-reliance could be better realized.

All male Boyds, young and old, bottled water three times a week. Peter had overcome his skepticism about the project and liked to work alongside his wife at the storage tank. Henry lent a hand in part because he also wanted to stay close to Ellen, who had declared him too healthy to require her daily attention at his longstanding sickbed. Blue Boy came aboard after abandoning the art world. None of his paintings had sold at the first Basha Kill art show and not even Nathaniel Bender, his best friend to say the least, could keep him away from contributing to the Boyd drinking water business.

At first the suddenly hard-working men used only the two blueberry carts to haul the bottled water the four miles to the Wurtsboro railroad station. Elmer then added to the fleet by cobbling together a third vehicle from a discarded rowboat, using the broken oars as handles, and for wheels two pneumatic tires that Gad had stolen from Nickey Bender's safety bicycle. Gad was the only one with the strength and stamina to push Elmer's so-called Great Conveyor, which carried as many full water bottles as the two carts combined, but he was neglecting his home schooling. That convinced Aida, who was making the lesson plans for Gad as well as daughter Handa, to at last authorize the costly but necessary purchase of a buckboard wagon and a mule from the livery stable.

The best wagon driver, Blue Boy, delighted in the new arrangement and named the mule "Salty the Second." Others could drive the wagon in a pinch because Salty the Second learned to follow the designated route with almost no guidance. Although not able to live primarily on blueberries and assorted vegetables like his owners, the mule was no meat eater, never balked at his working routine, loved the tender attention he received during off hours from Blue Belle and Handa, and paid for himself within two months. By that time, the Boyds were in the best economic shape of their lives, paying off back taxes, buying new Sunday clothes, and looking ahead to a bright future on Blueberry Hill.

Even though the drinking water came from the same source, the family decided to sell it under two labels. Sixty percent of the bottles were "Handy Spring Water," the logical name proposed by Blue Belle and backed by Chester, Elmer, Henry, and Blue Boy. The rest went by "Blue Rock Spring Water," favored by Aida, Handa, Peter, and Ellen because water under that name sounded more refreshing and harder to obtain and could be sold for ten cents more per bottle.

Both brands flourished near and far. "Isn't it absolutely marvelous," Handa exclaimed to her mother. "We're turning into actual entrepreneurs."

It was the railroad that made the new enterprise not only possible but also profitable. Still, as Aida acknowledged to every Boyd, living or dead, it couldn't have been accomplished without hard work. Bender businesses dwarfed Boyd blueberries and Boyd spring water, but the Benders couldn't dismiss this development. It angered Eunice Bender-Leach for months, but she could do nothing to stop it short of having her husband poison the spring or hold open hunting season on Boyds. Once resigned to the fact the enemy had enough money to pay their taxes and keep their house and land, she summed up the situation for her family: "We'll never get our hands on the whole Hill now. No longer relying on blueberries alone, those Boyd barbarians are thriving like camels in the desert, beaver in the marshes, largemouth bass in the Basha Kill. I'm afraid that barring a natural disaster such as the drying up of their spring, we are doomed to having their presence on the other side of Jackson for many years to come. Whether that means we should drink their water or not is another matter."

§

In June 1891 there was a natural disaster on Blueberry Hill during a violent pre-summer storm, but it affected only the Bender side. All the tall trees nearest the Bend had been chopped down earlier to protect the main house, so when lightning struck the tallest white oak and a substantial red oak that afternoon, one tree burned and the other blew into splinters but no structures or people were harmed. The Benders were inside the Bend toasting their good fortune when lightning filled the air again. A bolt struck the woodpile next to an outbuilding, creating a fire that flattened that building. The wind was blowing west, so the main house was spared. But the fire spread quickly through the Bender blueberry bushes and destroyed the carriage house, the grand gazebo, the stable, the barn, and the new four-room cottage Daniel Leach had built near Jackson for his daughter Berri and her banker-turned-accountant husband, Jonas Gadebusch. The couple escaped with minor burns, climbing in their desperation over the dividing wall to the Boyd side and laying low. A sudden shift in the wind resulted in only a few sparks flying after them over Jackson and none came close to threatening Blue Rock House. The stone wall was blackened on the Bender side but the Boyds didn't lose a single blueberry bush.

Aida, sounding much like the God-fearing institutionalized Mary, called this disaster for the Benders "God's will." While Blue Belle didn't go so far as to suggest that Ketanëtuwit or the spirits of Good Old Dad and Man had anything to do with it, all five of her brothers did. Nevertheless, Aida instructed her family to bring many bottles of Handy Spring and Blue Rock Spring water up to Jackson and hoist them over the top. Maybe two dozen bottles were relayed to and emptied on the burning embers of the cottage, but nothing could be saved but the chimney and a raggedy yellow-haired doll that Eunice had given her daughter long ago. Eunice and Berri thanked Aida for her family's neighborly effort, though it was ineffectual and, what Elmer called, "a waste of our good water supply." Daniel Leach and various male Benders were not only ungrateful but also suspicious since the Boyd side of the Hill had inexperienced no lightning strikes and no fire damage.

"How funny," said Aida. "The powerful Benders believe we can control lightning."

"Could be they are convinced the spirits of Handy and Man really did have a hand in this destruction of their property," suggested Chester.

"I prefer to think that Good Old Dad and his wonderful Lenni Lenape companion wouldn't hurt a fly, let alone a Bender," said Blue Belle.

"I prefer to think they would, out of their love for Blueberry Hill," said Elmer. "Of course, no Bender was actually harmed in the lightning fire, so perhaps you are right, little sister. Anyway, it's a good thing our favorite spirits at least spared the Bend itself. I know I once shot out some of its windows and that devil Daniel Leach designed the place, but it really is of good wood construction. Not to suggest it is superior to my...our...stone house, but I must give the devil his due."

"That's quite a generous statement coming from you, Elm," said Blue Belle. "I'm proud of you for being so magnanimous."

"You're weakening in your old age, Elmer," said Henry. "If the Bend had caught fire, I wouldn't have wasted a drop of our spring water on it."

"Me neither," said Chester. "I would piss on its ashes."

Jeremiah Bender arrived at the top of the Hill while the Boyds were recovering their empty bottles from the blackened ground where the Gadebusch cottage once stood. He had the nerve to suggest that arson was involved and that the ridiculous fire-fighting display was only done to cover the arsonists' tracks. Elmer instantly lost whatever magnanimity he possessed. He made sure Jeremiah was unarmed, then said he would never start a fire but fully expected Jeremiah, Alexander, Eunice, and Daniel Leach to end up burning in Hell. Jeremiah, though vastly outnumbered, began to curse in Elmer's face, calling him a *Homo neanderthalensis* fit only to live in a limestone cave.

Before Elmer could think of a fitting response, Chester stepped in, pushing his brother aside and getting in Jeremiah's face himself. After all, he had known Jermiah far longer and deserved first crack at the former butcher. Once up close, though, Chester saw how weathered that face was, now redder than Jeremiah's hair, which in uneven streaks was turning white. And Jeremiah's slightly contorted mouth reminded Chester that his No. 1 enemy had suffered at least one stroke. He wanted to back away but couldn't do it with Elmer standing directly behind him. Jeremiah shoved Chester, and Chester shoved back. They continued taking turns shoving for half a minute but both stayed upright. They knew their own strengths in old age, and those strengths didn't amount to much; they were like two toothless, clawless mongrel dogs nipping at each other.

Anna Bender had quietly trailed Jeremiah up the Hill and was a witness to the standoff between her husband and her former lover. Although she tried to avoid taking sides, she was not altogether successful. "Can't we just forget it, Jeremy," she said. "You know as well as I do that Chester would never burn down anything—certainly, not something as sacred as blueberry bushes. He adores blueberries, even ours. He was trying to put out the flames."

"Half-heartedly," said Jeremiah. "And he failed as usual."

Anna tried to get the two octogenarians to shake hands but instead Jeremiah spit against the wind, felt embarrassed that he had splattered himself, and stormed back down the Hill. He didn't look back to see if his wife was following, but he shouted to the sky: "Arson and adultery, adultery and arson. They go together like hand in glove." He seemed due for another stroke.

"I suppose he'll never forgive you," Anna told Chester.

"For shoving him back?" asked Chester.

"You know I don't mean that. I can hardly blame him. He's a proud man to say the least. It's all out in the open now. I not only was unfaithful but also acted with the full cooperation of his oldest enemy—you!"

"Go ahead and blame me. I'm the fool who fell for you."

"I couldn't put it any better myself," said Elmer. "Benders are poison."

"I blame myself more than you, Chester," Anna said. "The thing is, when I returned to the Bend from my mother's house in Tarrytown, he did forgive me for everything."

"How wonderful for you," said Chester, but he didn't like what his tongue was saying. "Now, once again, you can enjoy all the riches and special benefits that come from being wed to a proud robber baron and philanderer."

"I suppose, but that isn't enough. I really don't deserve to be forgiven."

"Of course, you do. All beautiful women deserve to be forgiven."

Elmer stepped around his brother to face Anna. He had calmed down considerably and seemed to want to make peace with her. "I always forgave Mary for whatever she did wrong, which by the way was never ever taking up with another man. In that regard, she was good. And she was good in many other ways. Nobody washed and cleaned like Mary, my poor dear Mary. I only hope and pray she can forgive me for sending her away."

"I'm sure she will in time," said Anna. "Will you excuse us." She took hold of Chester's right arm and pulled him away from Elmer and the burnt ground.

Chester went gloomily but easily. She led him to the outcrop she had named the Castle so many years ago. He brightened up some. He couldn't help but notice her fine form. She had bounced back from the "canal sickness"—which had made her skin scaly and caused her to temporarily lose her auburn shine—and gone on to age as gracefully as any woman could. She was a princess who never became Queen of the Bend—that would be Eunice Bender—but no matter how many years went by, he knew she would always be a princess in his eyes, which now had become wet.

"It hasn't gotten any better," Anna whispered to Chester once they were out of Elmer's hearing range. "Jeremy keeps wanting to take me down to the canal, which I'm certain he loves more than the Bend or, for that matter, me. He wants to do the impossible—bring back the old days. I see his puffy red head in that silly captain's hat and his lumpy body in those overalls, and I find myself wishing he would fall overboard and drown. Am I evil or what?"

Chester wiped his eyes with his shirtsleeve. "Of course. Nothing I can do about that."

"Are you so sure?" She touched his wrist, then his forearm, then his shoulder, and finally his chest. "You look fifteen years younger than Jeremiah."

"Must be from all those years I avoided most forms of work. I inherited my basic laziness from my father, who lived off the land without ever plowing or planting—happily, I might add."

"Oh, yes, surrounded by those cherished blueberries! But are you happy, Chesty?"

"I've had an up and down relationship with that fruit through the many years."

"You are working hard now in your advanced years. It's not just the seasonal blueberries anymore. Your drinking water business has taken off. I heard both labels are selling like hotcakes. I want you to know, Chesty, that I'm very proud of you. True, it took you longer than most, but you've come a long way."

"It's not my business per se. I help out as best I can. All of us Boyds are involved, but Aida is running it. She's the businesswoman. Her daughter Handa is second in command. Blue Belle was the one who thought of it."

"Yes, I know. It's such a wonderful story of perseverance. Your sisters are remarkable in their own ways. When I compare myself to those two women—and Eunice, too—I realize what little I've accomplished in my own life, and I feel inadequate."

"We are all inadequate in our own ways—Boyds, Benders, the entire human race."

"Aida is like Eunice, a self-assured, assertive, and highly capable matriarch. One can't help but admire them even if their strong wills and domineering natures can at times irk the likes of you and me. As for noble Blue Belle, she is beyond reproach. She stands apart from the rest of us, unique—ever so homely yet a lovely person, kind, generous, and brilliant to boot. But I can't be expected to fall in love with a tiny blind lady, can I?"

31
DEATH AMONG THE BENDERS

The 1890s were the Boyds' decade, certainly when compared to what was happening that decade to the Benders. After Walt Whitman completed his "Deathbed Editon" of the constantly revised *Leaves of Grass* in 1891 he wrote Blue Belle a brief note: "Dearest B.B.—*L. of G.* at last complete. No more hacking at it. No more mood adjustments. Ready for the Great Beyond. I bid you a fond farewell for I may not be able to do so later. 'Song of Myself' is done. May *Your Song of Yourself* ring out across the land for countless years to come." When news of Whitman's March 26, 1892, death in Camden, New Jersey, reached Blueberry Hill, Blue Belle gathered her family at Handy Spring and commemorated his life by sharing many tin cups of delicious water and quoting him extensively. She offered as the last two lines: *Give me of you O spring, before I close,/I with the spring waters laughing and skipping and running*. She never let on that her poet friend was writing about spring the season, not a spring like Handy Spring, and the other Boyds all listened in awe of both Whitman and her.

Through the decade, the Boyds experienced economic recovery and growth thanks to the efficient leadership of Aida, hard-working and surprisingly healthy aging family members, several excellent blueberry seasons, and especially the drinking water operation that the constantly flowing Handy Spring made possible. They suffered only a minor setback from the Panic of 1893, which otherwise caused five hundred banks to close, fifteen thousand businesses to fail, thirty-five percent unemployment in New York, and more than one-hundred fifty railroads in the overbuilt rail network to shut down. For a time, out of necessity, the Boyds transported most of their boxes of blueberries and bottles of water by D&H canal boats until the railroads rebounded thanks to bankruptcy reorganization and increased efficiency.

Alexander Bender, who had invested heavily in railroads and taken a railroad baron's daughter as his second wife, suffered the most from the Panic of 1893. He lost enough money to put a small dent in the family fortunes. Eunice said her family was fortunate that the lumbering, quarrying, and tanning businesses continued to bring in steady income while Jeremiah was keeping his head just above water running *Annabelle III* on the outdated canal. Alexander's health declined with the railroad troubles and did not improve after the trains were running at full speed again. Alexander had been a heavy cigar smoker his whole life, and Doc Tears said in 1895 that the damaged lungs were now cancerous. Alexander didn't believe it and he kept excusing himself from his wife and the other women to light up his stogies in the Bend smoking room with Daniel Leach. The old physician's diagnosis was confirmed by other medical men after Alexander succumbed to the cancer in 1896. Shortly thereafter Doc Tears himself died from what everyone agreed was "old age."

Alexander's funeral service at the Bend was well attended, even by Alexander's first wife Delilah and daughter Georgia, who came up from the South mostly for the reading of his will (a disappointment to them both because Alexander had thought at the end only about his sons Cal and James and second wife, Wilma). The Boyds were represented by Blue Belle, Aida, and Handa. Wilma Bender, not nearly as engrossed as her husband had been in the Blueberry Hill feud, had extended the invitation to all Boyds, but none of the males had wished to attend. They still clung to their bitterness over what the man stood for and didn't want to appear as hypocrites. The three Boyd women, though they had never gotten to know Alexander, wanted to see for themselves if those on "the other side" truly spared no expense when it came to honoring a deceased family member. They were duly impressed but all caught colds that lingered for weeks. The widow Wilma only lingered slightly longer at the Bend before she took a private car on the Erie Railroad to Buffalo, New York, to marry a company bigwig.

The Bender side suffered another loss in spring 1897 that was more dramatic, actually attracting some big city newspaper attention, but was considered less tragic by most Benders. After all, Alexander had been far more financially productive, serious, and loyal than Nathaniel Bender, an outlier in the family and then living in Wurtsboro's Hocking House. Natty had ventured to New York City in an attempt to revive the founding Basha Kill School. In the back room of a Bowery tavern, he put on a show that featured a dozen of his own soft landscapes and flamboyant bird paintings, an oil called *Drink or Drown* by Blue Boy, and Blue Belle's *Spirits Over the Basha Kill*, which anticipated the abstract movement of the next century. Neither Blue Boy nor Blue Belle attended the show. They were inactive members of the Basha Kill School, primarily because they were too involved with their family's business matters—Handy Spring Water, Blue Rock Spring Water, and BBB (Best Boyd Blueberry Co.).

The only active member of Nathaniel's Basha Kill School (and an overstimulated one to boot) called himself Chief Neversink. He created a disturbing canvas called *Redskin's Revenge* that depicted an Indian—naked except for a three-foot-high vulture-headed war bonnet and a loin cloth that failed to cover up the parts of the human anatomy it was supposed to—scalping a family of five. Nathaniel naturally refused to put the grotesque piece in the show. An enraged Chief Neversink, who had always been jealous of the attention Natty showed Blue Boy and even Blue Belle, arrived at the Bowery tavern with a large hunting knife that he plunged into the back of Nathan six times. Aida considered it fortunate that Blue Belle and Blue Boy had not attended the show, although Blue Boy believed if he had been there, he could have somehow saved his old mentor. The killer's obituary noted that he claimed to be three-quarters Lenni Lenape but in fact he was mostly Dutch with a touch of Irish and German blood and had not a trace of Indian blood. Nathan's body was shipped on the New York, Ontario & Western Railroad to Wurtsboro for burial near the crest of Blueberry Hill as he had wished. At the brief graveside service, Blue Belle said Nathaniel's life had ended far too early and called him "a lovely and loving spirit who cared for the human race the way the late Whitman had while also cherishing the great birds the way the late Thoreau had and appreciating the useful art of the world the way the late Emerson had." A few from the Bender side—Eunice, Berri, and Nickey—spoke but not nearly as graciously as the blind Boyd lady had done.

With the death of Nathaniel, who had understood and accepted people on both sides of Blueberry Hill, there was no Bender around to show the Boyds any consideration. The feud continued despite the best efforts of Blue Belle. The stone wall named Jackson stood out more than ever as the "impenetrable border" between families that had been at odds for better than half a century. Actually, there was one Bender showing consideration and something more for a single Boyd during that decade. For eight years in a row, Anna Bender and Chester Boyd brought their old bones to the valley for an annual rendezvous at the Hocking House. It was a not-so-well-kept secret that was either hushed up or ignored until November 1898 when their illicit meeting and another death fueled the flames of the feud.

§

Chester left Blue Rock House that cold November day bundled in an oversized wool coat that once belonged to his father. Snow already coated the ground and draped the sloping limbs of the blueberry bushes. Chester knew the snow was good for the hardy crop as it provided moisture, and if deep enough come winter it would help insulate the bushes from extreme cold. He also knew the early snow was good for him. While his eighty-seven-year-old legs could stand up to the mostly downhill trek to the valley, he could now cover much of the distance on Gad's five-foot steerable wooden sled. All the while descending, Chester pictured Anna underdressed but warm and waiting for him with open arms at the Hocking House, the respectable boarding house where the reliable management and staff never leaked out news of assignations.

Chester was pulling the sled along the towpath only thirty yards from the Hocking House when he thought he saw her standing on the porch. She was bundled in fur from her boots to her long coat to her ear muffs to her hat. He made out strands of almost auburn hair, though he could not make out her face. He cursed his old eyes. Still, who else could it be but the finest looking octogenarian in Sullivan County? With a burst of renewed energy and the optimism of a lover thirty years younger, he quickened his pace, soon swinging his arms with hands free. He had let go of the rope and left the sled behind without realizing it. It was of no importance now, and he didn't go back to retrieve it. So focused was he on what lay ahead that he was blindsided by two snowballs—one grazed his right ear and the other struck him in the Adam's apple. *Damn those jackanapes of Wurtsboro*, Chester thought.

"Beg your pardon, Mr. Boyd. I was aiming for your middle, but your big head got in the way. Hope I didn't hurt you any." Robert Bender stood ten feet away, rubbing his throwing shoulder. "Not so easy snowballing when you're fifty-six. Don't think I threw one of those since the wintery days of boyhood when Maurice and I had our brotherly snowball fights."

Chester had trouble swallowing for a moment so he didn't speak. Seeing one of Anna and Jeremiah's twins was unfortunate under the circumstances. He managed to shake his head without rubbing the two places he hurt.

"Stevie and Nickey used to have their share of...." Robert's voice trailed off.

Chester figured the man was still suffering from the loss of one son in that fierce panther attack so long ago, though the other one, Nickey, had gone on to become the first Bender to graduate from college, and Stevie's replacement, Oman, was getting highest marks in his class at the public school in Summitville. Fact was, Nickey and Oman, by certain standards, were doing much better than Chester's nephew Gad, who had avoided all formal education to labor for Aida and Handa in the Boyd water and blueberry businesses.

"Never saw a ninety-year-old man move so fast," Robert continued. "Where's the fire, Mr. Boyd?"

"Not ninety yet. And no fire." Chester's face still stung but he couldn't work up too much annoyance at being waylaid since he was on his way to his annual rendezvous with Anna. It suddenly hit him that he himself would never lose a son because he would never have one to lose. "Tell me, Robert, what brings you to town on this frigid afternoon?"

"You beat me to it. I was about to ask you the same question."

They stared at each other, neither ready to give an answer.

"You forgot something, Mr. Boyd." The voice was different but had the same pitch and tone. Maurice, Robert's twin, was close behind now, pulling Chester's sled.

"Oh, that," Chester said. The sun had popped out and he started feeling too hot in Handy's frayed winter coat. "It's nothing."

"I'm impressed that an old-timer like yourself can still enjoy sledding all by yourself," said Maurice. "No offense. You have weathered the years better than Pop, that's for sure. Poor man has had two strokes in case nobody told you"

"No, I didn't know about the second one. I'm...eh...sorry. Your father is resting at home, I take it."

"Hardly. He wouldn't stand for that. Robby and I wrapped him tight in a half dozen blankets and brought him here."

"Oh." Chester looked all around—even up and down the canal—but saw no wagon and no boat and no Jeremiah Bender. He felt as nervous as a boy on a first date, though he had never had a public courtship in his entire life. Of course, the date was with the wife, not the husband. "Where's your father now? You didn't leave him in the wagon, did you?"

"Of course not. That's no way for sons to treat a father. Pop is in the Pine Room of the Hocking House waiting. I doubt he is reading anything—it hurts his eyes too much—but, undoubtedly, he is smoking a cigar and admiring that evocative painting hanging over the fireplace. You know the one. It shows the D&H at a far busier time sixty years ago—idyllic as all get-out. Pop used to ask Uncle Nathaniel, may he rest in peace, why he couldn't ever paint a classical picture like that."

Chester suddenly felt like a snowman starting to melt. He stared at the Hocking House. Nobody was standing on the porch now. Anna must have slipped inside and retreated to an upstairs room. Under the circumstances that would be the wise thing for her to do, but he only hoped she had not run into her husband downstairs. "Jeremiah's waiting, you say?"

"Yes," said Maurice. "Waiting and smoking. We can't get him to quit. Smoking cigars did no good at all for poor Uncle Alexander, may he rest in peace."

Feeling dizzy and knowing he couldn't advance another step, Chester turned away from the Hocking House and slumped onto the sled. He was afraid to ask the next logical question. He wondered if it would be best to sit on the sled all night and freeze his old flesh to the bone.

"I can pull you the rest of the way if you want to pay your regards to our father," said Robert with a mischievous twinkle in his eye.

"Wouldn't that be the greatest surprise for Pop," said Maurice.

Chester knew the twins knew as well as anyone that he and Jeremiah had started the Blueberry Hill feud before mid-century and that the two old enemies hadn't spoken a civil word to each other in years. He could only hope that neither they nor their father knew why he had come to town. His thoughts pounded his head worse than the snowball. *How can I go to the Hocking House now? All optimism has drained from my heart and soul. But how can I make the mostly uphill journey back to Blue Rock House when I am so old, so tired and so...unfulfilled?*

"What is Jeremiah waiting for?" Chester finally asked.

"The wake, of course," said Maurice. "Isn't that why you are in town?"

"No. I...I just happen to be here on business. Did another Bender die or something?"

"No, we're all doing fine now, thank you. The wake is for the canal."

Chester sat up straighter and peered out at the water. "You mean the one right there?" he asked, pointing.

"Of course. The Erie Canal is still going strong, competing well with the railroads," said Robert. "We aren't so fortunate down here. The D&H is doomed. It is breaking Pop's heart. Weren't you a canal man at one time Mr. Boyd."

"You might say that. I did some canal work early on."

"Good for you. Pop has been a canal boat skipper for forty-three years. It's all over now but at least he gets to say his last goodbye."

"Yup," said Maurice. "Both the canal and the man will be gone soon. Uncles Alexander and Nathaniel already gone. We think it will all last, but nothing does. Such is life, is it not, Mr. Boyd?"

Chester didn't respond. He wasn't thinking about the late Benders. He saw it as some kind of victory that all his brothers were still alive except of course for Jacob, a casualty of the Civil War. He didn't want to know any details about the wake. He didn't want to have death on his mind...not today.

"You never did say what brought you to town," Robert said.

Chester bit his dry, cracked lip. He shivered and kept shivering. He wondered if the twins knew where their mother was this afternoon, the real reason she had come to town. She must have given Jermiah some excuse to avoid coming with him to the so-called wake for the D&H. Yet here they both were at the Hocking House—Red the Admiral of the Canal Boat Captains and *Auburn Anna,* the beautiful on-and-off adulterer.

"What business could bring you down off the Hill on a frightfully cold day like this?" Maurice asked. "Certainly not blueberry business this time of year. Spring water business?"

"Actually, not so much business. I like to get out of the house now and then." Chester wasn't foolish enough to say more than that. If he had only brought twenty-four-year-old Gad along to pull the sled, he'd be able to immediately hightail it back to Blueberry Hill. Instead, he had made other arrangements; Gad wouldn't come pick him up until morning. Yet, no question he still ached for Anna's warmth and didn't want to leave. The problem was how could he manage to enter Hocking House and creep up to Anna's chosen room without her husband and two sons seeing him?

"This is as far as I go," Chester said as he tried to get off the sled.

"Nonsense," said Maurice, raising an arm to keep him seated. "We'll take you right to the front door."

"But I...I'm not going to the Hocking House."

"No? Where are you taking the towpath to, then? Summitville? Ellenville? High Falls? Kingston?"

"Of course not. I was just..."

He had no explanation and it didn't matter anyway. Robert had taken hold of the sled's rope and Maurice now did the same. The twins pulled him along merrily as if he were one of their children, one of Jeremiah's grandchildren. He himself couldn't believe he was eighty-seven.

§

Mrs. Hocking, behind the desk in the Hocking House lobby, greeted the Bender twins and gave Chester what looked like half a wink and a nod toward the wide staircase. With Maurice holding his left arm and Robert his right, Chester entered the Pine Room as if being led to a jail cell. Bookshelves lined one wall of the room and nature paintings, including a couple by the late Nathaniel Bender, the other three. The grand fireplace and the enormous oil painting of the canal in its heyday commanded the room, and Jeremiah Bender, seated in one of two padded armchairs facing painting and fire, looked as if he were giving orders to the glowing flames. He wasn't reading or smoking, but he was drinking bourbon old-fashioneds and humming to himself out of one side of his mouth. The other side of his mouth was distorted by stroke. He did not act surprised to see his sons escorting Chester. He pointed to an empty armchair, and Chester sat when Maurice nudged him forward.

Robert advised his father not to drink too much because he was liable to fall asleep and miss the day's big event. Jeremiah scoffed at that possibility and waved both twins out of the Pine Room so he could talk with "good old Chesty" without their meddling. He quickly showed himself to be the opposite of a mean drunk. He poured Chester a drink, asked to be called "Red" again (though his hair was now all white), and explained the wake as if talking to a lifetime bosom friend. Jeremiah and his sons and other canal lovers would soon gather in front of the boarding house to begin their vigil. Sometime after dusk, Boat No. 1107 with a Captain Jacob Hensberger at the helm, would be passing by with the last load of Pennsylvania coal for New York City. Hensberger had left Honesdale's docks two days ago. The exact time the boat would reach

Wurtsboro was uncertain because there had already been delays—not enough water being let into parts of the canal; the Erie Railroad's dumping rock, dirt, and refuse into the canal at its Lackawaxen crossing; and Hensberger's decision to take the run slowly and with himself not necessarily being dry.

Chester sipped his old-fashioned as if it tasted bad. Applejack or blueberry wine would have gone down much easier. It was true that ages ago Jeremiah had been a friend, but they had been enemies for so long he wasn't certain how to talk nice with the oldest living Bender. Mostly he listened while wishing he was guzzling a beverage of his own choosing. Before long he started wondering what Anna was thinking and wearing upstairs. When Jeremiah gave his first toast to the D&H (there promised to be dozens more outside later), Chester managed to smile and click glasses with him. When the onetime butcher took credit for turning Chester into a fruitarian, they both shared a long laugh.

Occasionally the conversation drifted away from the canal, but Chester felt it safer to stick to that subject even if the canal's passing was not something he or his family would mourn. Soon enough, though, he was unnerved by the book he spotted lying out in the open on the nearest lamp table. It was Stephen Crane's romance novel *The Third Violet*, a much lesser work than Crane's famous war novel *The Red Badge of Courage* but one Chester had read in this very spot a year ago when Anna chose to sleep in on the morning after. He had a ridiculous urge to put the book back on the shelf where it belonged but instead turned away and tried to look into the fire without thinking. It got worse. Jeremiah, without any prompting, mentioned how Anna was back at the Bend helping Eunice bake a canal cake (whatever that was) for the wake but that the two women would be coming in the carriage at any moment to commiserate and comfort him and his canal pals.

"I'm afraid I won't be able to stick around, Jeremiah," Chester said. "I'm not really a canal man."

"You are to call me Red, remember?"

"I remember but I still must go."

"Balderdash! Blueberry bucket men and bottled water men are welcome, too. The D&H wake is even open to railroad men like my brother Alexander. I'm sure he'd be here if he weren't dead."

"I understand, and I'm sorry about your brother. Brothers, I should say. Nathan was always so nice to...you know my family."

"Not like me, eh? You hold a grudge, is that it? You can't stay because of me!"

"No, not exactly. You see, eh...Red, I came to town alone, and I best get home before dark. I don't walk or see so good anymore and there's all that snow."

"To hell with all that. Nobody sees or walks like they used to. We're all talk now, eh? But me and my boys will give you a ride to the Hill in one of our wagons when it's over. I wouldn't do anything less for an old pal."

"Pal?"

"That's right, pal."

"Look, I appreciate the offer but I can't stay."

"Why the hell not? It would mean more to old Red than you'll ever know."

What was making Jeremiah Bender so uncharacteristically friendly? Chester was so confused he set his glass of old-fashioned on the lamp table and told himself he had better not drink another drop. He listened to the fire crack like a whip or a hickory switch. He decided Jeremiah's amiability must be due to a combination of hard drink, tangled memories, two strokes, and deteriorating brain. Still, Chester was suspicious that Red hadn't truly gentled. It could be that come morning the Bender bastard would regret his bout of cordiality toward a Boyd.

"Let me fill your drink, pal," Jeremiah persisted.

"I really must go, Red. My family will worry about me. I've stayed too long already. I do wish you a wonderful wake, though. You deserve it."

Chester pushed against the armrests to raise out of his chair but stopped halfway up when Jermiah unleashed several words that struck like a blow to the kisser: "Sit down, Boyd oh Boy. You'll unequivocally hate yourself if you miss Anna when she comes down from the Bend with her special canal cake."

32

RENDEZVOUS AT HOCKING HOUSE

Chester was sitting in the Pine Room for another half hour listening to Red Bender's non-stop chatter about the good old days when he manned his canal boats with his young auburn-haired wife and their two fair-haired all-American twins aboard. Those twins, now full-fledged businessmen like their father, returned to take Jeremiah out onto the porch where he could sit bundled up on a rocking chair overlooking the canal. As soon as the Bender trio was gone, Chester returned *The Third Violet* to its place on the shelf and followed them out of the room as far as the lobby. There, he tapped the front desk with nervous knuckles, not sure what his next step should be.

"What goes?" he asked Mrs. Hocking.

The landlady peered over her spectacles but didn't say a word. She handed him a piece of paper folded into a tight ball.

"What is it?" he said, afraid to open it.

"From her. I don't care to be in the middle of a triangle."

"Huh?"

"Mr. Bender is on the porch. Mrs. Bender is in her room. You are here."

"He doesn't seem to know she's up there. He thinks she is home baking a cake."

"She came early, wanting to head you off before Mr. Bender arrived. She came in the morning on a wagon carrying lumber from their sawmill. The driver wasn't one to question her. As you know now, Mr. Boyd, you came too late."

"What should I do, Mrs. Hocking?"

"Read the note, Mr. Boyd, and ask nothing more of me. I like Mr. Bender, and I like you. You old men can't help but act like young fools. You don't know any better. It's what you have always done. You're like dumb mules pulling the canal boats! I adore Mrs. Bender but she is a married woman. She is to blame."

Chester didn't argue with her because he owed her and she was entitled to her own opinion. Besides, after all the hardships he had gone through getting down the Hill to town and having to deal with Anna's two sons and husband, he was in no mood to blame himself. He unfolded the note as if unwrapping a Christmas present and trying to save the paper. It read:

Change of plan. Can't be helped. Don't come upstairs. Wait for me in Pine Room. J. doesn't know I am here but he expects me. He doesn't expect you. If he sees you, tell him you are here for the wake. Even if he doesn't believe you, he'll explain the wake. He thinks I am home baking a cake with Eunice. He doesn't know Eunice can bake such a cake but I can't. He doesn't know me. Be safe. Stay down there. Read a book. [Burn this note in the fireplace].

Chester turned to look at the stairs. They were empty and inviting but he did not go to them. He looked at Mrs. Hocking but she was dusting off the front desk as if he had left dirty fingerprints on it. He returned to the Pine Room, where he reread the note two more times before tossing it into the grand fireplace and watching it turn brown to black in the yellow flames.

He did not sit. He was too restless. After weaving his way between the chairs, settees, and tables, he finally settled on going to the bookshelf. He rarely read anything at Blue Rock House, where the pickings were slim. There wasn't even a Bible anymore—it had left with Mary. Aida and Blue Belle had their Whitman, Thoreau and Emerson; Ellen her *Notes on Nursing,* by Florence Nightingale; and Elmer had recently picked up Thomas Hardy's *Jude the Obscure,* about a stonemason who wants to become a scholar. That was about it. Most of the titles on the Pine Room shelves were unfamiliar to Chester. Drawn again to Crane's *The Third Violet,* a romance set in Sullivan County and New York City, he stood there leafing through that book when Anna finally appeared in all her winter furs.

"Good, you're reading," she said as if praising a child.

'You told me to in your note," he replied.

"*The Third Violet* again? I know you like that writer character from New York City, Hollanden, who says: 'I don't like to see the world progressing. I shall go to Sullivan County for a time.' He does remind me of you, not wanting to see progress and all."

"I'm not a writer and I do want progress. I want to progress up the stairs. Jeremiah could come back in here at any moment. It's cold outside."

"No. He is having too much fun out on the porch. There are a dozen worn-out men out there giggling like schoolboys. A few wives are standing by with hot toddies and more blankets. The boat, the last boat, will be coming by soon. I can only stay a minute. I'll have to be out there when Eunice arrives with the cake."

"How did this all happen?"

"Jeremy never told me that the wake would be the same day as the rendezvous. I only learned it from Eunice yesterday. I couldn't risk visiting you at Blue Rock House and letting you know. Besides, I'm too old for trying to climb over Jackson."

"Damn that wall."

"Truth be known, I'm too old to be climbing all over you."

"No climbing necessary. You're...we're not too old."

"A year older than last year."

"All right. But we're still alive and relatively warm. That is to say we aren't dead. We have feelings. Jeremiah saw me but didn't seem suspicious. I think he believes I am here on Boyd family business. He was actually friendly to me in the Pine Room. He must be losing his mind."

"Those strokes he's had don't help."

"Suppose not. But your strokes have always helped me."

"Not so sure about that, Chesty."

"I was trying to be funny. Haven't you always asked me to be more amusing?"

"We've been together so infrequently. We've grown old, very old, apart."

"Yes, yes. Now you want me to reassure you that I'm not *too* old and am capable of making the first move for a change." He didn't move any closer to her but reached out with a quivering hand, not his dominant right one as that was riddled with the worst arthritis.

"Stay," she said, but she smiled and stepped forward. She left his hand hanging as she danced around it in an age-defying coquettish manner. When in range at last, she made the first move. She patted him on the head as if he were a dog, maybe the late coonhound Dred or the more recent Bender family bloodhound Teddy, whose namesake Theodore Roosevelt had led the Rough Riders during the Spanish-American War. "I'm so sorry things didn't work out this time," she said. "Sometimes the only thing we can expect is the unexpected."

"Why can't I go up to our usual room and wait?"

"That won't work. I know how disappointed you must be, as am I. But the room has been taken. All the rooms have been taken."

"What? How come?"

"The wake. After all the drinking and commemorating into the night, the canallers will be too tired to go back to their homes Most of them have rooms."

"So, what am I supposed to do? I came here alone thinking we'd have our room."

"I realize that, Chesty. But please don't be difficult. This is painful for me too. I've given it much thought, but I don't see anything you can do but go home right now and avoid this unfortunate mix-up. We'll have to make other arrangements."

"That so? I'll have you know that Jeremiah invited me to the wake and said I could get a ride home in one of the Bender wagons."

"Not tonight, dear. Nothing will happen tonight."

"Why not? You should have seen Old Red Bender in the Pine Room. It was as if all our differences on Blueberry Hill were forgotten."

"You haven't forgotten them, have you?"

"No." He looked over Anna's fine familiar form with young eyes. He didn't much approve of all the fur, even if it did keep her warm, but he was looking past it. What counted was the flesh and blood woman beneath all that animal hair and skin. The main thing he couldn't forget was that Anna, according to the law, belonged to Jeremiah. At the moment that seemed far worse than the Benders' lawfully occupying half of Blueberry Hill.

"You know, I'll have to cozy up to Jeremy out there," Anna said, even as she drew closer to Chester and he couldn't help but inhale her citrus scent. "The canal has meant the world to him, and I must...well, I owe this much to him—I need to be with him and support him all through the wake. For Jeremy, losing the canal is like losing his lifetime best friend."

"I understand."

"You do? Really?"

"No, but I don't believe I've ever had a best friend."

"You've had me."

"No need to remind me. I honestly don't know if I understand anything. I might be losing my mind just like your *Jeremy*. I'm nearly his age."

"Allow me to be completely honest with you, Chesty."

"If you must."

"To be completely honest with you, my sweet Chesty, I am *not* sorry to have married Jeremy. There, I've said it. He has given me so much, not just these furs and a multitude of jewels, but security, comfort, children, and a family home to die for."

"Gadzooks! Did you have to be honest on this day of all days?"

"Yes, but allow me to continue."

"I can't stop you, Anna."

"My attraction to you and yours to me is undeniable."

"You're telling me."

"But the man is my husband, and though in the past I have cursed the canal at times, today I will be there at his side to mourn its passing and commemorate its decades of memories. What good would it do you to see this? I won't be able to show you the slightest attention on the porch."

"Okay. But what about in our room later?"

"No, Chester. I told you we don't have a room."

"But are you saying Jeremiah will have a room?"

"I suppose I am. The fact is, Chester, I did get a room this morning but almost certainly it will be important that I share it with my husband tonight."

§

Anna left Chester with a kiss to the forehead that continued to burn after he lost sight of her. She went from the Pine Room to the back door of the Hocking House to meet Eunice, who would soon arrive at that designated spot with the special cake. The two women would then walk to the on-horse carriage parked in a pine grove and drive around to the front of the boarding house pretending to have just arrived together from the Bend. *Such silly deception*, thought Chester, nothing like the serious kind of deception he and Anna had been adhering to for eight years.

"To hell with romance!" Chester said to the fireplace. For a few moments he considered tossing *The Third Violet* into the flames, but he came to his senses. Stephen Crane couldn't be blamed for this romantic failure any more than the author could be blamed for the Civil War. Chester avoided the lobby, taking the narrow circular back stairs to the second floor. Not stopping there for even a peek at his "lost" room, he climbed the built-in indoor ladder and swung open the trap door that led to the roof. He had been on the flat roof of Hocking House enough times to feel nearly as comfortable there as he was on the porch roof of Blue Rock House.

He looked up teary-eyed, pressed his palms together with fingers pointed upward, and spoke to the clouds, which he imagined to be heaven's way of hiding its location. "Dear Ketanëtuwit—Please forgive me for coming up here and..." When a stiff wind struck the right side of his face, it was like being slapped by an invisible being, possibly the great Lenni Lenape spirit himself. He decided to play it safer and make his plea to a different immortal being, one more commonly consulted by white men. "Dear Lord Above—Please forgive me for coming up here and praying like this when I never take my prayers to church. But, you see, if indeed you see everything, I am an old lost soul standing here full of regrets about all the things I didn't do in my life. I've been pretty lazy and unmotivated through the many years; as a result, I have never amounted to much. I have earned no red badge of courage in the battle over Blueberry Hill, let alone the War Between the States, the Indian wars, or any other war you can name; I have only the red eyes of sorrowful cowardice in the fight for Anna Bender's affections. I'm not asking for much, Lord, only that you give this sinner, if I so be judged, the courage to take Anna into my arms tonight."

As he spoke, the clouds cleared away but only revealed a darkening sky. He looked out toward the canal and shivered, exposed as he was to the cold

November day without prospects for a warm bed. The angry wind out of the north grew strong enough to create ripples in the canal water. By dusk, a thin pale mist hovered over the water like dancing ghosts. When he heard a conch shell blast, he hurried to the front of the roof. From there he looked down at the porch roof, which hid from view Anna, Captain Jeremiah "Red" Bender, and most of the other participants in the wake, but he heard shouts of either sadness or joy, stamping feet, fiddle and banjo playing, corks popping, glasses clinking, and howling dogs.

All these sounds stopped or were drowned out by loud cow bells. Chester's eyes lost focus. He felt like screaming but his lips went numb, followed by the rest of him from the chin down. Only his ears seemed to work. They were ringing from the cow bells. Then he heard the heavy hoofbeats of towing mules—no, horses—plodding up the towpath. He rubbed his eyes. As the two-horse team came into view, Chester half expected to see the Headless Horseman on one of them—which would be fitting for the occasion. But both had only leather harnesses and thick ropes attached, as well as two cow bells each swinging from their necks. Leading the slow-moving horses was a towboy, who must have been ancient as he had a gray beard and was slightly hunched over as he shuffled along as if trying to make the outhouse before he had an accident. In one hand he held an as-yet-unlit lantern and in the other a metal container full of coal oil. Some on shore cheered him, but the biggest cheer arose when Boat No. 1107's bow slid into view, followed by its great bulk. A dark figure, Captain Jacob Hensberger no doubt, sat in the stern waving a bottle at the crowd, and the onlookers on the lawn held up bottles of their own or else glasses and mugs to salute this final passage. Jermiah and Anna must be doing the same from the porch. When the captain fell out of his chair, accidentally or for dramatic effect, Chester heard such laughter and undefined merriment from the people on the porch that he thought he was witnessing the beginning rather than the end of something terribly important.

The bearded towboy paused in his shuffling to light his lantern, and Captain Hensberger, an excellent showman even if bamboozled, picked himself off the deck and lit several well-placed torches that caused his boat to glow in the dark. Maybe they were forgetting how cold it was down below or maybe Anna and Jermiah were bundled in the same blankets and not feeling the chill in the slightest. On the roof, though, the cold pierced all the way through Chester's octogenarian bones, and he retreated inside. This time he walked through the hallways of the second floor thinking he might like to duck into one of the rooms reserved for others. Instead, he kept going and, in a sudden impulse, slid down the banister of the main staircase and practically into the lap of a stunned Mrs. Hocking.

"Don't tell me you are intoxicated, Mr. Boyd," she said, for she knew he had never needed alcohol to help him enjoy past rendezvous.

"Naturally, Mrs. Hocking, only naturally. I believed for a moment I was a kid again."

"No children are allowed in Hocking House tonight, Mr. Boyd."

"My sincerest apologies, Mrs. Hocking. I am myself again, sorry to say."

"I have seen you looking better. Are you ill?"

"Just cold, very cold. Allow me to reenter the Pine Room and warm my bones by the fire, if you please."

"Of course, Mr. Boyd. Be my guest. I don't expect any of my guests to be sober tonight."

In the Pine Room, Chester stopped at the bookshelf on the way to the fireplace and bypassed another perusing of *The Third Violet* for an older book he had never read, *Tales of the Grotesque and Arabesque, Volume 1*, by Edgar Allen Poe. He chose the same armchair Jermiah Bender had sat on earlier but kept the book closed on his lap, waiting to warm up before he began to read. When he finally did open the book, it immediately dropped to the hard floor. That sound didn't wake him, nor did the prodding of the man who came in an hour later to stoke the fire. In fact, Chester stayed put till dawn in that chair, experiencing his soundest sleep in many years.

When his eyes popped open. he remembered dreaming of Anna Bender without furs, blankets, or husband. It was not his true love's tender touch that had awakened him but the squeaky voice of housekeeper Miss Everhart, a nervous sort who reminded him of the gray squirrels that sometimes found their way into Blue Rock House but not a way out without assistance.

"You mustn't be here, Mr. Boyd," she said. "You must get up."

"Must I? What time is it?"

"Not so late, sir, but too late."

"What does that mean?"

"Something awful happened last night, out there." Miss Everhart pointed her long-handled dusting brush at the window, whose drapes were closed.

"Don't tell me the captain of the last canal boat fell asleep and crashed."

"Something much worse. It did involve a captain, though."

"What captain?"

"Captain Bender, sir. It was his heart, sir. It gave out at the celebration, the wake, whatever you call it."

That news brought Chester out of his chair. "Are you sure it was him?"

"Yes, indeed. His wife was at his side. They had been arguing heatedly about something. Of course, I only heard this, Mr. Boyd. I wasn't out there when it happened. I don't mean to spread false rumors about anyone, living or dead."

"What are you saying then? Is it a rumor or is Jeremiah Bender actually dead?"

"Deader than that canal."

Chester sat back down. He stared into the fireplace where only a few embers still burned.

"I'm sorry, sir, but you had better be on your way. I really must straighten up the Pine Room." She noticed Edgar Alan Poe's collection of short stories on the floor and bent dramatically to pick it up. Chester couldn't help but take note of her active backside despite the gravity of the situation. He thought she could have used a bushy tail. "Mrs. Hocking is having one of her conniptions this morning," the housekeeper continued as she dusted off Poe. "Nothing like this has ever happened before—I mean right on the Hocking House front porch."

"I wouldn't think so," Chester said, rising once more. "Has anyone been looking for me?"

"Not that I know of, sir."

"Have you seen Anna Bender this morning?"

"No, sir. She left with her sons and the, you know, gentleman's corpse in the middle of the night. I didn't see them go, but Mrs. Hocking told me the widow was in a terrible state, grieving even more than one would expect under these circumstances."

"Yes, trying circumstances—death at a wake."

"Yes, sir. That is what it was indeed."

Chester stepped aside because the anxious housekeeper wanted to dust the side table next to his chair and he had to pee something awful. "Goodbye, Miss Everhart," he said. "You've been a tremendous help."

33
THE RED BENDER MEMORIAL BASH

It came to light in Wurtsboro and both sides of Blueberry Hill that Jeremiah Bender suffered his fatal heart attack at the D&H Canal wake upon learning from his wife that Chester Boyd had come to the Hocking House that day for the sole purpose of fornication or, considering their ages, at least attempted fornication. Those on the Bender side pinned the blame for Jeremiah's death on Chester. They insisted that at age eighty-seven he remained an unscrupulous satyr bent on making Anna forget her marital vows. While she had rebuffed Chester's vile advances that day, the shock of hearing about them proved too much for Jeremiah's weak heart.

On the Boyd side, the consensus was that two people could not rendezvous unless they both wanted to rendezvous. At the same time Elmer, Henry, Blue Boy, and Peter could not see what their brother saw in Anna Bender and were sorry he hadn't showed better judgment, for his ill-advised rendezvous and the sudden death of his rival led to increased Boyd-Bender bitterness. Gad wondered why, if old folks could do things like that, why couldn't he. As for observers in the valley, they regarded the renewed hostility on Blueberry Hill as predictable and had no trouble debating who was most to blame and who might die next. Regardless, nobody had anything bad to say about Aida, the boss of the Boyd enterprises, or her able assistant, Handa. Handy Spring Water, Blue Rock Spring Water, and BBB (Best Boyd Blueberry Co.) continued to thrive, even as Chester sank into despondency despite the efforts of Blue Belle and Ellen to cheer him up.

Eunice immediately orchestrated a family-only funeral service for her latest late brother (after Alexander and Nathaniel had gone before him). It wasn't until the summer of 1899, however, that the Benders gave Jeremiah a proper send-off. They needed time to prepare for a no-expenses-spared extravaganza that newspapermen were already calling the "Sullivan County Party of the Century" and were predicting would not be topped until well into the next century. Maurice and Robert Bender and their wives, along with Eunice and Daniel Leach and all the younger family members, spent winter and spring turning the Bend—with renovations, additions, new furnishings, better gardens, and improved landscaping—into more than just a Sullivan County showcase. The house was the talk of upstate New York. And so was the early August party, which was meant to be a celebration of Jeremiah's life and his family's way of living on the Hill and received a brief mention in the society columns of three New York City newspapers. Eunice sent out hundreds of invitations and in each of them she insisted that nobody come to the Bend with the intention to mourn.

No Boyd, not even Blue Belle, was invited to cross over Jackson and attend. Chester, though, had a morbid fascination with the extravaganza and was determined to be an eyewitness. With his binoculars around his neck and Gad lending a much needed hand, the oldest living Boyd made it over the wall on the morning of the event. Trying to scramble up the rock outcrop that Anna had named the "Castle" proved too difficult, so he sent Gad to the top. The sightlines weren't right to see the Bend, his nephew reported, so Chester went with Plan B—taking up a spying position in one of the Bender hunting blinds. That didn't work out either. There were some good views from the blinds but none that allowed them to see much of the Bend. "Just as well," said Chester, who felt uncomfortable in these places where hunters fired down at white-tail deer and other harmless creatures of the Hill.

Gad had a better idea—a tree fort built by twins Stevie and Nickey Bender in the 1880s, two or three years before the killer panther of Long Swamp dispatched Stevie. Gad, now twenty-four, remembered being barred from the structure during his boyhood because he was the enemy. The twins, when they were playing frontier soldiers instead of cowboys and Indians, built the fort themselves in a tall red oak tree using the best Bender white pine lumber.

"It's much closer to the Bend than any of the hunting blinds," Gad told his uncle. "There's a ladder nailed to the side of the oak, at least there was. It led up to a high wood platform with three walls and a partial roof to keep out rain, cannonballs. and other projectiles. Not sure how well it has held up."

"How are the sightlines up there?" Chester asked. "How well can you see the house?"

"Pretty darn good I'm thinking, though, like I said, they never let me up there. Nickey did tell me once that from the tree fort they could not only hear their mother when she stepped out the back door to call them in for a meal but also see her. I just hope the fort is still there."

"Why wouldn't it be?" asked Chester, but he answered his own question. "Unless Daniel Leach cut down the red oak."

The tree, the fort, and the ladder were all still in place. Gad found the spot easily. There was more open space than he remembered. Only one rung in the ladder appeared loose, but he still doubted an old fellow like his uncle could make the climb. Chester insisted he could do it, mentioning how he still scrambled up the outdoor steps Elmer built to reach the porch roof back home.

"This is steeper," Gad said. "And two kids made this ladder. If you should fall...well, the Benders would find us and we'd be arrested for trespassing."

"What are you saying, Gad? You don't want to do it?"

"Sure, I do, if you do."

"Do bears shit in the woods?"

"Right, Uncle Chesty. I'll go first and scout out the view. Hand me those binocs."

Chester grumbled but passed his nephew the binoculars. Gad shot up the ladder, stepping over the one bad rung. The fort floor was splintered and not quite level, but solid. He felt it could support both their weights. From the fort's open end, he was surprised how much he could see with his naked eyes. With the binoculars he clearly saw the back of the two-story house, most of the manicured back lawn, and the entire rebuilt grand gazebo. A half dozen people, employees he believed, were walking around putting out checkered tablecloths and vases of flowers that didn't look wild. Three musicians stepped up into the grand gazebo with their instruments and found chairs. A woman, old but spry, came out the back door and began barking instructions. He identified her as Eunice Bender, Queen of the Bend.

"You see something else, don't you?" Chester called out.

"Plenty. It's early but there'll be a lot to see from here. We won't miss the party, Uncle Chesty."

"Who are you seeing now?"

"Not her yet. If you still want to come up, I'll come down and help you with the ladder."

"All I need is a little pull. The last step might be tricky." Chester spoke from the top of the ladder. When he reached out with his less arthritic left hand, Gad rushed over to him and grabbed the hand—not a second too soon, he thought. Chester freely gave him his other hand, too, trusting in him, and when Gad pulled, his uncle grunted but easily made that last step. Whatever fears Handy had, one of them wasn't heights. He walked steady across the floor, not bothered by the sway, took command of the binoculars, and stood straight and tall as he scanned the grounds like a ship captain looking out to sea with a spyglass.

"Excellent," Chester said. "Better than I could have imagined. Today I won't be blaming Daniel Leach for leveling so many trees on this side of the Hill. He left this wonderful oak."

"Not bad at all, is it?" said Gad. "Glad to have finally made it into Stevie and Nickey's fort after all these years."

"I suspect this is the only thing on this side of the hill not built by Leach. I love it. I'll be needing a few comforts from home. I plan to be here for the duration."

"I'm with you, Uncle Chesty. Tell me what you need and I'll fetch them."

"You're a good nephew. I made out a list earlier in case we found a spot like this. Here it is. Hurry, Gad. Like you said, you don't want to miss the party."

Chester manned the fort alone, but not for long. Gad had always been a fast runner. He returned from Blue Rock House with everything on the list—Chester's favorite wool blanket, a bottle of Handy Spring Water or maybe Blue Rock Spring (it was still all the same), a chamber pot, and a flat-bottomed paper bag loaded to the hilt with Boyd blueberries.

"I'll be all right up here," Chester told him. "No need to stay if you have better things to do."

"Aida and Handa would only have me picking more berries at the house. I'll stick."

"As you wish. My brothers think I'm crazy. Elmer said nothing would please him more than to see an all-day rain, wrathful thunder, and relentless lightning spoil the Benders' memorial party. Henry and Blue Boy went further, wishing for a full-fledged twister to rage on the Bender side of Jackson. Aida and Handa think I came here simply to avoid work. The taskmasters still expect me to pick at my age. Can you believe it!"

"Yes, sir. They think the picking gives you a purpose in life. They think the same about me and I'm young. But my mother and Blue Belle know the real reason you and I want to be here."

"Do they?"

"Yup. Anna Bender for you. They say she still occupies your heart and head and that you are dying to see her, even if it is only catching a few glimpses of her through your binoculars."

Chester lowered the binoculars so he could adjust the wool blanket and take a sip of water. He had never admitted to any member of his family that his obsession for Anna had grown despite the fact the widow was avoiding him like the plague and proving herself truer to Jeremiah's ghost than she ever had been to the living man. "A couple of smarties," he said. "Do you believe what they're saying, Gad?"

"Sure. I'm no kid anymore, Uncle Chesty. Fact is, I'm with you today for a better reason than not wanting to pick berries."

"How sweet. You don't want me to fall out of the tree."

"Yes, there is that. But if you want to know the absolute truth, I'm here pretty much for the same reason you are."

"Huh? You want to get a glimpse or two of Anna Bender? She is practically my age. Now, that's crazy."

"Not her, no offense. But have you seen Maurice and Judy's daughter, Betty?"

"Once or twice. Cute as a button, I suppose?"

"Sharp-witted, clever, independent-minded, and as lovely as a wild rose. Betty the Beautiful—that's what I call her. You aren't too old to see that, are you Uncle Chesty?"

"Hell no. We'll share the binoculars."

§

The guests at what later became known as the "Red Bender Memorial Bash," included onetime canal investors, unemployed canallers, former hoggees (yes, several were females), railroad presidents and engineers, assemblymen, local officials, businessmen, and farmers. They came from up and down the valley and beyond. The sun was popping in and out of the clouds as if teasing the party goers. Three different bands were taking turns playing lively beats at the grand gazebo, and the sound carried continuously to the ears of Chester, even though his hearing wasn't what it had been one year earlier, and Gad, who sometimes elected to dance with himself in the tree fort.

"Do you have to do that?" Chester asked, trying to hold the binoculars steady. "You're shaking the place."

"I should be down there on the lawn dancing with Betty the Beautiful," said Gad, but he didn't stop completely. He swayed to the beat, and the tree fort swayed with him.

"I'm not complaining, mind you. I'm glad to be here with you. Just afraid you might punch a hole through the floor with your feet. Wood looks to be rotting in places."

"I suppose. Wood does that. I imagine Uncle Elmer would be the only man alive who'd want to build a tree fort out of stone. That would be as funny as his stone outhouse."

"They sure are dancing up a storm down there on the lawn." Chester lowered the binoculars for a moment and rubbed his eyes as he stared at his nephew's feet. "What's funny is that in all my years on this planet, I never learned to dance. Looks to me you haven't either."

"What are you looking at me for?" Gad stopped his one-man dance and moved to the edge of the fort to peer below. "Weren't you able to spot her?"

"No." Chester went back to the binoculars. "A lot of those fat rich men bending to the will of the Benders are blocking the bejeweled ladies. Could be Anna isn't on the lawn at all. Maybe it is still too soon for a widow to start enjoying herself in public."

"I wouldn't know about that. But I didn't mean Anna. Sorry."

"Don't be sorry, Gad. I was only having fun with you. Betty must be the one in the blue dress dancing with that long, lean man in the three-piece suit. What a generous mustache he has and such a trim pointed beard."

"What? Give me those binocs, would you?"

Chester obliged. "Am I wrong?"

"Aw, your eyes must be deceiving you. Her dress is violet and she's dancing with her fat father, Maurice."

"My mistake—old tired eyes, you know." Chester chuckled and grabbed a handful of blueberries from the bag. He ate them one at a time, savoring every bite. When he was done, he reclaimed the binoculars. "Clouds are almost gone. Must be past noon. The sun has the Bend all lit up. Eunice must have ordered it. The rich folks are stuffing their faces. Must want to fill their bellies in case the rains come later."

"Is Betty still dancing with her father?"

"I'm looking at the house now. I forgot that the ever-industrious Daniel Leach added those two wings to the Bend. I know Berri and her husband, Jonas Gadebusch, are occupying one of the wings after their cottage burned down. Not sure about the other one. Lots of room for a growing family, though I'm sure they have plenty of guest rooms, too. I can see Anna's bedroom from here, not that I've ever been inside it, of course."

"Of course not."

"The curtains are drawn on her two windows but she wouldn't be up there now. That wouldn't do for a widow, whether grieving or merry. It is her responsibility to mingle with her late husband's friends and associates. Say, I wonder which room Betty sleeps in."

"I wouldn't know. I don't think you can see it from here."

"No matter. She's trying to be the life of the lawn party, isn't she?"

"I wouldn't put it that way exactly. It just comes naturally to her—you know, to shine and sort of stand out."

"She's not dancing with Maurice anymore. Who is that handsome young fellow giving her a whirl?"

"What?" Gad snatched the binoculars from his uncle. "That's only Nickey. That's okay."

"Right. They are first cousins."

"I wonder if Nickey actually asked her to dance. He has always been pretty shy."

"But he's about your age, right? We all grow up."

"Damn. I should be down there."

"You going to keep hogging the binoculars, Gad?"

"Sorry. A little while longer, please, Uncle Chesty. Don't worry. I'll let you know if Anna appears."

"Yes, do that. I'll tell your mother she should get you your own binoculars for your next birthday."

"Boy can Betty move, like a hummingbird. Her violet dress is flying about. She's creating her own breeze. Nickey doesn't know what he's doing. He's stiff as a board."

"Maybe she asked him to dance. Or don't young ladies do such things?"

"Sure, they do. I mean she would do that. He's shy and a...you know, safe choice."

"So, she wouldn't ask a bold Boyd like yourself to dance?"

"Wouldn't have to. I'd ask her first."

"I see. But what about other young men or old men for that matter. Would she ask them?"

"I don't think she'd ask you, Uncle Chesty. You don't dance."

"True. But would she ask some other older gentleman, say Blue Boy, another Boyd who isn't married?"

"Why all these silly questions. I'm sure she'd rather be dancing with me."

"I don't doubt that. I'm simply trying to gauge what kind of young lady Betty is."

"All right I'll tell you. I'd say, and others would say, too, she's the New Woman."

"New, huh? Meaning she smokes cigarettes, wears trousers, and rides bicycles?"

"No. I mean she does have a bicycle. Her father bought it for her. But I never saw her light up a cigarette, and she likes dresses, too."

"Right. Ever flowing violet dresses."

"Look, Uncle Chesty. I'll have you know that the New Woman isn't only about looks. She is intelligent, independent-minded, clever, funny and serious, interested in women's suffrage, opposed to the Philippine-American War, loves the taste of blueberries, appreciates modern literature and art."

"Is that all?"

"Is that all! Aw, you're kidding me again. I bet you didn't know she has talked about reviving the late Nathaniel Bender's Basha Kill School of Art with Blue Belle and Blue Boy."

"Not a Boyd hater then?"

"She'll get along with anybody, even those she disagrees with and considers old-fashioned."

"I suppose that would be me. I generally disagree with all Benders. And I don't approve of their monstrous house or any of the other structures they saw fit to stick up on *our* Hill. Well, maybe this tree fort is an exception."

"You never were opposed to Anna Bender."

"Never mind the merry old widow. What matters now is fresh young love. Would you say your Betty the Beautiful is a Boyd lover?"

Gad's face turned red and he lowered the binoculars. "You can't embarrass me, Uncle Chesty. I don't need to look at her anymore. Here, take the binocs. I'm hungry." He took a seat on the floor, crossed his legs, and helped himself to the bag of blueberries. "Nothing better in the whole wide world than fresh berries, eh Uncle?"

"Right. Along with Handy Spring water. Your Grandfather Handy would be proud of you, boy."

Chester scanned the dancers, focusing the binoculars for a minute on the pleasing Berri Gadebusch, who wore a frilly blue dress to match the color of the elaborate ribbon in her blonde curls. She had caught the eye of more men and women on the lawn than he could count, which shouldn't have surprised him, but he swung the binoculars away in disgust. Where was Anna? He doubted whether fifty or sixty years ago she could have been as beautiful as Berri was now. But it was close enough.

Chester kept pointing the binoculars at the windows of the Bend, but saw no movement behind them and suddenly felt tired. He was about to hand the glasses back to his nephew when something on the roof caught his eye and caused him to question his sanity. He kept refocusing, but there was no doubt about it—he was seeing a long, narrow boat, the kind that Jeremiah Bender once operated on the D&H Canal. Chester couldn't make out the name printed near the bow, but he was convinced he was seeing *Annabelle I,* the first of three boats that Jeremiah had named for a spouse who had resented being a "canal wife." He couldn't imagine how the boat ever got up there—a place where it would be seen by birds rather than fish.

"How could I have missed it before?" he said. "Up on the roof. It makes no sense, like putting walking shoes on a person's ears, a hump on a human back, a train engine on a canal, a horse or mule on a bicycle."

"Oh, that," said Chester. "Betty's uncle, Nickey's father, had it hoisted up there."

"For what purpose?"

"Betty told me Robert Bender wanted it on the roof to honor Jeremiah, the Admiral of the Canal Captains, as well as everyone else who made the D&H possible and profitable...for a while."

"Including himself, no doubt." Chester remembered reading an article in the paper about Jeremiah's favorite twin. Robert had served as towboy, bilge pumper, and bowman on some of his father's canal boats. He had reason to want to recognize the lads—and a few lasses, too—who had walked the towpath fifteen or more miles a day, six days a week, with mules or horses from late March until the usual December freeze. No doubt he was also hoping at this Red Bender Memorial Bash to gain support among the influential guests for the reopening of the moribund canal. Reportedly shipping on the canal could be done at half the cost charged by the noisy railroads, resulting in a savings of two dollars a ton. But was that enough to cancel out the slowness factor, reflective of a century about to close? Chester had no use for the canal but he could almost sympathize with Robert for wishing to bring back the past to restore any hope for the future…but only *almost*.

"Yeah, Betty's uncle is crazy about the canal. Her father is more sensible. Maurice Bender supports the railroad."

"I know; it's been that way for a long time." That same newspaper article had talked about Maurice, too. A onetime towboy like his twin brother, Maurice had showed enterprising skills in boyhood by selling cheap canal boat rides to children from Port Jervis, Cuddebackville, Wurtsboro, Summit, and Ellenville before turning against the canal life and becoming a totally grounded businessman. Maurice, like his late Uncle Alexander, had put his faith in the New York, Ontario & Western Railway and other railroads by buying valuable stock.

Usually one who avoided looking ahead, Chester wondered if the railroad would one day fall out of favor the way the canal had. Thinking about the future made him feel older and extremely sleepy. "That canal boat belongs on the roof, permanently stuck," he said. "It's obsolete. Of course, should there ever be a forty-day rain in the making as in Noah's time, the Benders will be all set." He pushed the binoculars into Gad's hands, lay back on his blanket, and closed his eyes to the present and the future. Where was Anna? He had never seen her dance in public in his life. He thought of her at rendezvous. No, she wasn't young, not like Berri or Betty, but boy could she *move,* perhaps more like a yellow-rumped warbler than a hummingbird.

"Watching how the rich and beautiful commemorate the death of one of their own has got you tuckered, huh?" Gad asked.

"Hush your mouth, boy. We don't like their type. We *look down* on them. You're a Boyd."

"Don't I know it. Should Anna Bender make an appearance, I'll wake you immediately."

§

Chester hoped to dream of Anna as she was before the D&H canal wake—warm and willing. Instead, his dreams were a jumble of nonsense and near truth, in which his father and the Lenni Lenape Man were performing the Blueberry Dance together while shaking turtle-shell rattles, Handa was fitting shackles around somebody's hairy ankles, Henrietta was landing a sperm whale while fishing in the Basha Kill, Blue Belle was teaching Walt Whitman how to spell anesthesia, Mary was sweeping phallic-like pine needles off the roof of Blue Rock House even as Elmer stood below dodging fieldstones falling like hailstones, Ellen was reattaching Peter's missing arm, and Jeremiah was flying through the clouds in a winged canal boat. He was remembering all this while waking up in total darkness except for a blotch of light coming from somewhere far off. He didn't know where he was, what time it was, or why a monstrous fly-like creature was peering at him.

"Wake-up, Uncle Chesty, wake-up!" said Gad, facing him with the binoculars still glued to his eyes. "You plan on sleeping all night."

Chester still heard the music coming up from below and at least remembered where he was—sitting in a rotting tree fort with his horny nephew like a couple of voyeurs. At least it wasn't raining. "What do you mean *all night*?"

"They turned the lights on at the Bend. I saw Anna. She came out and made an announcement, then raised her arms to the sky and the lights came on like magic."

Gad handed him the binoculars, and Chester peered through them toward the Bend. Indeed, there was light coming from inside every window in the house, from the grand gazebo, from torches planted in the lawn with the silhouettes and shadows of people all around. He thought he must still be dreaming.

"Amazing, isn't it, Uncle Chesty?" said Gad.

"How can it be? Nobody has brought electricity to the Hill."

"The Benders are generating their own electricity. Daniel Leach constructed a powerhouse next to the carriage house."

"Okay, a powerhouse. But what generates the power?"

"Not exactly sure. It's new to me, too. Betty told me a heavy gas engine is ignited by heating a red-hot ball with a blow torch. She never actually showed it to me."

'And it makes all that light?"

"Apparently. It's something to see, isn't it?"

"All right, Gad. I've seen it." Chester returned the binoculars to his nephew and rubbed his eyes so hard that they hurt. "Betty Bender has told you and shown you a hell of a lot, hasn't she?"

'I suppose."

"Don't lie to your uncle, Gad. How long has this been going on?"

"Awhile. Why should I lie. Something bothering you, Uncle Chesty?"

"You have been welcomed at the Bend—I mean by Eunice, Maurice, Robert and the rest of the surviving Bender family?"

"Not exactly. She comes up the Hill. We meet every two weeks or so at Jackson. She can climb the wall almost as good as I can. She's very able-bodied."

"Must be. Does your father and mother know about these secret meetings?"

"They aren't exactly secret, but nobody knows except you...well, maybe Blue Belle knows, too. She sees so many things without seeing."

"Nobody will accept you and the young Bender girl being so, you know, friendly."

"She's twenty-three, less than a year younger than me. We're both full grown."

"I'm not talking about age, Gad, or how grown up you two think you are. It's all about two families divided by a wall and years of hostility."

"Hasn't stopped you and Anna from getting together, has it? Betty and I don't go so far as to rendezvous at the Hocking House or anywhere else off the Hill."

Chester felt like slapping Gad, but he wasn't a hitter or a fighter and the impulse passed. "You got me there," he admitted. "But that's all in the past. The way Anna is now, our rendezvous days are over."

"The way Betty is now I hope it'll last forever and she never quits me."

"All right. I'll hope the same. But you sound worried."

"Worried? What do you mean?"

"Worried that she'll suddenly change and feel differently about you. Or maybe worried that her family will order her to stay away from you, a no-account Boyd, and that she'll listen because blood is thicker than love."

"Nothing like that exactly. But she's a free spirit who does what she pleases and isn't all together predictable. At the moment she isn't keen on marriage or even a long engagement. And children can wait. She doesn't want to be bogged down. Like I told you before, she's the genuine *New Woman*."

"Got it. So, you two do it right there in the blueberry bushes?"

"You're my favorite uncle, but I don't think I'll answer that one. I am a Boyd, but we can be gentlemen, can't we?" Gad narrowed his eyes and moved the binoculars back and forth hoping to spot his favorite Bender dancing in the moonlight.

"I reckon Anna once thought that was possible, me being a gentleman. Anyway, I wish you all the luck in the world with your Betty."

"Thanks, Uncle Chesty. I'm awfully glad it was Jeremiah who bit the dust at the D&H wake instead of you. Hey, speak of the devil!"

Gad had spotted something else lit up, not at the house but on a high but narrow rock outcropping beyond the powerhouse. He passed the binoculars to Chester, who had trouble finding the tall rocks, but once he did, he couldn't miss the larger-than-life, muscular and bearded bronze figure standing tall atop that natural pedestal. A statue of Jeremiah Bender had been unveiled. The sculptor had depicted him wearing a pea coat and a silly cap with the word "Captain" embroidered in gold and had him pointing at something unseen while holding what looked like a gigantic pocket watch in his other hand. Light generated from the powerhouse gave a solar red glow to Jeremiah's face.

"Can you believe it," said Gad. "Betty told me that her father and Uncle Robert had hired some famous sculptor from Albany to produce a bronze in a hurry. I never thought it would be so big and true to life."

"Too big. Look at that watch. No matter how big a time piece you have, you still run out of time. I truly have seen enough." Chester tossed the binoculars aside, accidentally or not knocking over the chamber pot, which fortunately was empty.

When the chamber pot began rolling down the uneven floor, Gad stopped its progress with his foot and picked up the binoculars for another look. "Statues usually last longer than men."

"Thank you for your wisdom, Gad."

"All I can say is, no matter what you thought of Jeremiah Bender in life, he looks pretty amazing now. All by himself he must be eight feet tall and the rock supporting him is at least twenty feet high. Heck, he's practically at eye level with those Canada geese headed for the Basha Kill."

"May they cover him with bird poop!"

§

Chester Boyd was a washout for the rest of the 1899 blueberry picking season and in late summer badly strained his back the one time he tried to help bottle water from Handy Spring. Trying to make it to the high, open air on the Blue Rock House porch roof became too difficult. He took to his narrow bed in his little claustrophobic room outdoing Henry when it came to shunning work on account of injury, frailty, and especially hopelessness. Ellen, the lifetime family nurse, now tended to him more than she did Henry, who was at least not gloomy in his endless suffering; Blue Boy, who hadn't been himself since the death of his artistic mentor, Nathaniel Bender; Elmer, who had gone into accelerated decline after wife Mary escaped in 1897 from the State Homeopathic Asylum in Middletown, devoured two handfuls of the appropriately named death angel mushroom, and died ten days later from liver failure; and husband Peter, who had proved himself to be the best worker of Handy's five sons and so healthy and understanding that he no longer needed to burden himself with fraternal jealousy or dwell on any manly deficiencies. Peter was, however, bothered by his limited relationship with his son; Gad worked hard with him for the good of the Boyd businesses but didn't confide in him, didn't look anything like him, didn't act like him, didn't necessarily look up to him, and only offered him insincere smiles and polite silences.

Gad couldn't relate to his mother any better than he could his father. Ellen was full of nursing instincts, of course, but lacked sincere maternal instincts. He knew she had given birth to him but sometimes when she looked at him or didn't look at him, he thought of himself as her adopted child. He was hard pressed to remember any long embrace, and he could not imagine her ever having allowed her one and only baby to suckle. Aunt Aida had been far more critical of him through the years, yet he had never felt his mother's complete support, not even after his return to Blueberry Hill from Oswego. For a bonified caregiver, she had a way of showing her love in small samples. She hadn't even liked the name his father gave him, preferring to call him *Sonny* (as if describing what kind of day it was) or *Boy Boyd* (as if he belonged to the whole family rather than her).

Gad did not find a substitute mother in either of his aunts. Aunt Blue Belle was like a mythical creature you wanted to believe in but could never be sure really existed except in the spirit world. She could read your mind and *not* hold your thoughts against you even though you knew many of your thoughts were unkind and impure. She could offer hugs, but hugging her was like grasping thin air or at least an insubstantial body light enough to blow away in the next strong breeze. Like her hero Walt Whitman she could celebrate nature, democracy, love, and friendship, but she did not speak out against the hatred, evil, and unfairness that persisted in the world and that meant never making a single mean comment about a Bender. In a way she was God-like, that is to say a God who created man, put him on Earth, and was content to watch him do whatever the hell he wanted because she was convinced his innate goodness would prevail in the end.

Aunt Aida held everything together—the house, the blueberry bushes, the fruitful spring, the traditions, the family—in the face of the Benders and the challenges of the outside world. Her five brothers had long submitted to her will or on rare occasion fought it out of weakness rather than strength. Behind her back, they referred to her as "The General" more than "Queen of the Hill," but they all knew they would be lost without her running the show on their side of Blueberry Hill. Gad could admire her all right when she wasn't ordering him about, but she often seemed distant and unapproachable, thus untouchable if not unlovable.

Daughter Handa, Gad's cousin, was so much like her mother that her uncles referred to her as 'Lieutenant General." Gad could think of her that way, too, even though Handa didn't always follow orders any better than he did when she thought she could get away with it. She had an independent streak that allowed her to think beyond blueberries and water. She imagined herself as the first Railroad Baroness, the entrepreneur who challenged and crushed the Bender empire, the first woman to became mayor of New York City, and the first woman to be elected president of the United States. She believed that her mother, upon learning of those deep-seated ambitions, would tell her to stop thinking the impossible like some silly girlish daydreamer.

Gad suspected, though, that Aida was all for Handa reaching for the stars and not being burdened with a husband and old-fashioned notions about what a woman's place should be in a man's home.

Gad once saw Aida take her daughter aside and give her a small, dead-serious speech: "I can't go on forever, Handa. Blue Rock House will all be yours one day, but you must have family to share it with. So many of us here today are old and worn and won't be here tomorrow or the day after tomorrow. Even if you find marriage unsuitable now and continue to do so in the future, you must at some point have a child as I have had you. More than one would be better. No point in taking chances and risk having the family become extinct. For the Boyds to boldly carry on in the 20th century and beyond, we must have not only production but also reproduction. Do you understand?"

"Of course, I do, Mumsy," Handa replied. "Marriage is quite unsuitable. I have too much to do here—more important things—with you. Strange young Nickey Bender once showed interest in me, especially after that panther ate his twin, but of course I would have nothing to do with him. Not only is he a Bender but he remains as helpless as a drowning pussy cat."

"But what about your duty to give us Boyd offspring?"

"I shall do my duty, Mumsy, no matter how great the sacrifice. No rush is there?"

"Certainly not, but time has a way of slipping away. I wouldn't wait too terribly long, dear."

The way Gad saw it, his cousin wasn't anything like his true love despite their shared opinion that marriage was out of the question, that all females deserved the same status as males, and that exceptional females should be recognized as superior. His Betty was the New Woman; Handa was the Reconstructed Woman.

34

DEATHS AND RESOLUTIONS

Aida and Handa shared a morbid joke on Christmas Day, 1899: The end of the 19th century was proving to be the "Boyd deadline." Three of Aida's brothers had died earlier that year, at least having the courtesy to wait until the blueberry picking season was over (that morbid joke was shared by Chester and Gad).

Elmer went first in late October, which was expected since his health had fallen with the temperature and he seemed intent in joining Mary in Heaven or somewhere close to it. Mary had been buried near the asylum in Middletown, but in accordance with Elmer's dying request, she was reinterred next to him in the family plot uphill from Handy Spring and directly behind the grave shared by Handy and Catawissa Manayunk. At the quiet graveside ceremony, Henry was suffering from consumption, and his coughing fits kept disrupting Blue Belle's touching tribute to Elmer and Mary. Blue Belle had been listing Elmer's accomplishments, all works of stone—most notably Blue Rock House and the family memorial cairn, whose growth would continue with the laying on of nonprecious stones. "I best return to my sickbed because that is to be my deathbed, and I mustn't take away from my brother's time," said Henry before he staggered up the Hill alone. It was seen as a noble gesture because it allowed Blue Belle to go on with the Elmer and Mary eulogy without further interruption.

Henry wasn't the next to go, though. In the room next to Henry's sickbed, Blue Boy became prostrate in early November, his bones and muscle aching from his tailbone to his receding hairline, his face continuously sweating, his hands swollen, his eyes watery, his appetite gone ("No more blueberries," were practically his last words spoken to his nurse, Ellen). By Thanksgiving he was gone, a late victim of the so-called Russian flu epidemic, which supposedly had run its course five years earlier. For how much time Ellen spent nursing Blue Boy, it was a wonder she didn't catch the highly contagious disease. But, as Peter suggested, nurses lived on until all their patients were buried.

It wasn't until the second week in December that Henry coughed for the last time. His last words were, "Why, Ellen, I may get out of bed this morning; I'm feeling nearly up to snuff." Quite a few blueberry bushes had to be cleared to accommodate the new graves. The family memorial cairn reached new heights, though not nearly rivaling the statue of Jeremiah Bender on the other side of the Hill. Despite being on the verge of tears and undoubtedly distressed over how fast members of the family were failing and falling, Aida noted to Handa how the family's expanding private cemetery was taking a toll on the valuable blueberry bushes. Handa, not one to cry or disagree with her mother, replied: "And, without doubt, we haven't seen the end of it. You still have two living brothers."

One of those living brothers, Chester, hadn't always seen eye to eye with Aida and Handa about family and business matters through the years. But he didn't hold it against them that they hadn't acted broken up when Henry stopped being sick and died, joining Elmer, Blue Boy, Handy, Man, and the first Blue Belle in eternal rest on the Hill. It seemed like Henry had been preparing for death most of his life. Chester spoke to all the living Boyds at breakfast the day after Henry went: "When tears start surfacing continuously like our spring water, right-thinking people come to realize unless they move on, they're going to drown in their grief. I sure don't want you all to drown before you get the chance to see my spirit fly up to Blue Heaven or spiral down to Red Hell. Save a tear or two for me."

The other living brother, Peter, shed his share of tears over the loss of three brothers but mixed in among the sobs brought on by sadness were tears of happiness. He finally had Ellen all to himself or would soon once Chester passed on, not that he wished to speed anything up. He loved his wife with a passion, loved his son with a passion, picked berries with a passion, bottled water with a passion, and each morning borrowed Handa's hand mirror and saw the passion in his own face. "I haven't felt this healthy since losing my arm in the Civil War," he told Ellen in bed on three occasions. Another time, while bottling water at a personal best pace, he told her, "Heck, my precious wife of mercy, I feel so darn good I half-expect my right arm to grow back." His revival amid all the dying alarmed Ellen at first but when she got used to it, she became delighted for the both of them. It was as if they were born again. She recalled how Mary once quoted Jesus Christ: "No one can enter the kingdom of God unless he is born of water and the Spirit." Not that Ellen wanted him or her to enter that kingdom anytime soon. "Don't you worry about the family businesses," she told Aida and Handa. "We'll keep all those bottles filled and next summer Petey and I will pick our tails off for you."

Chester marveled at the happy couple and also felt a tinge of jealousy, but he himself was no longer under a pall of gloom. He accepted the fact he couldn't possibly live as long as his father had; in fact, it wasn't something that mattered any longer. He decided to spend his last days not lying in bed mourning the dead and himself but sitting out in the fresh air on the Blue Rock House porch roof. Each day Gad, always obliging, helped him up those challenging stone steps so Chester could scan both the sky and the bushes with the new powerful binoculars he had received on his eighty-eighth birthday. He had given his old pair to Gad, who often sat up there with him. For his uncle's safety and comfort, Gad rigged up a heavily padded chair securely attached by wires to the chimney and equipped the chair with a belt that wrapped around Chester's waist. Chester was plenty safe now, whether alone or with his nephew on the roof, but his mind was slipping away—not exactly quickly but not slow enough for comfort.

Once Chester saw billowing smoke to the east and insisted that his late brothers Elmer, Blue Boy, and Henry had risen from the dead and burned the Bend to the ground. Aida told him that wasn't realistic and he *must* be realistic. Gad didn't see why. He suggested that more likely the great Lenni Lenape spirit, Ketanëtuwit, was behind the fire in order to return Blueberry Hill to its natural, pre-white man state. "Golly, I hope not, Gad," said Handa. "That would mean Blue Rock House was next." Blue Belle told everyone that Ketanëtuwit was a creator, not a destroyer, and that perhaps someone should investigate the cause of the smoke. It turned out Daniel Leach was having a controlled if mammoth burn to get rid of unwanted furniture, newspapers, and waste wood. Leach, Chester surmised, was too mean to die.

Another time Chester thought he could see the Jeremiah Bender statue all the way from the porch roof, which of course was impossible unless one was much, much closer, say in the dilapidated tree fort. He claimed to see a flesh-and-blood woman clinging to Jeremiah's bronze legs. She seemed to be pulling out her hair and wailing. Did Anna miss her husband that much? Chester tormented himself trying to answer that question until he convinced himself that the hair wasn't auburn and the backside wasn't prominent enough to belong to Anna. "It must be Eunice," he told Gad before asking him to hurry over to the tree fort to confirm the mystery woman's identity. Gad obliged. Chester said he would sit tight. He leaned back in his safety chair and looked up at the sky. A dozen turkey vultures were soaring, rocking side-to-side in the wind. Somebody had once told him that a flock of these birds was called a *wake*. He wondered if this was a sign that his time had come. But then he remembered that a "wake of vultures," was what they were called when in their nightly roost, often in large dead trees. A flock of them in flight was a "kettle of vultures." He felt better and fell asleep.

Gad, still a runner, completed his task before Chester could dream. After making sure his uncle was alive, Gad woke him up. He reported that no woman was anywhere near the statue of Jeremiah Bender but that he had figured out which window in the Bend belonged to Betty Bender. Chester congratulated him on his progress. Gad then excused himself from the porch roof, saying he had to run.

"Ah," said Chester. "Off to rendezvous with Betty the Beautiful?"

"No, sir," Gad said. "My Dad is teaching me how to play chess. He has developed a passion for the Game of Kings."

"Off with you then. I only know checkers, Game of Serfs, Peons, Peasants, and Other Simple Folk."

After Gad left, Chester remained on the porch roof for several hours alternating between seeing things in wide-awake dreams and seeing things through his binoculars. He didn't want to come down for the evening meal, even though Aida promised him all the sautauthig he could eat. Finally, Blue Belle helped her coax their brother down. Over the next week, Aida worried about him more than ever as the only place he wanted to be was on the roof despite the late fall chill and with near zero temperatures predicted by year's end.

"If he keeps going out onto the roof, he'll die of pneumonia for sure," Aida told Gad one cold afternoon, three days before Christmas, as she and her nephew warmed themselves at the kitchen stove. Peter and Gad had been sitting at the table engaged in yet another father-son chess match, but Peter had left to be with Ellen, who was feeling under the weather and had taken to bed that morning. Blue Belle was with Ellen, but Peter had announced that it was high time he looked after his wife. Meanwhile Handa, who for a change wanted a break from her Mumsy, was bundled up in her room engrossed in Stephen Crane's *The Third Violet*, which she planned to give to Uncle Chester as a Christmas gift.

"He'll die happy," Gad told Aida. "Uncle Chesty would rather die out there in the open air than in bed like Elmer, Blue Boy, and Henry. I'll take him up an extra blanket, if you'd like."

"What I'd like is for your uncle to live long enough to enjoy, or at least experience, another Christmas on the Hill."

"He's determined to do that, Aunt Aida. He has seen a lot up there on the roof but now wants to meet Santa Claus."

"Santa Claus! The crazy old fool! He's half blind. What can he see up there and not down here where it's warm?"

"He sometimes thinks he sees through his binoculars Anna over there at the Bend."

"Mercy! After all his disappointments with that woman, he still...crazy, just crazy."

"No. He's just old with his memories. He's not hurting anyone or himself."

"He's freezing himself to death! Chesty was always counting on outliving Jeremiah and that sure enough happened, but that hasn't done him a lick of good, has it?"

"I suppose not. But nothing to be done about it. He still loves Anna."

"Yes, old, but still crazy. Maybe everyone who gets old turns crazy. I'll find out soon enough, I suppose. But that's not my point. What I'm saying is how crazy it is to put one's faith in a Bender. Their women are as bad as their men."

"I don't know about that, Aunt Aida. Not all the Benders are..." Gad cut himself off and spun around to put his backside to the stove. He was thinking how Betty Bender touched him in spots he had never been touched before by any hands other than his own. His new woman had made a new man out of him. Uncle Chester and Blue Belle knew that—the first through private conversation, the second through blind observation—but Gad didn't believe Aunt Aida, his father, his mother, or Cousin Handa had any idea about his secret passion.

"I don't like to think of him as crazy," Aida said. "It could be more like that saying I never used to think about at all—there's no fool like an old fool who thinks he's in love." Aida also turned her back to the stove to warm her behind. "Something else occurred to me. Never mind him seeing Santa Claus. If Chesty lives a week beyond that he'll see the dawn of the twentieth century. Wouldn't that be something!"

"Actually, Handa told me he would have to live through the end of December and a whole year after that. The new century doesn't officially begin until January 1, 1901."

"That makes no more sense to me than him sitting out on the roof alone."

"Nevertheless, Handa read it somewhere and says it is so. You want me to take you outside and help you up the steps to keep Chesty company?"

"No thanks. It's frightfully cold out there. And in case you hadn't noticed, I'm no spring chicken myself."

"Nonsense. Anyway, you're no dead duck, either. The Boyd women are holding up far better than the Boyd men."

"Barely. I just don't complain about all my aches and pains the way Henry does...did. And your mother would never whine about her ailments. Ellen is simply a pure caregiver, born to look after all our broken men."

Not so much her own son, thought Gad, but this was no time to complain. "How about Blue Belle? She still looks...as lively as ever."

"Yes, it's unnatural. My little sister was old the day she was born. She's a rare bird who grows wiser without growing older. Sometimes I think she is aging in reverse...getting younger."

"That's a good one, Aunt Aida."

"I'm not fooling. If anyone ever discovers the secret to eternal life, it'll be Blue Belle. As for my Handa, as much as I love and respect my daughter, I sometimes wish she would act her age...younger. You Boyd men have caused most of my wrinkles, but she has given me a few herself."

"I know what you mean. When she throws her weight around acting like a know-it-all, you know, all superior, it gives me a fierce pain in the...eh... head."

"Oh, stop complaining, Gad. Anyway, I don't mean that at all. Nothing wrong with a woman being a strong person. But with my brothers dropping like flies around here, I worry about how we can keep going. We are running out of able bodies. I know Peter and you do your best most of the time, and Ellen tries hard, but we're at the point where I need to hire outside help. And looking beyond our immediate needs, we also need Boyd babies!"

"Can't help you there. You should be talking to Handa."

"I do all the time. And she talks back these days. But it can't be done by just talking."

"Don't I know it." Gad blushed at what he was thinking and what he thought his aunt was thinking. He had a sudden vision of Betty Bender sprawled out in the bushes on the Boyd side of Jackson complaining about the cold and asking to be warmed up fast as lightning. "I better go check on Chester," he said, racing out the kitchen door and feeling downright hot.

§

Chester saw Christmas but missed Santa Claus. The mystical white bearded figure also known as Father Christmas didn't show, not even in the guise of Handy Boyd's spirit. Chester was back on the roof for New Year's Eve. He was sitting up straight in his special chair wide awake because of the celebratory gunfire going off on the other side of Blueberry Hill. He wondered if Robert Bender or Daniel Leach had acquired a cannon or at least a howitzer. His entire bundled-up living family gathered on the rooftop with him shortly before midnight, and so too did the spirits of Handy, Henrietta, and Catawissa Manayunk, as well as the more recent ghosts of Mary, Elmer, Blue Boy, and Henry. And there, by golly, was Jacob, too. At least he saw them, and he knew Blue Belle did, too.

Although Chester didn't admit it to anyone, his powerful and no doubt enchanted binoculars allowed him to also spot the ghosts of some Benders, including Nathaniel, Alexander, and Jeremiah. In fact, he saw the ghost of Anna even though she was, presumably, very much alive and spending quality time with her children and grandchildren inside the Bend. He had no wish to see any other living Bender, especially not the ruthless, uncompromising, ageless Daniel Leach or the Hill desecrater's partner-in-devilry, Eunice.

Chester lent his one good ear to hear the after-midnight resolutions for the New Year whether or not 1900 marked the beginning of a new century.

Ellen went first. She resolved to help her husband Peter, brother-in-law Chester, and anyone else in need as long as she could manage to lift a single soothing finger. Aida and Handa didn't accept that resolution because Ellen had been relentlessly helpful all her life. She must resolve to do something she wasn't now doing, something that would improve her behavior, if that was even possible. After much pondering and shrugging, she made a resolution that stunned Gad: she promised to pay more attention to her son for the right reasons and not to criticize him for not living up to her altruistic standards. Peter stepped up next and resolved not to criticize his precious wife of mercy for being *too* helpful to others. Others on the roof found that resolve weak, so he added another: He would never again use the excuse of having only one arm for not giving his wife a full embrace as warm as sunbeams. "And the same for my one and only son," he added when he thought he detected a hurt look in Gad's eye.

Blue Belle resolved to continue being herself and never hurt a fly. Nobody objected to that. How could she resolve to stop doing something wrong when she did no wrong? Still, Blue Belle, humble but not shy, added that she would also try to raise the spirits of her beloved family by other means than quoting Walt Whitman's *Leaves of Grass* or Catawissa Manayunk's Lenni Lenape words of wisdom. That got gentle laughs across the porch roof; she was not only good, wise, and humble but also possessed a subtle wit.

Aida resolved to make an even bigger effort to promote Boyd blueberry and drinking water enterprises and to orchestrate a grand family awakening in all areas of life, despite the fact, as she now liked to emphasize, it wasn't technically a new century. Most of the others weren't exactly sure what she meant by "grand family awakening," but Handa emphatically said, "Ditto for me." Gad, for one, found his cousin's words unacceptable, because copying somebody else's resolution was not only cheating but lazy. Gad most likely was just teasing her, but she took it as a challenge. "All right then, meddler," she told him, getting in her cousin's face. "I absolutely resolve not to murder you this year." She expected laughter but nobody even cracked a smile. There had been too much death lately, "All right, all right," she shouted. "I further resolve not to have a baby this coming year. No reason I have to have one!" The response was silence, except from her mother, who couldn't hold back a deep sigh that was years in the making. It was not a sigh of relief.

"You can do better, I suppose," Handa said to Gad.

Gad shook his head. "I resolve not to have a baby this coming year, either," he said and that at least made Chester chuckle.

"Awful," said Handa. "You're deathly afraid of making a real resolution you know you wouldn't be able to keep."

"Hogwash," said Gad. But he had trouble thinking of something. He took a long time clearing his throat. Nobody was looking at him, except Handa. He suddenly became terribly shy, thinking nobody really wanted to hear from the youngest Boyd currently in existence

He was temporarily let off the hook. Aida and Blue Belle were urging Chester to make a resolution. The oldest member of the family grumbled for a minute or more before saying as matter-of-factly as he could manage, "You mean my very last resolution, don't you!" Silence followed on the rooftop, which didn't bother Chester, but after painfully twiddling his arthritic thumbs, he chose to say something more. "I resolve to lie around for eternity in my heavenly bed of nails and stone and oil paints with Henry, Elmer and Blue Boy beside me, with the Lenni Lenape Man sleeping with one eye open upside down on the ceiling, with Henrietta and Handy just down the hall of dreams tossing and turning on their bed of sunflowers and blueberries, and with an auburn-haired angel in a blue halo forever serving me berries and wine while fluttering large white wings that have been known to squeeze a dead man to life?" He drew blank stares; his family was clearly bracing themselves for what he might say next. They waited in silence, none of them ready to openly question his mental state.

"I am done," said Chester, and it looked as if the resolutions were done as well. But Handa spoke up as the others stirred, all ready to get off the roof and inside where it was warmer. "I suppose we ought to allow Gadzooks to say his piece," she said. "He has so much to resolve."

"Yes, I think we should," said Ellen with a smile directed for her son alone. "He has shown great patience."

"Of course, we should," said Aida. "We are all ears."

"Stand up, son, and project your voice," said Peter. "We all want to hear you. You are the future of Blue Rock House."

Gad stood up right away but went back to clearing his throat. He requested a sip of water but nobody had thought to bring a bottle of Handy Spring or Blue Rock Spring onto the roof. Standing up like this in front of his family (including whatever ghosts were present) made him feel as if he were a little boy again, one who could do no right by his mother, or father, or Aunt Aida, or that spirited pioneer of Blueberry Hill, Handy Boyd.

"Anytime now, Gadzooks," said Handa. "Uncle Chester has fallen asleep."

"Or maybe I'm dead," said Chester. "Either way, I'm listening. Take your time, Gad. There will be time enough for all of us to rest later."

Gad discovered he had excess saliva in his mouth, perhaps from his anxiety, but he had nowhere to spit. It would have to substitute for water. He swallowed hard, socked himself in the jaw, and decided it was high time he acted like a man despite the common assumption that the blood of Boyd males tended to be anemic.

"I have something to say," said Gad, as if that wasn't quite clear to his family. "I have never made a heart-felt resolution before, but I got one now." He stamped his foot for emphasis, hard enough to loosen one more of Elmer's roof tiles. Scanning the faces looking up at him, Gad wondered if he was expected now to make a bad joke, maybe resolve NOT to push Handa off the roof. If so, he would disappoint them, maybe shock them. "I resolve this year to stop fooling around, that is to stop being so irresponsible, so young, if you will."

"Hear, hear," called out Handa.

Gad heard her but ignored her. "I want you to all know that I have recently become engaged with—I mean engaged to—someone."

"A living female person?" asked Handa.

But Gad would not allow his cousin to steal his thunder. "You all know her name, but you don't know her. I didn't really pick her out. We picked each other. She is a woman of substance. She works hard, thinks positively, has her own mind, lives in the present moment but with keen foresight, and, amazing as it might seem, she loves me. Of course, I love her. She adds value to my life and to Blueberry Hill and to the world."

"My, my, son, who is this incredible woman you are no longer fooling around with?" asked Peter. "I never once heard you mention the name of any young woman."

"I wanted to be sure about her, about us. Her name is Betty, Betty Bender."

"Good God!" Aida and Handa cried simultaneously.

"Lord, save us!" said Peter. "Did you hear that, Ellen?"

"Yes, yes," said Ellen, putting an arm on her son's shoulder. "Can this be true? Isn't she the daughter of Maurice Bender? How in the world did you meet her, Sonny...Gad?"

"There are ways around and over Jackson, Mother. We aren't as divided on Blueberry Hill as you think."

"You two unequal love birds certainly aren't, not if you consider yourselves engaged," said Handa.

"We *are* engaged, cousin. I just told everyone and I'm not fooling."

"We almost wish you were," said Aida. "A Boyd engaged to a Bender!"

"The horror," said Handa.

"Like Romeo and Juliet," said Ellen.

Blue Belle rose up as if lifted by the wind. She stood next to the much taller Gad and gripped his elbow to show her support and perhaps to support herself. But she spoke to Handa and any other doubters on the roof: "Walt Whitman says, though he probably did not have a young couple in mind, 'Be not disheartened—Affection shall solve the problems of freedom yet; those who love each other shall become invincible.' Holy smokes! I beg your pardon. I've already broken my New Year's resolution by quoting Walt."

"We forgive you," said Aida. "And I don't know of any living thing that is invincible. As for you, Gad, you have, frankly, astounded us with your news of a...a most puzzling engagement."

"I'm not finished yet, family," Gad said. "There is more to my resolution than me saying I'll stop fooling around and am presently engaged. Here's the rest of it. I resolve to marry Betty Bender this year, the year that has already in fact arrived—1900. It *will* happen!"

"That remains to be seen," said Peter. "Have you asked her already?"

"Not exactly. But she knelt in our blueberry bushes two days ago and popped the question to me. Naturally, I accepted."

EPILOGUE

It was to be an early June wedding, for practical reasons to happen before the 1900 blueberry picking season got underway. That there would be objections on both sides of the Hill to a Boyd-Bender marriage was inevitable. But the protestations were surprisingly mild after several incidents and revelations. First, on an unseasonably warm afternoon in March, Anna Bender ventured to Blue Rock House after receiving a note from Blue Belle that Chester was on the verge of death and wanted to see her before he "kicked the berry bucket." Anna accepted and found Chester slumped in his special chair on the porch roof, held up only because of the safety rope around his waist. His eyes were closed and his mouth hung open, but he seemed plenty warm enough wrapped in four blankets, with wool hat, scarf, and mittens. On one side of him stood Ellen Boyd, with a thermometer in one hand and a homemade heating pad in the other. Kneeling on the other side was Gad, who was spending almost as much time with Chester as he was with his fiancée. Gad used a handkerchief with the initials B.B. on it (for Betty Bender, Anna assumed) to repeatedly wipe the blue saliva that trickled across his uncle's lower lip and onto his stubbled chin.

"Is he still with us?" Anna asked Ellen, with her fingers twitching above her old lover's face without quite touching the leathery skin. "He looks so far away...so out of this world."

Chester's eyes opened wide and lit up his entire face as if invisible hands had drawn open two curtains in a dark room. "Let's ask him," he said, managing a smile more pleasant than wry.

"It's me, Chesty."

"Yes, you are with me...again, though I can't ever remember you coming to Blue Rock House before. Welcome to the wonderful roof."

"Thank you. You seem...eh...comfortable."

"It is difficult getting him up those steps to the roof," Ellen said. "It takes at least two of us. But there seems to be no other place he can stand."

"I can't stand here either but I can sit, tied to my chair like the victim of a house burglary."

"You know you're not any kind of victim," said Ellen before turning to Anna and whispering, "Up here he must feel like king of his castle."

"Why don't we ask him," said Chester, grinning as if he were the wittiest man in the world.

Anna chose not to ask him how he felt. He was tied into that chair all right, but she had the uncomfortable feeling he could break through his restraints and pounce on her. "It's certainly a...eh...nice day for mid-March," she said, looking at the sky. It looked as if it would rain or they might get a dusting of snow. "Of course, one never knows about the weather this time of year."

"After all this time apart, I'd prefer we not talk about the weather. How are things on your side of the mountain...I mean Hill? It's more like a mountain to climb these days."

"Things are going well, thank you. More little Benders are on the way. Robert's son Nickey married a strapping Norwegian farmer's daughter with childbearing hips. I'm not sure Robert approved, but I'll be a great-grandmother next month. Berri and Jonas had their first child, a beautiful blond baby boy named Danny after grandfather Daniel Leach. Eunice is a grandmother at last. Berri promises her next child will be a girl and shall be called Eunice."

"The horror! Another Daniel and another Eunice!"

"I'll let you get away with that because I know you're sick."

"Just sick of being old. I've been taking my time dying. What brings you to the poor side of the Hill?"

"You want me to say *you*, don't you? But you'd be right. I came around on the buggy with Betty. She's down in the kitchen right now learning from Aida and Handa the secret of making the kind of blueberry pie you love."

"That Gad loves, you mean. I don't eat pie anymore, only a little sautauthig, the traditional Boyd dish. You'd better see to your intended, Gad, before Handa spills the beans about how you snore and usually forget to wash under your arms and behind your ears."

"Right," said Gad, laughing though his uncle wasn't. "And, Mother, I think you should take a break and visit your husband. I believe Peter might be coming down with a cold."

"What? Why, he is perfectly...Oh, yes. We should leave these two to talk in private." Ellen patted Chester's cheek and kissed Anna's forehead.

"Privacy not needed anymore," declared Chester. "Do I really need to say that at this stage of my life? But there is something everyone should know: Listen, Ellen. Listen Gad. I know you don't think I'm in my right mind at my age but what you don't know is that people have been saying that since I was knee-high to a bumble bee. Still, I'm only a raving lunatic when the moon is out. I do say things worth listening to on rare occasion."

"Of course, you do, Chesty," said Ellen.

"We love you even when there's a full moon," said Gad.

"All right then. Listen up." Chester reached out and groped at the air for a while before his right hand found Anna's right hip. He squeezed but she didn't dare move. He spoke looking up, perhaps up into her eyes but more likely at her breasts: "Through the four seasons, through thick and thin, through canal mist and hilltop rain, through rendezvous and rejection, through the feuding times, through the looking glass, and through the binoculars, I have always loved this woman from the bottom of my heart." He gave the hip another squeeze but wondered if she could even feel it. He had lost most of his strength, especially in his right hand.

She took his hand away from her hip but held it between her two hands somewhere close to her heart. He was struck dumb. He couldn't remember any such tender act ever occurring when they met for sexual adventure at Hocking House in Wurtsboro or at the Castle at the top of the Hill.

Anna smiled but at the same time she borrowed the handkerchief from Gad and wiped around Chester's drooling mouth. When she was done, Chester felt as if soon she would also have to wipe tears from his eyes. That didn't happen. She planted a surprisingly long kiss on his dry, cracked lips. His eyes closed on their own, and he trembled. It wasn't the kiss of death but he nearly slipped away to another world at that moment. Now that he wasn't looking at her, she spoke more freely.

"I don't know if you can hear me or not, Chesty, but I hope so, and I don't mind that Ellen and Gad can hear this, too, but I have always loved you. I loved my husband, too. I know it is possible to love two men at the same time, in different ways, of course. You and me couldn't make a big deal out of our love for obvious reasons, but we really paved the way by showing that a Boyd and Bender could be friends and lovers. And now my granddaughter Betty and your nephew Gad here are following in our footsteps and beyond by uniting in holy matrimony come June. That makes me so happy and so proud, as I'm sure it does you."

Chester didn't stir but he was at least still breathing. Gad assured Anna that Chester heard her and agreed with her but wasn't up to nodding. Ellen said that Chester had seen enough of the outdoors for one day. They undid the wires that attached the chair to the chimney, then moved the chair, with Chester still belted in it, to the edge of the roof. Gad climbed halfway down the steps, reached up and took hold of the chair as the two women guided it to the top step. He backed down slowly, struggling mightily to deal with the dead weight. It was a bumpy ride to the bottom of the steps but Chester didn't wake up. Peter came out of the house and he and Ellen took one side and Gad the other to lift the chair-bound Chester and take him to his room.

Anna stayed on the roof to catch her breath. She spotted Chester's binoculars, which he must have placed under his chair. She tried them out.

Everything looked fuzzy no matter how much she adjusted the focus. Finally, she made out what she thought was the Castle rising above the stone wall Jackson as if in a Gothic novel. On further study, she realized she was only seeing the dark clouds lingering above the crest of the Hill. Then came precipitation, not rain nor snow but irregular lumps of ice that kept growing. She couldn't remember ever seeing such enormous hailstones; they battered the roof like fieldstones. She froze, transfixed. Finally, Gad came running out of the house followed by Betty. They talked to her as if she was about to slip and slide off the roof. Gad was ready to catch her. She was definitely shaky and the steps were slippery, but she made it down safely. She felt better once she was inside and almost warm. Chester had been put to bed and lay under two blankets in peaceful sleep.

It was the first time that she had ever been in his bedroom, and he had never been in hers. But they had loved and they had endured. She bent over and kissed Chesty on the forehead. A funny sensation came over her, starting at her feet but shooting up her legs, her crotch, her belly, her breasts, her throat, her face, all the way to her head. It felt as if the room, perhaps the entire house, was leaning to the left and moving ever so slowly, as if gradually sliding downhill. Thinking she might slide with it, she took a seat at the edge of the bed, her backside even with the back of Chester's head. She listened to him breathe—not labored, not too faint—but couldn't turn to look at him. She imagined Jeremiah turning over in his grave, but she still didn't leave. She hadn't moved for ten minutes when Betty danced into the room hand in hand with Gad and announced that it was time to go home, back to the Bend.

"Yes, I should leave," said Anna. "I get the strangest feeling in this room. Do you feel it?"

"I feel nothing but love," said Betty, swinging Gad around in circles. "Is that what you feel, too, Grandma?"

"How strong is the foundation of this house?" Anna asked Gad.

"Solid as a rock," Gad said. "Uncle Elmer built Blue Rock House on a stone ledge. He built it to last."

"Oh, well, perhaps the wooden floor is warped."

"Could be," said Gad. "Elmer didn't like to work with wood. He was a stonemason."

"That might explain it," said Betty, clinging so hard to her finance that she brought them both to a standstill at the foot of Chester's bed. "On the other hand, this is the Boyd house. Everything on this side of Blueberry Hill must be a little warped."

Gad gasped. He had never heard Betty talk that way before, as if she believed all the Bender bunkum about the Boyd family. But she pressed herself against him, breasts and all, and began to caress the hairs on the back of his neck to show she meant no offense.

"Everything looks fine," Gad said, but he wasn't looking at her. Uncle Chester seemed so peaceful.

§

In April, Ellen went beyond the call of duty and crossed the wall to minister to Daniel Leach. He had shot himself in the foot at the annual Stevie Bender Memorial Rifle Shoot while explaining to his reluctant daughter Berri how the top-tang hammer block "safety" worked on his Model 1892 Winchester repeating rifle. Her husband Jonas, who was standing behind them holding Danny, was so startled to see his father-in-law hopping around on one foot that he nearly dropped the baby. Berri seized Danny and was too busy trying to soothe the bawling child to provide any aid to her wounded father. Jonas and three guest shooters carried Mr. Leach on a stretcher to the Bend. At the house, Eunice Bender Leach could not tend to her wounded husband because she was taking a long time to recover from the nearly fatal bite of a timber rattlesnake that had been making Jackson its home.

Other Benders were either too busy or too ill-equipped to deal with the ill-tempered patient. Nobody thought much of the heavy-drinking doctor in Wurtsboro who had replaced the late Ezekiel Tears and couldn't heal himself. It was Betty's idea to ask Ellen to help with Mr. Leach just before the soon-to-be-bride took a train to New York City for a week-long shopping trip (for starters she had in mind the purchase of a lacy white wedding dress for herself along with two sparkling rings for Gad and herself from Tiffany's). After Ellen started helping Mr. Leach, she soon took on Mrs. Leach, who was less crotchety than her husband but more demanding. Ellen couldn't stop going to the Bend daily until both Daniel and Eunice Leach were on their feet again. Peter made minimum fuss because he had learned he couldn't change his wife's caregiving nature and she did come to their bed every night without complaining of exhaustion or a headache. He couldn't image a more kindhearted person in the whole world than his precious wife of mercy except maybe Florence Nightengale and Blue Belle Boyd.

One of the first things Daniel Lecah did when he was up and about in early May was shoot three rattlesnakes residing in Jackson and blast a hole in the stone wall wide enough to accommodate a wagon. Gad and Betty now went back and forth to each other's houses freely, and, to the amazement of most Boyds and Benders, so did Aida and Eunice. The two former enemies were sharing plans for the June wedding, recipes, and their thoughts on what it was like to have the status of a matriarch.

Handa got in the habit of accompanying her mother to the Bend but not engaging Eunice in conversation. It turned out she had nothing against Eunice but liked to spend her time in the grand gazebo with quarry-owner and railroad advocate James Bender, one of the sons of Alexander and his first wife, Delilah. Both sons were still single. Unlike his brother Cal, who had soft hands, brainy talk, and classes in history and philosophy at Harvard, James had dropped out of school but was exceedingly handsome (favoring his Southern belle mother) and blessed with a rock-hard body that could stand up to any amount of hard work. What's more James had a soft spot in his heart for Handa and was drawn to her assertiveness, which Cal had seen as overbearing arrogance before he left for college. Handa insisted that her pledge to family that she would *not* marry that year was still intact, but she could not guarantee things wouldn't change in the 20th century. In fact, she on occasion imagined that if she played her cards right and James stopped playing around with all those amorous Wurtsboro women drawn to him, she might actually give birth to the first ever Boyd-Bender baby before Betty managed that feat with Gad.

Chester lived to see the wedding in June 1900. He was carried in his special chair up the Hill to witness the traditional vows, which took place at Jackson, now not only free of rattlers but also half-dismantled. Gad and Betty took the railroad west to an undisclosed location for their honeymoon but they promised Aida and Handa to return before the blueberry picking season reached its peak. While they were away, Chester stopped going onto the porch roof. It used to be a refuge, a place of peace and quiet and visions. Now, he talked crazy, afraid that if he went out there to sit without Gad, he would be forgotten and left to rot in the summer heat. He imagined not only his family and the Benders but everyone else in the Wurtsboro area departing— by train, resurrected canal boats, mule-drawn wagons, horse-drawn buggies, newfangled Mercedes motor carriages, high-wheel bicycles, hot-air balloons, weathered but still functional blueberry carts, and the Great Conveyor invented years ago by Elmer, though the wheels had long since fallen off. In his failing mind, he would then be alone, deserted even by the spirits of ancestors, both Boyd and Lenni Lenape. It was eternal loneliness he feared far more than death.

Chester was alive when the honeymoon was over. But while Gad returned with enough lingering high spirits to passionately pick berries without complaint, Chester could no longer recognize his nephew. Gad may as well have been a stranger who came to Blue Rock House uninvited like that deceitful soldier Mortimer Loomis who shot Peter in the arm or that phony phrenologist Professor Wadsworth who tried to steal Blue Belle's brain. In his last days Chester remembered having dreams of an auburn-haired beauty named Anna every night but he didn't remember that her last name was Bender or that she still lived on the other side of the Hill. He thought she had left like all the others, having flown off to Sleepy Hollow with a phalanx of storks. He died alone in bed on Halloween night. The Boyd survivors all said it was a shame Chesty hadn't lived until 1901, as if that would have made his long life more significant.

In the last year of the 19th century more berries than ever were picked on the Boyd side of the Hill thanks in part to the return of Gad but also to the participation, in varying degrees, of Handa's beau James Bender, young scholar Oman Bender, Nickey Bender, and Nickey's muscular Norwegian wife, who picked with her left arm while she held their baby Noah in the right. In the first year of the 20th century Aida and Eunice changed the name of BBB, the Best Boyd Blueberry Co., to BBBB (or Four B's), the Best Boyd Bender Blueberry Co. Profits nearly doubled. Likewise, the bottling business flourished, despite the fact the Blue Rock Spring Water label was eliminated. All the bottled water was now called Handy Spring Water, the source, and the Benders shared in the bottling and the drinking. The Benders brought new capital and life into those enterprises which was a good thing for that family as well as the Boyds because while the Benders benefited from railroad growth, the tannery business ended, quarrying and lumbering slowed down, and the freight-carrying boats would never operate again on the D&H Canal.

Some residents on both sides of the Hill called it a miracle that the long-standing family feud was over and that Benders and Boyds were living in relative peace. This is not to suggest that everything went smoothly between the former antagonists in the 20th century. There were ups and downs in relationships, diseases, deaths, births, accidents, storms, fires, draughts, financial disagreements, artistic differences, mental health issues, young women having abortions, young men going off to two world wars, and more. But nobody shot anybody else on Blueberry Hill, and both Blue Rock House and the Bend were still standing well into the 21st century, though the first needed a new roof and the second had lost a wing due to a night fire caused by either a Bender or a Boyd smoking in the same bed. Handy Spring water, brought by horse and wagon to the east side of the Hill, helped limit the damage of that blaze. The spring named for the pioneer of Blueberry Hill continued to be blessed, if not as a fountain of youth and hope than as an inundation of tradition and ancestral spirit. Nobody on the Hill—or off the Hill for that matter—seems to remember when Blue Belle Boyd finally stopped quoting Walt Whitman and drew her last breath. Perhaps she never did.

READERS GUIDE

1. Why is an Introduction, written by a fictional independent historian in the present day, included?

2. In what ways does Handy Boyd differ from the traditional image of a frontiersman?

3. Would the Boyd family have survived on Blueberry Hill without the Lenni Lenape Indian "Man"?

4. How does the death of Handy's wife, Henrietta, affect the rest of the Boyd family?

5. Why Does Chester Boyd become the friend of Jeremiah "Red" Bender in their early years?

6. In what ways is Blue Belle different from other members of the Boyd family?

7. What is the significance of the Boyds building a house made of fieldstone while the Benders live in a larger house made of wood?

8. How does the Boyds' blueberry business compare with the Bender enterprises?

9. Which family's approach to the land do you prefer?

10. What role does the Delaware & Hudson Canal play in the lives of the Boyds and Benders?

11. What role do the first railroads in Sullivan County play?

12. How does Nathaniel Bender differ from his older brothers, Jeremiah and Alexander?

13. Do the Boyds feel differently about the Civil War than the Benders do? If so, in what ways?

14. What does Blue Belle's friendship with Walt Whitman mean to her and the other Boyds?

15. How would you rate Handy Boyd as a husband and a father?

16. How does the "Panther Hunt" affect the family feud?

17. In what ways does Anna Bender's relationship with her husband, Jeremiah, change through the years? Her relationship with Chester Boyd?

18. Are Aida Boyd and Eunice Bender effective matriarchs in their respected families?

19. How does the Gad Boyd-Betty Bender relationship compare to the Chester Boyd-Anna Bender relationship?

20. What were the factors that brought the feud to an end?